*continued ...*

D0009668

### *A Most Unsuitable Man*

"Beverley turns a rejected 'other woman' into a fiery, outspoken, sympathetic heroine; pairs her with a dashing but penniless, scandal-ridden hero; and lets the fun—and the danger—begin. Once again readers are treated to a delightful, intricately plotted, and sexy romp set in the slightly bawdy Georgian world of Beverley's beloved Malloren Chronicles."
— *Library Journal*

"I found myself enjoying every minute of the relationship in this story of love, hope, and increments of witty humor. As usual, a Malloren novel is a keeper." —*Rendezvous*

### More Praise for Novels by *New York Times* Bestselling Author Jo Beverley

"A well-crafted story and an ultimately very satisfying romance." —*The Romance Reader*

"Jo [Beverley] has truly brought to life a fascinating, glittering, and sometimes dangerous world." —Mary Jo Putney

"Another triumph." —*Affaire de Coeur*

"Wickedly delicious. Jo Beverley weaves a spell of sensual delight with her usual grace and flair." —Teresa Medeiros

"Delightful ... thrilling ... with a generous touch of magic ... an enchanting read." —*Booklist*

"A stunning medieval romance of loss and redemption ... sizzling." —*Publishers Weekly* (starred review)

"A fast-paced adventure with strong, vividly portrayed characters ... wickedly, wonderfully sensual and gloriously romantic." —Mary Balogh

"Deliciously sinful.... Beverley evokes with devastating precision the decadent splendor of the English country estate in all its hellish debauchery ... a crafty tale of sensuality and suspense." —*BookPage*

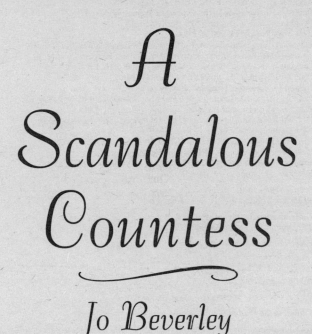

# A
# Scandalous
# Countess

## Jo Beverley

A SIGNET BOOK

SIGNET

Published by New American Library, a division of
Penguin Group (USA) Inc., 375 Hudson Street,
New York, New York 10014, USA
Penguin Group (Canada), 90 Eglinton Avenue East, Suite 700, Toronto,
Ontario M4P 2Y3, Canada (a division of Pearson Penguin Canada Inc.)
Penguin Books Ltd., 80 Strand, London WC2R 0RL, England
Penguin Ireland, 25 St. Stephen's Green, Dublin 2,
Ireland (a division of Penguin Books Ltd.)
Penguin Group (Australia), 250 Camberwell Road, Camberwell, Victoria 3124,
Australia (a division of Pearson Australia Group Pty. Ltd.)
Penguin Books India Pvt. Ltd., 11 Community Centre, Panchsheel Park,
New Delhi - 110 017, India
Penguin Group (NZ), 67 Apollo Drive, Rosedale, Auckland 0632,
New Zealand (a division of Pearson New Zealand Ltd.)
Penguin Books (South Africa) (Pty.) Ltd., 24 Sturdee Avenue,
Rosebank, Johannesburg 2196, South Africa

Penguin Books Ltd., Registered Offices:
80 Strand, London WC2R 0RL, England

First published by Signet, an imprint of New American Library,
a division of Penguin Group (USA) Inc.

First Printing, February 2012
10  9  8  7  6  5  4  3  2  1

Copyright © Jo Beverley, 2012
All rights reserved

Ⓤ REGISTERED TRADEMARK—MARCA REGISTRADA

Printed in the United States of America

PUBLISHER'S NOTE
This is a work of fiction. Names, characters, places, and incidents either are the
product of the author's imagination or are used fictitiously, and any resemblance
to actual persons, living or dead, business establishments, events, or locales is
entirely coincidental.

The publisher does not have any control over and does not assume any responsibility for author or third-party Web sites or their content.

## ACKNOWLEDGMENTS

Many thanks to author Margaret Evans Porter, who shared her knowledge of Georgian gardens and helped me find out when flowering tobacco came to Britain and how it was used.

# Prologue

*June 9, 1764*
*London*

"Huhn...?" Even through slitted eyes, Georgia, Countess of Maybury, could detect early-morning light—something she rarely encountered. Especially when she'd not gone to bed until past two in the morning.

"What?" She moistened her mouth, forcing her eyes fully open, prepared to glower at her lady's maid. *"Mother?"*

She pushed upright, sweeping tendrils of red hair from her face. At nineteen, she was still close enough to the schoolroom to be alarmed.

Loose hair? Why? No cap?

Now she remembered!

Dickon had come to her bed last night.

That was why she'd returned home so early from Lady Walgrave's ball. He'd insisted that they leave, eventually muttering, "Dammit, Georgie, I want to bed you."

She'd hoped his startling urgency promised a change, but the messy business had been as dull as always.

Lud!

Here she was, all disheveled in the bed where she'd lain with her husband.

No wonder her mother was frowning—her straight-backed, square-shouldered mother, who could make generals quake if she'd a mind to. What on earth was she doing here?

"Mother? Is this some dream?"

The Countess of Hernescroft sat down on the bed in a rustle of skirts and took Georgia's hand. "No, daughter. No dream. Rather, a nightmare. You must be strong. Maybury is dead."

"Maybury? Dead?" The words held no meaning.

"Your husband is dead, killed in a duel fought not two hours ago."

"Duel? Why would Dickon fight a duel?" Before her mother could answer, Georgia said, "Dead? He can't be dead. He was here last night!" She pulled back the covers as if Dickon might be hiding under them.

Her mother seized her hands, dragging back her attention. "Death can come in a moment, Georgia. You know that. Maybury is dead and you must rise and do what's necessary."

Georgia obeyed the pull of her mother's hands and climbed out of the big, high bed. But then she broke free.

"Dead? How can he be dead? A duel? No, no. He's the most easygoing man in the world!"

"Maybury met Sir Charnley Vance this morning and died of a sword to the heart."

"To the heart?" Georgia whispered, clutching her chest as if she too might be wounded there. Her mind felt blank. She shook her head. "No, no, no. It must be some mistake. A tease. He likes to tease."

"Would I be party to such a tease? The proof is at hand. They are laying out his body downstairs. You must dress and go down." The countess spoke to one side. "Something sober."

"I'm not sure there is any such, milady," Georgia's maid replied, her voice seeming far away.

"Then as pale and plain as possible."

"I need to use the chamber pot," Georgia said, grasping onto that natural need. See, life was as normal.

"Assist her," her mother commanded Jane.

"I don't need assistance." Georgia hurried into her dressing room and behind the screen.

*Dickon dead?*

He was only twenty-three. No one died at twenty-three.

Except in wars. Or sometimes of sickness. Or from falling off a horse, or drowning at sea.

Or in a duel.

A sword through the heart . . .

She sat on the closestool, hugging herself and rocking. Dickon. Her Dickon. Her husband, her friend . . .

"Milady," Jane called, "come on out now. Your lady mother awaits."

"Go away."

"Your mother—"

"Send her away."

"Oh, milady, do please come out. You can't—"

The screen was pulled aside. "Georgia, stop this." Her mother grabbed her arm and dragged her into the room. "Dress!"

Jane took over more gently. "There, there, milady. Let's have your nightgown off. I've your ivory lustring—"

Georgia twitched free. "Stop it, stop it, *stop it*! You're both wrong. You have to be wrong!" She escaped clutching hands and ran back through her bedchamber and into her husband's. "Dickon! Dickon, where are you? You won't believe what they say. . . ."

The bed was disordered. See, he'd just risen.

She ran toward his dressing room. "Dickon!"

His valet appeared in the doorway, a shirt over his arm.

"He's in there?" Georgia stepped forward, but tears ran down Pritchard's pale cheeks and he shook his head.

She mirrored him, shaking her head. "It isn't true."

"It is, milady. His lordship's . . . gone. I'm taking down a fresh shirt. The other one . . ."

Georgia kept shaking her head, but the truth was battering its way in.

*Her husband, her friend, her Dickon, was dead.*

"No!" She staggered over to clutch one carved bedpost, to stare at his bed, at the dip in the pillow made by his sleeping head, willing him back.

But he'd never be back.

She flung herself on the bed, weeping.

"Leave her for a moment," the Countess of Hernescroft said, grasping the maid's arm but looking at her daughter.

Such a radiant beauty, the countess thought, such a blithe spirit, and now this tragedy when she was not yet twenty.

Perhaps it had been a mistake to promote a marriage between Georgia and Maybury when the girl was but sixteen, but she'd been mature beyond her years and already driving men mad. It had seemed simpler to settle her early to a good-natured neighbor only three years older.

Georgia had been delighted to wed the new Earl of Maybury, whom she knew well. She'd been cock-a-hoop to leave the schoolroom and become mistress of her own properties ahead of her older sister. Maybury had never been able to manage her, however. They should have foreseen that and tied her to someone older.

"Shall I get a sleeping draught for her, your ladyship?" whispered the maid.

"Prepare it, but first she must come down to see the body."

"Oh, your ladyship, is that necessary?"

"Yes."

"Very well, your ladyship," the maid said, and left.

Lady Hernescroft grimaced at the thought of the

storm clouds gathering, but then she heard someone else enter the room, and turned.

Thank God. One of her sons, the Honorable Peregrine Perriam, had arrived, slender, elegant, and despite the early hour, perfectly dressed for the occasion in dark gray. Perry was distressingly dilettante, but he was a master at court and Town protocol.

"You must handle matters in society," she said quietly to him, "and control what is said. Unpleasant suppositions are already stirring."

"Poor girl." Perry was fond of his sisters, if perhaps less so of his brothers.

"Is it true, do you think?" she murmured.

"Georgie and Vance? He's not the type for fashion and boudoirs. Maybury invited him to manly affairs for his sporting abilities, but I doubt Georgie saw much of him."

"Logic won't carry weight when she's indulged in so many follies, some of them with men. You should have steered her to a better path."

"She had a husband," he pointed out.

"Who was not up to the task. What details have you gleaned?"

"At this hour, very little. I spoke with the men below. According to Kellew, his second, it happened last night at a tavern. There'd been a race and they were in their cups when Vance sneered at Maybury's driving skills. Maybury threw his wine in Vance's face and the duel was on. Dickon Maybury was a dolt of a driver, but I'd have said he was too easy natured to go to swords over it."

"Quite," Lady Hernescroft said. "Which is dung that will enable this weed to grow. Trivialities are often used to protect a lady's name in a duel, and what lady could be the cause here but Maybury's flighty wife?"

"The cats who envy Georgia's beauty and charm will delight in this. Wives have fled abroad in such situations."

"No Perriam will become an outcast. About your

work. Ensure that the right story greets the beau monde when it wakes today. I'll make sure the gentlemen below see her in all her raw grief and carry that tale to the clubs. Tell her maid to bring her robe."

She went forward to draw her weeping daughter up from the bed. "Come now, you must want to see him."

"Must I?" The wide, reddened eyes seemed like those of a child—a shocked child, bewildered by fate.

"You must. No need to dress. See, here's your maid with your robe." She herself helped her daughter to put on the pink silk. "No, don't attempt to tidy her hair. Come along, daughter. I will be with you."

Perry had gone to his allocated task, and she could trust him there. Lady Hernescroft thanked God her husband was at a race meeting. He was inclined to thunder, but this required a more subtle touch.

A mere two months ago Lady Lowestoft had fled after a similar duel, but all the world had known that she was the killer's mistress and that she'd run off with him. There was no true similarity, but vicious tongues would find one. Would it be best to take Georgia away from Town or compel her to face the world to put paid to any comparisons?

She guided her trembling daughter along the corridor and down the stairs of the fashionable Mayfair house to where Maybury's body lay on a chaise. His bloodstained shirt had been changed for a fresh one and his body covered to the neck with a red brocade coverlet. His eyes had been closed, but he did not look as if he slept.

At sight of him, Georgia made a choking sound, and Lady Hernescroft wondered if she would vomit and whether that would have good or bad effect.

Instead her daughter stumbled over, hands outstretched. "Dickon? Oh, Dickon, why?" She brushed brown hair from his temples but then flinched back. "Already cold. Cold!" She collapsed down, pink robe and Titian red hair spread over the crimson brocade. Lady Hernescroft was not poetical, but it was a striking effect.

"Oh, why, Dickon, my darling, why?"

Lady Hernescroft slowly let out a breath. Without any artifice, her daughter was putting on just the right show. Two of the four men were dabbing their eyes, and Kellew was sobbing.

After a few moments, Lady Hernescroft gently drew her daughter up and into her arms. "You must leave him now, my dear. Come with me. We'll get you a sleeping draught."

She guided Georgia back upstairs and helped the maid settle her in her bed.

Lady Hernescroft couldn't help but notice what a deplorable frivolity that bed was. The whole thing was painted white, with details picked out in gold. Cupids supported the four posts, and nymphs and shepherds frolicked on the headboard. Part and parcel with her youngest daughter's extravagant, frivolous life.

She and Hernescroft had expected the young couple to live most of the year at Maybury Castle, which lay close to their seat, Herne in Worcestershire. Even when they weren't at Herne to supervise, their various officers could, and Dickon's mother had continued to live at the castle.

Instead, as soon as Maybury achieved his majority and control of his large fortune, they'd moved to Town to become leaders of fashion. Visits to Maybury had been brief, and in most cases Dickon Maybury had visited alone. Georgia had lived in this Mayfair house, which was done up in the very latest style, leaving London only in the heat of summer for a Chelsea villa they'd named Sansouci.

Without care.

Carefree might seem all very well, but careless was to be deplored. Maybury had paid little attention to his estates, and Georgia had cared for nothing but amusement and fashion.

Lady May, they called her, as insubstantial as a mayfly, but darling of much of the beau monde.

The "beautiful world" could turn vicious in a moment, especially toward those it envied. As Perry had said, as soon as they heard the news, the jealous cats would be sharpening their claws, ready to shred Lady May's reputation.

The maid carried the sleeping draught toward the bed, but Lady Hernescroft put up a hand to halt her.

"Georgia, listen to me. You shall drink the potion and sleep a little, but then you will leave Town with me and return home to Herne."

"Herne? No, no, I'll go to Sansouci."

"Are you with child?"

Georgia looked away. "No."

Lady Hernescroft turned her daughter's tear-soaked face to her. "Pay attention. You said that Maybury came to your bed last night. No, don't weep again. Does that not mean you could be with child?"

Georgia wiped away tears. "Perhaps. But . . . but it's been three years, Mother. Why would last night make any difference?"

That was true. Three years and no conception.

If a miracle had happened, it would be revealed in time, but that in itself could cause problems. An heir conceived around the time of the husband's death was always suspect. Georgia must be carefully chaperoned so that many could testify that she could not have coupled with some other man after the duel.

Then there were the rumors about Vance. No matter the truth, people would speculate. . . . She should have told Perry to make haste to take hold of Vance so that he could assure everyone that the duel had been over driving skills and no lady was involved.

Perry would think of that on his own.

It was a damnable mess, however, and all her flighty daughter's fault. Her daughter, who did not yet grasp the situation.

"If there's no child, Georgia, Sansouci is no longer

your home, nor is this house, nor Maybury Castle. All will go to Maybury's heir, his uncle, Sir William Gable-Gore."

"What?" Georgia looked as shocked as at the death. "Everything gone? Everything?"

"Everything except your personal possessions."

"No...."

"Here, my dear. Drink this and sleep."

Georgia took the glass and sipped, then screwed up her face at the bitter taste. It seemed to act as a restorative, however, for she braced herself and drained the glass in one go.

That was one good thing—her willful daughter had never lacked courage. She'd need it now. Her path back to the world would not be easy, no matter how skillfully this crisis was managed.

The maid took away the glass and gave Georgia one of water to wash some of the taste away.

First Georgia must return to Herne and live quietly there in mourning, allowing the furor to die down. There would have to be a few visits from neighbors to scotch any rumors that she was, in fact, abroad with her lover.

Here in Town, Perry and others would make it clear that the duel had been exactly as it seemed—a folly of young men soaked in drink. If the truth was otherwise, it must be suppressed.

Ah. There would be an inquest, of unfortunate interest to the curious. That must be managed too, so that the Perriam name wasn't dragged in the dirt.

Lady Hernescroft looked ahead. In a year, Georgia would seek another husband, but this time he must be more suitable. An older man with necessary sternness.

Georgia drained the last of the water. "Last night, everything was as usual, delightfully so. I was at Lady Walgrave's ball. I was Lady May. Beaufort flirted with me, as did Ludlow. Sellerby composed a rhyme in adoration of my shoe buckles. Now I have nothing." She looked up. "How can that be?"

Lady Hernescroft had never been a doting mother, but that piteous question touched her heart. She embraced her daughter, kissing her unkempt hair.

"Your life has undergone a great change, Georgia, but you are not left with nothing. You have your widow's jointure, your own fine qualities, and above all, your family. Trust in your family. We will take care of you. We will keep you safe."

# Chapter 1

September 29, 1764
Herne, Worcestershire

Dear Lizzie,

Your letters have been a great comfort to me, and I can only beg you to forgive me for not replying. It seems I've slept through summer, hardly noticing the passing days, or even the blooming and fading of the flowers. I think I sank for a time into the grave with poor Dickon.

Something has awoken me now, however, perhaps simply that it's Michaelmas Day, when country servants consider whether they wish to stay in their employment or seek some other place.

I would certainly seek some other place if I could.

When I returned to Herne, I half expected to return to the schoolroom bedchamber I shared with Winnie. Instead, I'm installed in a handsome set of rooms, but in all other ways I could be sixteen again! I have no more say in the running of Herne than I did at sixteen, when I so recently was accustomed to managing three houses.

I have no money! In truth, I do, for I have my

*portion back, but it's returned to my father and he doles out a few guineas a month. I wasn't aware a portion could be returned, but I suppose anything is possible if all parties agree to it. The new Earl of Maybury was eager to shed the commitment to pay my jointure of two thousand for perhaps sixty years, even at the cost of twelve thousand now.*

*You will understand how bitter it is to have a pittance in my pocket. Father pays my bills, but I'm sure he feels entitled to question my purchases, and as all this is done through his clerk of accounts, you will appreciate how it galls me.*

*Thus far I've only purchased mourning clothes and a few essentials, but now I'm awakened, I'm tempted to order something outrageous. What do you think it should be?*

*A jewel-encrusted prayer book? A gold-plated chamber pot? I can see you laughing and shaking your head, and it makes me smile and cry at the same time. I would order a carriage now and race to see you, but I know you expect a new treasure at any time, so I'll restrain myself. I'd inflict myself on Babs except that she and Harringay are in France.*

*Ah, Versailles! Will I ever see Versailles again?*

*Yes, of course I will, you say, as soon as my year's over and I choose a new husband. I also hear your usual scathing comment on the French court, you country mouse.*

*May I beg an invitation to your country haven for Christmas, my dearest friend? Mother strongly recommended that I stay at Herne for my six months, and given the ridiculous stories circulating about me—Vance, Lizzie! Who could ever imagine me in his bed? When he killed my Dickon! My only desire is to run the foul wretch through with his own sword!*

*But by Christmas all fires of scandals will have*

*burned to ash, and I'm resolved to shed Herne along with my blacks. I have distinct memories of this place in winter. Huge chambers and marble floors in many rooms. What insanity to build in such a style in England.*

*Your Jacobean manor house is much better suited, and Dickon and I so enjoyed the one Christmas we spent at Brookhaven. I will know he's watching and smiling as I dote on your darlings, play hoodman blind, kiss beneath a mistletoe bough, and flirt with all the men. That is, if anyone wishes to flirt with me in dove gray and lilac, neither of which suits me.*

*You laugh again, but truly, both shades do odd things to my complexion.*

*When I leave you, I will return to Town for the winter season. No one shall prevent me, for I die for Town! Until I return there, I will not truly be alive.*

*Oh, see, a tear's blotted the ink, and it's not my grieving for the beau monde, but from imagining you shaking your head again, my dearest, dearest friend, and missing you so very, very much.*

*I look forward to your next letter and hope it contains news of your easy, safe delivery,*

*Your dearest,*
*Georgia M*

*December 6, 1764*

*Lizzie!*

*Have you heard the news? Dickon's mother has departed this life. I suppose I should express my grief, but as she was relentlessly unpleasant to me for most of my marriage, I will not play the hypocrite.*

*How unfair she was to blame me because we moved to Town, when it was Dickon who was des-*

*perate to escape as soon as he was of age and in control of his fortune. Yet it was to me she wrote, complaining of our extravagance.*

*Oh, but I complained of all that at the time. Did I tell you of the letters she sent after Dickon's death? I think not. Written in acid with a fiery pen. I tried to respond moderately, Lizzie, I truly did, for I understood the anguish of a mother who had lost her only child, but in the end I had the letters kept from me. I didn't return them, for I feared that would cause her greater pain, but I could not read any more of them.*

*She believes the foulest stories about me. I not only took Vance as a lover, but every single man in my court, and of course I seduced Vance into getting rid of my unwanted husband....*

*Oh, I will write no more of her, think no more of her! But alas, I fear I cannot visit you at Christmas. I won't play the hypocrite, but I must give my husband's mother the honor of at least a month of mourning.*

*If you and Torrismonde don't go to Town for the winter season, perhaps I may visit you in January. For now, I am gathering my shawls, thick stockings, and woolen mitts in hope of surviving to see you again.*

> *Your frozen friend,*
> *Georgia M*

"Perry!"

Georgia ran down the grand staircase to hug her favorite brother as soon as he entered Herne, but then she dragged him toward the stairs. "Don't shed a scrap of clothing until you're in my boudoir, or you'll die of the cold."

Laughing, Perry tossed his hat to a footman and went upstairs with her.

"I couldn't believe it when you wrote to say you'd visit," Georgia said. "In such weather and with Christmas a mere week away. Are you en route to visit friends farther north? This is so delightful, whatever the cause. It's months since your last visit."

"And that solely to see you. I like Herne as little as you do, Georgie."

"Kindred spirits. Here, come in. I manage to keep this room and my bedchamber tolerable, and thus I rarely leave them. Mother and Father aren't due to arrive for Christmas until the twenty-third. I suppose then I'll have to brave the dining room."

"Which they will keep as warm as possible, damn the cost." He shed gloves, scarf, and fur-lined cloak into the arms of Georgia's maid, Jane Nunn.

Georgia tossed her own warm cloak on the settee and then hugged him again. He was only a few inches taller than she, and of slender build. This led some to underestimate him, but he was strong and a skillful swordsman. Some also thought his stylish ways made him shallow, but there was more to Peregrine Perriam than met the eye.

"What refreshment can I offer? A meal, tea, ale, wine?"

"Tea now and any meal that can be thrown together. Soup would warm my bones."

"Tea and soup for my brother on the instant, Jane, and whatever else we can provide for a dinner. And make sure his room is as warm as mine."

Perry delayed things by going to kiss Jane's cheek. "As pretty as ever, and even more useful."

Despite her thirty-five years, Jane Nunn blushed. "Go on with you, sir. And if you want your sustenance you'd best let me be about my work."

"I could sustain myself on you," he declared, but he let her go.

"You tease her," Georgia complained.

"She likes it," he replied, and of course it was true.

Georgia sat, unable to stop beaming at him. "Is any woman safe from you?"

"All of them," he said, settling in the armchair, "for I've no mind to marry and I only dally with those who don't care about that."

"Wives," she said.

"Often, thus benefiting both them and their husbands, who are free to play elsewhere. Turning Puritan, love?"

"Lud, don't suggest such a thing! It must be the corroding effect of Herne."

"I don't suppose it's permanent."

Georgia turned serious, however. "You do know that I was a virtuous wife, don't you, Perry? I might have flirted—"

He held up a hand. "Of course I do, love. But I have bad news for you on that front."

He'd turned serious too, and Georgia gathered her shawl closer. She should have known only necessity could bring Perry so far from Town in winter.

"What?" she asked.

"Your scandal is raging again."

"Six months on? Why? How?"

"The dowager."

Georgia gaped at him. "But she's dead and buried!"

"And left poison behind. She took a week or so to die, making all decent arrangements, but also receiving visitors. She told everyone that she was dying of a broken heart. A heart broken by the wicked, barren trull her son had married."

Georgia grimaced, but said, "There's nothing new in that."

"Yes, there is," he said, and she heard the warning. "She claimed to have recently received the coup de grâce in the form of a letter Charnley Vance wrote to his second, Jellicoe, complaining that you'd seduced him into killing your husband by protesting love and promising to flee with him into exile."

"What?" Georgia shot to her feet. "Who would believe that? I seldom even met Charnley Vance, and I'd slit my own throat before I'd run off with a man like him!"

He rose too. "I know, I know, but enough heard about the letter from the lips of a dying woman . . ."

"Why?" Georgia wailed. "Why? She must have invented it to torment me from the grave. Oh, Perry, what can I do?"

He took her hands. "Nothing at the moment, love. Of course we're seeking the letter so we can prove it false."

"But if it never existed . . . This is so cruel. I'm innocent. I did nothing. Nothing!"

He took her into his arms. "I know, love. Everyone who truly knows you understands that you could never have dallied with Vance."

She pulled away to look at him. "But with others? Do people believe I could have dallied with other men?"

"Not those who truly know you, but . . . you made no effort to appear demure, Georgie."

"And for that I'm a harlot!"

"Flirtation? Wagering for kisses? Assignations in the garden during balls?"

"All in fun! Was I to be allowed no fun? Dickon didn't mind." She moved away. "I never thought you'd reproach me, Perry."

"I'm not reproaching. I'm laying out the truth of your situation. It's difficult, Georgie, and you're going to have to step carefully to survive."

"I'm here, aren't I? Moldering away at Herne in deepest mourning. I've remained here to mourn the dowager and all the reward I get is more hate. What more must I do?"

"Stay here longer," he said bluntly. "Out of sight, out of mind. The dowager's dead and that must be the end of her effect. That spurious letter will fade from memory, and in the spring you'll be able to emerge back into society."

"The beau monde will have forgotten?" she asked cynically.

"No, but your story won't be at the front of every mind, and other scandals will have occurred. Your friends will remind the world of your virtues, and you'll reappear in half mourning, reminding them of the truth. That you are a lady and a widow—the tragically young Dowager Countess of Maybury."

Georgia gaped at him. "No! I can't be."

"The death of Dickon's mother makes you the senior widow."

"At twenty? Oh, devil take it, that's cruelly unfair."

"Tush, tush."

"It's worthy of a curse."

"Remember, it might play to your advantage."

"Then I'll attempt to be grateful, but there's nothing for it. I must soon marry and shed the word 'dowager.'"

"As soon as you emerge, suitors will gather like drones around a queen bee when she flies from the hive."

She gave him a look. "Don't they all die?"

"A minor flaw in my simile, but trust you to pounce on it." He smiled at her. "If you remember to use your wits, Georgie, this will all turn out well."

Perry was a master of social wisdom. She had to believe him.

"I wish I knew where Charnley Vance was," she said. "I'd string him up by his thumbs until he confessed the truth about us!"

"I'd be alongside you with the hot pincers. Damnable that he fled abroad before the inquest and hasn't been heard of since."

Georgia turned to gaze out at the estate, which was a monochrome study in frost and black skeleton trees. "It's as if some malevolent fate seeks to destroy me. Why could that be? I truly can't think of anything I've done to deserve it."

"Of course you don't deserve this. You have a truly

kind heart. You're victim of an unkind twist of fate, that's all, exacerbated by your mother-in-law's bitter nature."

"And by my behavior," she said, turning to face him.

"Honest to a fault. Yes, a prim-and-proper countess would never be fertile ground for such nonsense, but . . . Ah, my sustenance."

Jane came in, followed by a footman carrying a tray loaded with soup, bread, and tea. "Dinner'll be up in a few minutes, milady."

Georgia directed the footman to put the tray on the small table she used for dining, and sat on one of the chairs there as Perry took the other and set to the soup.

"Thank you for coming, Perry. You could have written."

"It seemed worthy of a message in person."

"I do appreciate the sacrifice."

She poured tea for both of them and took a piece of bread from the plate.

"What are you finding to do with yourself here?" he asked. "You've never been at ease with idleness."

"In the better weather I meddled in the gardens, much to the annoyance of the gardeners, but now I'm pestering old Brownholme instead."

"Brownholme?"

"The archivist. You must remember him. He's been here almost as long as the dusty records."

"Oh, yes. It's not as if he's often seen. What have you been doing to upset him?"

"He's not exactly upset," Georgia said. "In fact, I believe I'm enlivening his dusty life a little. I'm writing an account of the adventures of our great-grandmother during the civil war."

"The beautiful Lady Hernescroft who persuaded a number of Roundhead officers to spare Herne?"

Georgia sipped her tea, smiling at him. "The beautiful Lady Hernescroft who slept her way through a number of Roundhead officers to persuade them to spare Herne."

"You can't be serious."

"The implications are clear in her letters and journals."

"'Struth!"

"Perhaps I shall publish my account. . . ." She laughed at his expression. "I won't, but I'll bury it in the family records and hope someone finds it a hundred years from now."

He laughed. "The beau monde has been the Slough of Despond without Lady May. Please say you'll let me read your account."

Georgia put down her cup. "Only if you suffer Christmas here with me."

"What? Outrageous."

"That's my price."

"You're a wicked wench. Oh, very well, but the adventures of the second countess had better be worth it."

"I think you'll find they are. Here's your dinner, and it looks very sustaining." Georgia smiled at the footman. "Thank the cook for me."

When the man had left, she watched Perry attack a beefsteak and fried potatoes. She'd enjoyed watching Dickon eat too. Men did it with such appreciation, and she'd planned the meals to please him.

"Why so sad?" Perry asked.

She slid from the truth. "I had hoped to spend Christmas with the Torrismondes."

"You still could."

"No, I'll not bring a scandal to their feast. Christmas has never been jolly here, has it?"

"Neither Father nor Mother enjoys the traditions."

"They arrive from Town on Christmas Eve, go to church on Christmas Day, dispense largesse, then return to celebrate the New Year at court." But Georgia smiled. "Which meant we could enjoy the rest of the twelve days, and especially Twelfth Night, without their interference. Will you stay for Twelfth Night?"

"Georgie, you know I can't. My place then is at court."

She sighed. Twelfth Night at court . . .

"Ah well, I'll make merry with the servants in the kitchens."

"You're angling for me to encourage you to return with me, but it won't do. The dowager's stories are too fresh. Wait until after Easter."

Georgia picked a fried potato off his plate and ate it, considering.

"No. If I must wait, I'll wait my full term. I won't return as the sober widow. I'll return when my mourning's over, as Lady May in full, glorious plumage."

Perry smiled. "You can probably carry that off." He put aside his empty plate and drank some wine. "Behave with discretion even then, though. Avoid behavior likely to upset the censorious."

She pulled a face at him. "Spoilsport."

"You want to find a good husband. Good husbands will shy off a scandalous widow."

"Only the most boring ones." When he raised his brows at her, she said, "Oh, very well. I'll try to be good."

"You will be good, or you're likely to be a dowager all your life." When she stuck out her tongue at him, he grinned. "Do you have a victim in mind?

"No, but I do have requirements." She counted on her fingers. "One, rich, so he can be, two, a man of fashion and elegance, plus he will be, three, generous with his wealth and delight in Town life. Four, an earl, marquess, or duke."

"No viscount or baron need apply?"

"Who would willingly step down the social scale? In any case, I'm looking upward. Don't you think I'd make a splendid duchess?"

She saw Perry make a quick assessment of the possibilities. "Beaufort?"

Georgia didn't reply, except with a smile.

# Chapter 2

"You've a cooler head than I," Tom Knowlton said. "I'm sweating on your behalf."

Lord Dracy didn't take his eyes off the two horses being walked nearby. "Comes from facing enemy shot while standing on a burning deck."

"Good God, did you really?"

"Once or twice."

"That sort of thing develops insanity?"

Dracy shot him a humorous look. "Undoubtedly."

He knew they were an unlikely pair. He was lean and solid from an active navy life, often on tight rations. His neighbor, Sir Tom Knowlton, had never known want, liked his comforts, and was prosperously round. Tom also avoided risk. He didn't ride spirited horses or travel in fast vehicles.

Dracy liked his comforts when he had the chance of them, but avoid risk? Risk added spice to life, and in that respect life had been bland since he'd inherited his cousin's barony and left the navy. Perhaps that was why he'd accepted this mad challenge.

He and Knowlton were standing in the shade of an

elm tree on the estate of the Earl of Hernescroft, where a private thoroughbred race would soon take place. The earl's famous bay mare, Fancy Free, was to race against the Dracy black, Cartagena, winner take all. If Fancy Free won, the earl would own both horses, which would be a pleasant addition to his famous string of race-horses. If Carta won, Dracy would own two fine thoroughbred mares instead of just one, which might be the beginning of the revival of the Dracy stud. If he lost, he lost all and would have no option other than return to the navy.

The unusual stakes had drawn some lions of the racing world to join the local spectators. The Dukes of Portland, Beaufort, and Grafton were here, plus the Earls of Rockingham, Harthorne, and Waveney.

Going on the betting, none of them expected Cartagena to win, but that was to the good. If—when—Carta won, Dracy's cash winnings would pay for the essential repairs to his stable block.

Cartagena was a four-year-old new to the racing world, but she'd scored two startling triumphs at recent meetings. After the second, Lord Hernescroft had scoffed to Dracy's face that she wouldn't beat Fancy Free if they met.

There'd been no easy escape, but Dracy hadn't wanted one. The do or die was irresistible.

"I grant you Cartagena's successes," Knowlton said, still fretting, "but devil only knows why you couldn't be satisfied with 'em. Handsome prize money and more to come. Why risk everything this way?"

"Because Carta alone can't restore the Dracy fortunes," Dracy said, adding, "as you know," for Knowlton had trampled over these arguments for days.

"You'll have the place in shape in time."

"A decade or so."

"Took years for your cousin to run it down."

"I'm not that patient a man."

"No, you're a rash one. What's to gain that's worth the risk?"

Tired of the debate, Dracy glanced around to be sure no one was in earshot.

The spectators—on foot, on horse, and a few on the seats of open carriages—had arranged themselves on either side of the beginning of the race, which would also be the end.

No one was too close, but Dracy spoke quietly anyway. "My inquiries tell me Hernescroft is particularly fond of Fancy Free. Born in his own stud and named by one of his daughters. The daughter's particularly fond of the horse as well. When he's recovered from losing the race, he'll negotiate."

"Stap me! You're playing for money? Now, that makes sense."

"I'm playing for a stud. Herne can keep Fancy Free in exchange for Gosling-go."

"What?" Knowlton exclaimed, attracting attention just as Dracy had feared. But then, flushing, he dropped his voice. "He might do it, mightn't he? He has two prime stallions and Gosling-go's the older."

"And a vicious devil, I hear, but it's not in the blood."

"You've checked his get?"

"I always plot a course carefully."

"Stap me," Knowlton muttered. "No wonder you draped yourself in glory in the navy."

"No more than most men, and none of it was careful navigation. Just blood and guts on the day."

Knowlton shuddered. "Why not buy ... But a stud like Gosling-go would be pricey, even if Hernescroft was willing to sell. Sired some winners. Eight hundred at the least. All the same, you've only the one mare. Why not just pay stud fees?"

"I'd rather get stud fees, and there are three older thoroughbred mares at Dracy that Ceddie hadn't bothered to sell. They might be able to drop a foal or two. None's produced offspring of quality, but it's always a gamble. Remarkable horses have come out of indifferent dams."

"It's still a mad chance."

"Life's all about the mad chance, Tom—at least for those of us born to make our own way in the world."

"Why didn't you tell me before?"

"Because you're an open-faced fellow and Hernescroft might have sniffed a rat."

"He might not care. He's sure he'll win."

Dracy looked across the track at the stocky, full-bellied earl. "He won't."

"You can't be sure—"

"Nothing is ever sure. Not even that we'll return safely to our homes from this event."

"Oh, I say . . ."

At least that gloomy observation silenced Knowlton and let Dracy study his horse.

Carta was perfectly conformed. Even his cousin Ceddie had seen that. The fool had ruined the estate with his taste for London life and the latest fashions, and he'd sold off his father's famous thoroughbreds to pay for gewgaws. He'd kept Carta, however, called the Midnight Jade then, hoping she'd eventually show well in races and sell for a high price.

Carta had been Ceddie's gamble, and now she was his, renamed for the best battle he'd taken part in. Do or die, then and now.

"Here we go," Knowlton said, as the jockeys mounted.

Hernescroft's man wore green and yellow silks, Dracy's black and red lozenges. The two horses eyed each other as if they knew everything rested on this contest of speed and stamina.

"The deuce!" exclaimed Knowlton.

"What?" Dracy looked around for some unexpected hazard.

"The Scandalous Countess. Over there, in men's clothing."

Dracy looked and saw a man cramming a wide-brimmed hat back on the head of a laughing, red-haired woman.

"You could object to that," Knowlton said. "She could jinx the whole thing."

"I don't believe in jinxes." Dracy returned his attention to important matters. Devil take it, Carta was starting one of her fidgets. Perhaps she objected to red hair.

"Got Maybury killed in a duel over her lewd behavior."

"Who?"

"Lady Maybury. The Scandalous Countess."

"She planned it?" Dracy asked, a scrap of attention caught.

"No, no. At least, I don't think so. Husband dead, Vance fled the country, but there she is, merry as a mayfly. Maybury was an amiable fellow."

"If he was amiable enough to let her stray, he should have been too amiable to challenge someone over it."

"Devil take it, Dracy!"

"I've no interest in Lady Maybury or her lovers. Calm down, Carta. Calm down. At this rate she'll burn off her energy before the race starts."

"Too high-spirited."

"There's nothing wrong with high spirits."

"A true beauty," Knowlton said.

"Isn't she just?"

"But too wild to handle."

"Jorrocks and she understand each other."

"Who? Damn me, Dracy, I was talking about Georgia Maybury."

"To hell with Georgia Maybury. They're readying for the off."

The buzz of conversation died away.

The horses would gallop eight times around the course, to make two miles.

Devil take the jade, right now he'd get top odds. She'd

bucked as if trying to unseat Jorrocks. The groom turned her in a tight circle, forcing her to behave, but men were shaking their heads.

Dracy glared at the starter, Sir Charles Bunbury, who was chatting to Hernescroft. Perhaps the glare was felt, for Bunbury turned and called for order.

"Here we go," Knowlton muttered.

Bunbury waved the flag.

"They're off."

Carta was caught in a fidget and Fancy Free took the lead, thundering toward the distant oak that marked the turning point of the course. Dracy took out his navy telescope and watched Carta close the gap as they turned the tree.

"Nothing in it," he muttered, but he'd expected that. This race wouldn't be happening if the two mares weren't closely matched. Damned closely. And Hernescroft's mare had two years' maturity and two years' more racing experience.

But Carta had youthful fire. She'd do her best to win, and no one could ask more than that.

As the horses galloped back toward them, the mass of men shouted and bellowed, threatening Dracy's hearing as much as ships' guns had, but he realized he was yelling too. Yelling at Carta to go, go, go!

When the horses pounded past him, Carta still looked full of fire. She pulled ahead, as if showing off for the crowd, but then Fancy Free caught up and pulled ahead. Carta pulled that lead back.

And so it went, around and around, nothing in it, nothing in it, Dracy's heart pounding in his chest, his throat raw with shouting. A mere breath lay between victory and complete defeat.

He was hoarse, and so must everyone be, but still they yelled, encouraging the horse they'd put money on, but also simply celebrating the magnificent, courageous beasts.

A higher-pitched call snapped his attention beyond the horses for a moment. It was that scandalous woman, waving her broad-brimmed hat, red hair tumbling out of pins, catching fire in the sun. Her companion shoved her hat on again. She laughed at him, unrepentant.

Dracy pitied any man who had the handling of her, but his attention was all back on the horses. One more turn, and then, nostrils flaring, necks extended, Carta and Fancy Free raced toward the finish line, first Fancy Free ahead by a nose, then Carta, then Fancy Free again. . . .

Dracy fell silent, too focused to shout. *Come on, come on, come on. A bit more, a bit more, my lovely. A bit—*

"Yes!" He threw his hat in the air, not caring where it landed. "By God, she did it! By a nose. By more than a nose."

Knowlton was jumping up and down, holding on to his hat and grinning like an idiot.

Dracy ran to Carta to give her all the praise she deserved, more purely exhilarated than during his fiercest victory at sea.

He congratulated the wizened jockey, aware of being backslapped and of men grabbing his hand to wring it. It wasn't just those who'd won bets. Men were celebrating with him because the race had been a fine one and because he'd gambled all and won.

Someone put a goblet of wine in his hand, and he toasted both horses and both jockeys. He passed the goblet to Jorrocks and had him drink. He praised Carta again. In her moment of glory she'd decided to be a perfect lady, posing like a black marble statue and accepting tribute.

"Oh, you beautiful jade!"

He was still grinning, even though he knew his scar would twist it. He'd a burn on the right side of his face that could make sensitive souls blanch, especially when he grinned and it created a snarl. He tried not to disturb strangers that way, but right now, he didn't give a damn. He grinned and laughed. This was a glorious moment.

He drained another cup of wine but then steadied himself and went to take possession of his prize.

Or rather, his bargaining chip.

Fancy Free's grooms greeted him with stony faces. They didn't want to see her go, especially to ramshackle stables like those at Dracy. Dracy had made sure they and the Earl of Hernescroft knew all about that.

The horse also seemed downcast, as if knowing her fate. He wished he could whisper that she needn't worry. That she wouldn't have to leave her luxurious home.

He bowed to the portly gray-haired earl. If Hernescroft had thrown a fit upon losing, he'd recovered. He didn't pretend happiness but offered congratulations.

"A damn fine race, Dracy, and a damn fine horse too. Damn fine. I regret she won't be joining my stables."

"They both ran well, Hernescroft. I assure you Fancy Free will be well cared for in my stables. They aren't as fine as yours, but she'll have the necessities."

The earl's jowly features twitched. "Perhaps she can stay with her familiar attendants for now, eh? Rest a day or two before traveling."

"By all means. I intend the same for Cartagena."

"Good, good. Would you take a celebratory glass of wine with me at the house? We can discuss the arrangements."

"Honored, Hernescroft." Dracy bowed again. "I'll just see to Cartagena's care."

"Have her brought to my stables. She and your people will have the best care."

Dracy's "people" were Jorrocks and a thirteen-year-old lad, and they'd be uncomfortable in grand surroundings.

"Thank you, my lord, but she's happily settled at the Bull nearby."

He turned away, intrigued by the earl's tone. Perhaps Hernescroft was already thinking along the right lines.

Carta was playing the coquette now, but in a well-mannered way, preening for her admirers and dancing just a little, as if to say she could do it all again, immediately.

"You minx," he said, rubbing her nose. "You beautiful, magnificent minx." Close to her ear he added, "I'm going to get you a fine stallion as a reward."

He sent her off to the Bull and told Knowlton, "I'm invited to drink wine with the loser."

"Gracious of him."

"Only what I'd expect." He strolled with Knowlton away from the dwindling crowd. "I suspect he's already thinking along the same lines as I. It's all going according to plan."

"You couldn't be sure you'd win," Knowlton complained.

"Fate's a capricious wench. I survived actions when men on either side of me died, and they'd done nothing to warrant their bad luck. I've seen winds change to favor one side or the other in battle. Some cry that God's favored them, but why should he? Neither side was good or evil, and wars are usually about money and land in someone's pocket."

"Oh, I say . . ."

Dracy regretted disturbing his friend. "In this case, I pray it's a stallion in my stables."

"Wish I had your nerve."

"No, you don't. You have all you want in life. You've no need to risk anything to gain more."

Knowlton smiled. "I admit it, but sometimes I think I lead a dull life."

"Give thanks for it daily. I hope for the same."

"You think to marry?" Knowlton asked, surprised.

Dracy had been thinking of life in general, but he supposed a cozy life would benefit from a cozy wife. One day.

"I've too much on my plate restoring house, estate, and stables to take on more at the moment."

"A wife can be a helpmeet, especially with the house. That's her domain."

"It's certainly not mine. Very well, if you think of a suitable lady with a tranquil temperament, frugal domestic talents, and a handsome dowry, let me know. One who won't mind my face."

Knowlton spluttered, and Dracy felt guilty again for upsetting him. Theirs was an odd friendship, but he truly liked Tom Knowlton and valued the entree to his cozy, normal world.

He slapped him on the back. "I'm off to my appointment with fate. Wish me luck. I'll report all to you over dinner at the Bull."

# Chapter 3

Dracy walked toward Herne through a dispersing crowd, but he was still frequently slowed by men wanting to congratulate him. He fended off a number of invitations to dine, or even to spend a few days at this place or that, but realized he was enjoying the spirit of the moment.

He missed the navy, especially the camaraderie enforced by crowded ships. He missed having friends and acquaintances in every port, especially those who shared his devil-may-care attitude to life. It didn't take long for any military man to realize how much of survival was up to chance.

He especially missed encounters with the men he'd first met as a cabin boy. Some were dead and the rest scattered around the world.

After nearly six months, he still struggled to fit into the sleepy Devon society around Dracy. The racing world was a better fit because it was manly and adventurous, with fortunes often in the balance. However, most of these men would return to lives as predictable and comfortable as Tom Knowlton's. They hadn't learned that anyone had only the moment, that disaster could strike with no warning, even on a sunny day.

They should have learned it—he met men, and even

some women, who teetered constantly on the edge of disaster, mired in debt, reveling in dangerous sports, flirting with fatal scandal. Every now and then one toppled over into the mire, yet the rest showed no visible awareness of their mortality.

Did they think they were gods?

He'd take the solid country gentlemen like Tom Knowlton over the beau monde any day.

But take a wife?

The idea was growing on him, however, especially now he'd won the gamble. Solitary life held little appeal. Perhaps a wife—a plump and practical one like Annie Knowlton—would know how to make damp, dusty Dracy into a cozy home. But she'd have to do it on a pittance. The stud, not the farmland, appealed to his temperament, and he was putting every spare penny to work there, and nearly all his energy too. Many a time he'd taken up saw or hammer to attend to a job.

A house was a wife's job, however, as Tom had said. He was sure Annie Knowlton took up duster and scrubbing brush alongside her servants. Perhaps a wife would know how to dragoon his handful of servants into hard work.

The right wife would know how to put cheap, tasty meals on the table and defeat the army of moths and other pests he housed. She would sit with him by the fireside in the evening, mending sheets as he worked on the estate books. And then in time, they'd go to bed.

How the devil would that go?

His bed partners had always been sophisticated ladies who by the very nature of things were demanding of those they favored. There'd been none of that since returning home. An impoverished baron didn't have the allure of a naval officer in a foreign port, and of course his appearance counted against him with some.

No, he wouldn't give much for his chances of any

sort of wife. One particularly sensitive lady in Devon had swooned when brought suddenly face-to-face with him.

Even Tom's wife was uncomfortable with his appearance. She was sorry for him rather than disgusted, but it had taken her a while to become at ease. Tom's children still weren't. If they caught sight of him they stared and clutched at an attendant. He'd quickly learned not to smile at them.

He wasn't one to mourn what couldn't be changed, but before leaving the navy he'd not been so aware of his disfigurement.

He passed through a yew hedge and paused to give due tribute to the great house known simply as Herne. The place was enormous, stretching left and right, ranks of windows gleaming despite the window tax. The front doubtless had pillars and porticos, but he was approaching from the rear. The back was still richly decorated, and a long terrace ran across the middle of the house, with stairs leading up to it.

There didn't seem much point in walking around to the front, but what were the appropriate entrances on this side? Three sets of glass doors led from the terrace into the house. The left-hand doors stood open. They'd do. He set off across a sea of lawn scattered with pale classical statues and then wove his way through geometric gardens.

He climbed the steps and crossed the stone terrace, pausing before a pair of gryphons, half eagle, half lion. As symbols of valor and magnanimity they were all very well, but as guardians they were rather easily circumvented. He walked around them and headed for the open doors, wondering whether it would be seen as a rude invasion.

Just then, a powdered and liveried footman stepped out to bow. "Welcome to Herne, your lordship."

Dracy nodded and went in, liking the feel of that.

Hernescroft had arranged for his comfort, and that augured well for making a good deal.

He was in an elegant room with a richly plastered ceiling, and walls covered with paintings. Probably not a drawing room, as they were generally on a higher floor, less easily invaded. This was for more public use. He wagered himself a shilling it was called the Terrace Room.

The footman led him down a corridor, then right and down another, until they'd moved beyond the main part of the house into a plainer part.

They halted before a plain door.

An estate room?

Not so promising.

When Dracy entered, however, he liked it better. This had to be the earl's office, but he clearly also used it as a comfortable retreat. Dracy's boots were treading on a fine carpet, and the furniture was all richly made and lavishly gilded, including a monumental desk. The walls here were also hung with paintings, but all of horses and races, alongside other sporting items. A small table might be used for private dining. Two upholstered chairs sat by the fireplace, and a settee nearby could be used by additional guests.

Dracy knew that noting all these details might seem odd, but it was an old instinct. Details were crucial in warfare, and especially in navigating unknown waters. Whether in the temperamental seas of the fashionable world or the more placid lakes of the country gentry, one wrong word could sink a man.

"Come in, Dracy, come in," said the earl. "Claret, brandy, port?"

"Claret, thank you," Dracy said, noting that the footman had left and the earl was serving the wine. So, a private discussion.

He'd studied all available information about the Earl of Hernescroft. Though portly and ruddy-faced, he was in excellent health. His heir, Viscount Pranksworth, was thirty-two years old and already father of two sons, so the line seemed safe. If that branch failed, the earl had three other sons, one in the army, one in the navy, and one a Town idler.

There were also two daughters, both well married.

Or in one case, widowed, Dracy remembered, and stained by scandal. An image of a laughing face and fiery hair darted through his mind like a shooting star. He blanked it out. This was no time to be distracted by a highborn doxy.

Dracy took the crystal glass and raised it. "To fine horses and fine races, my lord."

The earl raised his glass and repeated the toast. "Have a seat, Dracy. I've a matter to discuss with you."

Very promising. Dracy sat in one upholstered chair and the earl took the other.

"I play, I pay," Hernescroft said, "but there are methods of payment. Would you consider accepting a prize of equal value?"

Dracy took another sip of wine so as not to snatch the prize too quickly. "I would be churlish not to consider it, sir. Another horse, you mean?"

"Another horse?" Hernescroft's pouchy eyes narrowed.

Not another horse?

"What else, to be of equal value?"

"I don't have another mare to compare with Fancy Free, and I'd not offer less."

"So you mean a stallion?" Dracy did his best to pretend surprise. "I recollect that you do have two of quality."

His acting ability wasn't up to the job.

"Damn me! Was that your game? Gosling-go, I assume." The earl pulled a face. "Won't play, Dracy. Took exception to something a few days back and tried to kick down his stall. Broke his hock. Had to be shot."

"Dead," Dracy said, trying to conceal the blow. He should have kept himself better informed, but even a few days ago the die had been cast. "Most unfortunate, my lord. I heard nothing of it."

"I'd moved him to Lambourne to cover some mares there. Perhaps he objected to the relocation. I only heard the news myself yesterday."

Dracy drank more wine, replotting his course. "Then I regret I'll have to sell Fancy Free in order to purchase a stallion of quality."

"Put her up for auction? Not the way to treat such a horse."

"I agree, but I've less need of a fine mare than I have of a fine stallion. If you were to pay her value . . ."

The earl pinched his heavy lower lip. "Cash is damned hard to come by these days, Dracy. You must know that. The war, the prices. Things are bad all around." He pushed out of his chair and went to the decanter. "One of my younger sons has proven expensive."

He waved the bottle at Dracy, but he declined, wondering where this was leading.

The earl sat down again. "I could sell some unentailed land, but it's a wicked thing to sell land. Wicked. A betrayal of our ancestors who gathered it."

"I agree, sir," Dracy said, thinking of the unentailed land Ceddie had sold, but also trying to anticipate what was coming.

Lieutenant Arthur Perriam, RN's gambling debts were no surprise, nor was the earl's opinion about the sacred trust of land. Both had been part of his calculations. Hernescroft was steering a careful course of his own, however, and Dracy didn't like the fact that he had no idea what it was.

"I have another exchange to propose."

"Yes, sir?"

Hernescroft drank. Delaying?

"A different kind of filly, but worth more than Fancy Free. Much more."

Dracy chose to be merely attentive.

"My daughter."

"Your *daughter*?"

"Her portion's twelve thousand. You could buy a herd of stallions for that. You'll have to sign settlements for a widow's jointure of two thousand a year and give her generous pin money, but the twelve thousand will be yours, cash in hand, upon your wedding day. It's a more than fair exchange."

"It is indeed," Dracy said, feeling as if he'd been navigating a tricky shore and been ambushed by a dense fog.

"I'm speaking of my youngest girl, Lady Maybury. A widow, but ripe to marry again."

Titian hair.

Laughing, minxish beauty.

Wicked, wanton doxy.

Attached to that lady the word "ripe" was alarming, and this offer was astounding. He was no match for an earl's well-dowried daughter.

"You'll have heard of her," the earl prompted.

"She was pointed out to me at the race."

"Devil take the chit!" the earl exploded. "Dressed in breeches to boot. I'll give Pranksworth a piece of my mind for bringing her, but he'll say she'd have come anyway. Headstrong, headstrong. But," he added quickly, "not leather-mouthed and no true vice in her."

The fog had parted a little, but only to reveal jagged rocks.

"Not an attractive package," Dracy said, remembering his pity of the man who had to tame her.

Surprisingly, the earl laughed. "Is she not? Then why are half the men in England drooling after her? That's my problem, Dracy. She plans to marry again. Only natural at twenty."

"Twenty!" Dracy exclaimed. He'd imagined such a sinful jade to be much older.

"Married her off at sixteen. Maybury was well known to us and had just come into his earldom. He was only nineteen, but his mother and guardians were keen to see him wedlocked before he reached his majority and married a doxy."

Dracy kept the obvious comment to himself.

"Couldn't manage her, of course. Encouraged her in folly, if the truth is told. The fool liked her causing talk. Lady May, the beau monde dubbed her, but we thought she'd settle once she had children. That didn't happen, and then there was the Vance affair."

"Vance?"

"Sir Charnley Vance," the earl said. "The one who killed Maybury in a duel. You'll have heard of that?"

"Only a snippet, at the race." Dracy had the distinct impression that Hernescroft wished he'd not mentioned it.

"Ah, well, overseas when it happened, I suppose. Plaguey business all around."

"Was this Vance her lover, my lord? I wouldn't normally ask such a question, but as the lady is being proposed to me as wife . . ."

"She swears not, and I'd say that for all her faults, she's truthful. Never sought to hide any other sins," Hernescroft added with a scowl.

"Then why would her husband call this Vance out?"

"Devil alone knows. A greater piece of folly I've never seen. The story was Maybury had clashed wheels with a wagon during some madcap race. Vance taunted him and it exploded into a challenge. Men have met for less, but Maybury was an easygoing fellow, so people talked. Gossip always chooses the dirty path, and word spread that they fought over my daughter. Then that Vance was her lover. Some of the men who were present at the argument claimed her name came into it, but they all admitted to being deep in drink."

"I appreciate your frankness, my lord. Permit me to be equally frank in return. Your daughter's portion would be useful to me, and in monetary terms it's many times the value of Fancy Free. But when I choose a wife I'll choose one likely to give me tranquil days and make me a comfortable home." He suddenly thought of something else. "She's borne no children?"

"None."

"How long was she married?"

"Three and a half years."

"I would also want a wife who could fill a nursery. My apologies, but Lady Maybury fails to meet my requirements in any way."

"Does she indeed?" Hernescroft took something out of his pocket to pass over.

It was a miniature, and for a moment, it stopped Dracy's heart.

By God.

Here was the woman he'd glimpsed at a distance, but now she looked out at him with a mischievous invitation. Sparkling sea green eyes, full smiling lips, a flawless complexion, and that abundance of Titian red hair, in this case threaded carelessly with pearls.

True beauties were rare, but if the picture was honest, the wicked Countess of Maybury was one. His visceral reaction was a warning shot across the bow. A sensible man would turn and run, but he'd never been sensible in that way.

He forced his eyes away and looked at the earl. "Why would this woman want to marry me?"

"She'll do as she's told."

Dracy doubted that.

"You don't seem shy of a gamble, Dracy. No saying who was to blame for the empty nursery."

"A tranquil wife and comfortable home?"

Hernescroft chuckled. "Are you sure you want that? You've lived an eventful life and might not take to being becalmed."

He was impressed with the earl's insight. Dracy had cursed the condition of his new estate and the work it involved, but did he really aspire to live as placidly as Knowlton? Constant storms were unpleasant, but constant calm could drive men mad.

"What of the scandal? Will she be accepted back in society?"

"She's still my daughter, and nothing was proved against her. On our advice, she's spent her mourning year here, living quietly in seclusion, letting it all die down. She still has many friends and admirers. At least two of the men here today are drawn as much by the hope of seeing her as by the race. She'll probably soon be the darling of Town again, and there's the rub." The earl took another mouthful of wine and almost chewed it. "I'll have her tied to a solid, decent husband before she picks a blackguard."

"You know I'm solid and decent?"

"I've made inquiries."

Ah. The fog had almost cleared, but the jagged shore still threatened, and now an enemy warship had appeared.

Hernescroft had been playing as deep a game over the race as he. Had he planned to lose, even arranged to lose?

No, that would be against the earl's nature in all respects, but he could have seen a way where he would win, whatever the result. Win the race and gain Carta. Lose, and rid himself of a troublesome daughter while still keeping Fancy Free.

Tempting to call his bluff and take Fancy Free anyway.

Foolish, though. In strictly practical terms, twelve thousand pounds would be a gift of the gods. It would buy a prize stallion and a few good mares as well as dealing with most of the necessary repairs.

A widow's jointure of two thousand a year was ridiculously high for an estate such as his, but he could hope Dracy would be in fine state when that came due many decades hence. The generous pin money would have to be cut and any extravagance curtailed, but as he and his wife would be living quietly in the country, that shouldn't be a hardship for her.

She wouldn't like it, though, and a bitter wife was a hard burden.

Was he even considering this?

Yes.

It was a gamble, indeed it was, and one that would affect his whole life, but the sea was a chancier wench than any woman, and he had a way with women, even now.

He looked again at the miniature.

A siren. No, they'd been ugly and drawn sailors to their doom by song. Circe had been the beautiful enchantress encountered by Odysseus, but she'd turned his men into swine.

This one had turned a husband into a corpse.

"You can't be expected to make your decision without a meeting," the earl said, breaking the enchantment. "We'll be dining soon, and she'll be present. Join us. Only an informal meal for the men here for the race and those wives who accompanied them. You'll know the men from racing circles. . . ."

Dracy realized he was still staring at the miniature. He returned it.

"Keep it for now if you wish," Hernescroft said.

"No, thank you."

The earl laughed. "Wise man. But you're the type she needs. A man of iron, used to command."

"Keelhauling and the cat-o'-nine-tails?"

The earl laughed. "No, no, but a switch now and then might do her good. Kept her in line as a girl. Come along, then, come along, and judge for yourself."

A part of Dracy wanted to walk away from this treacherous bargain while he still had his wits, but he couldn't resist an encounter. After all, he was in no danger.

The scandalous Lady Maybury would have no interest in an impoverished scarred sailor, and once the earl accepted that, he'd find a way to pay the money.

# Chapter 4

*Dear Lizzie,*

*I couldn't resist the race. After all, Fancy Free is my favorite, for I named her when she was born. So I cajoled Pranks into letting me ride out with him.*

*Yes, of course, dressed in breeches. I see you shake your head, but I didn't want to be known. I wore a wide-brimmed hat and would have been completely undetected had it not come adrift. Twice. Very well, in the second instance I was carried away and took it off to wave it in excitement. I doubt anyone noticed, for all eyes were on the race. I didn't intend a scandal, not even a tiny one. I simply wanted to see Fancy Free triumph.*

*Alas, Lord Dracy's Cartagena won by a head against all odds, and now poor Fancy Free will have to move to Dracy's stables, which I gather are decrepit.*

*Do you think horses have the same sense of home as we do? When my mind turns to Belling Row and Sansouci, I can be quite cast down even now, nearly a year later. And I'm living in luxury. Imagine if I'd been compelled to move to a hovel in an alley!*

*I know, I know, that could never be, but this move will be the equivalent for Fancy Free.*

> *Moreover, I have control of my future, whereas the poor horse must go where she's sent. Lud, she's no more than a slave. Shall I start a movement against such cruelty? Yes, yes, I know it's folly, but I truly feel for the poor creature. . . .*

The loud knock at her boudoir door startled Georgia into blotting her letter. Before she could respond, her mother had entered the room.

"Georgia? Ah, there you are. You are to dress and go down to dinner."

Rising hastily she curtsied to her mother. "What? Why?"

Lady Hernescroft was a tall, gaunt woman with steel gray hair. Sometimes people said that Georgia resembled her mother in youth, which was positively alarming.

Thin lips grew thinner. "Because your father requests it."

*Orders,* Georgia interpreted, but she resisted. "You know I don't intend to mix with society until my mourning year is over, Mother."

"Then you shouldn't have attended the race. Having done so, you must correct the damage by presenting a more decorous picture at dinner."

"No one noticed," Georgia protested.

"Of course they did. And those who didn't have heard of it. In breeches! What were you thinking, girl? You will do as requested."

"I don't think it wise—"

"You question your father's judgment?"

Georgia instinctively said, "No!" That would be like questioning the word of God. But then she asked again, "Why? My attending dinner won't change anyone's mind."

Her mother still glared, but then, amazingly, her direct gaze shifted. Something was afoot. "It has to do with the race."

"My being there wasn't so—"

"Not your behavior, Georgia. The victor."

"Cartagena?"

"Lord Dracy! Despite the loss, your father took a fancy to him and has invited him to dine. You shall attend to his comfort."

"He needs a cushion for his chair, or a footstool for a gouty toe?"

"Don't be pert. Lord Dracy was in the navy until his cousin died in January. He's taken up his responsibilities but is sadly ill prepared for the highest circles. You shall ease his way over dinner."

Georgia bit back another pert comment, this time about choice of fork.

"Why me? Millicent will be there." Pranks's wife enjoyed fussing over guests and would resent Georgia supplanting her.

"Millicent will not be there. You know how sensitive she is when carrying. Your antics have sent her to her bed."

"Then I'm sorry for it, Mother, but surely . . ."

"There's another reason Millicent has absented herself. Lord Dracy was unfortunately scarred in battle. One side of his face is distorted in a way that must distress a sensitive lady."

"Whereas I'm tough as boiled leather?"

"*You* are not carrying a child."

Georgia told herself that wasn't a deliberate thrust. "I think it would be shameful to turn pale at the sight of a man blemished in defense of us all, even if I were with child."

"Do not criticize your sister-in-law because you are made of coarser stuff."

"Coarser? To seek to be kind to a hero?"

Georgia saw her mother make a big effort. Her lips even turned up at the corners. "You do have a good heart, daughter."

What on earth was going on?

"What exactly am I asked to do?" Georgia asked.

"Stay by Dracy's side and converse with him no matter how tongue-tied he is. Ease his way, advise him. . . ."

"On what?"

"Anything that arises."

A lewd vision popped into Georgia's mind and she had to struggle to keep a straight face. If only Dickon were with her. He'd laugh too.

"Have you other questions?" her mother demanded.

Only, *why*? Was this political? Her parents were constantly involved in political chess, especially now, with the king at odds with his ministry, and cabals scheming in every corner of St. James.

"Mother, what's truly behind this?"

"You are unpleasantly willful, Georgia," her mother said, but almost wearily. "If you will have an explanation, Hernescroft regrets the loss of Fancy Free. He hopes to negotiate an exchange of prizes. Some kindness to Lord Dracy might smooth the way."

"Ah, that makes sense."

Georgia considered the situation. She wanted to keep to her seclusion for the full year. Once she made a resolve, she liked to hold to it. However, Fancy Free's situation truly did concern her.

"Then I will attend," she said. "In Fancy Free's cause, I'll take the most tender care of our gouty tar."

"He's a naval officer."

Georgia ignored that. "And if he bellows across the dining table or spits on the floor I'll hint him toward better ways."

"Sometimes I despair of you!" her mother snapped, but closed her eyes and held back any other rant. "Remember, Georgia, you must also counter the impression of your appearance at the race. Dress modestly and behave with sober discretion; then perhaps our guests will carry away a good report of you."

She swept out, and Georgia indulged in sticking out her tongue at the door as it closed and muttering, "I'm as much a slave as a horse."

"You stop that, milady," said Jane, who'd been standing quietly in a corner.

Laughing, Georgia stuck out a tongue at her too, and then sat to add the latest news to the letter to Lizzie.

"Milady. You need to dress."

"In a moment." Georgia wrote quickly, ending with, *If this could reach you in time, I'd beg you to pray for me. As it is, I'll hold the letter back and report before dispatching it.*

She put the letter in a drawer in her desk and locked it, then surrendered to Jane. She shed her robe, then put on her stays for Jane to lace, regretting that "pray for me." It revealed nervousness. She'd explained keeping to her room last night as part of her commitment to avoid society for a full year, but she knew she'd grasped at the excuse.

She longed to return to real life, to fashionable life, but now, as the time came close, she sometimes felt slightly sick. How many people still thought she'd been Vance's lover, and thus the cause of Dickon's death?

She took out her feelings on the stays, pushing the flat, boned front into place. "What an imposition. I haven't worn a full corset in an age."

"You can't wear country stays to dine, milady. It's always obvious and gives a poor impression."

"I know, but this is so unfair."

"I warned against you going to watch the race, milady."

"Yes, you did, but it was worth it."

"You always say that," Jane grumbled, giving the laces a sharp tug. "But perhaps it's no bad thing for you to appear in a small gathering before going on to larger ones."

"You might be right. Beaufort is here, and Waveney."

"Lord Waveney is married now, milady, and his wife's here with him."

"Lud! Then I'll see if I can attract Portland, though he is rather dull."

"It's the ladies you need to impress, milady. Those are the ones who'll write letters and carry away stories."

"At least Millicent won't be there, sighing and tossing in reproachful comments. Though I suppose her sister will act as her proxy. Why Eloisa Cardross dislikes me so, I can't imagine."

"Yes, you can, milady. She's considered a beauty but can't hold a candle to you. Stand up straight, milady."

Georgia did. "Have I started to slump? Horrors! You would tell me, wouldn't you, if I had?"

"Always, for what attention you pay."

"You are my wise older sister."

Jane snorted, but there was a laugh in it, for they were friends.

Jane had just turned thirty when hired to be the new Countess of Maybury's lady's maid, and at first she'd seemed severe. Beneath a starchy exterior, however, lurked a wry sense of humor and a delight in fashion that equaled Georgia's. She'd soon become a friend and confidant, and she and Georgia had worked together to design the unique garments worn by Lady May.

Georgia knew she should have listened to Jane's sensible advice more often, but her adventures had seemed harmless and Jane's cautions stuffy. There'd been no serious consequences at the time, but those exploits had made it easy for vile-minded people to believe the worst.

The time she'd diced for kisses.

The goddess costume that gave the illusion of bare breasts.

Being caught kissing Harry Shaldon at Lady Rothgar's ball.

That had been unfortunate, but Dickon had made light of it, even claiming that he'd lost the right to the kiss at cards. He'd not reproached her afterward either.

Dear Dickon.

But that alone had made the story of her being Vance's lover credible to some. As if there were any comparison. Shaldon was a bold, sporting gentleman, but he was a gentleman. For all his birth, Sir Charnley Vance was not.

"Take my advice now," Jane said, knotting the laces. "Behave perfectly, for all eyes will judge you—"

"I know that."

"But do not show anxiety or shame. That duel was your husband's folly, no more than that, and though you've grieved for him most tenderly, you have nothing with which to reproach yourself."

Georgia almost argued, for she knew her sins, but what Jane said was mostly true. She was innocent—of anything really bad, at least.

"Now, what gown, milady? The cream lustring, the blue, the fawn with roses?"

"The gray tabby."

"That thing! It's hardly suitable for dusting, never mind dining with dukes and earls."

"It's my best half mourning. I won't dress in colors, Jane. I resolved to give Dickon the twelve months, and to renege on that simply because I mingle with the beau monde would be despicable."

"I doubt any of them are watching the date."

Georgia laughed. "They'll be counting the days as carefully as they count those to the birth of a first child. The gray. Hurry. To be late will make me all the more significant."

"Then put on the pockets and hoops whilst I get it."

Georgia was tying the second knot when Jane returned, her arms full of smoky cloth. It did rather look like a dark cloud.

"When you're finished with gray, milady, I'll say a prayer of thanks. It performs a miracle and makes you drab."

"Drab is exactly what we want now."

Jane passed over the skirt and Georgia put it on. Next came the bodice, which hooked up the front and reached modestly to her collarbone. She scrutinized herself in the mirror.

"Can you find that frilled insert, Jane? And the snood cap."

Her maid gave a snort of disgust but soon returned with the two linen items. The insert fastened around Georgia's neck and tucked down beneath the bodice, front and back.

"Positively nunlike," Georgia said. "This should smother any thoughts of the Scandalous Countess."

"A scandal it is that anyone call you that, milady, and you scarce more than a girl even yet. Sit you down and I'll fix on the cap."

"I don't think age plays a part," Georgia said, obeying. "There are girls at Danae House who were raped, but others who danced merrily along the path to disaster at fourteen." Danae House was a charity for disgraced serving girls.

Jane twisted up Georgia's thick hair and pinned it tightly. "It's not suitable for you to be involved with such as them."

"Is it wrong for Lady Rothgar to be a patroness, or Lady Walgrave, or the Duchess of Ithorne?"

"They're all older than you, milady." Jane shoved a last pin into Georgia's hair and added the snood, which covered all the hair at the back. Georgia tucked away as much of her front hair as possible.

"Jewelry, milady?"

To wear none other than her wedding ring would be eccentric, but what? "The pearl studs," Georgia said, taking out the plain gold ones she was wearing. "And my mourning bracelet."

When Jane returned, Georgia put in the earrings and then slid the mourning bracelet on her right wrist, pulling a face at it. The black and silver band held a crystal that protected a lock of Dickon's brown hair. It always made her think of his corpse.

She looked at the small portrait on her dressing table, which she much preferred. It showed him smiling and in fashionable finery, full of life and the joys it held. She kissed her fingers and touched them to the image, but the glass was as cold as his corpse had been.

She swallowed and stood to survey herself in the long mirror.

"Lud! Perhaps Beaufort and the rest won't even notice my presence."

Jane snorted.

Georgia put on her plain black shoes. "It might be pleasant to be ignored, like a ghost at the feast."

"There's an odd thought for Lady May," Jane said.

It was indeed. Georgia took the gray fan Jane offered and turned back to the mirror for a final check, tucking away a curl, smoothing away a crease in the bodice.

Delaying.

"Enough of this dithering," she said and left the room.

She went downstairs, but when she heard conversation from the Terrace Room, she halted three steps from the bottom.

She forced herself onward, but perdition! Her heart was beating faster than it should. She'd never been afraid like this before. Never. A burst of laughter felt threatening, as if they laughed at her. . . .

A footman was stationed in the hall, observing her.

To excuse another halt, she asked, "Has Lord Dracy arrived yet?"

"Yes, your ladyship, but I saw him just now go out onto the terrace."

"Thank you," Georgia said, meaning it, and turned to go onto the terrace by a different door.

A cowardly move, but she could cloak it in duty. Lord

Dracy was her charge, and it seemed he'd already fled
the company. Poor fish out of water. No, a beached tar,
like a beached whale.

Rotund, floundering, helpless.

Georgia went through an anteroom and out onto the
terrace, but then she paused.

There was only one man on the terrace, a gentleman
in brown country clothing who had his back to her. It
had to be Lord Dracy, but he was no gouty whale. Broad
shoulders, long, strong legs . . .

But what on earth was he doing?

Dracy had been introduced to the Hernescroft house
party and none of the ladies had fainted. Some had been
uncomfortable, however, so he'd relieved them of his
face by strolling out through open doors onto the terrace. After so much time at sea and in foreign lands, he
never tired of the English countryside.

He walked up to the stone balustrade, amused by the
fancy of being on the poop deck of a ship, with a fair sea
spread before him and a brisk wind making music in the
sails.

Instead of gray waves he was surrounded by the rolling green of a skillfully designed park, and the music
came from the twitter and song of birds. English birdsong was a rare treasure.

He inhaled with satisfaction and realized a sweet perfume rose from below. He leaned forward across the
wide coping to find the source. Ah, roses and a honeysuckle vine were climbing the wall. But what were the
tall, ungainly plants bearing pale flowers?

"I do hope you're not attempting to put an end to
your existence, Lord Dracy."

He straightened but took his time in turning. If that
mellow voice didn't belong to Circe, he'd be damned disappointed.

It did, and Lady Maybury, a teasing light in her big

blue eyes, was as perfect in the flesh as in the painting, despite a gray dress and a demure cap that hid most of her hair.

In fact, she was even more alluring.

In such a gray frame, she glowed with vitality.

He pulled his wits together and bowed. He almost said, "Lady Maybury," but remembered in time that she was supposed to be a stranger.

"You have the advantage of me, ma'am."

She dipped a curtsy. "The Countess of Maybury, my lord, Lord Hernescroft's daughter. He requested that I take tender care of you, so I fear he'd be most disappointed if you did away with yourself at the terrors of your first social event."

Heaven help him, a gentle wit, good humor, and most wondrous of all, no sign of a flinch at the sight of his face. She'd have been warned, but from the first she'd met his eyes with no hint of discomfort.

There was also no hint that she knew of a special connection between them. In general, he preferred honest dealings, but he'd avoid them for now and enjoy this pleasant moment.

"Hardly my first social occasion, Lady Maybury, but my first with fine English ladies."

"Frightening enough to send you head first off the balustrade, my lord?"

He smiled, testing her with the snarl.

Again, wonder of wonders, no flinch.

"I wasn't attempting suicide, ma'am. I merely wished to discover the magic of the perfume below. Roses and honeysuckle I recognize, but not the tall plants."

She came closer in a soft rustle of skirts and leaned out, but the balustrade was too wide to give her a view.

Dracy scooped her up and sat her on top, keeping an arm around her waist—for safety's sake, of course.

Her beautiful eyes were only a foot from his, the subtle tones of green and blue reminding him of some for-

eign seas. Her lashes were brandy brown and thick, and
even up close her complexion was as perfect as a rose
petal. It truly was.

And her scent . . .

Or was that the flowers?

# Chapter 5

Trapped by his arm, Georgia stilled, heart fluttering, unsure what to do but determined not to show it.

"I was warned you might be rough-and-ready in your ways, my lord, but this . . ."

His expression was slightly, irritatingly, amused. "Blame it on the navy. Are you offended?"

"And if I were?"

"I would instantly return you to the terrace, my lady, and apologize profusely."

"So tame?"

"You would prefer that I complete the offense and tip you over?"

She had to laugh. "You are certainly an original, Lord Dracy."

"Perhaps a gallant one? I hoped to prevent you from snagging your gown."

"It would be no great loss. In twenty-four days I'll be free of mourning and may well burn it. Very well, sir. I will trust you and lean."

She did so but hadn't anticipated that it would press the side of her right breast to his hand. Thank heavens for stays!

"Ah, the perfumed tobacco," she said, straightening

quickly. "I doubt you're smelling it now. It releases its scent in the evening. Restore me, please."

"And if I don't, what will you do?"

She counted on her fingers. "One, fend for myself. Two, send you the bill for my ruined gown, for I do have need of it for twenty-four days. Three, inform the world that you're a dastard, my lord."

"Four?" he asked.

"Three will suffice. Shall I begin fending?"

She saw the way he looked at her lips. Lud! He wouldn't!

"We are within sight of the house, sir."

"And if we were not?"

"I would probably slap you."

He laughed and said, "With reason."

He restored her to the ground, but this time she was more aware of being apparently weightless in his strong arms, of being settled back on the terrace with perfect care.

She fussed over the smoothing of her skirts, wishing she could smooth the rest of herself as easily.

"A perfumed tobacco," he said. "I've never heard of such a thing."

"It's a rare plant grown from seeds given to my mother. She has a fondness for perfumed gardens."

"Truly?"

She understood his skepticism. "No one has only one side, Lord Dracy."

"Some have too many. I like the idea of a plant that gives perfume only at night. A magical property."

"If it's magical, it's ordinary enough. I could have the gardener give you some seeds."

"Commonplace magic, so carelessly distributed. Are you an enchantress, Lady Maybury?"

"You cited magic first, sir, and merely because of a tobacco plant."

He leaned against the copingstone, irritatingly at ease,

even in command. "Clearly you haven't inhaled tobacco smoke after a long, hard day, or you'd not discount the magic of it."

Ah, there she had him. "As it happens, I have smoked a pipe."

"The deuce you have! Did you enjoy it?"

"No. It's vile stuff."

"One has to apply oneself to liking it at first."

Georgia flipped open her fan and wafted it. "I can't imagine why anyone would bother."

"Haven't you discovered that some pleasures take time to appreciate?"

Georgia raised her brows. "Applying oneself to the appreciation of a pipe, sir, seems much like applying oneself to the appreciation of brimstone."

The smile touched his eyes. "I've known people apply themselves to appreciating sea water."

She found herself smiling back. "Lud, don't remind me! I drank some once." She put on a shudder but then wondered if it was wise to be playful with this odd, scarred military man.

"Only once?" he asked.

"As I said, I don't apply myself to tolerating the unpleasant."

"No one likes sea water, but many find potent pleasures in a pipe. That didn't tempt you to persevere?"

"I have pleasures aplenty, sir, without choking for them. Come, we must return to the house."

She turned, but he said, "Wouldn't the ability to smoke a pipe be useful when you seek to play the manly part?"

She turned back. "You refer to my attire at the race, sir? If this is your notion of polite conversation, I tell you it is sadly off."

"Then, please, dear lady, teach me better ways."

She was being challenged again, in ways she hardly understood. She'd never met such a man.

"Are you truly out here because you're uncomfortable in the company of fine ladies?"

"Perhaps a little. I have no wish to disturb."

"No?" she asked pointedly.

"Very well. I don't always wish to disturb," he amended.

Georgia was aware of a strange temptation to linger out here bandying words with him, but she found the resolution to head back to the house.

He fell into step beside her. "You will be my guide in there, Lady Maybury? I truly am unused to this sort of gathering."

"Very well."

"You'll stay by my side?"

"I'll even elbow you if you commit a faux pas."

"Perhaps before?"

"I'm not a mind reader, sir. You'll have to learn by your mistakes like the rest of us." He stopped and she turned back. "Cold feet, Lord Dracy?"

"I merely wondered if you are usually so assiduous in obeying your father's requests. I'm sure he didn't expect you to go so far as saving my life."

"I'm sure he expected me to go as far as necessary to achieve his end."

"His end?" he asked, but he would know what she meant. She'd have her father's purpose laid out clearly between them before he leapt to any other assumptions.

"To retain Fancy Free," she said. "Will you accept some substitute?"

"Perhaps that depends on you, Lady Maybury."

"You'll be swayed by my kindness? A strange way of deciding a stud matter, but in order to save Fancy Free, I shall do my tender best."

"You tempt me to delay my decision. How long could your kindness last?"

"About two hours," she said briskly. "My engagement is only for dinner, sir, and I don't promise kindness even then. I am your mentor, not your comforter."

"I'd make a better Odysseus than a Telemachus."

She'd turned toward the house again, but she swiveled back. "I don't understand that."

"You haven't been classically educated."

"Lud, no!"

He laughed. "Such horror at the prospect. I too didn't get the usual tutoring past twelve, but I've always enjoyed the stories of the *Iliad* and *Odyssey*. Mentor was Odysseus's friend, not teacher. He was teacher to his young son, Telemachus. Odysseus himself was advised by goddesses, sirens, and enchantresses. More suitable, wouldn't you say, in our case?"

Georgia flicked open her fan again, wary of the currents beneath this exchange. "Didn't one enchantress turn Odysseus and his men into swine?"

"Circe," he agreed.

"My purpose is the exact opposite."

"The swine will be humbly grateful."

Perdition, her cheeks were flaming. "I didn't mean ...!"

"I was only teasing."

"But my words were careless." When had she last been so maladroit? "There's nothing swinish about you, Lord Dracy. Lud, that makes it worse! Oh, dear.... We'd best go in."

She turned to the doors but realized that they'd paused to one side, out of sight of those inside. How had that happened?

"Stay a moment," he said. "I've upset you, and your father might wonder what I've done."

She turned back to face him. "My father might have seen you tossing me around. Why did you come out here? I don't believe you're afraid of anything."

"Perhaps I simply have a fondness for fresh air."

"You mean fresh sea air? Was it very difficult to leave the navy?"

A sudden blankness told her she'd hit a spot.

"You're the first person to ask that, Lady Maybury."

"And the answer?" She very much wanted to know.

"I'm not sure," he said. "It was my free choice."

"Was it? You had no choice about inheriting the title. Your cousin's death sealed your fate there, and you would be expected to take up your responsibilities. A death ripped you from your familiar life." Too late, she realized she was speaking of herself as much as him. "Come. We'll cause talk, lingering out here."

She plunged into the Terrace Room as if it were escape.

Dracy followed Lady Maybury into the room, feeling the shift in the wind. Conversation ceased and all eyes turned to them. Everyone here had already seen his face, so the reaction was to the entrance of the Scandalous Countess. He had to fight the instinct to step in front of her as a shield.

Was this Lady Maybury's first appearance before the company? She might have joined him on the terrace through another door. If so, what he'd been told of her scandal wasn't false or overstated.

One blond lady's glance might as well have been an arrow tipped with spite. Ah yes, Miss Cardross, sister of Lady Pranksworth, the heir's wife. She clearly considered herself fine goods, but she'd shown otherwise by curling her lip at his appearance.

Would Lady Maybury be frozen out, here in her father's house?

No. Talk resumed, two women inclined their heads to her, if coolly, and here came two eager gentlemen. One was the young Duke of Beaufort, eyes bright. There was her destiny, to be sure. She'd make a stunning duchess.

Dracy searched his memory for the name of the other swain. He'd attended the race, but he hadn't encountered the man at any other race meeting.

Ah, Sellerby.

The Earl of Sellerby, but not quite at ease in this company. Whereas Beaufort's brown country wear looked well-worn, Sellerby's might rarely see daylight. Given that his conversation was all on London matters, he perhaps rarely ventured into the countryside.

A Town man to the core, and Lady Maybury was treating him like an old friend, thanking him for letters but chiding him for unsuitable gifts, all in a playful way. Perhaps he, not the duke, was her choice.

"Glad to see you on good terms with my daughter, Dracy."

Dracy turned to the earl. "She's a charming lady, Hernescroft."

"Aye." But the earl said it as if Dracy had said she had the plague. "I'll thank you not to make more talk about her."

"Talk?"

"Hefting her around as if she were a sack of grain."

"I hope I was somewhat more careful, sir, but I apologize. I merely sought to spare her gown."

Hernescroft leered. "And to get a feel of her, I'll be bound. Satisfied?"

He really couldn't punch his host. Aware of ears nearby, he spoke softly. "The Duke of Beaufort seems enamored, sir. I can't compete with him on any level."

"A fine match, but it'd leave our business unsettled."

"It's easily settled by cash."

"Damn me ..."

"Now, now, gentlemen." Here came Lady Hernescroft, smiling tightly. "The race is run," she said loudly enough to be overheard by all. "You must not continue to argue over the virtues of the horses."

"Or fillies," some lady said, causing a titter from someone and a further tightening in Lady Hernescroft's smile.

*What the devil did that mean?*

Lady Maybury seemed happily unaware as she enjoyed the admiration of three swains, for Sir Charles Bunbury had joined the group. Not a suitor, for he was married, but no wonder the other ladies looked sour.

Why didn't she do the sensible thing and sit with them to talk of housekeeping or fashion or whatever women talked about between themselves? Was she perhaps as wicked and wanton as rumor whispered?

Dracy made himself look away. "I asked Lady Maybury about the perfume near the terrace, Lady Hernescroft, and she said it was a form of tobacco."

The countess's smile became a little more genuine. "Ah, yes. Delightful, is it not? You are interested in gardens, Dracy?"

Hernescroft grunted and left them to it, and Dracy found himself enjoying the conversation, even if it was mostly a lesson on how to improve the Dracy gardens. People have many sides. He really should remember that.

"I will send you seeds, Dracy, and instructions for your gardeners."

His "gardener" at the moment was an old man who kept the overgrowth within bounds, where the sheep left any standing, but he thanked her. Perhaps he'd have time and money for a flower garden soon.

When he had a wife.

He glanced at Lady Maybury again. She'd acquired a fourth swain—another duke. Portland.

"Like moths to the flame," Lady Hernescroft said.

"You disapprove of your daughter's charms, ma'am?"

"Moths die in the flames, Dracy, and my daughter needs no more tragedies in her life."

Dinner was announced. Lady Hernescroft steered him over to her daughter. "I'll ask you to take Lady Maybury through, Dracy. Take good care of her."

"It will be my honor, ma'am. No matter what the storms."

Lady Hernescroft stared at him but then took the

other gentlemen away. Why the devil were the Hernes-crofts so determined to bring about this unlikely marriage? The money couldn't be an insuperable obstacle, and a union with Beaufort was too grand to be brushed aside.

"Storms?" Lady Maybury asked, and he looked back at her, struck again by the perfection of her face. A mask on a she-devil?

"A sailor learns to sense the wind, ma'am," he said as she took his arm. No one else was nearby, so he added, "I heard that there was some scandal blowing around you and now I see it's true. Unwise, perhaps, to snare four men for yourself?"

"You are not supposed to be tutoring me, my lord!" Then she surprised him by saying, "You're correct, however. It was simply that the men seemed more welcoming."

"You must be used to stirring jealousy in women."

She frowned slightly. "But I was married then, and it makes a difference."

"It does. Your road would be easier if you were less beautiful."

Unlike any woman he'd ever known, she didn't react to the description. Clearly she'd lived with it all her life.

"Yes," she said as they joined the procession to the dining room, "but I'd not willingly lose my looks, you know."

Oh, her wretched tongue. How had she said such a thing to a man so ruined in appearance? This event was straining her more than she'd thought. He was right about her behavior too, though he had no right to speak his thoughts on that.

As they walked to the dining room, she glanced at him but saw no reaction to her faux pas.

Her unfortunate words had risen out of an earlier moment. Before her mother had brought him over, she'd seen him in profile, from his left, his unblemished side, and she'd realized that he was beautiful. That he had been beautiful. An odd word to describe a military man, but his face at that moment had seemed classically perfect.

Perhaps he'd felt her gaze, for he'd turned and looked at her, shattering the illusion most horribly.

She'd returned her attention to her companions, trying to hide her distress. What had it been like to have a glorious appearance and then lose it? To look into a mirror one day and see oneself so horribly changed? Even as she thought it, she'd known her horror was all about herself.

Such a thing could never happen to her. She wasn't going into battle. There were other ways to lose one's looks, however. Smallpox could ruin a complexion, if it didn't kill you. Anyone could be scarred in a carriage accident. Burns didn't happen only in war. Poor Henrietta Wrothley had passed too close to a fire and her skirts had caught. The flames had been extinguished, but it was said she was horribly scarred all along one side of her body. She'd not been seen in society since.

"Why so silent?" Dracy asked quietly as they entered the family dining room, the one that seated thirty at most.

"Apprehension," she said honestly. "This is proving more challenging than I'd expected."

"Remember, I'm by your side."

When he took his seat to her left, Georgia wasn't sure whether to be glad or sorry that she could see only the ruination of his face. It was probably easier than a constant reminder of what had been.

And, oh dear, Eloisa Cardross sat opposite, alert for any misstep she could report back to her sister. At least Sellerby was at Eloisa's side. An eligible earl should distract her from her malice.

A glance around the table was less reassuring.

Waveney was leering at her, which was causing his pudgy wife to steam with fury. Mistress Fayne showed a greater appetite for scandal than for her soup, and she was a notorious gossip. Had she made that comment about fillies, and what had the resulting titter meant?

Throat tight with apprehension, Georgia merely stirred her soup and turned to the Duke of Portland, hoping for calm and boring conversation.

# Chapter 6

"It was as if the cats wanted to dine on her!" Dracy exploded as he entered the private parlor he and Tom Knowlton had taken at the Bull. All the way there, he'd burned over the poisoned darts some of the women had thrown at Lady Maybury during the meal.

"That Cardross woman, saying that a nunlike appearance looked odd on her. And Lady Waveney adding that it became her more than goddess garb. Why that caused smirks, I don't know, but it was foul. Poisonous snakes, the lot of 'em, and it didn't help that she had admirers. The Duke of Beaufort, the Earl of Sellerby, even Waveney was smiling at her in a way calculated to make his wife seethe. No wonder Lady Waveney came up with something about the theater. Did the damn woman appear on stage in breeches?"

"Lady Waveney? I haven't had the pleasure. Have some ale, Dracy."

"There'd be no pleasure, I assure you. A lazy, doughy sort of woman." Dracy filled a tankard from the pitcher. "But I meant Lady Maybury. Surely she's not in the habit of acting on stage?"

"Ah, I do remember something."

"A private theatrical?"

"Well, no, if I remember. One of the London theaters."

"Damnation. Someone needs to take her in hand."

Dracy remembered Hernescroft's comment about a switch and felt sick.

"I'd not envy anyone the task," Knowlton said.

"No?"

"Gads, no."

"She's very beautiful," Dracy said.

"But not at all comfortable."

Knowlton was completely serious, and he was right. The scandalous Lady Maybury was not at all comfortable, but Dracy remembered Hernescroft's astute observation. He might envy Tom Knowlton his comfortable life and comfortable wife, but he feared he'd be bored to insanity in a sixmonth by the same.

He took a deep drink of ale. Marriage to Lady Maybury was impossible in every respect, and she'd done her best to squash any stirring hope. She'd turned cool over the dinner and left him without a word or a speaking look.

But he couldn't let it go. It wasn't just her beauty; it was an illusion of friendship that grew out of their time on the terrace. He didn't think he'd ever spoken to a woman with such ease and enjoyment, and with damn few men.

"Hens coming home to roost," Knowlton said. "She was a wild one as I hear it. Took pleasure in attracting men, married or single, so of course the ladies don't like her."

"She can't help being beautiful."

Knowlton send him a worried look. "Word to the wise, Dracy. Lady Maybury is a lovely young woman. Enchanting, some say. Nothing but trouble, though, as such women always are."

Dracy refilled his tankard and sat down. "She's more vulnerable than you might think. She put on a performance of not noticing the looks and jibes, but I was sitting beside her. She was tense as a bow and hardly put a morsel in her mouth."

"So she don't like the bed she lies in, but she made it with her scandalous goings-on, and there's nothing you can do."

"I suppose not."

But mind, heart, and gut summoned him anyway. Summoned him to stand by her side on the burning deck.

Whom else did she have? At best her family disapproved of her and planned to cage her so she couldn't scandalize again. At worst she was nothing but a trading piece, and for a mere horse!

Perhaps Beaufort was a genuine admirer and would defend her, but he was young. Sellerby was a better candidate. That could be why Dracy had taken a dislike to the man. Handsome, elegant, at ease in the company even though he didn't give a groat for racehorses, and a favorite of Lady Maybury.

"Do you know the Earl of Sellerby?"

Knowlton screwed up his face. "Court type. Too high-flying for me, but I have met him. Ah, went with some friends to his London house to see his collection of classical statues. All modern molds, but correct to every detail, he claimed, and many from statues still abroad."

"Wealthy, then?"

"Have to be, I'd think. Thought about getting a few statues like that for my place. Annie might like it, as long as they were decently clothed, that is. I remember Sellerby mentioning a new type of plaster that can withstand the weather. Fired, like pottery. Could have a statue or two in the garden."

Dracy doubted the wisdom of introducing classical statuary to a cozy manor house, but he didn't say so. Instead, foolishly, he was wondering if Georgia Maybury would want such things at Dracy. If so, he strongly suspected she'd prefer the indecently clothed variety. So young, but so obviously worldly wise.

Which wasn't a crime in a widow . . .

"How did things go with Hernescroft?"

Dracy realized he'd stormed here ranting about Lady Maybury's treatment and spoken of nothing else. Now what to say?

He took a deep drink. "That's why I'm drowning my sorrows. Gosling-go's dead."

"The devil you say!"

"A few days ago. Had a fit of temper and broke a hock."

"That's a damn shame."

"Isn't it, just?"

"So you keep Fancy Free?"

Dracy disliked lying to anyone and especially to a friend, but he had to prevaricate. "We're looking for another substitution."

"But you need a stallion, and a mature one."

"I know that! Sorry to snap, but the past few hours have not gone as planned in any respect."

Knowlton nodded. "Hold out for the money. Hernescroft can raise it, and then you can take your pick. They say the Duke of Cumberland's failing, and he has a notable stud. Even Herod."

Herod was a notable stallion, but Dracy shook his head.

"I doubt a fair price for Fancy Free would cover Herod's price at auction. What do you think? A thousand?"

"More if the bidding's brisk."

But with twelve thousand in hand . . .

"The trouble is, Hernescroft holds the tiller. He knows now that I don't want Fancy Free. Might even suspect that I'm softhearted enough not to want to take the horse away from its familiar surroundings. If he insists that he can't raise the money, that it's Fancy Free or nothing, I'm on the rocks."

Knowlton looked aghast. "You think the Earl of Hernescroft's up to shady dealings?"

"He simply intends that things go his way, and at the moment I can't see my way forward. I might as well return to Dracy and put my winnings to work on the stables. Comes to a bit over three hundred."

"There's the roof of Dracy Manor," Knowlton reminded him.

Dracy almost said the roof could rot, but that would shock his friend to the core. "I'll arrange a patch or two. Don't preach at me, Tom. One way or another, I'm going to restore the Dracy stud."

"You need a roof over your head and food from the home farm."

"I know, I know. But it's a damned boring business, farming."

"Only in the good times," Tom said with feeling. "Can't you settle to a quiet life?"

Dracy drank some ale, knowing the answer was no. Damn a quiet life when a spirited redheaded lay to hand, bringing enough money to restore Dracy—house, estate, and stud. A spirited redhead he admired, and who stood beleaguered by enemies, needing a strong man by her side.

He remembered Lady Hernescroft's comment. Moths drawn to the flame died.

But what was life without risk?

*Lizzie,*

*The dinner was vile! Why didn't I expect that?*

*You were in the right, dearest, in doubting the wisdom of such long seclusion. I've lost my instinct for the beau monde and its ways. I couldn't even understand half that was said. A comment made about a filly was supposed to devastate me, but it meant nothing.*

*It's all Father's fault for ordering me to go down to dinner. If I'd planned to attend I would have studied the guest list and been better prepared.*

*Pranks's wife was absent, but her sister, Eloisa Cardross, ably stirred the pot. It's not as if I wanted the attention of so many gentlemen, but she took it as a personal attack and slashed back with a comment about my goddess costume.*

*Yes, I know you thought it shocking, but I was as well covered as any lady there. More!*

*Nasty cat.*

*No, not cat, ferret. She does have a rather sharp nose! Do you think she truly harbors hopes of Beaufort? Her portion will be good, but I wouldn't lay money on her chances. Sellerby, perhaps, if he could put up with her.*

*He was there, pretending to be a racing man. I teased him on it dreadfully, for he hardly ever mounts a horse. Even though my mourning's not yet over, he said a few things that could be of a wooing nature. Alas, I fear I will have to disappoint him. I have always enjoyed his company, and we share a great many tastes, but I will look for more than warm friendship when I choose again.*

Georgia stopped writing before she revealed more about a lacking aspect of her marriage. Dickon had been a friend too, but never more than that. It felt disloyal to even think it, but it was true, and in that respect she wanted better.

She now regretted allowing Sellerby to write to her and, especially, replying. In the early months she'd permitted no letters from gentlemen after the first one of condolence. She'd had them all returned unopened.

When she'd heard about Sellerby's efforts to sway the dowager in her favor, she'd written to thank him and from there slid into a correspondence. She'd enjoyed it, for he'd written all the best news of Town and he had a fine appreciation of arts and style, but it might have given him a false impression.

She was running out of space on her sheet of paper so she turned it sideways to write across, then dipped her pen.

> *Let me tell you of another lord—Dracy. Pray ex-*
> *cuse the crossed lines, but I don't want to burden*
> *you with the cost of an extra sheet.*
>
> *Dracy is an original—that is certain sure. I came*
> *across him leaning so far over the terrace balustrade*
> *that I feared he intended to throw himself off. But*
> *no, he was merely seeking to identify flowers.*
>
> *I suppose a life at sea doesn't provide much expe-*
> *rience of gardens. I'm sure I'd hate it, for I do love*
> *flowers. When I think of the ones in our London*
> *garden, and especially those at Sansouci . . .*
>
> *But I will not pine. All that is over and I will have*
> *other gardens soon.*
>
> *I expected a portly, weathered tar, but though he*
> *is browned and carries himself in a military manner,*
> *he is, in his own way, quite polished. And young. Not*
> *yet thirty, I'm sure. And with a fine, manly figure.*
>
> *He has much to learn, however. Would you believe*
> *that he lifted me, without request or permission, up*
> *onto the coping so I could identify the flowers for*
> *him! It quite flustered me, for he's very strong.*

Georgia ceased writing, brushing the tip of her quill across her lips.

Despite the scar, the briskness, and the lack of stylish manner, there was something about the man. He was so firm, so complete in himself. So confident and strong.

Such a shame about his appearance.

She was ashamed of her reaction there and resolved to do better if they ever met again. As a start, she could address the subject briskly now.

> *The poor man is badly scarred by a burn across*
> *the right of his face. The skin there is shiny and*
> *puckered and it twists up the right side of his brow*
> *and lips as if he's constantly in a sneer. I made a*
> *point to treat him exactly as I would anyone else, but*

*it is a sad injury, for I believe before he must have been a very handsome fellow.*

*I was supposed to assist him at dinner, but he managed very well on his own. I rather think he assisted me by anchoring me. That's a clever choice of words, isn't it, for a naval officer? He anchored me so I could ignore the catty ladies and leering Lord Waveney. He's married now and should desist.*

*When Mother led the ladies away, I had no intention of trapping myself with the cats, so I made my excuses and returned here.*

*I'm resolved to avoid the beau monde until I'm done with mourning, no matter what my father dictates. When I rejoin the world in Town, it will be in full glory and surrounded by friends. Face-to-face, in no time at all people will realize that their suspicions are idiotic.*

*Oh, talking of Town, which means gossip, I must mention that the Duke of Grafton was present, sans both mistress and wife. I've heard the duchess now looks elsewhere. Quel scandale, poor woman, but his behavior has been intolerable, vile man.*

*Talking of dukes, Beaufort flirted with me delightfully and spoke often of my return to Town, though worrying about my safety there. Fie for agitated silk weavers and the ever-restless mob. Remind me when we meet to tell you the story about Ulysses. It was a clever moment.*

In the tiniest writing, she managed to squeeze in:

*Fancy Free seems safe for the moment. She is to remain here until the Dracy stables are repaired, or until Father devises an acceptable substitution, but my part in that is done.*

> *Write back soon, my dearest friend,*
> *Georgia*

Georgia folded the sheet in three and then three again and took out the black sealing wax and her gold seal. It wasn't specific to the Countess of Maybury, as the design was a G surrounded by flowers, but Dickon had given it to her. When she married again, would it be appropriate for her to continue to use it?

She looked up at the portrait. "You wouldn't care, would you, love?"

As if he'd spoken, she wrinkled her nose at the black. Enough of that. Though her mourning wouldn't end for a few weeks, today felt like a new beginning. She searched her drawer and found red wax. She held it in the candle flame and dripped a blob over the join in the letter, then set the seal firmly upon it.

The seal would always be a sweet memory of Dickon, and she'd never marry a man who could object to that.

She sent Jane off with the letter, and then, in the spirit of new beginnings, she took a clean sheet of paper and began to make a plan for her grand return to the heart of the world in twenty-four days.

To London.

To Town.

To Life.

"Not go to Town?" Georgia stared at her father.

He was sitting in a quite ordinary upholstered chair in the family drawing room but gave the impression of being enthroned. Her mother sat nearby, mirroring the style.

Georgia felt diminished by being on a settee.

Her parents had traveled to Herne from Town for this discussion, which should have warned her something was amiss. She'd planned to set off to join them tomorrow, when her mourning would officially be over.

"Too dangerous," her father said. "By heaven, girl, you read the papers. The Spitalfields silk weavers smashed the

Duke of Bedford's windows to protest French silks, and the mob's gone wild about taxation, harassing anyone they take objection to."

"I don't wear French silk, Father, and I'm not connected to any discord."

"No, daughter."

That was the word of God, and though Georgia's jaw clenched with rebellion, to do more would be as futile as the mob's violence.

Choosing her words, she said, "I can't stay here, Father. It might look as if I skulk."

"Which would not surprise anyone, given your behavior."

"Where else am I to go? Some of my friends are still in Town—the Harringays and Arbutts, and Perry of course."

"Alas, no," said her mother. "He has traveled to Yorkshire."

"Yorkshire? Perry? He'd be as likely to head for darkest Africa!"

"Nevertheless, it's true. Carried there by the obligations of friendship. You may have read that the Earl of Malzard dropped down dead a fortnight ago. He left no sons, so his heir is one of Perry's friends, all unprepared for his duties."

"Unfortunate," Georgia said, meaning it in many ways. She'd been depending on Perry. "The Malzards seemed a pleasant couple. Who is the heir?"

"A brother, recently sold out of the army."

*A military man, like Dracy,* Georgia thought. She sometimes wondered how he was managing on his estate. He could know as little about that as he did about the beau monde.

She pulled her mind back to her predicament.

"Perry's bound to return south soon, Mother, and I look forward to hearing about his adventures in the wilderness, but I don't need him to be in Town in order to return myself."

"No, Georgia," her father stated. "Your safety is my sacred duty. It will not do."

"Then, where am I to go?"

She would not remain here—she would not—and this unexpected obstruction of her careful plans was intolerable. She'd disliked her year at Herne, but until now, she'd not felt incarcerated.

"Georgia does need to leave Herne, husband."

Georgia looked at her mother with wary surprise.

"For her to remain here could give the wrong impression. As if she fears a return to society. As if she were burdened by guilt. Perhaps she should visit Winifred. . . ."

"Hammersmith!" Georgia exclaimed, as appalled by that as by the thought of visiting her disapproving older sister.

"You speak as if that was the far north, when it's less than ten miles from that Sansouci you were so fond of. It's June, child. Everyone who can is beginning to leave Town for more salubrious parts, including your friends."

Georgia had no good argument to that. Even Perry visited friends in the country in the hottest months, and this was proving to be a hot year. Last year, when the duel had taken place, she and Dickon had been planning their move to Sansouci.

She'd envisioned her resurrection as a return to the Town life she'd enjoyed a year ago—to St. James and Mayfair, to court, parks, and theater. The best of that would be over now, however, for the king had already removed to Richmond.

But Hammersmith, haunt of scholars and Catholics? It seemed typical that her dull sister marry a man whose estate was on the fringes of Hammersmith.

Winifred, Lady Thretford, was two years older and had always resented Georgia's looks. When the union with the Earl of Maybury had become an issue, Winnie had insisted that she, the older sister, should become Countess of Maybury. Dickon hadn't wanted her, however. He'd wanted Georgia, and he'd wanted her immediately. Her parents had attempted to delay the wedding while they married Winifred off, but Dickon wouldn't hear of it.

And then, of course, when Winnie had married, it had been to a viscount, putting her eternally one step below Georgia. She'd compensated by assuming a moral superiority, even going so far as to send Georgia lectures on her behavior. They'd been at odds for years.

Winnie would want Georgia as a guest as little as Georgia wished to be there, but it seemed that Thretford Park was the only place she would be allowed to go. It was as least within traveling distance of Town, both by road and by water, so she put the best face possible on it.

"I shall enjoy a visit to Thretford, Mother, and delight to see Winifred's baby."

Her mother nodded. "I too wish to see little Charlotte. I shall accompany you there whilst Hernescroft returns directly to his duties in Town."

What a delightful journey that would be.

Perhaps her mother misinterpreted her grimace.

"Hammersmith isn't the wilderness, Georgia. Winifred shall entertain for you. A ball, I think."

"Mother, it's only six weeks since her lying in."

"An easy birth, and she assures me she's quite recovered. She will not mind doing her duty."

"Of course not," her father said. "A dutiful daughter, Winnie. An excellent idea, Lady Hernescroft. A ball will provide an opportunity for some people to meet out of Town, both allies and opponents. Within traveling distance, but not so much observed."

So that was it. Georgia was not dismayed. Everything in her world had an ulterior purpose, and she could turn this ploy to her own advantage. Once in Hammersmith, she would get to Town, one way or another.

"I shall need new gowns," she said. "I shall visit my mantua maker."

"You have chests of clothes," her mother objected.

"Old and worn."

"One year old, most of them, and many worn only once. Remember, you no longer have a husband's wealth to fund your extravagances."

"I have twelve thousand pounds," Georgia said, trying not to sound abrasive. "I will need my usual pin money, Father."

"What? That will drain your capital in no time. Two hundred a quarter should suffice."

Georgia swallowed a protest, calculating furiously. "If you will be paying my bills, Father . . ."

"Certainly not!" His cheeks were puce with anger. "You must curtail your extravagant ways, girl."

Georgia had spent two hundred on one gown, but arguing would be futile. "As you will, Father," she said, and saw surprised relief. He'd expected a fight? His children had not been raised to oppose his will.

Again she had that feeling of currents beneath the choppy water.

"We leave tomorrow," her mother said, "so go now and attend to your preparations."

Dismissed. Like a schoolgirl.

But Georgia said, "Yes, Mother," and rose, curtsied, and returned to her room like a good daughter.

"Politics," she complained to Jane as soon as the door was closed. "I'm a pawn on the board, but at least they haven't picked a husband for me. I feared that might be their plan."

"They might pick well, milady. They chose Lord Maybury."

"He chose me, but, yes, they might choose well. They'd have no more desire than I to see me wed to a man of lesser rank or fortune. But I mean to make this decision for myself. Thretford!" she said with disgust. "That's where I'm to go."

"It won't be too bad, milady. It's a pretty little estate. . . ."

"And within reach of Town!" Georgia laughed and hugged her maid. "Winnie's to entertain for me. A ball! At last, a ball!"

Jane hugged her back. "It gladdens my heart, milady, to see you in spirits. Will we have time to order new gowns?"

"It seems I can't afford it. Until I marry, I'm to have only two hundred a quarter. For everything!"

Jane looked suitably horrified, but rallied. "Then we'll plan the refurbishment of the old."

Georgia wrinkled her nose at the thought of that but then said, "No. No refurbishment. My best gowns are all memorably unique. Any attempt to make them look new will seem shabby. I shall wear them as they are, Jane, as they were. That will declare that Lady May has returned, intact, unchanged, unbowed."

Jane grinned. "Ah, milady, you've a fine, bold heart, and wisdom too. Wisdom beyond your years."

"I hope so, Jane. I know the stories still lurk, but what choice do I have but to face everyone bravely? I won't bury myself in the country, or even less, flee abroad. I will be myself. My conscience is clear."

# Chapter 7

Georgia survived the four-day journey to Hammersmith largely because she and her mother rarely spoke. Astonishing that her mother had not spent the time instructing her on the behavior necessary to restore herself in the eyes of the world, but so it was, and that was excellent.

It was even more astonishing that her mother didn't attempt to discuss Georgia's choice of husband. She began to think again that her parents had someone in mind, perhaps someone she'd meet at Thretford House. No matter. She couldn't be forced. In fact, as a widow she was free to marry whom she pleased, even when not yet twenty-one.

Despite the lack of friction on the journey, Georgia was heartily glad to arrive at Lord Thretford's estate near Hammersmith village, which lay on the River Thames. Thretford House was a stylish, modern building set in pleasant grounds, and Georgia determined to be easy to please.

After all, she could almost sense the city and had glimpsed the river, busy with boats. By boat on the tide it could take little more than an hour to be in the heart of the world, and that was a journey she intended to take as soon as possible on one excuse or another.

Winnie came out to greet them, looking both shabby

and improved. Her gown had an insert so it could meet at the front over fuller breasts, but the added roundness became her, for she'd always been thin and rather flat. There was something else, a glow. . . .

Her sister was finally content, presumably because of her baby.

"Mother, Georgia, how lovely to see you. I hope the journey was smooth?"

"As smooth as possible," their mother declared, climbing stiffly out of the coach. "Which is to say, not very, given the state of the roads. I need my room, tea, and rest, daughter."

"Of course, of course," Winnie fretted, her glow diminishing as she fussed her mother into the house.

Georgia followed, thinking wryly that she and her sister might have more in common now than they'd had in the schoolroom. They both were married women with parents who still attempted to rule as gods.

Winnie took them upstairs and showed their mother into a generous, well-furnished room. Thretford House wasn't large, and a few guests were to sleep here on the night of the ball. Georgia realized that the room given their mother was Winifred's own bedchamber. For the duration of the visit, she would sleep with her husband. Would she consider that a treat or a trial?

Dickon had slept in her bed only after coupling, and not always then. A warm body beside her had been pleasant, but he'd taken more than his share of the bed and was inclined to toss and turn in his sleep. She doubted she'd like it for many nights in a row.

Winnie made sure their mother had all she needed, and then took Georgia to another room. "It's rather small, I'm afraid, but we have only four good bedrooms in addition to our own, and with the house party . . ."

For a moment they were reflected in a mirror, but Winnie immediately stepped out of view. Georgia knew why. They were too alike, and too different.

Winnie's hair was closer to brown than burnished, and her chin receded. When younger she'd been prey to pimples, and though that stage had passed, some had left marks. The scars were almost undetectable, but Georgia knew the comparison with her own flawless skin still hurt her sister.

Georgia could take neither credit nor blame for nature, and it seemed unfair that it matter, but such was the way of things.

"I like the room," Georgia said, striving for harmony. "The view's delightful and I can glimpse the river in the distance."

"To have the house closer would be unhealthy. Everyone knows the river is foul."

"Surely not this far upstream?"

"Which is why Hammersmith is preferable to Chelsea."

So they were still scoring points, were they? Sanscouci had been—was still—in Chelsea.

Georgia held her smile as she unpinned her hat. "It's very kind of you to hold an entertainment for me so soon after your confinement."

"Father requested it," Winnie said, twitching the brown bed hangings to eliminate an imaginary flaw. "But it serves Thretford's purposes as well. He's striving to be a peacemaker between those who are contributing most to the discord."

"You expect the king to attend?"

"His Majesty? Of course not." But then Winnie caught Georgia's meaning. "Georgie!"

"He's the root of the problem and you know it. He can't reconcile with those who didn't want the queen listed as regent. What's more, I hear that he's a little ..."

She tapped her head.

Winnie turned pale and clutched a bedpost. "Georgie! Do not even *whisper* such a thing, even here."

Georgia hurried to her side. "My wretched sense of

humor. I'm sorry, Winnie. I promise I won't. Maundering in the countryside for so long must have touched *my* wits." Before her sister could shriek again, she added, "When will I be able to see your little darling?"

The distraction worked.

"As soon as you've refreshed yourself. Ah, here's your water. I'll return shortly and take you to the nursery."

Her sister escaped and the Thretford maid poured hot water into the china basin. When she'd left, Georgia washed her hands and face thinking this was going to be a very long visit, no matter how many days it lasted.

Jane arrived, along with the two trunks that contained Georgia's immediate necessities. The rest of her belongings were coming south more slowly by wagon.

Her mother had protested that. "Where is it all to go?"

"What point in leaving it at Herne?" Georgia had replied, not speaking the rest. That she would never return to Herne for more than short visits, and she truly wanted to shake the dust off her shoes. And off her gowns, her petticoats, her books, her small items of furniture . . .

"Jane, when you can, discover whether there's room here for all my belongings. I forgot how small this place is. I may have to arrange for them to be stored elsewhere until I marry again."

"Yes, milady." Jane closed the door on the departing footmen. "Do you want to change your gown?"

"Not yet. I dressed lightly today because of the heat." But then Georgia changed her mind.

She'd marked the end of her mourning four days ago by dispatching all her grays and lavenders to the vicar for the benefit of the poor. The blacks had gone that way six months earlier. She'd have liked to have traveled in pinks and yellows, but common sense had made her choose duller colors. Common sense need not rule now.

"A bright-colored gown, Jane. And light. See which is the least creased."

Jane unlocked one chest. "As hot as it is, milady, it must be right nasty in London."

"Don't talk nonsense."

"The sewers'll be stinking and disease spreading," Jane insisted, carefully unfolding layers of muslin. "Be grateful you're away from it and that the world will come to you."

"So it will. Remind me, Jane—I must check the guest list for the ball to be sure the right people will attend."

"Very well, milady. Here we are. The yellow stripe."

"Excellent." Georgia began to unfasten the blue and take it off.

She was soon in the yellow stripe gown with the white petticoat. Much better, but plain. Jane had found the cap trimmed with ribbons of the same color, which helped a little.

"The jewelry box, Jane. I'll wear the coral beads."

The coral closely matched her hair and made an improvement. Georgia added matching earrings and ring.

"There," she said, standing. "In fine trim to admire my sister's triumph."

"Now, don't you be like that, milady. A baby's a baby."

"Tell that to Anne Boleyn."

"Who, milady?"

"Henry the Eighth's second wife."

"Oh, her. But what . . . ?"

"She bore a healthy baby, but it was a girl. If Elizabeth had been a boy, Anne would never have gone to the headsman's block."

"But wasn't she up to things she shouldn't be, milady?"

"Perhaps, perhaps not. As mother to the king's son and heir, there would have had to be more proof."

*And if I'd had a son, I wouldn't have lost my life.*

Winnie hadn't given birth to a son, but she'd borne a

babe within ten months, so a son would surely follow. No one would be watching her waistline or suggesting that she consult a doctor, as Lady Hernescroft had with her.

She'd followed the suggestion, mortifying though it had been. Being told that she was a normal, healthy young woman had done no good. She'd suggested Dickon do the same thing, but he'd laughed it off.

"Nothing wrong with me, love, as you know every time I come to your bed! Put it out of your mind. We're young yet, and the infantry will come."

But the infantry hadn't come, and here she was.

Her sister returned and Georgia went to admire the proof of victory. In truth, there was little to see. The tiny creature slept in a gilded, lace-trimmed cradle, with the covers drawn up, and an embroidered cap covering her face to the brows. Georgia wondered if the child wasn't dreadfully hot, but she dutifully cooed and admired, pushing away jealousy as best she could.

She returned to her room with wounds newly raw. What if the lack of children had been her fault? What if she was barren? How could a doctor know?

What if she married again and it was the same?

Dickon had never reproached her, but men wanted heirs, especially men with titles and estates. She didn't want to run the risk of being a childless widow a second time, vulnerable to being exiled in one cruel moment.

During her marriage she had wondered whether Dickon came to her bed often enough, but frequency didn't seem to be the key. There'd been Maria the kitchen maid whose belly had swelled. She'd sworn it had been only the once when her Kentish swain had traveled up to London to see her. She certainly couldn't have sinned regularly, as her Michael had made great effort to get leave from his farm laborer's job that one time.

"I just missed him so, your ladyship," the girl had sobbed. "I missed him so."

It turned out that Maria had come up to London to earn higher wages in the hope that in a few years she could save enough for them to have a cottage of their own with a bit a land where they could grow some food and keep a pig.

What a crisis that situation had been!

The housekeeper had refused to keep Maria in the house even overnight for fear she'd corrupt the other servants, and Mistress Hownslow had been far too valuable to lose. Georgia had begged advice of Babs Harringay, who had told her about Danae House, a charity that provided help for female servants led astray.

Georgia had taken the girl there in her own carriage, ready to pay for her to be admitted, and been astonished to find herself talking to the Marchioness of Rothgar.

Lady Rothgar, it had turned out, had founded Danae House and recruited aristocratic ladies as patronesses. The price of Maria's instant admission had been that Lady Maybury become a patroness of the house herself. Georgia had done so willingly, for Maria's story was gentler than others'. Most of the girls helped by Danae House had been seduced or raped by the men of the family that employed them or by guests.

Each case was handled individually, but if a marriage was possible, a dowry was provided. That had been Georgia's participation. She'd provided a dowry for Maria and then added to the fund every month. The sums were so trifling. Ten guineas had enabled Maria and her swain to set up life together, but sometimes less would do.

It was satisfying to help, but the charity had always troubled her. Georgia entered her room with the old question rattling in her head. Danae House was proof that hasty coupling and even brutal assaults could result in children. So why had she, a virtuous, well-loved wife, never quickened?

Jane came in with a pile of ironed shifts. "How is the baby, milady?"

Georgia smiled at her. "Small. But if I'm to acquire a similar minikin, I'd best be about choosing a husband."

It was the only way. A woman without a husband was nothing.

She sat by the window to go over her notes. The top entries were the unmarried dukes. "Beaufort is still my first choice. He's only a little older than I and malleable."

"Go on with you, milady. If it's malleable you want, choose a doting dodderer."

Georgia shuddered. "Wrinkles and bad teeth. Never. There's the Duke of Bridgwater, but he shows no interest in marriage. They say one of the Gunning sisters broke his heart, but I suspect he's wedded to his canals."

"And producing a progeny of them, milady."

"Jane, you're a wit! I'll use that line one day. Bolton's unmarried, but gone forty and becoming rather odd. As for marquesses, alas, with Ashart gone there are none left unmarried. I might have to satisfy myself with another earl."

"You look for a good man you can love, milady."

"I will love the right man, Jane, but I couldn't love a man who would tumble me down the social scale."

Jane's lack of response was eloquent.

Georgia swiveled to look at her. "Don't you take your status in the servants' hall from mine? You're Countess of Maybury now. Do you want to become Viscountess Lowly, or Lady Down-in-the-Mud if I marry a baron?" A baron like Lord Dracy . . . She pushed that out of her mind. "Could you bear to rank below ladies' maids who were previously below you?" She saw Jane wavering and pressed home the point. "On the other hand, imagine being a duchess, ruling the roost."

"I'd not mind if you were happy, milady."

"I wouldn't be happy, so that's that." Georgia picked up her sheet of paper. "I shall go and speak to my sister."

Winnie was in her boudoir, setting neat stitches in a tiny gown, wearing spectacles. She looked dowdy but still content. She looked up over the lenses. "You have everything you require, Georgie?"

Georgia sat. "Yes, thank you. What a delightful little garment. Charlotte will look lovely in it."

That had Winnie smiling. Good.

"About the ball. Will you be able to add a few names to your list?"

"Of course, dear. I know you must want support."

Georgia's teeth gritted over two aspects of that sentence—pity and "must"—but she maintained her smile. "The Harringays are in Town, for Babs refuses to be separated from her husband, and he does something very important in some government department. And the Torrismondes' estate is not far to the west."

"I will certainly send them invitations."

Georgia moved on to the next point. "Have you invited any dukes?"

"Newcastle, Bedford, and Grafton."

"Perhaps we could add Beaufort? And Bridgwater?"

Winnie looked at her. "For your support, it's the duchesses that matter, and those two are unmarried."

Winifred wasn't stupid, and there was no purpose in denying it. "Perhaps I aspire to become a duchess."

"In light of the past, you may wish to aim lower."

"May" was not "must," but close enough. "I did nothing to cause that duel, Winnie, and I carry no blame."

"That isn't how the world sees it."

"Then I'll change what the world sees. As to a husband, I'm in no hurry," she lied. "I wish my second marriage to be perfect."

Winnie's gaze sharpened and Georgia realized what she'd heard—that her first marriage had not been perfect.

"I mean, of course, that I hope my next marriage will bless me as you have been blessed, with a child."

"Ah, yes. But, Georgie, there's no way to know. Unless you marry a widower with children."

That was a new idea, and Georgia considered it. "Are there any young widowers with children?"

"Everdon," Winnie said. "And Uxthorne, though as his poor wife bore five babies in eight years he might be too . . . productive."

"Lud, yes!"

"And every child a daughter. You would need a widower with sons in case the fault lies with you."

"It doesn't! A doctor assured me of that."

"Good heavens. Can they be sure?"

"I'm sure." Before they fell to quarreling, Georgia passed over her sheet of names. "There are some other gentlemen. Mere earls, you'll see."

Perdition. As Thretford was an even lowlier viscount, there was a jab in that which Georgia hadn't intended. "I don't want to overburden your house," she said, and then realized that too might sound like a slur.

Winnie's smile was tight. "As long as the weather holds, my guests can enjoy the terrace and gardens. We hang lanterns in the trees, and more float in the lake. It's very pretty."

For Winnie to call the pond a lake . . . But Georgia had never thought of floating lanterns on water. One day, when she had a house again, could entertain again . . .

Soon.

"I look forward to seeing it. The ball and house party will be a great deal of work for you—don't deny it, Winnie! Please let me assist with the preparations." When her sister looked suspicious, she added, "I'm longing to arrange a social event again, yes, but I'm trying to ease your burdens too. You have little Charlotte to take care of."

Winnie thawed. "Could you supervise the writing of the invitations, then? And perhaps the flowers? You always had a gift for flowers."

*And still do,* Georgia thought. *I am unchanged.* But she smiled as she said, "Of course."

# Chapter 8

She set to her duties and left the house in search of her sister's head gardener. She inquired about what flowers and greenery the garden could provide, and as they discussed the possibilities, she thought of something.

"Do you have nicotiana planted here?" she asked. "I believe my mother's gardener sent seeds."

The elderly man pulled a face. "I do, milady, but off in a corner. Nasty, ungainly things."

"But with a glorious perfume after dark. Would it be possible to move some into pots and place them where people will stroll?" When his scowl deepened, she added, "They need not be in sight."

"I can try, then, milady. And if they die, it'll be no great loss."

Georgia kept her temper. "I'm sure you want Lady Thretford's entertainment to be a success. Where is the nicotiana?"

Sullenly, he took her to a small patch behind some foxgloves and delphiniums. She sent him off to his duties and then touched a pale trumpet blossom.

"I hope moving doesn't kill you, but you deserve to be more widely appreciated. And I shall make a note to send some seed to Dracy Manor."

She smiled as she strolled around the gardens, admiring some places and noting lacks in others. She often thought of that time on the terrace at Herne. Sometimes she could almost feel again his hands on her waist. Remember being effortlessly lifted up onto the coping and confined, boldly close.

She shivered in the memory of a frisson, but all memories of that day were darkened by his damaged face. She'd suffered a few unpleasant dreams about hot tar falling on her face and woken in a sweat, having to run to the mirror to be sure she was unblemished.

A part of her wanted to meet him again, to see if that sense of connection and friendship was real, but on the whole she was happy to have him in Devon restoring his crumbling inheritance.

She returned to the house to check on the work of two clerks who were writing out the invitations. She looked over Winnie's list and paused on Sellerby's name.

He'd continued to write letters, even though she no longer replied, and he'd sent her an exquisite bottle of gilded Venetian glass in the shape of a heart. Completely unsuitable between friends, and she'd received it on the very day her mourning ended, which had added to her discomfort.

She'd returned it and heard no more, but then she'd left to travel south. Perhaps a letter pursued.

She did not want him at her ball.

Alas, a tick indicated that an invitation had already been written. She riffled through the pile, found it, and slipped it into a pocket, then flipped through the rest so as not to be obvious.

*What?* She picked up another sealed invitation and hurried to her sister's boudoir. "Lord Dracy?"

"Dracy?" Winnie looked up from the baby in her arms. "Mother suggested his name. To help him in society, she said."

"He's in Devon."

"Mother said he was in Town. Isn't there an address?"

Georgia looked. "Marton Street. I was sure he was in Devon."

Winnie shrugged. "An invitation can be flattering even if the person can't attend."

"I certainly hope he can't!"

"Why? Is something wrong with him?"

"No . . ." Georgia could never put her revulsion over his appearance into words. "Nothing at all. It's only that . . . Oh, of course. Fancy Free. Father's still trying to sweeten the pot."

"You're babbling like an idiot, Georgie. Sit and explain."

Georgia sat but was distracted by the infant. Charlotte was still hardly visible amid shawl and cap, but there was something delightful about the tiny hands and the big eyes fixed on her mother.

"She's lovely."

"I think so," Winnie said, smiling at her child and making little kissing movements. "And healthy, which is a blessing. They're so vulnerable at this age. So why is Father sweetening the pot? And what pot?"

"It's all about Fancy Free," Georgia said and told the story.

"What a tangle. But if Lord Dracy's establishment is as ramshackle as it sounds, I'm not surprised Father doesn't want a fine horse sent there."

"Cartagena's a fine horse, and she isn't harmed by it."

"Perhaps it's a matter of what one's accustomed to. People live contented lives in cottages, but we could not. Even a manor house would be uncomfortable after growing up at Herne. But a manor house would seem a palace for many."

It was an excellent point. "It works in the other direction too, doesn't it? A cottager wouldn't be comfortable here, and we wouldn't like to live in a palace."

"Certainly not St. James's!" Winnie said, and they both laughed. The old palace was a collection of drafty rooms and corridors.

"No wonder Their Majesties have abandoned it for Buckingham House," Georgia said.

"Would you like to hold her?" Winifred asked.

Georgia realized she'd been looking at the baby as she spoke.

Instinct was to deny all interest, but she did want to hold Charlotte. She moved to sit beside her sister on the settee and took the baby into her arms. "So light." The big eyes fixed on hers, and Georgia smiled. "Good afternoon, my pretty."

The baby opened and shut her mouth, making Georgia laugh with delight. "She's trying to talk!"

"Not yet, I think, but she is very quick and clever."

"She's perfect," Georgia said, and meant it, feeling an oddly intense pang.

For the first time she wanted a baby in a physical, yearning way. Before, it had been a matter of fulfilling her duty and proving there was nothing amiss with her, but now she simply wanted. She touched a tiny hand, and the baby grabbed.

"So strong."

"Not too strong," Winnie said. "She will be a perfect, pretty lady."

*You may be what you want,* Georgia thought at the baby, *and your aunt will make sure of it.*

"So Dracy is to be pleased," Winnie said. "If he attends, I will do my best. But to what purpose? Does Father hope he'll accept less than the real value of the horse? That doesn't seem quite right."

"It won't be a lesser value," Georgia said, still entranced. "But Father has no mare as valuable as Fancy Free." The baby blew a bubble, making Georgia laugh. "If your uncle Arthur hadn't been such a fool," she said in a singsong voice to little Charlotte, "your noble grand-father could give Dracy the value of Fancy Free and be done with it."

Winnie snatched her baby back. "Don't criticize our brother in front of her!"

"Why not? To lose over ten thousand at cards, when his naval officer's income plus his allowance is only a thousand a year? Father should have let him sink to debtors' prison instead of paying the debt so he could stay afloat in the navy. Lud, two fleets."

"What?"

"The Fleet Prison and the naval fleet. I must work that into an epigram."

"Georgie, it doesn't serve for a lady to be too clever."

The baby squawked and Winnie fussed over her. "Hush, my darling, hush. Your aunt didn't intend to up-set you."

Georgia rose and moved away from mayhem before she responded to that.

Lud, a baby could make a vast amount of noise.

"Margaret!" Winifred called, which didn't help mat-ters, except that a buxom maid hurried in and took the baby away. As blessed silence settled, Winifred said, "She must need feeding. I have an excellent wet nurse."

"I was only saying that Arthur's made things difficult. He should at least admit his folly and show some shame. Then Pranks went ahead and commissioned all those new statues for Herne, and the mirrored wall. And Fa-ther himself—"

Winnie clapped her hands over her ears. "Georgie, don't! We can't have discord in the family."

"Then the men should behave better," Georgia snapped. But then she said, "I'm sorry, Winnie. Perhaps we should show reverence to our father."

"Perhaps?" Winnie queried, lowering her hands. "Re-ally, Georgie."

"But why our brothers?" Georgia persisted.

"Because they're men."

Her sister was close to tears, so Georgia swallowed an argument. She'd met very few men worthy of reverence, and as for them being cleverer, many would fall apart without a woman to cope with life for them.

"I remember the horse business now," Winifred said, anxiously picking up that conversation. "It happened not long after Charlotte arrived, and I was paying no attention to gossip, but I think Thretford said Dracy was after Gosling-go."

"What?" Georgia exclaimed, completely distracted. "Dracy intended all along to trade? The cunning rascal. What a shame the nasty creature had to be shot. Gosling-go would have been well served to end up at Dracy, with rotting straw and a leaky roof. But Fancy Free must be spared, so Dracy must attend and not be uncomfortable."

An idea began to stir.

"Is he very uncouth?" Winnie asked.

Georgia said, "No," for that did seem unfair, even if he had manhandled her without permission. "But he has a bit of the salt air and rigging about him, and seems to want only to be walking his fields and mucking out his stables."

"Then if he attends, I pray he cleans his boots!"

Georgia laughed and made her farewells, but as she returned to her room she wondered if Winifred hadn't been serious.

As for her idea . . . She considered it carefully and then went to her mother's bedchamber.

She found her mother writing letters, which seemed to be her main occupation here, nearly all to Georgia's father, who sent missives back many times a day. Georgia was realizing that her mother was more active in politics than she'd imagined, and might even be the steady hand behind her father's irascible temper.

Where was the reverence there?

If her mother's counsel was important, however, why was she lingering at Thretford?

To keep an eye on her wayward daughter?

She dipped a curtsy. "Mother, do you think it safe for me to travel into Town one day soon? I could go by river."

Her mother continued to write. "There's no need."

"Lord Dracy," Georgia said.

Her mother did look at her then, slightly alarmed.

Georgia laughed. "What are you imagining, Mother? That I'm enamored of him? I've just learned he's in Town and invited to the ball. I thought he'd returned to Devon."

"I believe he did so, but if you say he's returned . . ."

"I'm only going by the invitation. I wonder if he has suitable clothing, if his bow is elegant and his dancing up to snuff. I was asked to assist him," she reminded.

"Ah, yes . . . He could be summoned here."

"That won't provide him with finery."

"And you wish to visit some establishments yourself," her mother said. "This is as much for your improvement as his." She considered, however, as if it were a weighty matter of state. "We certainly don't want Lord Dracy embarrassed."

"Certainly not."

"Very well." Georgia's triumph was soured when her mother added, "I shall come with you."

"You wish to supervise Dracy's polishing, Mother?"

Her mother looked as if Georgia had suggested a swim in the Thames. "I wish to talk to your father. There's only so much that can be put in writing. As we'll go our separate ways, you'll need your maid to accompany you, and a footman. Unless," she added, "Dracy will be able to meet the boat and escort you."

Georgia hesitated on that. She'd grasped an excuse to get to Town without truly thinking of the consequences. A brief encounter with Dracy to advise was one thing. Having him as escort for hours was quite another.

"You've taken him in dislike, daughter? He offended you with his rough ways?"

Georgia had to say no to that, and she was ashamed of her reaction to his appearance.

"I won't mind the escort of a footman if Dracy is otherwise engaged."

"I shall write and ask." Lady Hernescroft took a new sheet of paper and wrote a line. But then she gave Georgia a look. "You are not to go jaunting about."

"Of course not."

"I'll have your word on it."

"Mother! Why would I?"

"I have no idea. I just know your ways."

"I'm fully aware that my behavior must be above suspicion, and I certainly have no desire to become entangled with a mob, or to venture into dubious areas."

"I should think not, but ..." Georgia feared her mother was about to cancel the expedition, but she said, "I pray Dracy is free to be your escort. He'll not allow your games, and with your maid to preserve the proprieties, no one can spin scandal out of it."

Georgia didn't like the reminder that some people might still try to spin scandal out of nothing, but she wouldn't give up a chance of Town.

"I'll have someone check the tides and hire a boat, then," she said. "For tomorrow?"

"If that fits with Lord Dracy's commitments. We should hear back from him in a few hours." Lady Hernescroft dipped her pen and wrote some more. "And I'll summon the family barge here. A boat, indeed." She looked up. "If Dracy's wardrobe proves inadequate, take him to Pargeter's."

"Pargeter's! I've always wanted to see the fine garments gentlemen cast away."

"You might consider casting some of yours to the ladies' equivalent."

"And meet one of my unique gowns at an event? How embarrassing for all."

"I believe they generally alter them sufficiently." Her mother signed her letter and sanded the ink.

"That wouldn't work with my most notable creations, Mother. In any case, I intend to wear some of them again."

Lady Hernescroft paused to stare. "Not the goddess costume, I hope."

Georgia immediately wanted to wear it, perhaps even for Winnie's ball, but she could recognize insanity. "No, not that one, Mother."

The peacock, however . . .

"You've given up all notion of new gowns?"

"What choice do I have? My pin money won't allow for it, and I won't attempt to refurbish a gown in the hope no one will recognize it."

"Your strength is both a blessing and a curse, Georgia. I can only pray that heaven wins." She folded and sealed the letter, then handed it over. "Have this sent."

Georgia took it and left, bemused by her mother's comment. How had talk of gowns led to talk of heaven and hell? In any case, gowns were more to the point.

She gave the letter to a footman and then hurried back to her room. "Jane, you must find the peacock gown. I will wear it to the ball."

"You were going to wear that sprigged primrose, milady."

"Which I'd never worn because it was too demure."

"Demure is what you need, milady, and everyone will remember the peacock from last year."

"That's the point. I said I was going to return as Lady May in all her glory, and that isn't sprigged primrose! The peacock gown is perfect, and the whole beau monde will remember it. And, Jane, we're going to Town! Tomorrow! Just for the day this time, but we're going to

Town. We can visit your sister and learn all about the latest fashions."

"That'll be grand, milady," Jane said, beaming as widely as Georgia as she left on a peacock hunt.

Georgia did a little victory dance and then hugged herself for pure delight.

Jane's sister Mary Gifford was her mantua maker. She'd been a simple dressmaker, but Jane had urged Georgia to commission her to create a winter gown of green velvet. She'd done that so well that she now made all Georgia's gowns and also worked for a select few other ladies, making her much sought after and able to charge high prices.

The peacock gown had been her tour de force. The gown was made of clear dark silk embroidered on the front to look like iridescent feathers, but its finest feature was the saque back, embellished to look like a furled peacock tail.

Then there was the *embrun de mer*, constructed of layers of fine voile in shades of green—hence the name "sea spray"—that was swathed around the bodice instead of fitted to the solid base of the stays, as with most gowns. It had a casual, almost transparent effect even when worn over stays and petticoat.

Mary and Jane had both been uncertain about the goddess costume, but she'd insisted and it had been the star of the Olympian Revels two years ago. She'd portrayed Aphrodite in a classical robe, but one draped to leave her upper body mostly naked—or so it had seemed. In fact, she'd been covered to the neck in flesh-colored cloth. Such fun, and Dickon had been so proud of her.

Of course, people threw it up now as if she truly had been naked. She was going to have to be demure, for a while, anyway, but at least she was to visit Town. And soon she'd enjoy her first ball in a year and dance in her peacock gown.

As for Lord Dracy, she resolved not to let a trace of her unease about his disfigurement show. He'd been wounded in the service of his king and country and deserved all honor and kindness. Especially when he'd provided an excellent excuse for a visit to Town.

# Chapter 9

D racy stood beneath the stone arch of the York Stairs, watching Lady Maybury approach, aware of a heart that beat too fast for the situation. A few weeks in the sanity of the countryside hadn't restored his mind at all. She'd haunted his dreams, and even in the day he'd fallen into trying to imagine her as his wife, in his home.

Ridiculous, but he'd repaired the roof with her in mind, and even had the window repaired in the drawing room. That could have waited, but a drawing room was the lady's domain.

And here she came, a different woman from the one in his memories, and even less fitting for his dreams.

Her broad straw hat was trimmed with pink ribbons and flowers, and her hoop-spread gown was made of a pink-striped material. A bold choice with her loose copper hair. Moreover, she and her mother were arriving not in a common Thames wherry, but in a gilded barge rowed by six liveried men, two powdered footmen in attendance, and the Earl of Hernescroft's escutcheon on the side.

She inhabited a different world from his, and he'd best remember it.

He descended the stairs to meet the boat, but slowly, so that Lady Hernescroft had already taken a footman's hand to step out of the barge and he could offer his hand to Circe.

That open, sparkling smile hadn't been imagined. "Neatly done, Dracy. I see hope for you yet."

"Hope, Lady Maybury?"

"Of your social agility." She paused so her maid could fluff her skirts back into place. "I was surprised to learn you were in Town."

"Suffering in the cause. Let's haste away from the stinking river to the slightly less stinking streets." He bowed to her mother. "Your chairs await, Lady Hernescroft."

Lady Hernescroft did not demand his escort but swept ahead on the arm of the footman. Delightful to have a lady's mother as ally.

The waiting sedan chairs were plain, but they too were not common ones, available for hire. They were Hernescroft ones, and the armed chairmen were in the earl's employ. Perhaps the family also had gilded, escutcheoned ones, but in the present climate with the people restless in hard times, the aristocracy did not draw attention to themselves on the London streets.

The ladies sat inside, the doors were closed, and the party set off with Lady Maybury's maid and one footman walking behind. Dracy chose to walk by the side of Lady Maybury's chair, even though he couldn't see above her chin. Probably as well. His heart was still unsteady from a brief exchange and a smile.

They soon arrived at Hernescroft House, where the chairmen carried them into the safety of the house and set down the chairs in the grand hall.

When Dracy handed Georgia out, she asked, "Is something amiss?"

"Perhaps I'm awed by my surroundings."

She looked around at the portraits on the paneled walls. "Ranks of disapproving ancestors. They certainly awe me."

"You've always felt that way?"

"I've only visited here a few times," she said.

"Why?"

"I married at sixteen, remember? What cause had there been for me to come to Town before then? We all came for the coronation."

"How old were you?" he asked, thinking that with her bright eyes and tumbling hair, she looked a girl still.

"Just sixteen and longing to do more than watch processions and illuminations. Of course, not long after that I married, and soon my husband reached his majority and we removed here to enjoy delights to the full."

"I shall spend my time in Town with Hernescroft," Georgia's mother interjected.

Dracy started. He'd forgotten Lady Hernescroft entirely. Detecting a smirk, he wanted to point out how little hope there was.

"I depend upon you to keep my daughter safe, sir."

"It will be my honor, Lady Hernescroft."

"And, I'm sure, your challenge."

She swept away, and Lady Maybury said, "Are you up to the challenge, my lord?"

"Always and anywhere."

She eyed him. "I could go to extremes to prove you wrong."

"You would only force me to extremes to prove my mettle, my lady."

Perhaps she sensed danger.

"Alas, I can't accept any challenges just now. I am condemned to be good. Come into this reception room so we can discuss our plans for the day." When he hesitated, she sent him a mocking glance. "My maid will attend us, Dracy, so you needn't fear that sort of challenge."

He followed her in. "I'm rarely fearful, Lady Maybury, and then only with due cause."

"I believe you're taunting me, my lord, but I will be strong and resist. Now, are you adequately equipped?"

He grinned. "For what?"

That pretty color rose, but she wasn't dismayed. "Naughty man. For war, sir, for war. In other words, my sister's ball."

"A wooden battlefield and toy weapons."

"Don't deceive yourself. The weapons are real and can draw blood."

She was serious, so he responded that way. "A point, but why would anyone target me? Or do you speak of yourself?"

Her flush was not so pretty. "The ball won't be like that dinner at Herne. I go into this skirmish prepared."

"With me as your guard."

"I rather thought I was to protect you," she said.

"Perhaps we can stand back to back."

"Rather awkward, is it not?"

"But an excellent defensive position when attacked."

"Very odd at a ball, however."

"It's a pass in some dances."

She startled him by laughing. "Oh, how delightful this is! This is the first enjoyable conversation I've had in an age!"

"You live at your sister's house in silence?"

"Of course not, but the conversation . . . With my sister it's all babies, and with my mother all politics. But to business, Dracy. Do you have a suit of clothes for an elegant ball?"

"No, but I doubt it matters."

She seemed truly shocked. "Of course it matters! You'll be dreadfully ill at ease if wrongly dressed."

"I might be dreadfully ill at ease in silk and lace."

"Nonsense."

"I see I'm not so much to be guided as dragooned. I suppose I might become accustomed."

"Accustomed? I warned you before, sir, that my commission was of limited duration. But for the nonce, I do intend to dragoon you—into high fashion. You will enjoy the ball, Dracy, and out of your gratitude accept my father's exchange so poor Fancy Free won't be compelled to sink to life at Dracy."

"Dracy Manor is not the Slough of Despond, you know."

"Not for those accustomed, I'm sure. You wouldn't want to live in a cottage, Dracy, and I wouldn't want to live in a palace."

"No aspiration to be queen?"

She laughed. "None at all, even were it possible. But are you attempting to distract me, sir? I repeat, do you have a fine suit of clothes?"

"No," he said, "and thus it must be. Unless you really do know magic, I must attend the ball in plain clothes or stay away, for such things aren't acquired in an afternoon."

She grinned at him. "Perhaps Pargeter's is worked by elves and fairies, then, for it will provide."

"What's Pargeter's?"

"A place where valets sell their employers' finer cast-offs. They wear the simpler garments around Town but have no call for embroidered silk and velvet. Do you have a valet?"

"No," he said, feeling dragooned indeed. "And no need of one."

"Hire one, immediately if possible. And remember to reward him with finery if you want his best work."

"I have no need of a valet, Lady Maybury. A footman will do for occasional assistance."

"I detect rebellion! Or should it be mutiny in your case? A hanging matter, that, but I'll let you off. If you plan a dull life, that's your concern. Mine is to smooth your way at the ball, so you can't attend in shabby state. I've always wanted to explore Pargeter's."

"Then, of course, we must go."

"Don't 'must' me, Dracy," she said, "especially in that tone. I'm making light of an imposition, for I'd much rather spend the next few hours with my mantua maker."

"Then I most humbly beg your pardon and grovel in gratitude."

She frowned. "Are you cross? What an exasperating man you are. Promise me something."

As imperious as the queen she didn't want to be.

"What?"

"Why so wary? It's a minor matter. I labor with a purpose—to help Fancy Free. Promise me that if you're comfortable at the ball, you'll spare the poor horse at a price my father can afford."

Damn the woman, and damn her father who'd come up with this device. He wanted to tell her the truth, here and now, but if he did she'd shun him forever.

"Is it so hard a thing?" she demanded.

"You're very tender of the sensibilities of a horse."

"They have feelings. Will you consign her to suffering in order to squeeze every last guinea out of your lucky win?"

"Dracy can use every coin. . . ." He reined in his temper, but now he wanted her even more. She wasn't afraid of him or of any man. She'd always give as good as she got.

"Very well, Lady Maybury, I accept your bargain. If I'm comfortable at your sister's ball, I'll take your father's bargain. But only if we seal it with a kiss."

"A *kiss*, sir? My maid is present."

"You wouldn't agree if she were not."

"We'd not be here together if she were not."

"Precisely. So what danger in a kiss?"

He watched her struggle between outrage and temptation. He wasn't surprised when temptation won or when she controlled the payment. She rose on tiptoe and put a light kiss on his lips. "There, the pact is made."

That butterfly contact had been like fire, and perhaps she'd felt it too, for despite her light words, she'd turned away.

"The pact is made," he repeated, knowing then that

he was going to fight his damnedest to win Georgia Maybury for wife, for all eternity and beyond.

"To Pargeter's?" he said.

She hesitated in an interesting way, sliding a thoughtful look at him. But then she turned and briskly led the
way out of the room, once more assuming command.

Georgia wasn't quite sure what had happened. The kiss,
of course, which had been naughty of him, but nothing
of significance. Men and women kissed in games and in
light wagers all the time.

That had been a startling kiss, however.

Only because he'd made it daring, almost wicked.

She should remember that Dracy was the man who'd
picked her up without permission and flirted with her in
a very daring way. He didn't bend to her every whim.
Instead, he challenged her.

"Do you want your chair, Lady Maybury?" he said in
the hall.

It would be sensible protection against dust and dirt,
but Georgia felt a need to experience the London streets
more directly. "No, we'll walk. It's not far."

As they left the house, she pulled down veiling on her
hat to protect herself from dust. "Pargeter's is in Carlyon
Street," she said, turning right.

"At least you're no fragile bloom," he said. "Do you
often walk around Town?"

"Are you criticizing me, my lord? Suggesting I'm
made of coarser stuff?"

"Lady Maybury, no one could ever describe you as
coarse."

"Thank heavens for that. I feared a year of rustication
had ruined me completely. Why are you not rusticating,
Dracy? I thought it your intention."

"I was ordered to pay attention to my duties in Town."

"Were you? By whom?"

"By you."

She felt her cheeks heat. "How very presumptuous of me, to be sure. But I'm sure I was right."

"Are you always sure you're right?"

"Except when I'm wrong," she said lightly. "And I'm right about the ball. Fair warning—it will be as much about politics as about me. Thretford aspires to play peacemaker. He, my father, and a few others need an excuse to bring some important men together on neutral ground."

"Coroneted brigades on a very slippery wooden battlefield. You alarm me."

"No, I don't," she said.

"I beg your pardon?"

She met his eyes. "Nothing alarms you, Lord Dracy."

"There, Lady Maybury, you're wrong."

"Perhaps you alarm me, my lord."

"There, Lady Maybury, you might be right."

A shiver went down her spine.

"How odd you are today," she said, walking on briskly. Whatever she'd expected from this day, it was turning out otherwise. She realized with surprise that his face hadn't disturbed her. The damage was still extensive, but she'd made it worse in her mind so that now it seemed at least tolerable.

There were other aspects as well. When she'd first seen him waiting at the York Stairs, distance had given a new perspective. She'd been struck by a nobleness of bearing, and when he'd descended the steps, by an ease of movement. It was easy to imagine him on the deck of a ship, in command, or strong and agile in battle.

"Carlyon Street, didn't you say?"

His words brought her out of her thoughts, and she saw they'd arrived at the street. "Yes, and we need number sixteen." She walked along, eager now to have this task done. "Here we are. How very discreet, to be sure. Only a small plaque." She mounted the three steps. "Knock."

"What a shame they don't allow females into the military."

She raised her veil to see if he was truly cross. She couldn't tell.

"Am I commanding you? Dickon—my husband—sometimes complained of that." She gave him her prettiest smile. "My dear Lord Dracy, of your kindness, would you ply the knocker?"

Dracy wanted to kiss her again, or spank her, in equal measure. She truly was a Circe, and could wrap him around her pretty fingers with ease.

The damnable thing was that he might not mind as long as she was his.

He rapped the knocker, and the door was opened by a middle-aged maidservant who dipped a curtsy and took them into a small but well-furnished reception room.

When the maid left, Circe looked around. "I might think we'd come to a private house by mistake."

"You haven't visited a similar establishment for ladies?"

"Faith, no!"

He wasn't sure her horror was feigned.

"What do you do with old gowns?" he asked, genuinely curious.

"The simpler ones I give to Jane, but the others are stored."

"Why?"

"Am I to sell them and meet another lady wearing one? Embarrassing for her and me. Am I to pick them apart and try to reuse bits and pieces? Perhaps you think I should burn them."

"I think you should wear them out."

She laughed, but said, "It will please your frugal soul to know I mean to wear some of them again during the next few months."

Her tone stung, but she was right. He did have a frugal soul. It came from never having had money to squander.

A short, portly man came in, looking exactly the part in an elaborately curled bagwig, face paint, and a cloud of perfume.

He bowed. "My lady, my lord, you honor my establishment! Jeffrey Pargeter, most humbly at your service. How may I assist you?"

Dracy saw Lady Maybury prepare to command and spoke first. "I need a suit suitable for a summer ball, sir. Alas, short notice makes it impossible to have something made."

She put her oar in anyway. "Until recently, Lord Dracy was in the navy."

"An honor to assist a hero, my lord," said the unctuous Pargeter. "If you would come with me, sir, we can ascertain your measurements and discover what we have that might suit."

Dracy went, certain that Georgia Maybury itched to come with him. He smiled. He had no objection to being managed by a lovely woman, but she needed to learn that she wouldn't always be in command.

# Chapter 10

Georgia frowned at the door. "I'm not sure why I'm here."

"I'm not sure either, milady," Jane said. "Lord Dracy seems well able to manage his affairs."

"But he knows nothing of style and fashion."

"Mr. Pargeter will advise him, milady."

Georgia took a restless turn around the small room, then sat and picked up a magazine. "*The Lady's Almanac*. I'm surprised it isn't *The Gentleman's Magazine*, or some such."

"Would a gentleman accompany another here, milady?"

"And if he did, he'd be allowed to go with him into the innards of the place. There could at least be some goods on display. As it is, I'll learn nothing. Sit down, Jane. What color do you think would suit Lord Dracy best?"

"Blue, milady," Jane said, sitting neatly on a hard chair. "Not navy blue. A bit brighter, like his eyes."

"Are his eyes bright blue?" Georgia asked, but she knew they were. "Perhaps it comes from looking at the sea."

"Mostly the sea's gray, milady."

"You have no romance in your soul."

"I'm only speaking the truth."

"A dangerous habit, that. What of his hair? He'll need it to be curled and powdered."

"Perhaps a wig, milady?"

"It is hard to imagine him sitting still for hours," Georgia agreed. "A wig, then, but good wigs aren't come upon in a moment. . . ."

"Milady, Lord Dracy's not a doll for your dressing."

Georgia looked at her maid in surprise. "Of course not. But I need him to feel at ease at the ball for the sake of Fancy Free. There can be nothing so awful as being inappropriately dressed."

"There can be any number of more awful things, milady, and I don't know how you'd know how being inappropriately dressed feels."

"Jane, are you cross with me?"

Jane sighed. "No, milady, not cross. But you're treating Lord Dracy as an amusement, and he's not like your usual gentlemen. He's . . . he's been in the navy most of his life, living hard, fighting, killing even. You need to watch yourself."

"You're referring to that kiss," Georgia said. "It was nothing."

"If you say so, milady, but I don't mean that."

"You think him too rough for gentle company? Then I'll polish him like a brass pot until Fancy Free is saved."

"You won't *change* him, milady."

"I don't want to! Lud, why are we talking this way? Yes, I used Lord Dracy as an excuse to come into Town, but what harm in that?"

"You might have raised some hopes."

"He'd never be so foolish," Georgia said, but didn't entirely convince herself. "If you're right, it's unfortunate, but I'm sure he'll soon see that he's no candidate for my hand."

"It's to be hoped so, milady."

"Don't put on that dismal face. I'll magic him into form for the ball, and guard and guide him on the night, then with Fancy Free safe, I'll wave him off to his muddy acres."

Jane still had that look—the you'll-come-to-grief-if-you-go-on-this-way-milady look.

"Perish it, there's no reason for us both to kick our heels here. Your sister's establishment is only a few streets away. Go there and enjoy some time together until I join you."

"I can't leave you unchaperoned, milady."

"I don't need a chaperone to walk a few Town streets. When Dracy's business here is done, we'll join you there."

"Remember, milady, you must cause no new talk."

"How could I in that time? Go, Jane!"

"I don't think—"

"Go, or I shall become cross."

Jane rose. "On your head be it," she said, and left.

What on earth had she meant by that?

Alone, Georgia's irritation slowly melted into liberation. Here she was, at liberty in Town. She could leave here now and go where she wished, do as she wished. . . .

She wouldn't, for she needed respectability, but the possibility put her into a good humor. She picked up the magazine again to consider the latest styles. She'd chosen not to receive magazines at Herne, for they would have been depressing, so this was a treat.

She browsed, noting with relief that there'd been no revolutions in style in the past year, so her old gowns would not make her a laughingstock.

There were small style details, however, and some novel ways of trimming. She could have that style of point lace put on her blue instead of scalloped, but would that be shabby refurbishment?

She settled instead to ideas for new gowns. That saque embroidered with summer flowers was pretty, but what if some of the flowers were silk ones, attached as if scattered there. What if they were arranged in garlands?

Would a background of green lace in a leafy effect be too much?

A skirt gathered up into billows of lace was absurd, but if it were silk gauze embroidered with spangles it could be pretty. Even better in a color other than white. A soft brown with copper spangles?

She stored both ideas for when she was married again and could indulge.

She studied a plain blue villager dress. If the skirt was hitched up at the side, as if caught up for work . . .

The door opened, and Dracy returned followed by Pargeter and three employees, each holding up a suit of jacket, waistcoat, and breeches, hung together so that they lacked only the man inside.

"I thought it wise to seek your advice, Lady Maybury," he said, perhaps drily.

Choosing diplomacy, Georgia asked, "Which does Mr. Pargeter recommend?"

"He refuses to give weight to any of the three but says all should fit after minor alterations."

Georgia rose to inspect the offerings—a dark blue, a light blue, and a gray with embroidered flowers.

She took the lighter blue and passed it to Dracy. "Hold it in front of you, my lord."

It was close to the color of his eyes, which really were a very fine blue, but she twitched a finger. "The gray."

When he was holding the gray, she stepped back and considered. "I wouldn't have predicted it, which is what makes fashion so interesting. Will it be recognized, Pargeter? I rather think that dark blue belonged to Lord Ashart."

"You have a keen eye, milady. We've altered the trimmings—we're most careful about such matters—but a true connoisseur of fashion notices these things. In the case of the gray, however, it has only been seen in Ireland. Never worn in Town, I assure you, and again, altered."

Georgia nodded and turned back to Dracy. "You approve?"

"I'm in your hands. It's of little interest to me."

"Would you go on board ship improperly dressed?" she demanded.

He smiled. "You win that point."

She nodded. "Complete your purchase, my lord, and we'll move on to other matters."

He went, leaving Georgia unsettled, though she wasn't sure why. She remembered Jane's vague warnings, but she couldn't believe Dracy was a danger to her.

It must be the other thing Jane had said—that he was a military man. He'd fought battles, which must mean that he'd killed. He would have lived a hard life at times, which was probably why he was impatient with her. She couldn't help the fact that she'd always lived comfortably, and she certainly didn't wish it otherwise.

He was so different from other men she knew—from Dickon, Perry, Beaufort, and the rest. Men who'd been raised to elegance and style. He was also different from the rougher men, the sporting men like Shaldon and Vance. Their dangers were chosen.

That didn't make Dracy a danger to her.

Not at all.

Certainly not during a walk to Mary Gifford's house.

Having satisfied herself on that, she was able to greet him easily upon his return and leave the establishment without a qualm.

Perhaps he felt differently. As the door closed behind them, he asked, "What's become of your maid, Lady Maybury?"

"I gave her leave to visit her sister nearby. Don't fret. We'll join her there forthwith. Do you need a wig, Dracy, or will you use a coiffeur?"

"I have a wig. Isn't it unwise to be with me without a chaperone?"

"No."

"Then why are you pulling down your veil again?"

"Against dirt and dust. Are you saying that you are dangerous, my lord?

"In ways you can't imagine," he said.

He was trying to put her off balance, and she'd have no part of it. "In a naval sort of way, you mean. But we're safely on land, aren't we?"

On the street, with people around. Ridiculous to need the comfort of that. She dragged the conversation back into safer matters. "Your wig. Is it suitable?"

"I believe so. Should I have it powdered?"

"Most of the gentlemen will be white, and many of the ladies."

"Including you?"

"I only powder when it's essential. For court and such."

"Wise, when your hair is such a glorious color."

"Why, thank you, my lord."

He smiled back, but said, "It can hardly be news to you. I'm not being courtly, am I? I apologize, though I do like plain speech. I wonder why white hair is so valued. After all, it's a sign of age."

Georgia was happy to switch to a triviality. "A question I've never asked! Now I think on it, I don't know when the fashion started. I don't believe they powdered back in the Restoration."

"They wore those long, curly wigs. Too much hair to powder, perhaps?"

"Where fashion commands, nothing is impossible," she stated. "The periwig did make men look romantic, though, even the most unlikely ones. There's a portrait at Herne of my grandfather in jowly middle age, and he was a hard, harsh man by all accounts, but with that mass of curls, he could almost seduce me."

"Until the wig came off," he said.

"I think I'd decline the honor even before then."

"Wise lady. We men are all hard and harsh beneath the lace and curls."

"My husband wasn't."

He halted. "My apologies . . ."

"No, no," Georgia protested. "I didn't mean it as a reproach. But Dickon was very sweet natured, very generous, gentle. That's why it was so awful. . . ." She hurried on, taken unawares by a spurt of grief. "My apologies again," she said, grateful that the veil hid tears.

"When did you last walk these streets?" he asked.

"Oh." Georgia stopped again. "The day before. When my husband was still alive . . ." She swallowed and forced a brighter tone. "He would have enjoyed a visit to Pargeter's. Simply for amusement's sake, of course."

"Of course. No secondhand clothing for him. He was a merry soul?"

"Yes. Yes, he was."

But the sadness wouldn't be suppressed, and Georgia saw why. She must have been directing their steps unconsciously, for they were not on their way to Mary Gifford's establishment. They were at the corner of Belling Row, where her house was.

Had been.

"We've come the wrong way," she said, turning.

He grasped her arm. "Memories?"

"It doesn't matter."

"Yes, it does. What lies down this street?"

She resisted, but then said, "My house. What was my house. Our house."

"Show it to me."

"No."

"Please."

She frowned at him. "Why?"

"Because you need to exorcise these ghosts. They'll linger otherwise, eating away at your heart."

"Eating . . ."

"Perhaps too strong, but you'll be better without them."

The clattering city seemed hushed and, yes, filled with ghosts.

"Can you avoid this street forever?" he asked.

"Perhaps . . ."

She couldn't, however, and he was correct about the ghosts, so Georgia straightened her spine and walked on.

Belling Row was like many other terraces in Mayfair, lined with tall town houses, each with shiny black railings in front and neat ranks of small-paned windows. She'd never considered such details as intently as she did now.

One particular house came closer and closer, and her heart pounded.

"I'm not sure if Dickon's uncle . . . the new Lord Maybury," she corrected, "has kept the house or sold it." Her throat felt tight, her mouth dry, but she forced herself to keep speaking. "Most people prefer to rent, you know, as they only spend a few months in Town. We lived in Town as much as possible, so we owned the house. Leased, that is, but a long lease . . ."

As they walked down the street, Dracy let her talk, tossing in only a word or two, wondering whether she grieved more for the loss of her homes than for the loss of her husband. That would be shallow, however, and despite Georgia Maybury's frivolity, he didn't think her shallow. Young, yes. Pampered, yes. But surprisingly clearheaded and strong.

Perhaps husband and homes were, for her, one great void?

She fell silent in front of a house indistinguishable from the rest.

"This is it?" he asked.

"Yes. Impossible that I can't walk in." But then she moved on. "I don't want to be seen gazing at it like a lost soul.

"It's one house among a street of them."

"I suppose there are a great many similar ships," she snapped, "but don't you pine for the one you left?"

He weighed his answer but gave her the truth. "Not at

all. For some of the people on it a little, but there were others I was glad to be shot of."

"Then you don't know what it's like to lose a home. Homes."

"No," he admitted, "I don't. What other homes?"

"Maybury Castle," she said, "but I never cared much for that. And Sansouci."

"Without care?"

"My house ... Our house. In Chelsea, by the river. We'd be there now. . . . I mean, when London became intolerably hot. The gardens ... The new Lord Maybury has kept Sansouci. He's probably there now."

He could offer her no comfort except for the illusion of country and garden. "We could walk in the park. Would it take us much out of our way?"

She shivered as if she'd been lost in thought. "No," she said, and turned toward the grass and trees.

Dracy went with her, struck by the situation of a childless widow. Overnight, Georgia Maybury had lost not only her husband, but her homes. She'd been evicted as thoroughly as a dismissed tenant from a tied cottage and allowed to take hardly anything with her.

The new Lord Maybury would have taken possession of everything she'd considered hers. Not just three houses, but the furniture, china, paintings, carpets, jewelry—everything except her clothing and such, and items specifically given to her.

No wonder she was obsessed with regaining all she had lost.

"It's a cruel system," he said, "but how else could matters be arranged?"

She didn't pretend not to understand. "No other way. I know that."

She walked as briskly as before, but now as if fleeing something. He wanted to take her into his arms and comfort her.

She did pause in the end, in the shade of a tree. "So unchanged," she said.

"The park?"

"Everything. The house, the park, Pall Mall . . ." She turned to him. "If you returned to the navy, nothing would have changed there either."

"I'd doubtless be on a different vessel, if I was lucky enough to get a posting at all. Peacetime's the very devil."

She cocked her head. "What was the name of your last ship?"

"The *Pickle*," he said, and got the result he wanted—a real smile.

"Are you teasing me?"

"No, on my honor. The grand names are preserved for the grand ships. There's a *Ferret* and a *Haddock*."

"And you don't pine for the *Pickle*?"

"Not at all."

"What of your childhood home? Did you pine for that when you went to sea?"

"Not that I remember. My parents died when I was ten and I went to live with my aunt and uncle at Dracy Manor. I'd visited it before and I liked it, especially the stables, but I never felt it was my home. After all, it never was."

"So no loss, no wrench."

"A small one. For a pony."

"What was its name?" she asked.

"Conquistador. Its real name was Homer, but that was too sober for a ten-year-old."

"I like horses, but I've never been fond of riding."

"Perhaps you should try riding astride," he suggested. She smiled. "Perhaps I should."

"Dracy is mine now," he said, needing to try to convey it to her. "It is my home now, and also my responsibility, my duty."

"That I do understand," she said. "I hope it brings you joy."

*Only with you in it,* he thought.

"I assume Green Park isn't summoning painful memories," he said.

"Ah, that's interesting." She didn't seem upset by the subject. "Of course—this isn't lost to me. I can walk here exactly as I did before, enjoy it as I did before. Thank you for that, for reminding me that so much is still mine to enjoy. The parks, the theaters, the shops, court. How foolish to dwell on the few small losses when Town remains and all will soon be just as it was. I need only remarry."

As he'd thought, she was intent on restoring things to the way they had been. He was sure she'd repossess that Belling Row house and Sansouci if she could. But it could never be, any more than he could restore his handsome face.

When would she realize that?

It was early days yet for her, he reminded himself.

"I'm considering a duke," she said lightly, walking out of the shade to cross the park. "I would like to be a duchess. I wouldn't confess as much, but we're friends, aren't we?"

Ah, a direct challenge, "only friends" implied. Georgia Maybury was no fool, and she recognized that their intimate conversation had broken down barriers, so she was deftly rebuilding them.

"I will be honored to be your friend, Lady Maybury," Dracy said, adding, "always."

No lie in that. Friendship in marriage was his ideal.

"How delightful. You remind me of my brother Perry, you see. The Honorable Peregrine Perriam." She was building a stronger barrier, moving him from friend to brother. "I can talk to him about anything," she went on, "and he understands me as few do. He shares my love of Town, court, fashion, theater. . . ."

She prattled on, brick upon brick. The damnable Peregrine Perriam sounded as much a fribble as Cousin Ceddie. Doubtless he too squandered his all on fashion.

As Georgia Maybury was accustomed to do.

As she couldn't wait to do again.

Every word from her lips raised the barrier between them.

Georgia had been so intent on making sure that Lord Dracy harbored no foolish hopes that she'd lost track of her surroundings. "Ah, the Queen's House. You know it, I assume."

"I've not yet entered it," Dracy said.

"You've been presented, though? At St. James's?"

"Yes."

"Of course you have. Do forgive me. I don't know why I'm fussing over you like a duck with one duckling."

That made him laugh. "Hard to see myself as small and downy, but you may fuss over me all you wish."

"A dangerous invitation, Dracy. I might feed you worms."

"From your mouth, Lady Maybury, I might even eat them."

Georgia laughed, but matters were sliding in the wrong direction again.

"I'm too good a *friend*," she said, emphasizing the word, "to torment you so."

"Then I'll be too good a friend to tease."

"What do your friends call you, my lord?"

"Dracy," he said.

"I mean, what were you christened? Not Dracy Dracy, I assume?"

"No."

"Then what?"

"We'll have to be much better friends for me to tell you that."

"You exasperating man! Now, of course, I'm eaten with curiosity. I shall guess. Tom, Dick, or Harry?"

"Too commonplace."

"Methuselah."

"My parents tried to ensure longevity?"

"Lazarus."

"An attempt to enable me to rise from the dead?"

"Gog."

He laughed. "With a brother, had I one, called Magog?"

"Tell me," she demanded.

"No."

She considered him. "If you tell me, I shall permit you to call me Georgia."

"Not a large enough bribe."

"Then that wasn't permission." Georgia tossed her head and walked on, but she was smiling from the exchange. As a friend, he was delightful. She remembered what he'd said.

"You have no brothers?" she asked.

"Nor sisters either."

"That must have been odd. Did your parents not mind their only child going to sea?"

"They were dead by then, but I was always intended to follow in my father's footsteps."

"Did you say you joined the navy at twelve? That must have been horrible."

"Not at all. I wasn't cast onto the waves without care. I started out as cabin boy on a ship captained by an old friend of my father's, and I wasn't at all reluctant to go. Is that honest answer enough to reward me with permission to use your name?"

"No."

"Why not?"

Because in some way it would be intimate instead of friendly.

"Because it would be inappropriate," she said, "and I need to be appropriate at all times."

"Poor Georgia." She glared at him, but he wasn't driven off. "You said that I'm like a brother to you."

"Then on those terms, sir, you may." She saw it score and smiled. "In private only."

"So you plan private moments. I'm all expectation."

Lud! She was seeking something quelling when clocks began to chime.

"My stars! Is that two o'clock? I only have another hour before returning to the boat!"

"Then we must make haste." He grabbed her hand and set off at a run.

Georgia shrieked, but then she hauled up her skirts and ran with him, laughing at the childish absurdity of it.

Abruptly she hauled back. "Stop, stop. I insist!"

He obeyed. "What's amiss?"

Georgia fussed with her skirt. "One does not run in the park."

"Not even when in a hurry? Ah, I see. We're observed and disapproved of. But you are veiled."

"So I am." She looked at Bella Tresham and stuck out her tongue. "Come. We still must make haste. I wish to have time to look over the dolls."

"Dolls?" he said. "You are quite young, but . . ."

"Fashion dolls," she said, hurrying out of the park. "Do you know nothing?"

"About such things, less than nothing." Dracy tossed a coin to the lad who'd swept dung off the road for them. As they crossed, he said, "Explain fashion dolls."

"A mantua maker can't make up gowns to show to her customers—that would be too costly—so she dresses dolls. There are illustrations, but nothing shows a style so well as a doll. They can be sent into the country too, so that distant ladies can see the latest styles."

"You played with these dolls at Herne?"

"Cease your provocation, sir. I didn't request any. It would have cast me into the Slough of Despond to think of fashion when I had no need of it. But now I must catch up. Here we are."

She'd stopped at a two-story, double-fronted house

where one window displayed a gown and some trailing bolts of cloth.

"A mantua maker," he said. "My naval friends would never believe it."

"New experiences broaden the mind. If you promise to be good, I'll ask Mary to send out for some ale for you as you wait."

He raised her gloved hand to his lips. "Thank you, Georgia. Then I promise to be very, very good."

That really shouldn't have caused a panicked flutter in her heart. But it did.

# Chapter 11

Georgia became so lost in fabrics and patterns that Dracy had to insist she leave, because her mother would be waiting. She pouted at him, and then regretted it a little. But what right had he to disapprove of her?

She traveled back to the stairs in a hired chair, reading one of the two magazines she'd borrowed. She must remember to arrange a regular delivery.

Her mother was already in the barge and glaring, but Georgia didn't care. For the first time since Dickon's death she had felt free, free to come and go and to choose her amusements.

Before she boarded the barge, she paused to thank Dracy. "You've been the perfect escort, my lord."

In some way he had. In particular, he'd helped drive some of the ghosts and fears away.

"I'm at your service as long as I'm in Town, Lady Maybury."

"Easy enough to say when I'll be in Hammersmith."

"But I'll join you there at the ball."

"I look forward to seeing you in full finery."

"Do get in," her mother said. "We must be off."

Georgia turned and entered the barge with the assistance of a footman.

"You will be at hand to serve as escort and adviser,

Lady Maybury?" Dracy said. When she hesitated, he added, "After all, we have a bargain."

He was challenging her, and belatedly she remembered other aspects of today. A run through the park. A kiss.

"Fancy must certainly be free," she said lightly and settled on the seat beside her mother. "I will do my duty."

The boatmen were casting off when she remembered something. "Dracy! Do you know how to dance?"

He sent her a crooked grin. "Have no fear, I can execute a hornpipe with the best." As the barge pushed off into the river and the men began to row, he linked his arms and executed a few nimble steps.

Georgia stared, muttering, "Hornpipe . . ."

"I'm sure he knows the rudiments of other steps, child," her mother said, giving her an arch look. "You seem on good terms with Lord Dracy."

"I did my duty, Mother, and was as pleasant as I know how whilst providing him with adequate clothing. I wish I'd remembered dancing, though."

"He's not at the antipodes. Write a letter recommending a good dancing master. Pargeter's provided?"

"Yes, though I wasn't allowed to explore. I saw a suit of Ashart's there. I remember thinking at the time that it was too dark a blue for him."

"You can't have spent the whole time on that," her mother said.

Georgia resented being interrogated, but there'd be no point in rebellion. "We strolled in Green Park for a while and then he accompanied me to my mantua maker. He was very obliging."

"And his disfigurement? You seemed at ease with him."

"I don't mind it at all," Georgia said, determined that that be so. "Do you know that he's an only child, Mother, and now an orphan? I wonder what family he has."

"Very little, I think. Both Cedric Dracy's parents were dead, and he too was an only child."

"Lud, it's a dismal family pattern. Poor constitutions?"

"Cedric Dracy's parents were drowned crossing from Holland some years ago. Eight, perhaps. The sinking of the *Brightly Bess* was much talked about."

"What of the current Lord Dracy's parents?"

"Perhaps some naval incident. You must ask him."

"No, no, it was only idle curiosity. Do political matters go well, Mother?"

"It seems the nonsense is coming to an end. Perhaps Winifred's ball will be an opportunity to settle matters. Most fortuitous that your return to society provides the excuse."

"I'm honored to be of use."

If her mother caught the dryness, she ignored it.

Why, she wondered, was the queen so powerful in chess when women had so little power in the world? Georgia suspected that her mother was more politically astute than her father, but she could have any effect only through him.

Georgia remembered the few occasions when she'd felt strongly about some issue and persuaded Dickon to go to Parliament to cast his vote. If she'd been able to go, she might have made a speech on the subject. She could probably have swayed the house through charm if not by eloquence.

Largely out of mischief, Georgia asked, "Do you think women will ever be able to take seats in Parliament?"

"Take seats?" her mother exclaimed. "Stand in elections? Completely improper, and men would never vote for a woman."

"If women had a vote . . ."

"Enough of such foolishness, Georgia. Women have enough to do with their homes and children. Men have more time on their hands for things like speeches and negotiations. Though they can't always be relied upon to use good sense."

Georgia bit back a laugh, sure that was the explanation for the amount of time her mother spent on her father's politics. This was an interesting discussion, however.

"What of the situation of Lady Rothgar?" she asked. "She's also Countess of Arradale in her own right, and the earldom of Arradale has a seat in the House of Lords. She maintains that she should be able to take it, and I can't see why not."

"Lady Rothgar has a great many odd notions. Feeding her baby with her own milk whilst continuing with all her activities. Writing to the newspapers on legal matters."

"But why is it odd to want her seat in Parliament? She's not allowed to send a deputy, so the earldom is deprived of influence."

"Which is why titles should always descend in the male line," her mother said. "Anything else leads to irregularity, and there's enough of that in the world from other causes. The behavior of the Americans is quite absurd, and if we're not careful, unnatural women like Lady Rothgar will bring disorder here. Only consider: she has traveled north to deal with matters on her estates herself at a time when she should be by her husband's side in Westminster. Why she couldn't send a deputy there, I have no idea, but to add to it, her babe must go with her. It's to be hoped it survives."

Georgia wasn't sure that hope was sincere. She'd forgotten that Diana Rothgar was a particular irritant to her mother.

She said, "Amen," and took refuge in her magazine. Her mother opened a book—an account book of some sort. She was probably going over the Hernescroft accounts, just as she herself had gone over the Maybury ones. Left to Dickon, all would have been chaos and senior servants would have been sliding aside funds for their own use. Were all men as lazy about such things?

Were the great estates being held together by women rather than men? Interesting notion. Who was overseeing the books at Dracy?

No, she would not offer to do that for him, though she missed that part of her former life more than she'd realized. There was something satisfying about facts and figures, about putting them in order and good sense. She needed a husband who would allow her that task, but how to find out was a puzzle.

Like Dracy's name. What could it be that he disliked so much? Moses? Esau?

Boaz? Wasn't there a saint called Chrysastom, or some such?

Men sometimes took their mother's surname. Blatherwick? Peabody? Pickle?

"Did you cough?" he mother asked.

"No, Mother," Georgia said, biting her lip.

She couldn't wait to share her suggestions with Dracy when they met at the ball.

Georgia was inspecting Winnie's collection of bowls and vases when a footman found her. "The Earl of Sellerby has called, milady."

"Oh, perdition . . ." Georgia muttered under her breath, but she could hardly refuse to see him when he'd come all the way from Town. She was guiltily aware of the invitation she'd torn up and tossed into Winnie's "lake."

"I'll be there shortly," Georgia told the footman and hurried to her room to take off her apron and tidy herself. "I wouldn't put it past him to propose," she said to Jane. "What am I to do?"

"Reject him, milady?"

Georgia stilled, realizing something. "I've never had to reject a suitor before."

"You only have to say no, milady. Kindly."

"I suppose so. And perhaps he won't. He understands

correct behavior, and he would have to apply to Father first. Unless he's done so. Stars and angels, Father wouldn't have approved him, would he? Without a word to me?"

"Even if he has, milady, you can still say no."

"Yes, of course I can. But I don't . . . I do hope I can come through all this without having to openly defy my father."

Jane put a hand on her shoulder. "It won't come to that, milady. Lord Sellerby is too fine a gentleman to distress you."

"It distresses me to receive such devotion, especially when I can never reward him as I wish. You will come down with me, Jane. That should give him the hint."

"Very well, milady, but you favored him for a good two years before Lord Maybury's death."

"Are you my conscience now? Desist! I know my faults. But I was married then, so there was nothing to it. He was excellent company at the sort of occasions that Dickon disliked. Performances of ancient music, lectures on art, philosophical soirees . . . Oh, come. Let's dispose of him. There's so much to do."

Sellerby waited in the small drawing room, and Georgia paused to admire his plain but elegant appearance. Correct in every detail, as he had not quite been at Herne. Gray cloth with chased silver buttons, his dark brown hair neatly dressed, narrow ruffles with just an edge of lace. A ring and a gold pin in his neck cloth.

Perhaps she should reconsider him.

"Sellerby," she said, offering her hand. "How kind of you to come so far out of Town."

He took her hand and kissed it. His lips actually touched her skin, which was not quite comme il faut.

"My dear Georgie, you know I would travel to the Indies for you."

She'd permitted him to use her name years ago. Another regret.

"The Indies?" she said, sitting in a chair so he couldn't attempt to sit beside her. "Would you bring me back rubies?"

"As big as pigeon eggs."

She chuckled to make light of it. "I hope you bring me something of greater value. The latest on-dits from Town. How goes the Grafton tangle?"

He obligingly shared gossip, and Georgia had only to toss in the occasional comment and relax. He clearly wasn't here to propose.

His conversation was so easy, and he knew just what topics would interest her. He was handsome. . . . No, not quite that. She realized his face was ordinary, but his style and manner made it seem a little finer.

"When will you move to Town and be au courant yourself, Georgie? I confess to surprise that you've roosted so far away."

"I wished to visit my sister and see her baby. And now I'm assisting her with her ball." She winced, but the word was out.

"Ah, yes." He smoothed one ruffle. "I have not yet received my invitation."

"I wonder where it went," Georgia said, praying not to show guilt. But, perdition, there was a way out of it. "Of course you are invited, Sellerby."

"Your first ball in your new life. May I claim the first dance?"

*No,* came strongly in her mind, for the first dance was always seen as significant. She responded playfully, however. "Now, now, Sellerby, you can't expect that. It will play out on the night."

"No reward for your most devoted servant?"

"I reward Jane very well, I assure you, my lord."

Did annoyance tighten his smooth features? If so, it passed.

"The witty Lady May. Your world awaits. I will do your bidding and await the night along with all your court, but may I remind you how very well we have danced together?"

It was true. He was possibly the best dancer in the beau monde and had always been a favorite partner, but he was wooing her, even with discretion. It would not do.

"I won't forget," she said, but rose. "You must excuse me, Sellerby. With my sister having so recently given birth, I'm shouldering much of the work of the ball."

Obediently, he rose. "Then the event will be a triumph, as all Lady May's entertainments are. What will we all call you when you remarry, I wonder?"

Lady Sell was probably in his mind, she thought wryly. It hardly had a ring.

"Perhaps the time for such names will be over," she said, moving toward the door. "I will soon reach my majority."

"Such hoary age."

She smiled at the joke, so when he removed something from his pocket and pressed it into her hand, she took it.

"A mere nothing," he said," but a gift of the heart."

He left before she could thrust it back at him, and in any case she could tell it was a pair of gloves, which was an unexceptionable gift.

Damn the man, though, for trapping her like that. "I fear he's going to persist with his suit," she said.

"I believe you're right, milady. But no matter. You have only to say no."

"Yes, but . . . He'll pester me with gifts and I'll have to decide whether to return them or not."

She untied the ribbon and spread open the paper. White silk gloves, as she'd thought. Short ones, beautifully made—but with embroidered hearts along the cuff.

"A gift of the heart, indeed," she said, and gave the gloves to Jane. "Take those away. I have work to do and only twenty-four hours in which to do it."

# Chapter 12

The next evening, Georgia was considering the arrangement of her hair when someone knocked on the door. She sent a prayer that it not be her mother.

Her friend Lady Torrismonde entered, elegant in yellow silk.

Georgia flew into her arms. "Lizzie! It is fine beyond anything to see you at last."

Lizzie Torrismonde laughed, hugging her back. "You could have come to visit us at any time these past few months, you know."

"I know, I know, but I decided to complete my full term at Herne. How well you look!"

Lizzie wasn't a beauty, but she was lovely, with fine skin and thick light brown hair. Two babies hadn't changed her slim figure, but they'd increased her air of contentment.

"You're wearing the peacock," Lizzie said. "It deserves another showing. I think it's my favorite of all your special gowns."

Georgia rotated to show off the furled peacock tail that made up the saque back. "But should I go for the peacock eye aigrette, or scattered jewels?"

Lizzie settled on the settee. "As if I know better than you or Jane. What did you wear last time?"

"Jane? What did I wear in my hair then?"

"The aigrette, of course, milady."

"Then I shall do the same. Clever Lizzie." Georgia sat so Jane could fix it, but turned on the bench to face her friend. "You've understood my purpose. I will appear as I was, unchanged."

"You're ready to face the world?"

"Of course."

"So why are you late to go down?"

"The hair," Georgia said, but then pulled a face. "You know me too well. I'm nervous. Isn't that absurd? Lady May, nervous about entering a social occasion? But the guest list isn't as cozy as I hoped. Thretford's insisted on any number of political people. And their wives."

"Ah."

"Indeed. Lord North is to be here, and Anne North has always disapproved of me, as has Lady Shelburne. Thank heavens Pranks remains at Herne, his vinegary wife with him."

"Georgia . . . ," Lizzie chided.

"She is! She hooks onto every new whisper about me. She's sent a deputy, would you believe? Her sister, El-oisa Cardross, arrived today without warning, and she's as spiteful as Millicent because she sees us as rivals in beauty. Poor Winnie has so few rooms, she murmured about Eloisa sharing with me, but I put my foot down, so Eloisa is in a tiny room intended for a maid. I suppose I shouldn't have been so firm. . . ."

"Georgia, you're too kindhearted. Anyone who turns up uninvited and unexpected should be grateful not to be sent to the nearest inn."

"Perhaps so. She brought letters from Millicent for us all. I don't know what was in the others, but I was sweetly reminded of the shame I'd brought on the family and how it was important to avoid more scurrilous attention. She even reminded me of that letter the dowager had trumpeted, and that it would not have been forgotten."

"The nasty cat!" Lizzie exclaimed, and from her that was extreme condemnation.

"She is. And I won't excuse her on the grounds of being with child. I'm sure it doesn't turn you into a harpy."

"Of course it doesn't. I hope you burned the letter."

"Instantly. I wish I could burn every bit of foulness, but whispers and rumors can't be burned."

"They can be extinguished," Lizzie said, "or simply die for lack of fuel, which is the case with you. You have only to avoid creating any new dramas tonight."

"So boring!" Georgia said instinctively, but then she wrinkled her nose at her friend. "Don't worry, I'm determined to be the epitome of demure."

Lizzie laughed.

"I can be," Georgia protested.

"In that gown?"

"It's not much lower than yours."

"But that little extra makes all the difference."

Georgia swiveled to study her bodice. Her breasts did swell up beautifully above the flat front, and her delicate sapphire necklace drew attention there. "There's nothing outrageous about it."

"But epitome of demure?"

Georgia swiveled back. "Very well, I won't attempt demure. However— Jane, are you finished?"

"As best I can with you twisting this way and that, milady."

"Yet you work wonders. Thank you. Now, the mourning bracelet, please."

Georgia was already wearing the locket that held Dickon's picture, pinned amid the silver lace that trimmed her stomacher. That wasn't for show, but simply to have Dickon with her in some way. She knew he'd watch over her if he could.

The black and silver bracelet didn't really go with her ensemble, but that would make it all the more noticeable. She had Jane fasten it on her right wrist, and then she looked at her friend. "Yes?"

"Yes," Lizzie said.

"It's so lovely to have my wise friend back by my side. Have I thanked you enough for your plentiful letters? You saved my sanity."

"Your letters were a delight too, especially in the winter when I was as big as a whale with Arthur."

"Oh, how is he now? He must be . . . heavens, is he five months old? I long to see him."

"Then you must visit. He's at a charming stage."

"But keeping you in the country."

"I enjoy the country, and when you have children, you will too. It's much better for them."

Georgia avoided talk of children by rising to put on gray silk shoes. If nature had worked as it should, she'd have a child, and if it had been a boy, she would still have most of her life. The Town house, Sanscouci, and Maybury Castle, at least for the next twenty years.

The question burst out. "*Why* do some couples have children easily—sometimes too easily—and others have none? It's so unfair."

"It's God's will," Lizzie said.

"Then why does God will it so?"

Lizzie rose to take her in her arms. "That's too deep a question for me, love. But when you marry again, I'm sure he'll provide."

"Not with a second Annunciation, I pray."

"Georgia!" But then Lizzie hugged her. "Oh, you haven't changed, and I delight in that. Certainly if anyone appears in your bedchamber in angel guise, be very, very suspicious."

"Do you think any seducer has tried that trick? 'But, Father, it was the Angel Gabriel!'"

They all burst out laughing, and Georgia could hold on to a bright smile as she left the room to face both friends and foe.

*    *    *

Georgia descended the stairs to the hall, chatting to Lizzie, striving to be as carefree as in the past, which was hard when pricked by avid glances. She was accustomed to being the center of attention, but not in this way. For most guests this was a first sight of Lady May since her husband's death, and they were all passing judgment. And finding her wanting?

Had they expected her to attend in deep mourning, or in muted gray? She realized she was touching the locket and lowered her hand, but it was comforting to think of Dickon with her. He'd understand the peacock gown and approve as well.

Damnation, she would not cry.

She sought friends below. Harringay was over there, talking to Waveney, who was an admirer but could be more trouble than benefit now he was married. Babs Harringay must be here somewhere. She saw the Duke of Bridgwater, a possible suitor. He was paying no attention to her at all, probably absorbed in talk of canals.

Mr. Porterhouse's smile was open, so she smiled back. He'd been one of the pleasantest members of her court and could always to be relied upon.

Dracy.

Where was Dracy?

Lizzie's amiable, ordinary husband came to meet them, his eyes warm with appreciation of his wife. Of his wife, Georgia realized. Not of a spectacular gown or spectacular beauty, but of her. Had Dickon admired her most for herself or her style . . . ?

No, she wouldn't have such thoughts, especially here and now.

Where the devil was Dracy?

A quick glance around didn't find him, and she was dismayed by how much that mattered. She realized she'd expected him to be waiting, as on the York Stairs ready to hurry to her side, to be her anchor. Lud, she was clinging to the Torrismondes like a nervous child. Porter-house was talking to the Berrisfords; Waveney was with his wife.

Eloisa Cardross came over in extremely low-cut pink, smiling prettily. "Such a lovely house, is it not?"

"Charming," Georgia said.

"Exquisite floral arrangements."

"Thank you."

Eloisa looked at her.

"I assisted my sister by managing the flowers. I'm pleased that they please you."

Eloisa looked as if she wished she could bite the words back.

"I suppose you miss having a home of your own to manage," Eloisa said. The words could be sympathetic but weren't.

"I miss my husband more."

"But are hungry for another, I'm sure."

"You must have a healthy appetite for your first," Georgia said. It came out more cattily than she'd intended, but completely in response to Eloisa's catty tone. "I'm sure you will have your pick of the dishes," she said, to sweeten it.

"If you leave any for any other lady!" Eloisa snapped and swept away.

Georgia stared after her. She'd known Eloisa was jealous, but not how viciously. She must certainly leave Thretford for Town as soon as possible. To add to her problems, Lord Sellerby approached. "My dearest Georgia, in full bloom. Or should I say plume?"

She had to smile at that. He could be witty. "Birds of a feather, Sellerby," she said, admiring his suit of lilac silk. "Thank you for coming. I know you won't disappear into a political huddle at the slightest excuse."

"Not with you as my lodestone," he said, that light in his eyes.

Georgia had to do something about that. "You know

you can't monopolize me, Sellerby. May I ask you to be kind to Miss Cardross, who may not know many here? You may remember her from the dinner at Herne?" She took him over.

"How could I notice anyone in your presence," he murmured, but was too civil to show anything but delight.

The Bryght Mallorens arrived, so Georgia went to greet them, wondering if she could promote a match between Sellerby and Eloisa. Eloisa was beautiful, which was important to Sellerby, and her portion would be reasonable. Presumably she'd be happy with an earl in her dish. Yes, two birds with one stone.

Lord Bryght's full name was Arcenbryght, which Georgia felt a weighty burden to place upon an infant. Some ancient British prince or such. He had shoulders broad enough to bear it. He was a fine figure of a man, which made him an odd match for his wife, Portia, a petite redhead of no particular beauty from a very ordinary pedigree. Despite the mismatch they seemed a devoted couple.

Pairings could be so very odd.

Georgia knew Portia Malloren through Danae House, for she was also a patroness and sister-in-law to the founder, the Marchioness of Rothgar. Georgia didn't know Portia well, for the Bryght Mallorens shared the Torrismondes' enjoyment of country living, but the couple were safe company. The three of them talked of nothings such as the weather and the prospects for the harvest. Then Lizzie and her husband joined them.

Georgia wondered if Lizzie was hovering protectively, but Torrismonde wanted to discuss canal building and Lord Bryght was a well-known supporter of Bridgwater's enterprise. Soon the two men went off to speak to the duke.

"Canals, canals, canals," said Lady Bryght, rolling her eyes. "I hear of little else."

"They do seem to be important," Lizzie said.

"And becoming profitable, but Bridgwater's obsessed."

"All men have their obsessions," Lizzie said. "Digging channels for water to flow through seems harmless enough. Oh, I see Mistress Wayworth. Do excuse me."

Georgia smiled at Lady Bryght. "Speaking of obsessions, Lizzie and Maria Wayworth can talk forever about glass houses and the production of tropical fruits."

"I confess, I'm content with my hardy orchards and berries. I wish I were there now to tend to them."

"You're fixed in Town?" Georgia said. "That's unusual for you."

"And unwelcome. The political chaos wreaked havoc with trade and 'Change so Bryght felt he should be on hand to watch over the Malloren interests. I was torn, for we didn't want to bring the children to Town, but in the end I left them and came with him. I didn't expect to be away so long."

*Children.* When last they'd spoken Lady Bryght had only a son.

"I'm sorry. I'm sadly out of touch. You were expecting . . ."

"Last June, yes, when you had no interest in such matters. Again, my deepest condolences."

Portia had written, as had all Georgia's friends and acquaintances. Such a mountain of black-edged paper.

"Thank you. It was a hard time. Do you have girl or a boy this time?

"A girl, Joanna, and she has Bryght's dark hair rather than my carroty color."

"You can't expect another redhead to be so dismissive."

"There's red and then there's red," Portia said. "Your coppery shade is lovely."

Georgia smiled and waved her fan, not wanting to get into that, for Portia Malloren's red was closer to orange and went along with a great many freckles.

"And your son?" she asked dutifully, but wondering if she was to hear of nothing but babies, babies, babies all night.

After a few minutes of the brave, kind, clever Francis Malloren, Georgia plunged into the only topic they had in common. "Have you had an opportunity to visit Danae House while you've been in Town?"

"Not opportunity so much as necessity. Diana had to go north to attend to some problem on her estates and she made me promise to do her weekly inspection. If it weren't for that . . ." She looked sharply at Georgia. "Is there any way you could take over that duty?"

"Of course," Georgia said, but then she grimaced. "Except that I'm stuck out here."

"Why?"

"Father thinks London unsafe."

"It's still restless, I grant, but the rioting seems to have stopped. Of course, I argue in my own cause. If you could take over until Diana returns, we could go home to Candleford. We've only been delaying for this."

Georgia's heart actually pitter-pattered with excitement. Here was an excuse to visit Town weekly. Or even move there?

"When's Lady Rothgar expected back?" she asked.

"Impossible to know what issues she might have found or how long the journey will take. With a baby, even! I do think . . . But it's not for me to criticize. She'll return as soon as possible, I'm sure, having left Rothgar behind."

Indeed, the Rothgars seemed hardly able to bear to be apart. Had she ever felt like that about Dickon? She couldn't remember it. She touched the locket, feeling as if she betrayed him.

With a start, she realized Lady Bryght was still talking about Danae House. ". . . is particularly busy. Such hard times. It's as if war created prosperity and peace has created poverty and unemployment. That seems all wrong, but . . . Oh dear, I shouldn't talk serious matters here."

Georgia hoped she hadn't seemed bored.

"I don't see why not. Most of the men are talking politics. Or canals," she added with a smile.

"Danae House?" Lady Bryght persisted. "Is there any chance . . . ?"

Georgia made the decision. "Yes. I've kept an eye on things before from Chelsea when summer took most of the patronesses to estates. Alas, wickedness and folly know no quiet season."

"Thank you!" For a moment Georgia feared Portia would hug her, right there in the hall. "I feel as if I've shed a burden. As for season, love knows no season either."

"Nor rape," Georgia said, "and summer sorrows grow from spring assaults."

"There are some who are led astray by love, like that maid you brought. I feel some sympathy for such as they. How hard it must be to wait for years when love and desire run like fire in the veins."

Georgia tried to find the right expression in response to that, especially as Lady Bryght had glanced at her husband with such a look. She could only say, "I suppose it must."

*When love and desire run like fire in the veins?*

Georgia knew she'd never felt like that with Dickon, never found days apart intolerable, and now it seemed worthy of tears.

"Georgia!"

Georgia turned with relief to buxom Babs Harringay, dark curls bobbing, dimples deep in round cheeks. She greeted her friend and made the two ladies known to each other, glad to be back to normal matters. Within minutes, however, the two mothers were talking of children, of their charms and mischiefs, their feeding and clothing, and the unpleasantness of being separated from them.

Georgia excused herself and moved away, smiling,

greeting, but seeking Dracy in all seriousness. He could be depended upon not to speak of nurseries.

She strolled from the hall into a reception room, pausing to talk to friends and flirt with suitable gentlemen and doing her best to ignore piercing looks from others. As soon as they became accustomed to her being as she'd always been, incapable of squalid sin, all would be well.

Remembering where she'd found Dracy at Herne, she went out onto the rear terrace. Alas, no beached tar leaning over the copingstone, but then he'd have no need to do that here. The shallow terrace was but four feet up from the lawn, and the balustrade only hip high.

She returned through the library, which was set for cards, but still saw no sign of him. Impossible that he would have backed out. A man like that feared nothing.

Or did he simply disguise fear well?

Perhaps people here thought her fearless, and in the past they would have been correct. Now, however, she had to at least admit unease. People did not smile as warmly at her, nor rush to be in her company. This wasn't the world she remembered.

Ah, Beaufort! Here he came, glowing with pleasure, soothing her pride. As he kissed her hand, he even flushed slightly in a most endearing way. Then Lord Everdon joined them, perhaps with courtship in mind. Her court was increased when the Duke of Richmond came to flirt. Two dukes, even if one was a mere seventeen. All was as it should be after all.

She allowed Richmond the first dance—the formal minuet—mainly to tease the others. As she walked onto the floor, she saw Sellerby ask Eloisa to dance, so perhaps her plan was working there. If only Dracy would arrive, the evening could be perfect.

She smiled at Richmond. "This will be my first dance in a year, Duke. Thank you for the opportunity."

He blushed. "The pleasure and honor are all mine,

Lady May. The world has been dull as November without you in it."

"A clever turn of phrase, Duke, and charming as well."

He blushed even more.

The music started and Georgia happily lost herself in the pleasure of the stately dance, knowing she executed the movements to perfection. Well satisfied with that, she granted the first country-dance to Beaufort, who seemed almost giddy at the honor. She stepped and wove and turned, unable to stop smiling. Lady May was back, and her world was just as it ought to be.

When that dance ended, she saw Sellerby approaching. She would have to grant him a dance, but she was growing worried about Dracy, so she excused herself with a smiling apology and went in search again. When she saw her brother-in-law, she asked, "Is Lord Dracy here yet?"

"Dracy?" Thretford asked. "Oh, your father's protégé, the naval man. No idea, my dear. Perhaps he's lost his way, not being used to navigating on land."

He chortled at his own joke and moved on to greet a late guest. Not Dracy. She circled the house again, but then returned to the dancing to find Sellerby standing out, waiting for her. He took her hand. "I feast my eyes on Lady May!"

He really was ridiculous at times. "Do eyes have teeth, then, Sellerby?"

He chuckled. "Clever girl. Only lashes."

"All the better to whip me with? Come, come, this is an odd line of speech."

"You leapt from feast to teeth, my dear Georgie, but I assure you, if I were ever to whip you, it would be a very gentle chastisement."

"If you were to . . ."

"When you are mine. But come, let us join this dance."

His words, his sense of ownership, made her rebel. "I regret you must excuse me, Sellerby. Something has disagreed with me. . . ."

She hurried away, as if suddenly in need of the ladies' room, hoping her abrupt exit hadn't been noticed and added to talk about her.

She made her way down a corridor, but the house was filling beyond capacity, and the sweaty, perfumed space made her feel truly unwell. She escaped onto the terrace to inhale fresh air and steady her panicked heart but stayed out of sight of the windows. In his present mood, Sellerby might pursue, and he was becoming very strange.

They'd enjoyed that sort of badinage many a time, but whips? And *when* you are mine? She'd never given him reason to think that.

Oh, he'd meant nothing by it and she'd overreacted because of the pressure of this event. Even though it was going well, she still felt on trial. She'd make it up to Sellerby in due course. For now, no one else was on the terrace so she could linger, breathing in fresh air and regaining her composure. Soon one or more admiring gentlemen would find her and she'd return to the dance escorted and in good spirits.

She'd organized the flowers out here, so she surveyed her work. Urns had been placed in the corners, all holding tall white blooms and trailing variegated ivy. Pale colors always worked well for night events, for they caught the light, whereas colored blooms turned gray and dull when the sun set. To increase the effect, each urn also held a tall lamp in a frosted shade. Pools of light, but leaving shadowy corners such as the one in which she stood, so useful for trysts.

Alas, no trysts for her tonight, here or in the gardens below.

The colored lanterns in the trees were charming, but she could take no credit for them. Winnie had used them before and her people had known just what to do there and with the lights on the pond. She'd like to see the pond now darkness was settling, so she walked to the front of the terrace. Delightful! The bobbing lights in colored glass were like jewels on black satin.

But where were her swains? She was in full sight of the dancing room now and should have been swarmed.

Oh, that was ridiculous. Richmond and Beaufort knew better than to seek another dance so soon after their first, and Sellerby thought her unwell. He'd have chosen another partner. If Dracy had been here . . .

She remembered the perfumed tobacco. She'd wanted some in the urns, but the gardener had claimed he had only two healthy plants. She'd wondered if he'd deliberately damaged the others, but there'd been no means of knowing. She'd told him to place the two near the central steps down to the garden. She walked to the steps, unable to detect the sweet, distinctive perfume. Devil take the man. But then she caught the scent, a very faint scent.

She put a hand on the low copingstone and carefully leaned forward.

"Do please tell me you're not attempting to put an end to your existence, Lady Maybury."

Georgia straightened quickly but took her time in turning, aware of a speeding heart.

He'd come.

Then, as she faced him, her heart went into full gallop.

Dear heaven, the man was gorgeous! The embroidered gray and powdered wig in some way enhanced the active energy that seemed not of her fashionable world. Even the scar, starkly clear and undisguised, and the cynical twist it gave his face, made him more, not less. . . .

*Breathe, Georgia, breathe.*

# Chapter 13

Dracy kept his composure, but it wasn't easy when faced with Lady May in full, glorious plumage. She looked just like that miniature, but in the round, in the flesh, and more.

The most round, most eye-catching flesh was her breasts, rising plumply above the tight front of her stiffly embroidered bodice. That bodice covered her nipples, but surely only just....

A peacock-feather fan rose to block the view.

He looked up. "My apologies, Lady Maybury, but to ignore such wonders would be unforgivable."

Her lips twitched, and then she chuckled, sweeping the fan aside. "Look all you want, sir, but if you ogle the other ladies so boldly, you may come to grief."

"I doubt any match you in magnificence."

"Dracy, you've been taking lessons in flattery!"

"Only for use with other ladies."

"Training in a nimble tongue too, I see. But not in punctuality? You're late."

"I was delayed by a visit from a friend. He was quite amused to find me in such finery."

"A naval friend?"

"No, from Devon. He's keeping an eye on Dracy for me and reported that nothing is worse than it usually is."

She chuckled as if that were a joke, but those had been Tom's words, with reproach implied. Tom had been worried about Dracy lingering in London, and even more so when he'd found him in finery, about to set out for a ball held by Georgia Maybury's sister. He'd put Tom off, but he'd have to calm him down tomorrow.

"Do I detect nicotiana?" he said.

"I've educated your nose!"

"My nose is humbly grateful."

She chuckled again. It was good to see her in light spirits. The event must be going well.

But then why was she out here alone?

"Mother sent my sister some seeds, but the gardener planted them in an obscure corner. I think he must lack all sense of smell."

"Or isn't out in the garden as it grows dark?"

"I hadn't thought of that. I'm tempted to summon him here now."

"He's doubtless in his worthy bed, in preparation for rising with the dawn."

Clearly she hadn't thought of that either.

"When we frivolous creatures will be seeking ours. We live in different worlds, don't we?"

One of the many things he liked about Georgia Maybury was the way her agile mind caught an idea and leapt onto another. Some might see it as a magpie quality, but her mental leaps were always to the point.

"There's rarely any lying abed in the navy either," he pointed out. He could add, *or in struggling to restore a ruined estate*.

"Then you're well away from it," she declared. "I'll leave the gardener to his world of sleep, especially as he did obey and plant at least one down there. I was trying to see."

"I could pick you up again."

"You wouldn't dare!"

"A challenge, Georgia?"

Her chin went up when she said, "Yes," but her eyes were bright.

She probably wanted him to pick her up again, whether she knew it or not, so instead he looked over the low balustrade himself. "Two, but spindly specimens."

"Because he originally planted them in a poor spot and probably moved them roughly."

Dracy straightened. "You have a great interest in things being where they should be. First a horse, now a plant."

"Why not? Plants thrive in one location and shrivel in another."

"You are truly interested in gardening?"

"The home is the lady's responsibility, and a garden enhances a home. Don't imagine me on my knees grubbing in the soil as my mother sometimes does, Dracy. I merely issue orders."

"That I can believe, but Lady Hernescroft?"

She walked past the steps and continued along the terrace. "I think perhaps you put people into narrow slots."

"I'm learning not to. Your mother promised me seeds, and my home certainly needs enhancing, but I have no terraces."

"Then erect some," she said, as if it were as simple as planting seeds.

"I have other demands on my purse for now."

She was so easy to read. He saw her think that odd, but then accept it as part of his very different world. Just as well he didn't harbor too much hope of installing her as mistress of Dracy Manor.

"Are there any beds against the house?" she asked. "The perfume would rise at night to enter an open window."

"Into the bedchamber, perhaps," he said. *Where you and I lie tangled in sheets, contented and entwined.* Perhaps his tone was too easy to read, for her eloquent fan unfurled and wafted. That was always a lady's defense, feeble though it was.

"What sort of house is Dracy?" she asked.

He gave her the truth. "A simple manor house, badly neglected. My cousin spent his income on his London home."

"He did mostly live in Town, so that's not unreasonable."

"He shouldn't have mostly lived in Town. Not when he had an estate to run and a house that needed care."

She halted and looked him in the eye. "Are you criticizing me and my husband, Lord Dracy?"

He hadn't been, intentionally at least, but it was a point. "You do seem to be birds of a feather with my cousin."

Her jaw dropped. "With *Ceddie Dracy*? If you make comparisons like that, sir . . ."

He raised a hand, laughing. "Don't challenge me to a duel." Gads, that wasn't a good joke to toss at her. "Why? Where's the difference?"

*"Where . . . ?"*

"I see I've truly offended you. My deepest apologies. I met my cousin only once from the time I went to sea."

"Your cousin, sir, was a fop of the silliest sort. He mistook price for value and indulged in all the most expensive follies. He had no taste or style and lacked the good sense to seek the advice of those who did."

"Blasted with all guns! Poor Ceddie. At least, I might feel sorry for him if he'd not beggared Dracy in the process. If he'd squandered it all on paintings or statues I might have been able to sell them, but he bought fripperies and friends, neither of which are worth a farthing now."

"I can imagine. A sad burden to inherit."

Perhaps unthinkingly, she'd put a hand on his sleeve.

Dracy struggled with a jolt of pure lust.

From a hand on a sleeved arm.

But also from the genuine concern in her beautiful eyes—eyes that looked at him without a flinch. Then there was her perfume and her breasts. . . .

"My lord." She removed her hand.

He looked up, knowing he'd revealed too much—his desire, yes, but perhaps his deeper feelings.

"I hope I haven't misled you, Lord Dracy, by my pleasure in your company. I hope we're friends, but we can never be more."

"Never?" he asked, trying to hide all reaction.

"Never. Please believe me on that. If I think that will be difficult for you, we cannot even be friends. I'm no Barbara Allen."

The pure steely honesty conquered his heart. Many beauties enjoyed their conquests and collected broken hearts as trophies, as with the Barbara Allen of the song. Not Georgia Maybury, who truly would avoid him if she thought his heart in danger.

"'Struth," he said lightly, "I'm not the type to die for love, but you have a rare beauty and entrancing personality, and I can't imagine a man alive who wouldn't respond to that, friend or foe."

"I hoped you'd be immune!" she said, not reassured.

"Perhaps if I were to wear a blindfold," he teased, "and you were to cease wearing your magical perfume?"

It hung in the balance, but then she laughed, shaking her head. "Admire and inhale, then, but don't fall in love. I already have a surfeit of unwanted devotees. On strict terms of friendship, I'll risk my toes and dance the next set with you."

"You do like to live dangerously, don't you?"

"Often," she said and led the way back into the house, light of step, graceful, and surely smiling.

Dracy followed, considering the fabulously beautiful, fabulously expensive back of her gown, and their conversation.

Different worlds and broken hearts.

Why did he even hope at all?

At least he'd returned her in good spirits. When he'd arrived and wandered the house in search of her, he'd heard gossip. Lady May, too beautiful for her own good. Or that of her husband's. Not a trace of shame. For all the attention dukes were paying her, he heard people say, she wouldn't snare one now.

He was particularly concerned by that *now*. It had been as if the scandal were new, not a year old. Where were all her dukes? He faced no competition as he led her into place for the next dance.

Georgia dipped a curtsy, hoping Dracy wasn't too poor a dancer. She'd needed escape from the situation on the terrace, and sooner or later she'd have to dance with him, but she was prepared for another cause for sniggers from her detractors.

As they completed the first turn, she gave him a scathing look. "Hornpipe, indeed."

He smiled at her. "I can dance a fine one, but you shouldn't underestimate a naval officer. We are often obliged to do our duties on shore."

"Which involve dancing?" she asked, turning in the other direction.

"Pleasing the local population as best we can. Especially the ladies."

The rascal! "One in every port, I hear," she said, and danced away in a long hay, touching hands to ladies and gentlemen as she wove through the dance.

*Damnation.* Might he take the tone of her comment as jealousy? Rather, it had been pure irritation. Why would no one be what they were supposed to be tonight?

Instead of being tiresomely adoring, Sellerby had turned threatening. Instead of being ill at ease, Dracy was gorgeous, elegant, and even charming! He danced as well as any man here, and many of the women were noting it. If they'd been shocked or appalled by his face, they'd overcome it. They smiled, they blushed, and a few swayed closer than the dance required. She knew the reputations of those women and had no doubt they were plotting how to get him into their beds. And people criticized her behavior as wanton!

She couldn't be jealous of a man she didn't want, but all the same, his words churned in her mind, along with their implications. When the dance brought them together again she said, "I don't suppose ships are often in port."

"But when they are," he said, amused, "it can be for months."

To add to her strain, Sellerby was standing against the wall, staring at her coldly. Lud! She'd cried off dancing with him and returned with another. That was impossibly discourteous. How could she have been so thoughtless?

When she danced with Dracy again, he asked, "What's amiss?"

"Nothing," she said, and moved on in the dance.

When the dance ended, however, he said, "A nothing called Sellerby? He's been staring at you throughout the dance."

"It doesn't matter."

"He offends you?"

He looked so dangerous that she grasped his arm. Then hastily let it go. So many eyes were on her. "I'm at fault. I feigned illness when I was supposed to dance with him. When I returned, it was to dance with you. I will give him the next and my sweet apologies."

"And charm him out of his sulk."

"Georgia!" Thank heavens, here came Babs—but her attention was all on Dracy, and she had that look in her eyes.

Georgia wanted to warn him, but warn him of what? Babs was a flirt and adored handsome men, but she was lustily devoted to her husband, even though he was a stocky, short-legged man with a bulldog face. Marital matters were endlessly, frustratingly exasperating.

In any case, Dracy had dallied with women all around the world. Let him handle this.

"Lord Dracy, I believe," Babs said, eyes sparkling.

"Ma'am," he said, merely inclining his head. "I don't believe we've been introduced."

"Ooooh! Was I just spanked? Introduce us, Georgia. I want to dance with this masterful man."

Despite himself, Dracy was looking amused, but Georgia wanted to send Babs to perdition. She performed the introductions coldly, adding, "Where's your husband?"

"Talking politics," Babs said, impervious to chill. "Your sister and mother are attempting to harry more men out to do their dancing duty. You should wander by the doors. You'd suck them out like nails to a magnet. But I'm away with my prize."

Babs hooked arms with Dracy and left. Perhaps he resisted for a moment, but not for long. Babs was probably just the sort of woman he really liked, the sort of woman he'd danced and dallied with in ports around the world, and doubtless done more. Sailors were notorious.

"Now, what has you in a glare?"

Georgia turned to Lizzie. "Men, marriage, everything."

"Poor Georgia. I need a word with you."

Now what? Lizzie was worried about something, but Sellerby was approaching. Georgia owed him the next dance, but Lizzie came first.

She gave Sellerby her sweetest smile. "My deepest apologies, Sellerby. My friend has need of me. The next dance—I promise it to you." She turned to Lizzie. "My room."

She led Lizzie out of the room and up to her bedchamber.

"Lord Sellerby looked fit to murder you!" Lizzie said.

"And with reason. I'll appease him. What's amiss?"

"Sellerby, for one. I'm sorry, Georgie, but he's implying that you and he are engaged to marry."

"What? Devil take him!"

"Georgie!"

"Don't 'Georgie' me. A good curse clears the air. There, I feel better already. I shall return and deny it."

"That's difficult until faced with it, so I came up with a plan. As soon as we're in the midst of people, I'll mention the engagement and you can be appalled."

"Thank you. I don't know how to bring him to his senses!"

"I'm not sure he has any senses where you're concerned."

"He needs another object of adoration. I've tried to steer him toward Eloisa Cardross."

"Is love so easily steered?"

"He doesn't love me or he wouldn't pester me so."

"Now, that makes no sense," Lizzie said. " 'Tis the nature of love to pester."

"Dickon never pestered me."

"He had no need to. The marriage was proposed and accepted."

"He did pester me with gifts," Georgia said. "Truly, Lizzie, I think the world's run mad! People thinking I would bed Vance. Sellerby talking nonsense. Babs drooling over Dracy."

"Babs enjoys playing with handsome heroes, but you know she's madly devoted to Harringay. Lord Dracy is a handsome hero, isn't he? The scar's quite shocking at first, but then . . . it isn't."

"If you start flirting with him I'll know the world's turned on its axis."

"You seemed very happy in his company."

"*No,*" Georgia said. "Dracy has many fine qualities, but he's impossible."

"Why?"

"He's poor and a baron. I know it sounds shallow, but I couldn't be happy in that situation any more than I could if married to a bishop."

Lizzie chuckled. "I must confess, a less likely bishop's wife is hard to imagine."

"You see? I must return and give Sellerby his dance."

"I'd think you'd want to avoid him," Lizzie said.

"But I was maladroit. I refused a dance with him earlier on the excuse that I was unwell. I was merely concerned about Lord Dracy, you see. But then I returned to dance with Dracy."

"Oh, that is bad."

"So I must dance with him now. What a tangle this is becoming. Lizzie, tell me the truth. How do people regard me tonight?"

"With great interest. I'm sure it can't be comfortable, but they are only assessing you anew."

"That's the sum of it?" Georgia asked, sensing more.

Lizzie grimaced. "Some do think you should still be wrapped in grief."

"After a year? How long should my mourning continue?"

"I know it's not reasonable, but remember, no one ever saw you in mourning. Lady May disappeared and now she returns, just as she was."

"I never thought of that! I did as my parents thought best."

"And perhaps it was, but it will take people time. Once they see you dignified and poised . . ."

"Dull, you mean. I think it vastly unfair. Dickon would never have wanted it."

"Fairness butters no crumpets."

"Shouldn't that be 'fair words'?"

"Both apply. Have a care, dearest."

Lizzie was serious, which made it worse.

Georgia sighed for her freedom to be herself. Lost, along with everything else, for simple lack of a son.

She knew it wasn't the time, but she had to talk to someone, and Lizzie would leave at dawn to return home.

She sat in front of her mirror as if to tidy her hair. "I need to marry again, Lizzie, but I fret about children. What if it was my fault? Men want an heir, and I don't think I can bear to disappoint again."

"It could well have been Dickon's lack. Only consider Lady Emmersham. Ten years barren as Mistress Farraday, but when she married Emmersham, a babe within the year."

"Within the seven months," Georgia pointed out. "Lud!" she exclaimed, swiveling to face her friend. "Do you think they planned it that way?"

"Planned what? Waited until . . . ? *Georgie!*"

"Don't shriek at me. It makes sense. Emmersham needs an heir, and even if he was mad for her, he wouldn't want to marry a barren woman. . . ."

"No," Lizzie said.

"Quite, and so—"

"I mean, no, you must not. You can't even *think* of trying out a husband before you wed."

Georgia hadn't, but now . . . "If I don't conceive, I've lost nothing."

"Nothing? Your honor, your virtue. You must not—"

"Stop *must*ing me! In any case, it would be more a case of a potential husband trying out me. Only think, Lizzie. Rather than marrying and then waiting every month. Being disappointed every month. Disappointing . . ."

Lizzie rushed over to hug her. "I knew it was an anxiety for you, love, but not how much. But you can't—you can't. Only think on it. If you don't conceive with one man, will that settle it? If not, how many men do you sin with and for how long before you resign yourself to being barren?"

Such an ugly word, "barren."

She pulled free of her friend and fussed with her skirt. "I don't know, but if that day came, I'd marry a widower who already has an heir. Lord Everdon would do. He's wealthy and shares many of my tastes, and he's not too old. Not yet thirty, I believe."

"By then he might not want you, nor would any other man. People would be bound to discover a string of liaisons. You could end up too scandalous to wed."

"Then I'll be the scandalous Lady May all my life, free as a bird. But then," she added, regarding herself in the mirror once more, "are peacocks ever free?"

"They're notoriously foolish, which you are not."

Lizzie was truly distressed, so Georgia turned to her friend, smiling an apology.

"I'm full of follies and fancies tonight, aren't I? Don't fret, Lizzie. I'm sure I don't mean a word of it. Come, we must return below. Apart from poor Sellerby, if I'm away too long, someone will put a foul interpretation on that."

They slipped back down so as to reappear as if from the ladies' room. Georgia looked around for Dracy but didn't see him. She assured herself Babs was to be trusted, and in any case, she owed poor Sellerby his dance.

Where was he?

Stokesly invited Lizzie to dance, and Georgia suddenly found herself alone, unpestered by a single gentleman anxious to dance with her. She couldn't remember such a thing ever happening before. Even Sellerby was staying away. She saw him on the other side of the room looking at her in a strangely cold way. He wasn't the only one.

Cheeks heating, she strolled toward the open doors, attempting to look at ease, but aware of being watched in a newly unpleasant way. When she smiled and inclined her head to Lady Landelle, that woman returned the reverence awkwardly and quickly looked away.

"Georgia, am I fortunate enough to find you free?"

She turned gratefully to Lord Harringay. "You are."

"The world's gone mad, but to my advantage."

He led her to join the end of the long-ways dance.

Georgia kept up her smile, but she was desperately trying to understand what was going on. People were definitely cooler than before. Or rather, more people were
cooler. Even Richmond's smile was uncertain as she
caught his eye.

Why? Because she'd been absent with Lizzie? Did
people think she'd been off with a man?

She wanted to confront someone and shake the nonsense out of them. Instead, she smiled and danced as if
she hadn't a care in the world. When the dance was over
she'd find someone to explain it all.

But perhaps she'd imagined it, for here came Sellerby.

Georgia smiled and offered her hand. "I would have
given you that dance, Sellerby, but failed to see you. The
next is yours."

"Your debt has grown, Georgie. I claim the supper
dance."

The choice of partner for that was considered significant, and Georgia remembered Lizzie's warning. "My
deepest apologies, Sellerby, but I'm already promised to
another."

His smile quenched. "You should have preserved it
for me."

He was speaking for the people nearby, damn him.

It was no effort to look blank. "Why?"

"You know why. My dear Georgie, we . . ."

"We *what*, my lord?"

"The matter is private as yet, I know, but—"

"Any private matter of yours is no concern of mine,
sir!" A mistake to speak so sharply. She tried to sweeten
it. "Come, our dance is about to begin."

Coldly, he bowed. "I regret, I am promised to another."

Her words thrown back at her. Georgia smiled and
curtsied. "Alas, sir. Perhaps later."

She managed to walk away calmly, but she was seething inside. He'd turned a simple matter into a scene, and

perhaps caused the coldness all around by his lies. Was she now a heartless jilt as well as a wicked adulteress?

Winnie intercepted her to mutter, "Why must you always create scenes?"

Georgia flicked open her fan. "That was all Lord Sellerby's fault."

"When you play fast and loose with a man . . ."

"I have never played fast, or even slow with him!"

"Everyone knows he was a chief member of your so-called court, and you corresponded with him from Herne during your mourning."

"How do you know that?"

"Millicent remarked on it."

Her delightful sister-in-law, who'd watched like a hawk for any wrongdoing.

"I fell weakly into kindness because he supported me to the dowager." She'd had enough of this conversation and saw an escape. "Ah, Porterhouse. Thank you!"

Porterhouse blinked, for he'd merely been passing by, but he was far too well mannered to deny her and led her to join the ongoing dance. He was such a good and amiable man, she might marry him if only he had rank and fortune, but at this moment, probably even he wouldn't want her.

Had she imagined coldness all around her earlier? She found it hard to tell. In her sister's house with her powerful parents present, few would be willing to be overtly discourteous.

As they strolled off the dance floor, however, Porterhouse said, "I feel I should warn you, Lady Maybury."

"Warn me?"

He led her to a quiet part of the room. "People are talking."

"Alas, I've grown accustomed to that, my friend."

"But there's a new story. About Vance's letter. The one the dowager Lady Maybury claimed to have seen."

Georgia waved her fan and smiled as best she could,

but she knew it couldn't reach her eyes. "Old news and old nonsense."

"Georgie, someone here claims to have actually seen it. Or to know someone who has. The rumor is muddled. . . ."

"As rumors always are. But here, tonight?" Georgia couldn't resist scanning the room. "Who?"

"I don't know. It could all be false. . . ."

"It has to be false. Such a letter couldn't exist."

"But many are believing it. I regret distressing you, my dear, but I thought you should know."

She smiled at him as warmly as she could. "Thank you. There was *nothing* between me and Charnley Vance, Porterhouse."

"I'm sure not," he said, but she suspected even he had a glimmer of doubt. "I'm afraid I must seek my partner for the supper dance. Shall I escort you to your mother?"

Refuge of the wallflower and the outcast.

"Thank you, but no. I have a partner for the dance."

He bowed and walked away, leaving Georgia feeling alone in a completely new way. People were believing this ridiculous rumor, which meant they had been ready to believe it. Even after a year, most of the beau monde still thought the worst of her. She needed to return to Town, to regain her life, but for the first time she really wondered if Town would accept her.

And she had no partner for the supper dance.

She'd intended to grant it to Beaufort, but she saw he was paired with Lucy Pomeroy. Richmond was looking delighted by pretty Miss Horstead. And there was Sellerby, watching her with what she could only call a smirk. Was he preparing to offer as her last chance?

She'd rather eat glass.

# Chapter 14

"Our dance, I believe, Lady Maybury?"

Georgia turned, feeling faint with relief, but she addressed Dracy with a touch of annoyance. "Ah, there you are, my lord. I thought you'd abandoned me."

"Never, Lady Maybury, I assure you."

She remembered that she shouldn't encourage him toward a broken heart, but at the moment she was too weak to do anything but cling to his arm.

He led her forward, but she held back. In the square room there were two lines and Sellerby was asking Miss Cranscourt to dance. The middle-aged lady was blushingly grateful, and Georgia waited until they took their places in the right-hand line before moving to join the left.

"Lord Sellerby is to be avoided?" he murmured.

"Eternally."

"I thought him a favorite of yours. Indeed, I've heard mention of an engagement."

"He lies!" Georgia heard it come out as a hiss.

"Swords at dawn?" Dracy asked, amused, but then said, "I apologize. An unfortunate reference."

"Believe me, Dracy, I would punish Sellerby if I could."

"Peacock feathers at dawn, then. My money would be on you."

He made it all light, and that soothed her. "That's as foolish as being flogged by eyelashes."

"What?"

They had to separate, however, to stand opposite in the line.

Beaufort was in this line, just a few down from Dracy, and Everdon farther along. She might have seen that as promising a little while ago, but now she was too aware of the way many people weren't meeting her eye.

The dance began, and she focused on Dracy alone. He danced so beautifully, even dressed well with a little encouragement, and had a rare ability to create the illusion that she was safe.

She was shocked at the direction of her own thoughts. *No, Georgia. You could never be happy with him, or indeed, make him happy. He'd lose patience with your frivolity and need for the beau monde. You'd resent any attempt to restrain you, and you could never be a country wife.*

He deserved better.

And she deserved better than a cold shoulder from so many.

When the dance ended, she kept up a smile but was seething underneath. Of course he noticed.

"Are your teeth gritted behind that smile?"

Everyone was flowing toward supper, but Georgia wasn't sure she could swallow a morsel. Had Dracy heard the story about the false letter? From whom?

She suddenly wondered if she could track the poison to its source.

"Let's not rush to eat," she said. "We can go on the terrace for a while."

"The best food will be gone."

"I can survive that. Can you?"

"There are many kinds of feasts," he said and went with her through the open doors, but his tone reminded her of all her good resolutions. She'd warned him, even more bluntly than she'd warned off Sellerby, but this could undo her good work.

"I've changed my mind," she said, turning to follow the rest. "There's roasted lobster."

He caught her wrist. "Tell me of the new rumors."

His hand was hot, and he'd grasped her just above the mourning bracelet. Georgia had the strange notion that he and Dickon had formed an alliance in her cause.

"Perhaps a *friend* can help," he said.

He'd used that word deliberately, telling her that he remembered and understood.

Perhaps he'd done the same with his talk of women around the world. That boastfulness wasn't natural to him. Perhaps he'd wanted her to know that she was only one of many and needn't carry his feelings as a burden.

"You navigate tricky waters well," she said.

"I hope so." He released her but said, "Tell me what's happened to distress you, Georgia."

She moved along the balustrade, out of hearing of the house. "Did you hear of the letter supposedly seen by my mother-in-law, the dowager Lady Maybury?"

"No. I know nothing of the dowager either."

"I suppose you were still at sea last December."

"Shore based, but I had no interest in this world."

"I mean the dowager Lady Maybury, my husband's mother. She approved me as his bride, but with the belief that Maybury and I would live at Maybury Castle, under her eye and management. We clashed from the start, of course, because I'd been trained to run a great house and expected to do so."

"And were in the right," he said, but then added, "My apologies."

"For what?"

"For thinking you truly a peacock. It never occurred to me that you ran anything. Of course you did, and well too."

"I hope so. We came to terms of a sort on management, but once Dickon—Maybury—achieved his majority, he wanted only to leave the castle and live in Town. I wasn't reluctant, but in his mother's eyes it was all my doing, even though she could then rule the castle supreme! Of course she wanted to rule him."

"Of course."

She looked at him. "You're wondering why I'm rambling on, but there is a point. Before Maybury died she disliked and resented me, but afterward I was a wicked harpy from hell." Before he could speak, she waved a hand. "I understood. Her only child had been killed and she had to blame someone. As there were those noxious rumors, why not me?"

He took her hand, and weakly, she allowed it.

"When the new Lord Maybury took possession, she had to leave the castle. A smaller wound, but still a wound. She took up residence in Cheltenham and made it her life's work to inform everyone she met, everyone she wrote to, of my perfidious wickedness. She even wrote to me, but after the first letter, I had them blocked. I didn't have them returned. It would only have deepened her pain."

"You're a remarkable woman, Georgia Maybury."

"Remarkably disastrous, it would seem. I don't know if it was deliberate, but her stories grew in detail and ferocity. I didn't know it at the time, but from telling everyone that I tempted men to folly with my wanton ways, she progressed to asserting that I'd taken Vance as my lover, and then that I'd conspired with him to rid myself of my husband!"

She had to pause to gather her composure.

"I truly think she became addled toward the end," she said, "for then she told anyone who visited her that she'd seen a letter from Vance which said exactly that. That I'd seduced him into killing my husband with the promise that I'd run off with him when I was free, taking the Maybury jewels with me. It would all be laughable if so many people hadn't believed her. That was in December. I thought the madness had died with her, but now this resurrection tonight."

"How?" he asked.

"I'm told that someone here is claiming to have the letter and intends to reveal it publicly. That would explain the growing coldness, but why would anyone spin such a wicked lie? Why would anyone hate me so?" When he squeezed her hand, she realized she was clinging to his. "It's so unfair," she said. "Oh, how weak and paltry . . ."

"But true. It's unjust and unwarranted to boot. Are you sure this is happening?"

"Porterhouse, bless him, told me directly."

"Good man."

"I don't understand *why*, though. What does anyone gain by this?"

"Bringing down Lady May," he said. "Pure envy— that's my speculation—and probably a woman. We can find her, you know."

"That's what I thought. There are only about a hundred people here, and she's among them."

He smiled. "As I said. A remarkable woman."

"To want to find the person who wishes me ill?"

"To think quickly of action when attacked."

"You underestimate women. . . . Lud! Winnie will kill me if I cause a grand scene."

"I'll defend you. Do you have any suggestions as to where we start?"

"I can think of three prime suspects."

"Who?"

"Lady Waveney, Lady North, and Miss Cardross."

"Waveney," he said. "He paid you too much attention at the Herne dinner, which brought out the harpy in his wife. Miss Cardross resents the fact that men ignore her when you're in the room. I'm sure she's the center of attention in her home area."

"I'm told she's called the Gloucester Rose. Lady North simply disapproves of my shocking ways. When I look at it that way, there are probably any number of people who see me as a smallpox carrier, infecting the beau monde with wickedness."

She bit her lip on tears, and he raised her hand and kissed it, pressing his warm lips firmly to her knuckles. "Don't give our poisoner an added victory, Georgia. Be strong. Let's set about our hunt."

She let him turn her toward the house but said, "How?"

"We simply follow the crumbs. Do you have allies who would help?"

"I would have said many, but now I'm unsure. The Torrismondes and Harringays will always stand my friends."

"Porterhouse?"

"Perhaps, though I'm not sure he'd hunt with us. I'd like to say Beaumont and Richmond, but I'll not put them in an awkward position."

"Even six should be enough."

"But what do we *do*?" she asked. "I can't bear to make things worse."

"Doing nothing could make it worse, but detection should stop any further malice tonight."

"Further . . ." Georgia balked at even entering the house.

"Courage," he said. "You shall have the say about any action once our villain is found."

He glanced around, then raised her chin so he could kiss her. A simple kiss. A comforting kiss.

A friendly kiss.

Why, then, did her toes curl with pleasure?

She pushed gently away from him, knowing he was her anchor yet again. "Thank you. To the hunt, then."


Dracy accompanied Georgia Maybury into the supper room, alert for clues. There were sliding looks aplenty, some cold, some disdainful, some disgustingly amused, but he caught no one looking triumphant. They were hunting a clever devil, then.

Now that he knew what was going on, he could understand some things he'd heard. There'd been murmurs about Georgia all night, but the change had been in the last hour.

He remembered hearing one man say, "What's good for a man like Vance . . ."

Another had been more like Lady North and wondered if Lady Maybury was suitable company for his wife and daughter.

Dracy had been in a group when Titus Cavenham said that he'd heard Vance claim to be her lover just before the duel. Cavenham was an ass, but he wouldn't lie about such a thing. Someone else had pointed out that what Vance claimed had nothing to do with truth, so Georgia had allies, but the men would remember Cavanham's words.

Dracy would have defended her if no one else had, but he had to admit that he hadn't been entirely sure. He believed in her essential goodness, but a naive and willful young wife could be seduced by a clever man. Vance didn't sound clever or attractive, but he'd known women attracted to similar men.

Now he refused to believe it. Their recent discussion had wiped away all doubts. Lady May was innocent, vulnerable, gallant, and besieged, and he would stand by her side and slay her enemies, even without hope of reward.

"I don't see the Harringays or Torrismondes here," she said, scanning the supper room. "There are more tables on the side terrace."

The side terrace was narrow but set with urns of flowers, shielded by an awning, and lit by lamps. As soon as they walked out there, someone called, "Georgia!"

They were being hailed by three ladies, and Georgia led the way to the table.

He'd danced with black-haired, buxom Lady Harringay and was introduced to Lady Torrismonde, a pretty lady with brown hair and a warm smile. A petite redhead with freckles was Lady Bryght Malloren. In the past weeks, he'd learned that any Malloren was a force to be reckoned with, but this one seemed harmless enough.

He seated Georgia and went off to forage, with a particular eye for lobster.

When he returned, the other three gentlemen were seated with their ladies. He knew Harringay and Torrismonde from Town, but not Lord Bryght. He was a surprising match for his wife—tall, dark, and as formidable as his eminent brother. Dracy had been approached by the Marquess of Rothgar and sounded out about his political stance. An unnerving experience for someone still unsure of it.

He was surprised that Lord Rothgar wasn't here, dabbling in peacemaking and politics. Was Lord Bryght his deputy? There was no way to know, as the men avoided political subjects in the presence of the ladies.

Did the women truly lack interest? He'd met some around the world who were very interested indeed, and there were women who ruled nations. The czarina Catherine ruled Russia, and the empress Maria Theresa ruled Austria, Hungary, and a great many other places. He'd visited an African country ruled by a queen.

Without politics, or anything that could connect to it, the conversation was all gossip and trivialities, and he left it to Georgia to raise the subject of their villain when she thought the time right. He couldn't help noticing how she relaxed into froth and badinage, like a mermaid returned to the sea. She positively shone and was quick with wit and bon mots.

This moonlit, sea-foam world was her natural milieu. To snatch her from it would be as evil as to trap a mermaid on dry land, but he wasn't strong enough to entirely give up hope, especially when so many enemies circled.

She'd be safe at Dracy, murmured the devil. Tom and Annie would befriend her, and he'd guard and protect her. Together they could make Dracy a haven where she need never fear an enemy again.

# Chapter 15

Georgia waited until the Mallorens left the table before speaking of her problem. They might have been willing to help, but she couldn't be sure, especially of Lord Bryght. The Mallorens were always playing a deep game of their own. There was certainly no excuse to embroil the couple in her personal problems.

The Harringays moved as if to leave too, but she said, "Stay a moment." Once they'd settled again, she continued. "You'll have heard the whispers about the letter."

Babs and her husband grimaced, as did Torrismonde, but Lizzie said, "What letter?"

"I didn't want to upset you, love," her husband said and gave her the story.

"That's wicked! There can be no truth to it at all."

"Of course not," Torrismonde said, "but some people will believe anything spicy."

"Cats," Lizzie said.

"That's to malign cats," Georgia said. "Rats, let's say. Lord Dracy and I were speaking about this, and we want to try to find the rat, here, tonight."

"Here, tonight?" Lizzie echoed, looking alarmed.

But Babs leaned forward. "An excellent idea. How?"

Dracy spoke at last. He'd been very quiet. "Georgia

doesn't intend to make a grand affair of it, but only to warn the culprit that they've been detected."

"We want to trace the story back," Georgia said. "If you can each approach the person who told you and find their source, then ask that person and so on, we'll have threads enough to trap a rat. In an hour, we'll gather on the main terrace near the steps and share what we've learned."

"But I don't want to talk to people about such foul stuff," Lizzie protested.

"Don't be a rabbit, Lizzie," Babs said. "You can frame it as outrage and make it clear that it's all lies."

"Ah," said Lizzie, straightening. "That I can do."

"But not too much outrage," Georgia said. "I've no desire to stir a furor or to ruin Winnie's ball. Are we all agreed?"

Everyone said yes, but Dracy said, "You can't take part. No one's going to talk to you about this."

Georgia wanted to protest, but he was correct. "Then will someone please dance with me? Not you, Dracy. Not two dances in a row. That would be as good as an announcement."

"I'm willing if you are," he said, but as a joke, and the others laughed.

Georgia feared he hadn't spoken entirely in fun.

Torrismonde offered to partner her, and they all rose.

Harringay gave the hunting call, "Tallyho!" and Babs dragged him away, hissing at him to be more subtle about it. Georgia strolled inside with the other three, truly dreading a return to the company. How had a simple ball come to this?

As they approached the dancing, Dracy said, "You could speak to Porterhouse. He'd tell you who told him."

She smiled at him. "You understand my frustration. I'll do that."

Then they had to part, and she sorely missed her anchor.

\*       \*       \*

Dracy watched Georgia and Torrismonde stroll over to where Porterhouse sat with two ladies. He had no thread to follow because he'd only overheard conversations and never been told anything directly, so he went to the smoking room. It was the main location for intense political discussions, but some men were also using it for its purpose, so the smoke hung in the air despite open windows.

Tobacco, he thought with a smile. He'd be haunted by it all his days, in all its forms, but smoking men also gossiped.

He saw Newcastle walk away from Georgia's father, leaving the earl alone for a moment. Even better. "A word with you, Hernescroft."

"Of course, Dracy. You are interesting yourself in the new ministry?"

"Not at all, sir. I am interesting myself in your daughter. You'll have heard the new rumor."

The earl's face reddened. "Damned scandal, and at my elder daughter's ball. Nothing to it, of course."

"Of course, but it would be interesting, don't you think, to follow the thread back to whoever started the filth? Can you remember who told you?"

"My wife," Hernescroft said. "You'd best ask her."

Dracy thanked him and did so, finding Lady Hernescroft in the drawing room, where many of the older ladies were resting. Two were asleep.

"Follow the thread?" she said. "Excellent idea. I heard it from my daughter, Lady Thretford, and she heard it from Miss Cardross. Do you want me to ask her where she got it?"

"If you please, ma'am."

She nodded. "I'm pleased to see you so engaged with my daughter's good, Dracy."

"I hope I would do as much for any lady, ma'am."

"That's not, however, how the heart behaves."

"It's how my mind behaves." He paused, then spoke

his mind. "May I ask why you support a marriage between me and your daughter, ma'am? She'd be better protected from ill winds by someone like Beaufort."

"Not in my opinion, and there's the question of Fancy Free."

"I'm surprised such a minor matter concerns you."

"It is not minor to Lord Hernescroft, and his interests concern me."

He wanted to demand, *Shouldn't your daughter's interests concern you more?*

He must have shown his feelings, for she said, "You have much to learn, Dracy. In a marriage it's often the small accommodations that are more effective than the large."

"But if large are necessary?"

"Then the marriage was ill planned. You think the accommodations between you and Georgia would be large?"

"Vast. She's a hothouse plant and I have no glass houses at Dracy."

"Twelve thousand pounds will build some," she said. "And many pampered plants do better in a more natural setting, if hardened off appropriately first."

"How, exactly, do you suggest your daughter be hardened off?"

She didn't react to his caustic tone. "Slowly, Lord Dracy, slowly. But don't take too long about it or the growing season will be over."

She swept off, leaving Dracy clench-jawed. He'd like to marry Georgia if only to save her from her heartless family. For now, all he could do was hunt down her enemy.

He returned to the smoking room and, as he'd hoped, heard two men gossiping. "In his own words . . . And the letter is to be published and put on display at Rope's Print Shop."

He interrupted them. "You speak of the letter relating

to Lady Maybury, sirs? I must warn you that it's mere malice, with no substance."

"Indeed? And how would you know, Dracy?"

"In the same way you think you know it's true. Someone told me. May I ask who told you?"

"Not if it's going to lead to blood."

Dracy remembered not to smile in reassurance. "I'm a very peaceable fellow, Morgan. I merely wish to discover where this weed has grown from."

The other man, Dormer, spoke up. "From the lady, sir, and her reputation."

Dracy looked at him. "Peaceable though I am, I cannot stand by to hear slander—"

The first man hastily interrupted. "I had it from Sir Quarles Cork."

Dracy bowed, said, "Thank you," and cruised in search of Sir Quarles, whom he thought he remembered as young, big-bellied, and hearty. If he had the right man, he was here because he was a neighbor, not for political reasons.

He found him in the card room and observed until a hand ended.

"A word with you, Sir Quarles, if you would be so kind."

Cork looked surprised, as well he might, but he rose and stepped aside.

"I won't keep you from your game, sir, but I'm tracking down the source of the lie about a letter from a man called Vance?"

"A lie? Do you say so? Had it as a certainty from . . . Now, who was it? I remember. Pretty Miss Pierce. I did think it a bit of a warm subject for her, but of course, she was only expressing her shock."

"Of course," Dracy said. "My thanks, sir."

Miss Pierce. That meant nothing to him, and he couldn't imagine questioning a young lady, so he went in search of Georgia.

She was dancing with Lord Bryght, which was probably a good strategy, given the Malloren reputation. She was giving a skillful impression of untroubled pleasure, but Dracy wanted to go around the room and wipe the expressions off all the faces. He spotted Lord Sellerby standing with two older women but watching Georgia most of the time. He'd defended her once before and could be recruited again. But then Dracy remembered how she'd tried to avoid him and gave up the idea.

Pray God he didn't become as insanely besotted as Sellerby. The man had had years to be bewitched out of his senses. Perhaps Tom Knowlton was right and he should escape to Dracy Manor as soon as possible.

The dance was ending, so he went to Georgia to mention Miss Pierce but was intercepted by Lady Hernescroft.

"Eloisa Cardross claims to have heard the story from Lady Waveney."

She walked on, leaving Dracy puzzled as he joined Georgia.

She thanked Malloren and smiled at Dracy. It didn't reach her eyes, but he realized she was less worried than angry. "Are we any further along?" she asked.

"I have two interesting strings, but nothing at the end of either yet. Do you know a Miss Pierce?"

"Of course. A Grenville connection. Brunette in pale blue, over there with her mother."

"Too young for me to accost. She told the tale to a Sir Quarles Cork."

"I think I'd terrify her too. I'll ask Lizzie." They went in search of her.

"Your mother traced it back as far as Lady Waveney. What of Porterhouse?"

"Had it from Carlyon, so I put Harringay on that trail. I truly think we'll catch the rat."

"And it cheers your heart."

She smiled at him. "It does. Dance the next with me?"

"Your toes are still willing to take the risk?"

As he'd intended, she smiled at that reminder of an earlier, lighter moment, but as they returned to the dance, she sobered.

"After this one," she said, "we compare notes."

There was such a fierce light in her eyes that he said, "Remember, no bloodshed."

"Alas, no, but I'd like to see some."

Georgia danced with Dracy, aware that it could be their last. There were few left before dawn, and after this event he should return to his duties in Devon. It was all for the best, but she'd miss her friend. When the dance ended and they strolled out onto the terrace, she said, "Have I saved Fancy Free?"

He looked a question at her.

"Remember? If you enjoyed the ball, then you'd accept whatever exchange my father offers."

"Ah, that. It's certainly not been boring, so I can promise to do my best."

His words seemed guarded, as did his expression, but they were coming up to the others.

"Eloisa Cardross!" Lizzie said as soon as they reached her. "I can't believe she'd stoop so low."

"You're sure?" Georgia asked, looking at them all.

"Three lines lead to her," Harringay said.

"Perhaps four," Dracy said. "Lady Hernescroft had it from her. Miss Cardross passed the blame on, but I remember that Lady Hernescroft used the word 'claimed.' She didn't believe it."

"My mother is a very clever woman."

"Miss Pierce had it from her," Lizzie said. "How busy she must have been. I want to tear her hair out!"

Georgia had to laugh. "Dear Lizzie, you're usually the most peaceable of us all."

"Not over something like this. What are we going to do?"

"Confront her with her lie," Georgia said, "but I do feel a little sorry for her."

"You feel sorry for everyone!" Babs exclaimed. "What excuse do you have for such spite?"

Georgia sighed. "She was expecting to spend the spring in Town, but Millicent demanded her company during her delicate time, so she was trapped at Herne, which is enough to turn anyone sour. Then Millicent fed her stories about me."

"That's no excuse," Babs said. "Now, how do we deal with her?"

"*We* don't," Torrismonde said. "Six accusers would probably terrify her out of her wits." He looked at Georgia. "Are you strong enough to confront her?"

"I'd resist any attempt to prevent me, but I'd like support."

"I go with you," Dracy said. Georgia knew she should object to such a tone, but she wanted him by her side.

"We might need extra ladies in case she does throw a fit," Georgia said. "Babs? Lizzie?"

"Of course," Lizzie said, "but where should we be?"

"There's the problem," Georgia said. "The whole ground floor is being used for the ball, and I don't want a public scene. I wonder how susceptible she'd be to a mysterious tryst. In her bedchamber, even . . ."

"She wouldn't!" Lizzie protested.

"She might," Babs said. "She'd do anything to hook a titled suitor. So if the tryst was with a duke . . ."

Georgia put her hand over her mouth. "That's positively wicked, but she deserves it. Very well. We'll forge a billet-doux and have Jane give it to a footman we can trust. If she slips upstairs, we have her."

"Which stairs?" Harringay asked.

"I don't think she'd use the servants' stairs, but there are two others." She looked up at the house. "My room is second from the left there, and hers is two windows along. She'll have to pass mine. I'll wait there, and if she takes the bait, I'll wave a handkerchief out of the window."

"A mind made for conspiracy," Dracy teased. "Do I wait with you?"

Georgia prayed to stop the blush. "In my bedchamber, sir? Certainly not. You can wait out here with everyone else."

Georgia hurried away, fleeing, in fact. For a moment there, his question had dangled like a golden apple of temptation.

She was halfway up the stairs when she realized she had no plain paper on which to write her note. She detoured to her brother-in-law's office, praying not to be caught, and rummaged in drawers until she found some plain sheets. She slipped out, feeling like a thief, and hurried to her room.

Once there, she had to light a candle, and nervousness made her fumble the tinderbox.

With the flame burning steadily, she sat, uncapped her ink, prepared her pen, and considered how a man's handwriting looked. Perhaps she should have brought Dracy along to write this.

She hadn't received many letters from men. A few scrawls from Dickon when they'd been apart. He'd used a clerk for anything more formal. There were those long letters from Sellerby. He had an elegant, flowing style. Sir Harry Shaldon had sent her a few billets-doux. Strong strokes that used a lot of ink.

She practiced on one sheet, adding a heavy hand to an even script. She decided it would do and indulged in excess.

*Dear Lady,*

*Bright star in the firmament, I am slain by your beauty, your goodness, and your charms. I cannot bear to leave this house without speaking, but where? Would you grant me the greatest honor a*

*man can ever attain and trust me for a few moments
in the privacy of your chamber? I have ascertained
where it is. Please forgive me for that boldness, angel of my heart.*

Georgia glanced at the clock. It was almost half past
two.

*I will await nearby at a quarter to three, and if I
see you enter, I will know I have hope.*
                    *Your newest, most ardent admirer,*
                    *B*

She let the ink dry, pleased with her work, and then
folded it neatly. She melted sealing wax and dripped it,
then applied her own seal. Quickly, she pressed on it to
smudge the impression, but a seal, even a smudged one,
looked more formal and impressive.

She rang the bell and Jane soon hurried in. "Is something amiss, milady?"

"No, but you look as if you've been enjoying yourself."

Jane blushed and adjusted her mobcap. "No harm in
a bit of fun when we can snatch the time. What do you
need, milady?"

Georgia gave her the letter. "It's to go to Miss
Cardross, but she mustn't know who sent it. Is there a
footman who'll keep his mouth shut, at least for now?"

"Charlie's a good sort, milady."

"Good. Tell him he's to slip it to Miss Cardross and
say it's more than his job is worth to say who gave it to
him, other than that it was a titled gentleman."

"Very well, milady, but are you up to mischief?"

"This is a very serious matter, so don't fail me. I'll tell
you all about it later."

When Jane had left, Georgia extinguished her candle
and went to the window. The illuminated garden looked
lovely from here, and the lights floating on the pond

could be admired to the full. She would like to know just how that was done.

She could see her five friends on the terrace, chatting as they waited. A few other people were out there, but the music continued for the dance. The ball was winding down, but no one would leave until dawn provided light.

She moved over to stand by her door, listening for footsteps. She hoped Eloisa would come, for she needed an enemy to fight. Still, she knew much of the damage would linger unless she forced Eloisa to confess her spiteful lies. She wasn't sure she could do that to anyone.

Ah, someone was coming. The footsteps went past, and a door along the corridor opened and shut.

Georgia hurried to the window and waved her handkerchief, and then she returned to open her door. She waited until Dracy joined her and then went to knock on Eloisa Cardross's door.

Eloisa opened it eagerly, but then gaped.

Georgia went in. "A word with you, Eloisa."

"What? Who? I'm innocent!"

Georgia was startled but then realized that Eloisa thought they'd found out about the tryst.

"Innocent?" Georgia said. "We have proof that you've spread malicious lies about me during this ball."

*"What?"* Eloisa exclaimed, but the new tack had changed her completely. Now she was bold. "Are you here to protest your innocence, Georgia? That won't wash."

"I *am* innocent. Of everything. I know Millicent will have told you things—"

"No excuses," Dracy said, cutting her off.

True, she'd been about to plead Eloisa's case for her.

Dracy took the reins. "Miss Cardross, we know you have deliberately spread a lie this night about a letter that would incriminate Lady Maybury if it existed. We require you to put right the wrong by telling as many people as possible that you were mistaken."

Eloisa had stared at him throughout, but now she laughed.

"Has she duped you too, Lord Dracy? I haven't lied about anything." She turned to a drawer, opened it, and took out an unfolded letter. "There—read that. It does, as you say, incriminate Lady Maybury of the most heinous sins."

# Chapter 16

Georgia snatched it out of his hand and worked through the execrable handwriting.

*My dear Jellicoe,*
*I write to you a broken man, exiled, penniless, and without friends through the machinations of a coldhearted woman. You know what she promised me, that we would be happy together, well funded by her jewels. Once I'd rid her of her husband, however, she laughed at my expectations, writing to say that I'd liberated her to marry the man she truly loved. Spring by name, but winter in her heart. Of your kindness, can you send me funds to the Hartmann bank here, else I must shoot myself.*

*Vance*

"Lies," Georgia said as Dracy took it from her. "Every word is a lie."

"It seems genuine to me," Eloisa said, smirking.

Georgia had to admit that it did. The letter itself had the battered appearance of one that had traveled far and been handled by many hands.

Dracy turned it to inspect the address and place of dispatch. "Cologne, and addressed to Major Jellicoe."

Georgia couldn't read his expression.

"You see!" Eloisa said.

"But it's all lies," Georgia protested again, feeling as if she'd fallen into a nightmare. "I made no pact. I rarely exchanged a word with Charnley Vance!"

"I know that," Dracy said. "Either Vance wrote this for his own malicious reasons, or it was forged to do you harm."

"*Forged?* By the dowager?" Georgia shook her head. "Impossible. She'd have shown it if she'd had it."

"So she never had it," he said.

"That letter is real," Eloisa snapped, "and it identifies you, Georgia, as if your name was stated. How long can you keep up this pretence? Faith! You sent that letter to bring me here! *You* are the forger, Georgia Maybury, and wicked to the core."

Georgia wanted to slap her, but Eloisa probably did believe every word, and the letter . . . the letter was a disaster. Now she truly was ruined.

"You'd be wise to guard your tongue, Miss Cardross," Dracy said. "This letter is a forgery, and by spreading word of it, you're an accomplice to a wicked act."

Eloisa went from triumphant to stricken. "I didn't . . . She . . ."

"A wicked act," he repeated. "Who gave you this letter?"

"I don't know!" Eloisa cried, pale now. "It was brought to me by a footman."

"The cover," he demanded.

She scurried to the drawer and produced the sheet of paper. Georgia wasn't surprised that Eloisa had crumbled. Dracy was terrifyingly stern.

He looked at both sides of the paper and then handed it to Georgia. "Do you recognize the hand?"

She studied the name on the front and the single sentence inside. *Use this as you see fit to right the wrong.*

"It's carefully written," she said. "As in a child's copy-book."

"A way of disguising the natural writing." He looked at Eloisa, who was sniveling into a handkerchief. "You may want to consider how Georgia's family will regard your actions."

"You won't tell them. Georgia, please!"

"Come, Lady Maybury." He steered her out of the room.

Georgia heard Eloisa burst into tears but could take no comfort from it.

"I have no defense! I know the letter is false, but others will believe it. Thus, they'll see me as my husband's murderer!"

He grasped her shoulders. "You can't fail now, above all times. We are going below, and you will be Lady May, disdainful of all suspicion."

"I can't!"

"There's no limit to what we can do if we are brave enough. Remember, you are innocent."

She stared at him. "You believe in me?"

"Completely."

"Why? You hardly know me."

He smiled. "I know you well enough for that. I knew you were honorable at our first meeting."

She remembered. "At Herne. Yes, you did. It strengthened me then, when the challenge was so small."

"Let it strengthen you now. Anyone who knows you knows all foul rumors to be false."

She laughed a little. "Then very few know me."

"A wise woman told me once that the human heart can cherish only a few. Too wide a circle makes a shallow pond."

"Which makes the beau monde little better than mud." She took a deep breath. "Very well. I am restored. At least the lions can't actually eat me."

"Rats," he said. "At worst, they can only nibble."

"I believe I've heard of people nibbled to death by rats, sir. But onward."

Lizzie and Babs were waiting around a corner. "What happened?" Babs asked. "We heard some yells, and you look dreadful."

"Full of dread, yes. Eloisa didn't invent the letter. It's real and unfortunately it looks believable."

"Forged, of course," Dracy said, giving Babs the letter.

Georgia wanted to protest, but it was already done.

"Forged!" Lizzie gasped. "That's a hanging offense."

"Only forging money, I think," Babs said, reading.

Georgia turned her mind to the encounter. "I wonder why she didn't show people the letter but only spoke of it."

"Too bold for her," Dracy said. "She's a rat that wanted to stay behind the wainscoting. You saw her face when I mentioned the reaction of your family."

Georgia did, and felt pity, but only a little.

Lizzie was reading the letter too. "Oh, Georgie, what are you going to do?" From her expression, she was thinking of such things as fleeing the country, or at least scuttling back to Herne.

"Find out who's behind all this," Georgia said, "and stamp the rat into the ground."

"You must burn that letter," Babs said.

Dracy said, "Trust it to me. It's evidence. I won't let it escape."

Georgia longed to burn the vile thing to ash, but she wouldn't squabble over it now. "Very well, but we must all return below, and not in a group."

"Are you sure?" Lizzie asked.

"What else can I do? Go."

Lizzie and Babs left, and Georgia turned to Dracy. "We can't go down together either."

"Very well, but meet me on the terrace."

"I shouldn't."

"In full view of others. We can't dance again, but we need to discuss this further. And I can't abandon you to the rats."

She shivered at the thought. "Very well. On the terrace, shortly."

With her new knowledge, Georgia expected an attack of some sort, but of course that wasn't the way of the beau monde. She passed through the house and out onto the terrace without any interruption at all, almost as if she didn't exist. Cold or even angry looks would have been a relief. Even though it would ruin the dress, she wished she had a warm woolen shawl.

When she joined Dracy, she said, "It's as if I don't exist."

"You exist for me and for your true friends."

"That's a very little world."

"Plague take the person behind this."

"Eloisa—"

"Not her. Whoever sent her the letter, here, where she'd be unable to resist speaking of it."

"I hadn't thought of that." Georgia looked back at the pretty, illuminated house. "There's another person there who hates me. Why?" she asked, turning back. "Why? I swear, I've never intentionally hurt anyone. Or unintentionally, to my knowledge."

"I believe you. You have a kind heart. May I fight in your cause?"

"A duel! Never!"

"No, no. A poor choice of words. Fight to vindicate you. We must find the sender of the letter and the forger who created it, but above all, we must find Sir Charnley Vance. Then I'll get the truth out of him."

She smiled at him, but sadly. "Dear Dracy, but many have tried to find him and he's eluded all of them. Perhaps he did shoot himself in Cologne."

"Even corpses turn up. Who might know Vance's hand?"

"You think you can prove that letter a forgery?" she asked, allowing a flicker of hope.

"It *is* a forgery, so why not?"

"Sent from Cologne?"

"Perhaps that's forgeable too."

"I had one thought," she said, "though perhaps because I want the letter to be false. . . ."

"Tell me."

"The writing is rough, but the language, the phrasing, is not. I hardly knew Vance, but I don't think he'd express himself in those words."

"Ah. When I think about it, you're right. We need to find this Major Jellicoe and discover if Vance wrote any sort of letter to him. Do you know him?"

"No, but he served as Vance's second at the duel. His regiment shipped to India a month later."

"In July." He took the letter out of his pocket and tilted it to catch a little light. "I thought so. Dated October the nineteenth."

"Vance fled the country within hours of killing my husband, so he wouldn't know that Jellicoe was no longer in London."

"Convenient for the forger as well. Who else might know Vance's hand?"

Talking about it so purposefully was helping her, so she applied her mind. "Sir Harry Shaldon was in the same sporting set as Vance and my husband."

"Then I'll find Shaldon, and if not him, others in that sort of man's world."

"Dracy, you have work to do on your estate, and I'm sure it will reward you better than a wild-goose chase. Why are you so sure I'm worthy of all this?"

"Because I've known many wanton ladies, and you don't have their ways."

"Perhaps I'm a skillful deceiver."

"My dear Georgia, you're an open book."

"Am I indeed?" she protested.

"Even your father offered that you are honest."

"Did he? When?"

He looked a little embarrassed to admit, "When we spoke once of your many charms."

"I'm surprised he thinks I have any. Oh, enough," she said, disliking her own tone. "I should return, but it's too Arctic in there for me. Let's walk to the edge of the terrace. The lights on the pond showed very prettily from my room."

He walked with her but said, "I intend to find out all about that duel as well."

Georgia touched the mourning bracelet, wanting Dickon with her now more than ever before. Idiocy. If he were here, none of this would be happening. But she couldn't speak of the duel now, perhaps not ever.

She halted at the balustrade at the closest point to the pond. "They're not so effective from here."

"But still charming."

He was standing behind her, big and strong, like a guard against all the malice in the house. Some of the aching tension inside her leaked away, but she still felt hollow.

The letter must be proved false. She must be proved innocent. She couldn't bear exile from all she loved.

"The candles bob on the water," he said. "I wonder how they're supported. We could stroll down and look."

Leave the terrace and go into the darkness?

"It rained earlier," she said. "The grass will be damp.

"By the time you rise tomorrow, the servants will have cleared it all away. Will you allow a damp hem to bar you from enlightenment?"

She was being dared. In the past she wouldn't have hesitated. . . . So she wouldn't hesitate now. The pond was no more than twelve feet away.

"I don't suppose I'll wear this gown again, anyway," she said as she turned and walked toward the short flight of steps. "Twice is once too many."

"A sorry waste," he said, by her side.

"It's done me little good tonight. You see the folly of wearing a grand gown twice."

"The back is beautifully worked with great skill. It deserves to be appreciated."

He was criticizing her for extravagance, as she'd predicted he would. Proof positive they would not suit.

"You could hang it as a work of art," he said.

"That would be very odd."

"People hang tapestries."

"Then I'll do so," she said, raising her skirt to go down the shallow steps. "When I have houses to decorate, that is. The grass *is* damp," she pointed out. "My shoes will stain."

"You mean you wear shoes more than once?"

"What an odd mood you're in, Dracy. Dark gray silk goes with a number of gowns. One need only change the buckles to suit."

"What buckles do you wear tonight?"

She raised her skirt and pointed a toe into the light of a lantern.

"Sapphires?" he asked.

"Merely chips."

"Set in gold."

"No, pinchbeck!" she snapped, fighting tears as she picked her way over to the pond. This was too much after everything else. She needed him to be her friend, not to sneer at her over her gown and her buckles.

She concentrated on the pond. "Little wooden boats. How clever. Do you think the candles are glued in place?"

"I'd spear them on spikes, and tie them as well."

"Perhaps I could create a naval battle." *When I have a lovely house to ready for parties.*

"Perhaps you could."

She turned to him. "How?"

"Merely by being you." He added, "Helen."

"I do recognize a reference to Helen of Troy without it being hammered home, but I don't appreciate it. She was the death of a thousand men or more. I'm only accused of one."

"Georgia." He took her hand, but she snatched it free, and then regretted it.

"Excuse my mood," she said, swallowing. "It's been a trying night. Let's plan a pond battle."

He looked as if he'd persist, but then he looked back at the pond. "It can't be done. The ships would have to maneuver, and those ones are fixed. I suspect they're tethered to the bottom."

"They could be untethered."

"Then they'd float around at random and simply collide. Hardly a battle."

Georgia concentrated on the problem. "Servants with long black poles," she said. "One per boat. About twenty would do, all dressed in black so as to be almost invisible."

"Twenty servants," he echoed. "Their poles would get in each other's way."

"Plague take it.... Ah, perhaps the sticks could merely nudge, then retreat."

"You're very inventive."

"I enjoy such things. The boats would be ships, accurate in their details, with rigging and sails. I'd need cannon fire.... Fireworks!"

He grabbed her hand and dragged her away. "You'd end up igniting the neighborhood, you madwoman."

"But it would be magnificent! Will you be my naval adviser?"

Too late to take the words back.

"We must return," she said quickly, returning to the steps. "People are probably already talking of my disappearance into the dark and putting the worst interpretation on it. I think I see the attraction of a fit of the vapors. It might stir sympathy."

"Have you ever had one?"

"No."

She raised her skirts and went up two steps, but hesitated.

Ahead, Thretford House glowed with candlelight, and music floated out. Inside, some were still dancing and others would be talking.

About her.

"Ah, the tobacco," he said behind her.

She turned, finding him on the step below. By chance, the nearest lamp lit the left side of his face, putting the scar in shadow.

She touched the rough skin. "So tragic."

He covered her hand with his. "It could have been much worse." But then he met her gaze. "What are you doing, Georgia?"

"Being driven mad by tobacco, I think. Kiss me?"

"Why?"

"That's looking a gift horse in the mouth!" When he only waited, she said, "Because I want it."

"And that is reason enough?"

"Yes."

"How many men have you kissed?"

She thought about it. "Perhaps ten."

"How many of those kisses did you enjoy?"

"Why all these questions? If you don't want—"

He put an arm around her and drew her close, so that she was pressed to his warm, strong body. He held her eyes as he slid a hand up her neck and into her dressed curls, as his fingers played in her hair, and then as he lowered his lips to hers.

Perhaps it was the touch on her scalp that alarmed her. She pushed back, but he kissed her anyway, and her push lost all its strength. Pressed to him, her mouth hotly joined to his demanding one, she could do nothing but submit.

And be devastated.

She had never, ever, been kissed like this, by the whole man and a hot clever mouth.

She surrendered, and then she explored—with her own mouth, with her own tongue, with her hands beneath his jacket, sliding over the silk of his waistcoat to delight in his hard, vibrant body. Shivers ran through her, but of pure pleasure.

She could do this forever, and ever, more deeply, more hotly, forever and ever. . . .

He was the one to break the kiss, but he didn't let her go. He held her, breathing deeply, resting his head on hers.

Georgia pushed back again, but this time to look at him.

"None," she said.

"What?"

"I have kissed no one, until now."

"Your husband . . ."

"Not like that."

He stroked her face with his knuckles. "Poor Circe. Poor husband."

"Do you think . . . ? No."

"What?"

She eased out of his arms, even though it made her feel chilled. "A foolish thought," she said, smoothing the front of her gown and looking away. "That kisses like that might have something to do with conception."

"Very little is required for conception. It's an animal business after all." He turned her back to him. "Georgia, I would never reproach you with barrenness."

"Dracy, don't! It can never be."

"I don't accept that."

She turned to hurry up the steps now, hating that she'd forgotten all her resolutions and hurt him so.

When they reached the terrace, she made herself face him. "That kiss was wonderful, and I thank you, because now I know another thing I must have in a husband. But he can never be you."

"Why not?" Now the light shone on his scar.

"We have nothing in common."

"We have a great deal in common, and kisses like that aren't commonplace, you know."

"They can't be unique to you," she protested. "To you and me."

"No? Think carefully about what you're throwing away, Georgia."

In this unreal magical moment she did—and saw another obstacle.

"It would be seen as an admittance of guilt."

"Of course it wouldn't."

"No? Why else would Lady May wed an impoverished baron?" It was harsh, but the truth, and she saw it hit him.

"All the more reason to clear your name completely," he said at last.

She shook her head, torn between laughter and tears. "Oh, Dracy . . . What on earth is your name anyway?"

He stared at her and then smiled back. "Humphrey."

For a minute, she was nonplussed. "Unfortunate, I grant you."

"As a cabin boy I was tagged with Fry. I was small, but I grew. Since then, I've insisted on Dracy."

Laughter won, though there were tears in it, and she collapsed against him as she surrendered to it.

# Chapter 17

Dracy kept an arm around Georgia Maybury, knowing the giggles were a large part tears, wondering why the devil he couldn't wipe away all her burdens with one mighty stroke.

That rarely happened in life, however, and burdens must be borne. Not such unjust ones, however. Somehow he would clear her name, even if that freed her to become a duchess.

She recovered and blew her nose, apologizing.

"I was honored to be your giggling post."

"Don't! You'll start me off again. We really must go back, but I refuse to do so looking as if I've wept. Do I?"

She angled her face to the light and he took the opportunity to study it. "No. But dawn's touching the sky and a few people are coming out to see it. We could join them so you don't have to face the light."

She looked around, assessing everything. "Very well. I think I see the Harringays."

They were indeed in one corner, half hidden by an urn. As he and Georgia came closer, they saw they were enjoying a kiss.

"Mad for each other," Georgia said.

"A blessing."

"Is it? Never to want to be apart?"

"It seems a pleasant image of marriage," he said, "unless it becomes an obsession."

The Harringays emerged, grinning with pleasure, and weren't at all abashed to know they'd been seen.

"The perfect way to greet the day," Babs said, but sobered. "How are you, Georgia?"

"Ready to greet a new day," Georgia replied, "though with no great hopes of it."

Babs hugged her. "All will be well. But what are you going to do? Will Miss Cardross leave here, do you think?"

"Lud! She may not. I can't exist beneath the same roof."

"Come to Town," Babs said. "You can stay with us."

Dracy watched the struggle, knowing better than to offer her refuge in Devon. Would Georgia really choose to plunge into the lion pit? *No, rat pit,* he amended. Of course she would.

"Very well," she said. "I already promised Portia Malloren that I'd oversee Danae House. But I'll stay at Father's house."

"I suppose that would be best," Babs said. "But we can visit frequently. The Arbutts are there, so you will have some other friends." Bab's bit her lip on that unfortunate comment but at least had the wit not to make it worse by apologizing. "The Torrismondes have already left," she said. "Lizzie looked for you."

"We were inspecting the lights on the pond," Georgia said. "It's cleverly done."

"Truly? Come, love, we must go and see."

She dragged her husband away, and Georgia gave Dracy a rueful smile. He couldn't resist. He took her hand, interlocking their fingers as they turned to watch the pearly light begin to break into orange and pink.

Georgia should free her hand but lacked the resolution just now. She gave thanks for something to concentrate on that gave a degree of anonymity amid the company.

Men took her hand in the dance, or to lead her in a formal way, or to kiss. They didn't intertwine fingers like this, imparting warmth and strength.

When she remembered that he would leave soon, she wanted to weep for loneliness and vulnerability. So tempting to hide away, even to run back to Herne, but nothing was more likely to condemn her in the eyes of the world. The only way was to be bold, and that she could do.

"The end of night," he said.

"Which is always welcome."

"Night can be full of pleasures, you know."

She slid him a look. "There'll be no more wickedness in the night, my lord."

"I can be as wicked by daylight, I assure you."

She shook her head at him.

"Doesn't it say somewhere in the Bible that the devil works at noon?" he asked.

"It says the devil never sleeps."

"But then, nor do the brighter angels."

She bit her lip.

"Now what did I say to amuse?" he asked.

"Only a silly joke about the Angel Gabriel and the Annunciation. Ah," she said, as the sky flared. "Perhaps the angels dance at sunrise."

"Perhaps they do," he said and she felt an angel-wing kiss against her hair.

When the sun was up, they wandered back into the house, among the last to do so, which on Georgia's part was deliberate. She'd managed to avoid the worst of the gauntlet after all. Carriages were rolling to the front of the house and yawning guests were piling into them. Some were going down to the river to catch the last of the tide.

"How do you travel?" Georgia asked Dracy.

"I came by boat but have been offered a place in a returning carriage. I should seek my benefactor."

Georgia prepared to take a calm farewell but wondered whether she'd see him again. He'd said he'd seek the truth of the duel, but he'd also spoken of his duty to his estate, and presumably the matter of Fancy Free would be settled now.

"Ah, there you are." Her mother came up to them. "A word, if you please. Apart."

Georgia sent Dracy an apologetic look, but her mother said, "You too, Dracy."

Bemused, Georgia followed her mother inside.

"How you could cause *more* talk, I do not know," her mother said. "Not only ridiculous stories about a letter, but you were seen out in the garden, kissing!"

Georgia flushed with shame as if she were sixteen, but she rallied. "By whom?"

"By Eloisa Cardross. Who will not hesitate to speak of it."

"Oh—" Georgia managed to bite back a curse, but of course Eloisa would seek some way to strike back.

"Lady Hernescroft—" Dracy said, but was cut off.

"Don't try to take all the blame, Dracy. I know my daughter. There's only one thing for it. We will put it around that you were sealing a commitment."

"What?" Georgia exclaimed, turning to Dracy. Had he somehow contrived to compromise her, acting in the same way as Sellerby? But he looked as stunned as she was.

"Lady Hernescroft . . . ," he began again.

"Of course nothing need come of it, but we will make it known that such a union is under consideration."

"So then soon I'll be a jilt," Georgia objected.

"Not when matters were never certain. I assume you will play your part, Dracy?"

"I will serve Lady Maybury in whatever way *she* requests, ma'am," he said.

His words mollified Georgia. In any case, he couldn't have planned this. She'd been the one to ask for that kiss. There was no one else to blame.

"Very well, Mother, though I doubt many will believe it."

"On the contrary," her mother said, looking grim.

Of course, it was the same point she'd made herself—the beau monde would assume that having been caught out in her wickedness, she'd accepted the only man who'd have her. She wanted to pick up a nearby vase and hurl it at the mirror. Dracy took her hand with great firmness, as if warning her, and then raised it for a kiss.

"It will be an interesting diversion, Lady Maybury."

"A great imposition on you, my lord."

He smiled. "You know it's not."

"Then it should be."

"Georgia," her mother chided.

Georgia spread her hands. "It seems I have no choice. We should give the froth more substance, my lord. I'll escort you out to your carriage." As soon as they were away from her mother, Georgia said, "This is intolerable!"

"We should have expected Miss Cardross to try to pay us back."

"Yes, and I deeply dislike being stupid. Don't feel you must linger in Town because of this. I can act out my misery at your absence."

"Remember, you're a poor liar. I can stay a little while, and I do want to investigate the letter and look into the matter of the duel. I sense that is the root of everything."

"Of course it is," she said impatiently, "but there's nothing new to learn about it."

"We'll see. I hope you'll tell me what you know."

She hated talk of the duel because it cast Dickon in such a bad light. Drunken and foolish. "My brother Perry knows as much as can be known, for he investigated it at the time. I assure you, if he hasn't dug up a detail, it's not to be found."

"A fresh eye often spots something new, and an outsider can see things that others don't."

"Then I wish you well with all my heart. I dearly long

to be proved innocent." She realized she was turning the mourning bracelet and stopped.

"If there's any way in the world," he said, "I will prove the letter false and you a virtuous wife. And I will stand by your side."

"Dracy, you mustn't. . . ."

A footman hurried over to say that Lord Dracy's coach awaited.

He kissed her hand again. "Until we meet again, Lady May."

She watched him go, beginning to dislike that name.

Dracy returned to his lodging at the Crown and Cat off the Strand and rolled into bed. By the time he rose, fashionably late to the noon bells, Tom Knowlton had been out and returned.

He shook his head to see Dracy eating breakfast so late. "Ruin your constitution," he said.

"This is not my normal regimen, I assure you, Tom. Sorted out your legal business?"

"Going well," Tom said.

Dracy suspected his friend's main purpose in traveling to Town was concern over him. Knowlton's lawyers were in Exeter.

"How was the ball?" Tom asked, taking a seat.

"Much like any other," he lied, hoping Tom wouldn't get a sniff of Georgia's new scandal. With luck he'd return to Devon before he heard about the spurious betrothal. "An elegant small house, illuminated gardens, a tolerable supper."

"And Lady Maybury?"

"Splendid in a peacock gown. The main business, however, was political."

Tom had country opinions on politics, mostly irritation about the mishandling of everything in Westminster, so that set the conversation off on a safe track. When Dracy had finished his breakfast, they went out to stroll about St. James's—palace, square, and park. They eventually dined at an excellent chophouse for a modest amount at a long table with good company.

Dracy wanted to plunge immediately into his quest to vindicate Georgia, but all the same, he enjoyed such a normal day and Tom's steady company. He'd put the matter so out of his mind that he was startled to hear "Maybury" from a little way down the table.

He turned that way and heard a pinch-faced man in shabby clothing say, "Up to her old tricks. Or rather, her old sins return to burn her."

*What business is it of yours, you devil?*

"A great beauty, I hear," said a younger man.

"So was Delilah," said the crow.

That set up a debate about the appeal and peril of a beautiful woman. Dracy found Tom giving him a very eloquent look.

"Later," he said, and mentioned a new type of Thames wherry to distract.

When they left the chophouse to stroll back to their inn, Dracy said, "It's only a matter of someone stoking the old fires. And nothing to it either."

Tom held his silence.

"Look, none of it's true. I know it. You might trust my judgment."

"My brother almost married a gypsy girl, convinced she'd make an honest wife."

"Perhaps she would have done."

"Filched his silver spoons before the knot was tied."

"Very well, I take your point, but up until that duel Lady Maybury was a respected wife. Flighty, perhaps, and inclined to mischief, but I've not heard anyone suggest a prior sin. It's the duel, Tom. Everything else flows from there. If Maybury had killed himself in that carriage race, she'd have lost her husband and her homes, but she would have been a tragic widow, not a scandalous one."

"But he didn't," Tom said. "He was killed in a duel with a man some believe to have been her lover."

"But why? Why believe that? If . . ." He'd been about to say "Annie," but that would be too close to the bone, so he chose Lady Swanton, a virtuous wife of a Devon neighbor. "If Sir James Swanton were to get himself killed in a duel—yes, I know it's unlikely—would anyone believe for a moment that they'd fought over Lady Swanton, still less that she'd been sneaking into the victor's bed?"

"Lady Swanton hasn't acted a breeches part at Drury Lane."

"'Struth, did she? Never mind; that's not the same thing."

"Maybe not, but she sold kisses for a guinea apiece. Perhaps the people who believe the stories know her better than you do."

Dracy crossed the street between two wagons, frustrated by everything. A breeches part at Drury Lane. Selling kisses. She did need reining in. . . .

But he didn't want to be her jailer.

He wanted to be her lover.

As they cut down Crock Lane, he remembered saying that a new eye saw new things.

"Tom, that duel was nearly as odd as one fought by Sir James would be. It was given out as being about Maybury's inability to drive a team, but the rumor of it being about Lady Maybury began nearly as soon. I need to find out why."

Tom shook his head. "Bewitched. Come away back to Devon with me, Dracy, and clear your head of her."

"I'm not bewitched," Dracy lied. "I truly do have business to complete here, but I will return soon, within a fortnight of a certainty."

"I'd ask for a promise if I thought you'd make it."

A fortnight, and he'd already been away from Dracy almost that long. He couldn't neglect his primary responsibility indefinitely.

"Then I give it. I'll set out to return to Dracy within a fortnight."

"Good man."

Dracy laughed. "You sound like someone whose friend has sworn off gin! I'm in complete control of all my wits and appetites, I assure you."

That sparked a new question in his mind. Men do rash things when drunk, but why did the duel go ahead when everyone had sobered up? He wouldn't distress Tom anymore, however, so he said, "A shame to sit by the fireside on your last night in Town. The Mitre Inn has a nightly entertainment of acrobats and such, and serves good ale."

Tomorrow, Georgia would arrive in Town, and Dracy couldn't help but be glad that Tom would have set off back to the West Country by then.

# Chapter 18

Georgia stepped into the barge to travel to Town thinking how happy she would have been only a few days before. Now it was a test of her courage.

Her mother had removed to Town herself the day before to begin the battle to overcome the new scandal, so Georgia had only Jane and one of Winnie's footmen to attend her. Dracy was to meet them at the York Stairs, and he and the chairmen would be adequate escort. But it wasn't attack by a mob she feared. Unless, that is, the beau monde could be considered a mob.

She had no choice, she reminded herself as the barge moved into the river downstream. She couldn't stay at Winnie's house, even if she wanted to, with Eloisa Cardross in residence, not without doing something she'd regret.

Although she'd retaliated in one way.

Eloisa had tried to be included in the move to Town, but on that Georgia and her mother had been of one mind. She could do as she wished, but there'd be no place for her at the Hernescroft House in Piccadilly. Doubtless letters would fly to Millicent at Herne, and howling reproaches would fly back, but letters from distant parts were so easily ignored.

Unless they came from Cologne, bearing wicked lies.

Who, she asked constantly, hated her enough to fabricate such a thing?

And what might they do next?

Despite the shrouded threat hanging over her, she had to move to Town. It was that or accept defeat and slink away forever. Never. Justice had to prevail, but the river seemed sluggish today, as if even it was reluctant to carry her.

Oh, nonsense. It was a tidal river. Once in a while it shrank almost to mud, and not because of human foibles. It would carry her to the York Stairs, from whence she would go to her father's house. From there she'd go about Town, enjoy the company of the friends she still had, and pray the world would come to its senses.

After all, Dracy had the letter. It could not be published or displayed in some print-shop window. As Eloisa had claimed that it would be, its nonappearance should deflate the story. Eloisa would certainly not dare to come forward as sole witness to the letter's existence.

All the same, Georgia traveled in sick dread until she saw Dracy awaiting her as promised, her steady anchor in the storm. She smiled as he handed her out of the barge. "Thank you."

He kissed her hand. "I'm your trusty knight. Come, your chair awaits."

He escorted her to the chair and handed her in. It was so like the last time she'd visited, and yet all was changed. Did London truly smell worse, or was that her imagination? It always stank in summer, and this year had been unusually hot.

The smell faded somewhat as they moved farther from the river, but there were others in its place. Sewers, horse dung, perhaps even dead cats and rats. She'd spent too much time in the countryside, that was all, and was now more sensitive to the stink.

She was carried into the house and Dracy handed her out into the tiled hall. It seemed chilly, but only in comparison to the heat outside, and she took courage from the ranks of Earls of Hernescroft looking down on her. She was a Perriam, they seemed to be saying, and must not falter.

She turned to Dracy. "Thank you for your escort. Can you return for dinner?"

"I've no need to leave. Lady Hernescroft was kind enough to invite me to lodge here for the while."

"Here?" she exclaimed.

"I believe there are enough rooms."

Georgia regretted her sharp response in front of the servants. "Of course, and I'm delighted, my lord. Ah, here's the housekeeper to guide me to my room. Till dinner, then, Dracy."

She escaped smiling, but jangled between delight and alarm. Much of the alarm was because of the delight. She liked the man too much, and meeting him morning, noon, and night would do nothing for her sanity.

"Heavens above," she said to Jane as soon as they were alone in the bedchamber, "I've known too many women who have married rashly and regretted it."

"What are you talking about, milady?"

Georgia ignored that, looking around the room. "So darkly decorated. Oh, for a home of my own. For silk wallpaper, pale paint, and gilding. And," she said, flipping rust-colored velvet, "flowered hangings."

Jane didn't answer, and Georgia knew her maid wasn't fooled by her light manner. She knew the full extent of the situation.

She was resident in Town again, she reminded herself. The first step back.

She raised the window to look out. Not swathes of green, empty but for animals, but only a small walled garden, and beyond, house roofs and church spires, implying people of all kinds, people from all around the world. This was a rich and fascinating world, and it was hers.

She sat to write a note to Babs to announce her arrival. Within half an hour, Babs was hugging her and blessedly acting as if nothing was amiss.

"How splendid this is. With Harringay flitting from club to coffeehouse to residence stitching together agreements, I'm sadly neglected. And I met Dracy below. You're sharing a roof. How delicious. It will lend credence to the match."

"It's only pretense," Georgia reminded her. "Tea, please, Jane."

"Then do let me help you amuse him. He's very toothsome."

"He's a scarred ex–naval officer, more accustomed to warfare than drawing rooms."

"Which probably explains the toothsomeness. He sends shivers down my spine. And through other places."

"Babs!" Georgia exclaimed, cheeks hot. "Does Harringay know?"

Babs smiled, showing her dimples. "Harringay knows me. Having a dashing man as escort puts him on his mettle, which is completely delightful."

"Babs!"

"Dear Georgia, in some ways, you're such an innocent! If you ever need advice, come to me."

"That book you had was bad enough."

"Positively wicked!" Babs agreed. "Harringay and I enjoyed exploring the possibilities."

As the book had contained illustrations of couples doing extraordinary, seemingly impossible, things, Georgia blushed even more.

"Oh, I'm sorry," Babs said, becoming completely sober. "I can only imagine how painful it must be for a widow to speak of such things. I'll talk scandal instead. Did you hear that Mistress Benham has run off with her footman? Oh dear. You won't want to talk scandal either."

"It's not my favorite subject, no, but if the lady has truly done that, it's a different case than mine."

"She certainly has. Benham's a brute, of course, but one wonders how she'll survive. Perhaps poverty is tolerable in the company of the beloved."

"I doubt poverty is ever tolerable," Georgia said. "Given that, can love last?"

Jane returned and set down a tea tray. Georgia thanked her and sent her away before Babs said something else outrageous.

But Babs took a cake and asked, "What's happened to Eloisa Cardross?"

Georgia told her.

"She should have been made to confess in public!"

"To what?" Georgia asked. "She would claim only to have spoken of something that appalled her, and anything she said now would only extend the interest in the letter."

"True, alas. And to think that someone forged it. It was like loading a pistol and putting it in her hands, not caring whom she shot."

"Except that the only possible target was me."

"I don't know how you can be so calm about it."

"I have no *choice*, Babs. I can only carry on as if nothing is the matter and hope it becomes true."

Babs looked doubtful, but said, "Well, then, have you heard about the masquerade?"

"A masquerade?" Georgia said, grateful for a change of subject. "Vauxhall or Ranelagh?

"Carlisle House. Madame Cornelys is engaged by the Whigs to host a grand masquerade on the theme of peace, prosperity, and patriotism."

"I heard nothing of this."

"It's a suddenly hatched plan."

"When is it to be?"

"Three nights from now."

"So soon!" Georgia was panicked by the lack of time to prepare, but then she saw another problem. "Should I go?"

"Of course! What point to being in Town if you skulk here?"

"Lady May never skulks. Jane! Oh, I sent her away. We must begin immediately to design a costume. Three days! It can't be done."

"Yes, it can. And Lady May's costumes have always outshone others."

Thus stirring envy and hatred. Georgia gulped some tea, wondering if this time she should wear something conventional. "What will you wear, Babs?"

"Nell Gwyn again. I love that part."

"How is that connected to peace, prosperity, and patriotism?"

Babs winked. "She was cheerful and generous and served the king right mightily."

Georgia laughed. "That'll pass muster."

"So what will you be?"

"Perhaps a goddess of peace."

"*Not* the goddess costume," Babs said, actually looking alarmed.

"Of course not. Do you think I'm mad? I was thinking of normal, classical robes, both concealing and conventional. Who was the goddess of peace?"

"I'm not sure there was one."

"That probably explains the whole of human history."

"Perhaps you should avoid goddesses," Babs said. "What about Britannia?"

"Wasn't she modeled on one of King Charles's other mistresses? Too racy a connotation."

"You could go as a saint."

"People would say I'm a papist."

"Good Queen Bess?"

"The virgin queen? A protest too far, I fear, and I'm sure there'll be a dozen of them. The men will have the easier part. Most of them will resurrect the togas and robes they keep for the Olympian Revels."

Babs grinned. "I wonder if Ithorne will repeat his per-

formance as a lowly shepherd. Very fine legs. You could
cover yourself in sheepskin and go as one of his lambs.
That's a symbol of peace."

"Oh, Babs, you tempt me."

"Remember that he's married now."

"I do, and . . . Ah!"

"You have a costume idea?" Babs asked. "What?"

"A secret." Georgia grinned. "A million apologies,
Babs, but I must shoo you away, summon Jane, and go to
my mantua maker immediately. There's not a moment to
lose!"

"Why can't I come?" Babs protested.

"Because my costume will be a secret!" But Georgia
hugged her. "A Cornelys masquerade on the theme of
peace. I feel sure that is a good omen."

Dracy went to his room and made himself settle to some
legal papers he needed to review. Ceddie had not only
drained the estate but left the administration in a tangle.
Because he'd loved Town, he'd transferred all the estate
business to a London firm, and Dracy was in the process
of moving it back to Devon. He was going over everything in case he had questions to put to Lacombe, Bray,
and Pugh, because he wouldn't trust any of them further
than he could throw an anchor.

He expected word from Georgia about their activities
for the day, but when an hour had passed he went down
and asked the footman in the hall.

"Lady Maybury has left the house?"

"Yes, your lordship. In haste." That alarmed, until the
man added, "She wished you to know that she has an
appointment with her mantua maker and would return
for dinner."

Her mantua maker. Why should he be surprised?
Lady May returned to Town and her first thought was of
new clothes. He had to accept who she was instead of

constructing an imaginary woman who'd settle cozily in Dracy Manor.

He thanked the footman, tempted to linger in the hope that she'd soon return. Instead, he'd pursue his quest to set his scandalous countess free to wed a duke.

He returned to his room for his gloves and hat, considering his course for the day.

He'd already sent a note to Sir Harry Shaldon and heard back that the man was out of Town. He'd have to find another person who might know Vance's handwriting, but without help he'd be poking around blindly. He also needed to find a forger, but again, he had no knowledge of such matters, and a criminal wouldn't be easily unearthed. He was beginning to think his offer to vindicate Georgia rang hollow.

For the moment, the best he could do was glean, and the snatch of gossip at the chophouse made him think much might be learned that way. The favorite gathering places for gentlemen in London were the coffeehouses. They all had their particular clientele, and much business was done there. Last week he'd attended an auction of goods from India at Jonathan's Coffeehouse in Covent Garden, simply out of curiosity.

He had no need of a mercantile or scholarly coffeehouse, however. He needed one where the idle gentlemen of the beau monde sipped and gossiped. He knew a few of those.

As he returned downstairs, the footman was opening the door to a gentleman elegantly dressed in olive green, with a striped waistcoat, clocked stockings, and high-heeled shoes.

Lord Sellerby, in his natural plumage.

"Lord Sellerby for Lady Maybury," he said and stepped inside.

The footman allowed him so far but placed himself in the way of progress. "Her ladyship is not at home, milord."

Sellerby's eyes narrowed as if he'd question that, but then he saw Dracy. "My lord!" he said and bowed, but if looks were daggers, as the old saying went, Dracy would at the least be bleeding. He must have heard of the possible betrothal.

"My lord!" Dracy echoed, crossing the hall and trying to hide an unwarranted sense of victory. "A pleasure to see you again."

"You are leaving?" Sellerby said. "May I walk with you a while?"

Dracy would rather go straight to his task, but there was no polite way to refuse, and perhaps the man deserved an opportunity to vent his bile. Better on his head than Georgia's. They set off down the street, Dracy having to moderate his stride to Sellerby's.

"You are enjoying your dalliance in Town, sir?" Sellerby asked.

"Well enough, Sellerby, though I'm unable to dally all the day. My estate makes demands on me."

"And soon will drag you back to Devon, I have no doubt. I'm sure you find this milieu mere froth after a life on board ship."

"Only in parts," Dracy said, wondering where this meandered. "Riots are distressingly solid, and the streets are hazardous at times."

"They are indeed, sir. They deprived me of my valet last year. Sent the poor fellow out on an errand—a mere few streets—and he was discovered a corpse, struck over the head."

"Shocking, and you have my condolences."

"Indeed, he was a superlative valet."

Dracy assessed Lord Sellerby as one who saw nothing but his own interest. No matter, except that he wanted Georgia.

"I heard the most amusing rumor last night," Sellerby said.

"Yes?" Dracy asked, plotting a course to detach himself from his shallow companion.

"I heard—but you will be so diverted, sir!—I heard you were to wed Georgia Maybury. Of course I immediately disabused all."

"How extraordinarily kind, sir," Dracy said, "but perhaps unnecessary."

"Of course, of course. As I said, most amusing."

"Or perhaps based on truth? After all, I am a guest in Hernescroft House."

Sellerby halted to look at him. "You are residing there?"

"In the circumstances it seemed suitable."

"My dear Dracy!" Sellerby recovered and strolled on. "You are new to Town, sir, and even new to England in a sense. You can't be faulted for a poor understanding of the beau monde."

"So kind of you, sir," Dracy said, fascinated.

"In particular, you may not be familiar with the ways of ladies such as Lady Maybury, the navy being a manly world."

"There were times ashore," Dracy suggested.

"But not, I'm sure, in the highest circles."

Dracy didn't correct him.

"You may not understand, therefore, when a lady is being playful."

"You refer to Lady Maybury in particular?"

"The most playful of them all, sir. If she has paid you some attentions, even flirted a little . . ."

"Even kissed me in the gardens at Thretford House?"

Sellerby halted again, and his hand tensed on his gold-topped cane. Dracy planned the best reaction to a blow, keeping in mind that it could be a swordstick.

However, Sellerby relaxed into a smile. "Playfulness, sir, as I said. That gives even more point of my warning."

"I might find such playfulness enchanting."

"Quite so, but it would be an error to take it seriously."

Enough was enough. This madman needed to be sunk before he distressed Georgia.

"Is the Earl of Hernescroft being playful when he discusses a union with me? Or the countess merely diverting herself by inviting me to lodge at Hernescroft House?"

Dracy could see Sellerby long to hurl an accusation of lying in his face.

Of course he didn't. That might provoke a duel, and a man like Lord Sellerby would hide under a table at the hint of violence.

"My dear Dracy, I fear the whole family plays with you, though why, I cannot imagine. Have you done them harm? Ah, the horse race!" Sellerby chuckled. "Hernescroft was not best pleased by his defeat. My dear sir, only think. What possible connection can there be between you and Lady Maybury, especially after only two encounters? Whereas I have been her friend and often welcome companion for years. We share all interests and tastes."

"It does seem unfair, doesn't it?"

"Incredible, let us say. Am I in error in thinking you inherited a ruined estate and have no other means?"

"No, that's about the sum of it."

"Do you have any idea how much Georgia Maybury spends on a single gown?"

"As she has enough to last years, it won't matter."

"*Won't matter!* By Olympus, she never wears a grand gown twice!"

Sellerby was hitting too close to the bone for comfort, but Dracy wouldn't show it.

"I gather the gown she wore to her sister's ball wasn't new."

"She has just emerged from mourning and will need time to design and commission new wonders."

"She designs them herself? Then she's much to be admired."

Sellerby waved a dismissive hand. "For the most part it's her maid's work, and the maid's sister, Mistress Gifford, but Lady Maybury has perfect taste."

"I agree with you," Dracy said, thinking of a kiss.

"She won't marry you," Sellerby stated impatiently. "I merely seek to spare you embarrassment."

"So kind, sir. May I spare you in turn? Once free of scandal, I predict she'll marry Beaufort."

He expected that obvious truth to stagger Sellerby, but the man smiled slightly. "Will she ever be free of scandal, however? I would wash her clean in an instant if I could, Dracy, but some of the stain has gone too deep. Her true friends will stand by her, but I don't count Beaufort among them."

"Then there'll be other suitors."

"Willing to overlook all? No, no, she will, in due course, marry me."

Such overweening confidence. But then Dracy saw something else.

A sneer?

No, a touch of amusement.

By all that was holy, could Sellerby have decided to set some stains deeply in order to remove the competition? By means of a letter, revealed at the Thretford ball? A wild idea, especially when Sellerby had worked hard to weaken the scandal by trying to sway the dowager Lady Maybury in Georgia's favor.

"You give me food for thought, Sellerby; indeed you do. I thank you, but I must now be on my way."

Sellerby bowed. "A delightful interlude, Dracy."

Dracy bowed back. "Positively illuminating, Sellerby."

He walked briskly away, not caring about direction, sifting through his thoughts.

Sellerby had stood as Georgia's friend in the matter of the dowager, but that might have fixed the idea of an incriminating letter in his mind. If it had actually existed then, and Dracy wasn't sure how, Sellerby might even have managed to steal it. Purely to protect Georgia, he was sure. However, when he saw Georgia beginning to triumph over scandal, and thus being courted by the likes of Beaufort, he'd had a weapon.

It was damned hard to believe. Sellerby, for all his foppishness, wanted to marry Georgia. He'd never want to fix the stains of scandal on his wife.

And yet, and yet . . . there had been something in his manner, and he was so damnably confident, despite Georgia's attempts to warn him off.

Dracy realized something else. If his speculation was true, then Sellerby must have taken the letter to the ball in case of need. It would have been a cold-blooded, calculated plan. In that case, the man might try again, heaping scandal upon scandal until only he remained willing to marry her. It would be an insanely destructive course, but Dracy had known men driven beyond reason by passion for a woman.

If any of this was true, Sellerby didn't truly love Georgia—he only burned to possess her. What was more, he didn't know her. She'd beg for bread in the streets before marrying any man out of desperation. Dracy might not have spent a great deal of time with her, but he knew that.

He realized his footsteps were taking him back to Hernescroft House, where he could warn Georgia. She probably wasn't there, however, and he shouldn't distress her with such half-baked suspicions. He'd think on it. Even if Sellerby was so vile, he wouldn't strike again yet.

The better way to serve her was to clear her name, and he revised his plan. He didn't need coffeehouse gossip. He needed men who'd known Sir Charnley Vance and who might know where he was, or at least illuminate his character. That meant a haunt of sporting gentlemen. He turned his steps toward the White-Faced Nag tavern.

# Chapter 19

He'd visited the Nag a number of times because it was popular with racing men and so he'd generally find an acquaintance. Today he spotted Lord Yately, a spare man in his thirties who owned a few thoroughbreds for amusement, and Sir George Mann, a swarthy Welshman of the same stamp. Sir Brock Billerton of the massive belly was interested only in the gambling aspect. He hailed Dracy warmly. He'd been one of the few to have bet on Cartagena, so he'd won a splendid amount and considered Dracy a friend.

Dracy called for ale and joined their table. He was introduced to two other men, one of whom had the brash honesty to ask the cause of his scars. Having explained and endured the usual praise of his bravery, he settled to mostly listening, curious as to whether any of these men had heard of the new scandal.

It wasn't mentioned, nor was the supposed betrothal. No surprise there, for these men spun in a different orbit, and there were as many of those in London as there were planets and stars. The conversation was all about racing and horses, but then a newcomer brought Georgia's name.

"Lady May's back!" Jimmy Cricklade announced as he joined them. "Saw her alight from her chair not more than two hours since."

"Tallyho!" hooted Mann, making Dracy clench his fist.

"You'd have no chance with her," sneered Billerton "Likes a court beau the like of Sellerby."

"Wonder if she'll set up her court again," a young man asked with an eager eye.

The man next to him shoved him. "What would you want with dallying in a lady's boudoir telling her what pin to wear in her gown?"

Clearly the young man might want that sort of thing a great deal, but he had the sense to keep his mouth shut.

The men joked about Lady Maybury's court, and Dracy decided to risk raising Vance's name himself.

"Was Sir Charnley Vance part of her court?"

All the men laughed.

"Not one for boudoirs, Charnley Vance!" said Yately. "His fine ladies visited his lair, not he theirs."

"Fine ladies?" Dracy asked, surprised. What little he'd been able to learn about Vance didn't fit that picture.

"Any number of 'em," said Billerton. "For all their silks and airs, many a duchess—or a countess," he said with a wink, "likes a low adventure. And I heard Vance was particularly well-endowed."

"Gads yes," said Mann. "Saw him take out the snake once and wave it. I suppose some women like a monster."

He sneered and a murmur of disgust ran around the table, but Dracy knew that Vance's action had been a boast that touched men where it mattered.

Hung like a horse and women chasing him because of it, even fine ladies.

Not Georgia, he was sure, but he now saw why the story had been so easily believed. If ladies of the beau monde were known to have adventured with Vance, why not the flighty Lady Maybury?

That made his task even harder.

"Remember another like that," Yately said.

"Like what?" Billerton asked.

"Well hung. Friend of Vance's, as it happens. Man called Curry."

"Snakes of a feather hang together?" Cricklade said and laughed at his own joke. The rest only smiled at best. "Curry!" Cricklade said to recover. "Remember him. The Marquess of Rothgar did away with him in a duel, snake and all."

There was a flurry about the duel, and indeed, Dracy thought, it must have been an event of note when a man of Rothgar's status was engaged in a fatal meeting.

"I heard tell," said Mann, in a portentous manner, and then waited for attention, "that Curry might have been put up to it."

"Put up to it?" Yately asked.

"To kill the Dark Marquess. He has enemies enough."

"Then they chose the wrong means," Yately said. "Devil with a sword, Rothgar is. That Curry must have been a fool to attempt it."

"Money," Mann said. "That'd be it."

Dracy decided he'd heard enough about the distinctly unpleasant carryings-on in the so-called beau monde and took his leave, little the wiser in any way that was useful.

There were hours to go before dinner and he needed to find out more about the letter. He was carrying it in his pocket to keep it safe, so he took it out to refresh his memory about the address. Major Jellicoe, Fellcott's Coffeehouse. It was common enough for men to use such places to receive their correspondence, and Fellcott's would not be out of his way.

He went there weighing the wisdom of it, for he didn't want the letter to be real. However, as he'd said to Georgia, it was always better to know the truth.

He insisted on speaking to Fellcott himself, but neither the man nor his servants remembered a particular letter from six months ago, not even one from abroad.

"Major Jellicoe certainly used Fellcott's for his correspondence, my lord," the proprietor said, seeming eager to please.

"Do you remember the man?" Dracy asked.

"Oh, yes, sir. Remarkably well set with a booming voice. Generally well disposed, but not a man to cross, if you know what I mean."

"I heard that he was involved in a fatal duel a while back."

"That he was, sir, but only as a second. A nasty business. An earl dead, and Jellicoe's principal fled for fear of the noose. Jellicoe himself stood in some danger as accessory, but the jury at the inquest decided the duel had been managed as it should be."

"A sorry business, all the same," Dracy said, feeling like slapping himself in the head. Inquest! There had to be a record of that somewhere. "I thank you for your help, sir."

He left, feeling he might at last be on the trail of something solid. He had no idea where records of inquests were kept, so he returned to Hernescroft House to consult one of the earl's people.

When the footman on duty in the hall offered him a letter, his heart somersaulted with hope that it was from Georgia. It wasn't, but it was almost as welcome. Lady Hernescroft wrote that the family was to attend a musical evening at Lady Gannet's, and he was invited to join them. Family must include Georgia, so he'd spend some time with her today.

He had a footman take him to Hernescroft's Town secretary and asked Linley about reports of inquests.

"A particular inquest, my lord?" Linley asked.

Dracy had to admit it, though he'd probably seem idly curious. "The one into the death of the Earl of Maybury."

"We have a copy, my lord. I will have it sent to your room."

In minutes, Dracy had a bound, handwritten transcript of the inquest into the death of Richard, Earl of Maybury.

It began with the account of the duel itself, with depositions from those there. Lord Kellew had stood for Maybury, and Major Jellicoe for Vance. Sir Harry Shaldon had also been present, though it wasn't clear if he was attached to either man or a bystander.

The three accounts were consistent. There'd been no pistols involved, so the two men had fought with swords from the first. It had been agreed from the start that the seconds would not fight.

The bout had lasted some five minutes with no blood drawn, and in his testimony, Lord Kellew had reported his hope that the matter would end with no harm done. However, Vance had delivered the fatal thrust.

Dracy read over Kellew's exact words on that. "Vance thrust to the heart and then stepped back."

Stepped back. Accidents happened in sword fights, and some were fatal, but in such a case, wouldn't the culprit rush forward in remorse and attempt to help?

He read the other testimonies, but none mentioned that detail. The coroner, damn him, hadn't pressed for more detail of Vance's actions.

The next deposition was from the surgeon who'd pronounced Maybury dead of a sword thrust that had penetrated the heart. The coroner had then noted that Sir Charnley Vance was not present at the inquest and was reported to have left the country. If he were to return, he was obliged to present himself to give his account.

Then, right at the end, the coroner had asked the witnesses about Vance's words and actions. All three men agreed that he'd been calm throughout, and that after killing Maybury, he had paused only briefly before turning to mount his horse and ride away.

On paper it sounded cold-blooded, but Dracy knew that shock could affect people in odd ways. He remembered one man whose closest friend was killed at his side. He'd carried on as normal for hours before completely breaking down.

Perhaps Vance had turned pale and no one had mentioned it. Perhaps his step back had been of horror at seeing what he'd done. Perhaps he'd ridden away and collapsed only when he thought himself safe from observation.

Dracy read the report through again, but the words offered nothing new.

The jury had confirmed the obvious—that the Earl of Maybury had died from a sword thrust to the heart, delivered, in the course of a duel, by Sir Charnley Vance, who had then fled the country. The coroner repeated his hope that Sir Charnley would return and give an account of himself, and that was that.

It was almost the dinner hour, so Dracy tidied himself and returned the document to the secretary.

"Was there any attempt to prosecute Vance?" he asked.

"No, my lord. The due processes of dueling appear to have been followed, and with Vance out of the country there would have been no purpose. If he ever returns, measures might be taken. But not by the family."

No prosecution by the Perriam family because there must be no underlining of a connection between Vance and Georgia.

"I gather great efforts were made to locate Vance," he said.

"Yes, my lord. Particularly by the Honorable Peregrine Perriam."

The idle, Town-loving fop. Dracy had no opinion of any work he might have done.

He thanked Linley and went toward the front of the house, to the anteroom where the family and guests would gather before dinner. Georgia would soon be there, and the question rose again. Should he share his suspicion about Sellerby? She had long knowledge of the earl and could better judge the probability, but it went against the grain to accuse someone of such behavior without proof.

When he entered the room, she was already there, and his heart betrayed him with a thump.

She was talking to an elderly gentleman while her parents conversed with Lord Bathhurst and George Grenville. This was a political gathering, then, but perhaps also a way of presenting Georgia to a few people.

He studied her but saw no distress. When she noticed him she smiled, so he joined her to be introduced to Sir George Forster-Howe, a neighbor from Worcestershire and member of the Commons for a riding there.

"Navy, eh?" Sir George said. "Good man. A sorry wound, that."

"Could be worse," Dracy said, and the man nodded.

"True enough, true enough."

"Did your morning go well?" Dracy asked Georgia.

"Exceedingly so, but I do apologize for my neglect." She smiled at Sir George. "I promised to act as guide to Town for Lord Dracy but then abandoned him. I plead the Cornelys masquerade, however. So little time to assemble a costume."

"And what are you to be, Lady Maybury?"

"Now, now, Sir George. In the best tradition, it will be a secret. Do you attend?"

"Not me, my dear. Old age and masquerades are a poor match."

"Sir George, you're not old! I see the youth in your eyes."

He chuckled. "We all remain young at heart, Lady Maybury. Would that it spread to my joints."

Dracy wondered how much of her charm was effort and how much simply her natural kindness. In either case, perhaps she could conquer the beau monde, one person at a time.

She turned the charm on him. "What will you wear to the masquerade, Dracy?"

Dracy hadn't even known there was to be a masquerade, and he wasn't overly fond of such events, but he said, "In the best tradition, it will be a secret, Lady Maybury."

She chuckled and rapped him with her fan.

Dinner was announced, and she went in between him and Sir George and then sat between them at table. The dinner was informal, and the talk intensely political. It became clear that Sir George was to be encouraged—and perhaps charmed?—into supporting some measure to do with taxes. Dracy knew he should pay attention, but he was absorbed by the woman at his side.

She said little but was clearly following the discussions, and he suspected she could make some succinct remarks if she thought it appropriate. Lady Hernescroft was a full participant, even if she did occasionally cloak her own opinion as if agreeing with something said by the earl.

Clever women, both of them.

Lord Bathurst caught him unawares by asking his opinion on the reduction of the navy. It was an easy subject, however.

"I'd like to believe in eternal peace, my lord, but I'm too attached to facts. France will strike again, and there's trouble brewing in the American colonies. How is Britain to defend herself and her interests without an ample navy and the trained men to man the ships? We should be building, sir, not scrapping. And planting oaks for the future."

That set up a debate, which fortunately moved on to the colonies, on which he could be silent.

"Do you plant oaks at Dracy?" Georgia asked.

"Yes, and I'll plant many more, even though it will only benefit future generations."

Sir George's age hadn't affected his hearing. "Good man. Too much land wasted on fancy trees, that's what I say. Tulip trees, indeed. And drooping willows too weak to survive."

Dracy was happy to talk about trees and other agricultural matters, leaving Georgia to politics. Different worlds, but they did connect, as with oaks and the navy.

The meal over, the two ladies left, but the conversation at the table continued along political lines. Dracy excused himself. Georgia would be returning to the business of her costume, and he wanted to speak with her. He was only just in time, for she was already coming downstairs.

"Lady Maybury, may I have a moment of your time?"

"Hours of it, my lord, as soon as the masquerade is over. I do apologize, Dracy, but I'm driven by necessity, I assure you."

How could he insist without raising speculation, which in Georgia's case could too easily turn to scandal? She was in no danger at her mantua maker's, and there'd be opportunity to lay out his thoughts about Sellerby in the evening.

"I bow to necessity, ma'am, and look forward to this evening."

"As do I," she said with a smile and hurried away.

No point in cursing their separation. In fact, he needed to be busy too, and on the same matter. If Georgia was braving the world at a fashionable masquerade, he must be there to guard her.

He sought out Lady Hernescroft and asked her about the event.

"But of course you must attend, Dracy, to lend credence to our little device."

"Wearing what, ma'am?"

"Most of the gentlemen will wear variations on classical robes, so you may do the same. I'm sure we can supply something."

"Thank you, ma'am, but I believe I can find something myself."

Insane to feel he should try to match Lady May, who was apparently famous for her originality, including a damnably indiscreet goddess costume, but he did. A naval friend had encouraged him to look up a brother who was an actor at the King's Theatre, and this seemed just the moment. Edward Nugent was amenable and gave him access to such a vast collection of costumes that Dracy could only plead for help.

"A nautical theme," said Nugent and rummaged around. "Here you go, and here, and here. A mask? I know just the person. You'll need to use this glue for your facial decorations, which must be warmed. Don't worry; it rips off without taking too much skin."

Nugent packaged it all up but then insisted on Dracy going with him to a tavern for some ale. Dracy enjoyed himself too well and had to rush back to Hernescroft House to tidy himself for a beau monde musical evening.

He joined the company a little late and apologized.

"Enjoying the diversions of Town, Dracy?" Georgia asked, the minx.

"I admit, with good company it can be tolerable."

He was trying to decide why she looked different. Her yellow silk gown brought out all the warmth of her complexion and the glory of her hair. It was prettily embroidered with white flowers, and he noted the occasional clever touch of silver thread. Perhaps the difference was an effect of simplicity, even though the gown probably cost more than many people made in a year.

Her hair was gathered up in some magical way and set with small silk flowers. She wore pearls in her ears, at her throat, and on her right wrist. Pearls on her buckles? At the moment he could see only the toe of a white satin shoe.

Then he realized her hands were tight on her white silk fan.

"Do you have to attend this?" he asked quietly.

"I can't stay at home every night. It shouldn't be unpleasant. Lady Gannet is a cousin of mine, and the company will mostly be connections."

He should have realized that the Perriams would manage this first Town event with expertise.

"Will Lord Sellerby be there?" he asked.

"I shouldn't think so. Why?"

"I need to speak to you about him."

"Is he still spreading that absurd story? I would never have imagined that he could be so densely persistent. But he's my burden to bear, Dracy. Pray don't concern yourself with him."

The carriage was announced and he could say no more.

When he realized that Lady Gannet's house was only a street away, he thought the carriage ridiculous, but he supposed the ladies couldn't walk the evening streets in silks and jewels, especially not with the threat of disorder lurking in every shadow. What had Sellerby said? His valet attacked on a short mission.

They alighted to enter an elegant house where music already played, and went upstairs to a drawing room. This was no fashionable crush. The thirty or so guests could be comfortably seated in the ranked chairs.

He and the Perriams were greeted warmly by Lady Gannet and then by others. If anyone here thought Georgia a wicked harlot, they didn't show it. When everyone took their seats, Dracy realized opportunities for private moments were unlikely, especially if he didn't want to cause talk.

At least the music was excellent.

Three professionals performed—a slender flautist, a barrel-chested baritone, and a plump harpist. After the harpist had been applauded, the company all went down to the dining room to take supper at a long table while a trio played out of sight.

The conversation here was mostly of music and other arts, about which Dracy knew little, but he was willing to learn. He relaxed his vigilance over Georgia, for no one here wished her ill, but he couldn't help watching her.

Their supposed betrothal gave him some excuse. He realized that she was using charm and apparent ease with all the skillful intent of an admiral and that she was salting it with a touch of youthful innocence.

The gown! The aspect that had puzzled now came clear. The low bodice was topped by a frothing tumble of fine lace so that no part of her breasts showed. She'd doubtless had that detail whipped together today at her mantua maker's with this demure effect in mind.

Georgia Maybury was a mistress of her art.

She even had musical talent.

After supper, everyone returned to the drawing room, and now the guests entertained. Georgia performed third. Her musical skills weren't professional, but she played the keyboards well and sang a light ditty about a girl seeking a lost linnet and enjoying a flirtation with the youth who helped her. It suited her sweet voice and also augmented her illusion of youthful innocence.

She was only twenty, he reminded himself, and she was reminding everyone of the fact.

He, however, had another vision for his foolish fantasy—Georgia at Dracy, playing and singing like that for him alone. Or for a small gathering of neighbors. Or, in time, for their children.

Impossible, but it was as impossible for him to think it so.

He was more and more sure that his ideas about Sellerby were ridiculous, but as they took the short journey home he hoped for the opportunity to lay them before Georgia. She should be warned. However, she parted from him with no more than a smile and a "Good night," and went upstairs with her mother.

He was snared to take brandy with Lord Hernescroft. He went, expecting an awkward discussion of betrothals, but after a cursory "Betrothal business going well, is it?" it was all horses. Dracy escaped as soon as he could and went upstairs, dissatisfied by his day. He paused outside a door not his own. This was the door to Georgia's room, and he indulged for a moment in visions.

Was she still up, perhaps sitting at her dressing table as her maid brushed out her hair?

Or was she already in bed, tucked under the covers, sweetly, innocently asleep? He was falling under the illusion of her performance tonight, but he didn't find sweetness or innocence unsuitable.

The house was quiet.

The corridor was deserted.

It would be easy to go in, and he even had an excuse of sorts.

Would she scream?

No, she'd be too aware of the consequences of that. She'd be outraged, and with reason, but it still took fortitude to walk on and enter his own room.

He halted just inside the door.

Georgia Maybury was there, sitting in the armchair that faced the door, waiting for him.

# Chapter 20

She was more substantially covered than she had been at Lady Gannet's, but a high-necked nightgown covered by an encompassing robe of pale green was not dressed. Not at all.

He shut the door behind him. "Georgia?"

"Don't take any foolish notions, Dracy. You said you needed to speak to me."

"And you think this is the moment?"

"Are you angry? Then I'll leave." She rose, frowning at him. "I truly don't mean anything by this. Please don't leap to the wrong conclusion."

"Of course not," he said, struggling to find the right response, which wasn't easy when her light perfume had invaded with her. Though her presence was torment, he didn't want her to leave.

"Please, sit down again. I do have something important to say."

She did so, but this time perched and wary.

Sweetly innocent.

It was so easy to forget that Lady May was young and that her only real experience of the world was as a cherished wife.

"About Sellerby?" she prompted.

"Yes. He called on you this morning."

"I was told."

"I was just leaving, so we walked a ways together. He hasn't taken your words to heart, and he hasn't given up hope. He finds our supposed betrothal incredible."

"With reason," she said, clearly not meaning it to be a blow.

"He claims your rejection was part of a game, a game you and he have played for years."

"Oh, the deuce. He is impossible."

"I agree, but you encouraged him, didn't you?"

"Not in this," she protested. "Before . . . before Maybury died, he had to have known that any flirtation was a game. He would profess his devotion too strongly and I would scold him. He would offer too rich a gift and I'd scold him again. He would then offer a suitable one, and I would accept. A game, yes, but not one that could lead to marriage. I was devoted to my husband and Sellerby knew it. I tried to find him a bride any number of times, but he never pursued any of them."

"Because he was in love with you."

"But I was married."

"Love isn't ruled by good sense."

She shrugged, and he wondered if she'd ever known true love. She probably had been devoted to her husband, but had she loved him?

"Did the game continue after your husband's death?"

"Of course not. How can you think such a thing?"

"My apologies. I merely wonder why he appeared at Herne, in full devotion after a year of separation."

"I assure you it was a year of separation," she said. "But we did correspond in the latter months. He attempted a correspondence from the first, but I'd have none of that, not from any gentleman. In December, however, there was the issue of the dowager and the letter and I learned that he'd gone to great efforts to try to make her see sense. I wrote to thank him and fell into a correspondence. I confess, I did enjoy hearing a little of

Town amusements. There was nothing in my replies to encourage him to think it a courtship."

"Still less a favored one, but it can be easy to shape matters to suit oneself."

She spread her hands. "All I can do now is avoid him when possible and make the situation clear when we meet. Thank you for warning me that he might persist."

She rose, but he said, "Why don't you consider him as a husband? He's wealthy, he's an earl, and he shares your interests."

She furrowed her brow. "I don't know. I like him, or I used to, but I don't *feel* anything for him. I feel for him as I do for my brothers."

"You said the same about me," he pointed out.

She flushed. "And you must be as a brother to me."

She walked to the door and he went ahead to make sure the corridor was deserted. "All's clear."

She hesitated, looking at him, inches apart.

Dracy suppressed a smile.

She might speak of brothers, but Lady May wanted a kiss. She didn't admit it, perhaps even to herself, but that want could be the main reason she'd come to his room.

"Good night," he said.

A betraying frown flickered, but then she hurried over to her own room.

He realized that her presence had so befuddled him that he hadn't told her of his suspicions.

Georgia entered her room and leaned back against the door, heart racing, legs unsteady. Why, oh why, hadn't he kissed her? She hadn't known until that moment how desperately she wanted to reexperience the passion of his kiss.

He was being honorable, of course, especially when she couldn't have made it plainer that they could never wed.

A brother, indeed! She didn't feel about Lord Dracy as she did about even her favorite brother—but that changed nothing, and she should never have gone to his room like that.

She tossed aside her robe and climbed into bed, but as she extinguished her candle and slid under the covers, she thought again of that moment, and the kiss that hadn't happened, squeezing back tears. Why did everything conspire to make her unhappy?

She didn't sleep well and rose feeling heavy-headed.

"You stay home today, milady," Jane said. "There's no need for you to be at Mary's all the time."

"There are constant adjustments to be made."

"Then go along later, milady. Rest this morning."

Georgia took a leisurely breakfast but couldn't imagine sitting at home for hours. Then she realized what she wanted to do.

She quickly wrote a note.

"Jane, take this to Lord Dracy. I owe him some time as a Town guide."

But Jane returned to say that he'd left. "Summoned to the Admiralty, milady, by an important-looking letter."

"Heavens, he can't be ordered back to sea, can he?"

"I don't know, milady, but it's unlikely, isn't it? We're not at war as best I know."

"Of course," Georgia said, but was disturbed by the flat panic she'd felt for a moment. At sea or in Devon, he would soon be out of her orbit, and infuriatingly, he wasn't available for a tour around the Town.

"Oh well, I'll write letters for a while, and then we'll visit some shops until dinnertime. After dinner, I'll visit Mary's to be sure all's well."

She wrote to Lizzie, to Clara Allworthy in Wiltshire, and to Anna Long in Ireland. Repeating the same news was tedious, however, especially when she left out a great deal in her letters to Clara and Anna. The shops didn't prove as amusing as they should, and when she realized she was being avoided by some ladies, she retreated back home to safety.

Oh, but she hated this, and hated the people who'd brought it about. Her situation wouldn't be nearly as bad without that wicked letter. Eloisa Cardross and who? Who hated her so? When Dracy didn't appear for dinner, she could almost have cried.

"Dining at the Admiralty, I assume," she said, striving for indifference. "What they can want of him, I can't imagine."

"Have sense, child," her mother said. "He's now a lord. A mere baron, but that gives him a seat in the House. They'll want to ensure that he casts his vote in favor of the navy."

Georgia supposed that was true, but she knew he'd cast it the way he thought right, not to order.

They were eight to dine today, including two wives who were so meticulously polite that it was an insult. Georgia coped in the only way she could, by being calm and unaffected, but gave thanks when the event was over and all the guests had left.

She was leaving the drawing room when her mother said, "We are invited to an exhibition at the Danish embassy tonight. Do you wish to come?"

Georgia knew she should. Should again present a sweet, innocent appearance and charm people back into their wits, but she couldn't face it. "I've felt out of sorts all day, Mother. I'll go early to bed."

When she returned from Mary Gifford's Georgia played cards with Jane for a while and then did prepare for bed early. She dismissed Jane but couldn't settle. She tried to read but too often went to the window to peer out, hoping to see a carriage approaching, carrying Dracy home.

It was both foolish and wicked, and tonight she had no excuse to visit his room, but temptation danced through her. She could come up with an excuse.

Where on earth was he? It was gone eight o'clock. Admiralty business couldn't last so late. For a man who didn't care for Town, he seemed able to enjoy it very well.

She sat to read a new book of poetry, forbidding herself from going to the window. The verses were quite good, and when she heard something out in the street, the clock said almost ten.

She hurried to the window but saw only three gentlemen walking away. Perhaps they'd simply been walking past, but had she heard a knock at the door?

She pulled her wrap around her and crept into the corridor, listening.

Voices in the hall.

As she went to the top of the stairs, the voices became clearer. Dracy's and probably a footman's.

"I was attacked in the street," Dracy said. "Thieves. Any chance of bandages?"

Georgia ran down the stairs. "Bandages! What's happened?"

Dracy stared up at her, and she remembered how she was dressed, but she couldn't retreat, not when his buff waistcoat was stained with blood. She ran up to him. "What's happened to you?"

"Footpads. I'm all right."

"Not if you need bandages. You're covered with blood!"

"Not covered . . ."

There was a slur to his voice.

"Dracy, are you *drunk*?"

"Guilty as charged, ma'am."

She rolled her eyes, but she'd dealt with Dickon in a similar state. "Come, I'll assist you to your room. Get washing water," she ordered the footman, "and something that will make bandages. Come along."

"And brandy," Dracy added.

"You don't need more drink," she said, trying to put her arm around him.

He fended her off. "You don't want blood on your

gown . . . or whatever that thing you're wearing is. I'm steady on my feet."

"More or less," she muttered, as he made his way carefully up the stairs. He couldn't be seriously wounded, however, and her heart rate began to settle.

He paused at the top to get his balance on the newel post. "Where're your parents?"

"Mother went to the Danish ambassador's house, and Father was to join her there. I chose a quiet evening."

"Scared?"

"Not at all."

"You're a bad liar, Georgia."

"And you are stupid with drink. Come along."

Again he fended her off and made his way to his room. He turned the knob and went in.

When she followed, he said, "Don't."

"Don't what?"

"Come in. I might ravish you."

Her heart thumped. "You're wounded!"

"The one doesn't preclude the other. Though my arm might make it tricky." He sat on the bed, cradling it. "If I attack you, sweet Circe, hit my left arm."

Georgia stared at him but knew he was serious. Drink had loosened his restraints and he wanted to ravish her. She was both thrilled and terrified.

"What's wrong with your arm?" she asked from the safety of the door.

"Cudgel."

"Is it broken?"

"No."

"Can you be sure?"

He flexed it, so he was probably correct, even though he winced.

"What happened to your side?"

"Knife."

"You could have been killed!" She stepped forward, but at that moment the footman entered bearing hot water, followed by Jane bearing bandages and giving Georgia a ferocious frown.

"He needed help," Georgia protested.

"He has it now. Let Jem tend to him, milady."

"He's drunk."

"All the more reason to let Jem tend to him, milady."

"Good idea," Dracy said and waved his right arm grandly. "Ladies, leave the ship! There are likely to be sights unsuitable."

Georgia giggled. "Very well, but I'm returning to make sure you'll survive the night."

As soon as the door shut, Jane said, "Don't you be so foolish, milady."

"It's my duty."

"Then come and get decently dressed."

"Jane, cease your fussing. I'm covered neck to toes, and to reassemble myself in stays and petticoats would be ridiculous. In any case, he's too hurt to molest me."

Jane muttered, but Georgia shooed her off to bed and hoped she went.

For her part, she couldn't wait to return and make sure Dracy was all right.

Drunk! She covered her mouth on another chuckle. He always seemed so neatly put together that it was delightful to see him loosened by drink.

But he'd been attacked!

She crossed the corridor and opened his door just a crack. "Dracy, do you need a doctor?"

"No, thank you. Go away, Lady Maybury."

She closed the door and returned to her room. Was he being rational? Men often overestimated their health. She heard footsteps in the hall and looked out to see the housekeeper, Mistress Crombie, march into his room.

"My own salve, milord, efficacious against bruising."

"I thank you, ma'am. Any possibility of coffee?"

"Of course, milord, but if I may offer a word of advice. It's unwise to walk the night streets of London alone."

"I'd certainly have been better alone than with that linkboy," Dracy said. "Are they often in league with thieves, ma'am?"

"I suppose that can happen, milord, but most men know where they're going."

"A profound observation, ma'am."

Mistress Crombie left him then and closed the door.

Georgia paced her room. Linkboy? In league with thieves? He truly could have been killed! When his coffee arrived she'd be able to visit him and hear the full story.

She heard the footsteps and the opening of the door.

"Pour me a cup, Jem, and then you can go."

Soon two footmen left the room, closed the door, and walked away, gossiping quietly about the wicked state of the streets.

Georgia gathered her nerve and slipped into Dracy's room.

"How are you?" she said, but then stopped. She hadn't thought that he too might have changed into his nightwear and be a lot less clothed than he normally was.

He was sitting propped up on the bed, coffee in hand, in his nightshirt. Not even a robe. His lower legs were very hairy, his feet rather noble and strong.

He was watching her, inscrutable.

She would not be maidenly. She hurried to the bed. "Are you all right?"

He toasted her with his coffee. "Enchanted unto madness by you, Circe."

"Still silly with drink, I see. Where were you to become so addled?"

"Easy enough to achieve all around the Town."

"Unfortunately true. How are your wounds?"

"Minor."

"Your side?"

"A mere scratch."

"Your arm?"

"Hurts."

She sat on the edge of the bed. "Are you sure you don't need a doctor?"

"Yes. Could you put my cup on the table?"

She did so but returned to her perch, finding him adorably boyish in drink. "This will confirm your low opinion of London, I fear."

"It certainly hasn't improved it, but . . ."

"But?"

"I know better than to blindly follow a linkboy, so it was my own fault."

"How many attacked you?"

"Three."

"Three against one? How did you escape?"

"My sword kept them at bay, but I called for help and some gentlemen ran to my aid. If the cudgel had hit true . . ."

"Cudgel! Dracy . . ."

"A glancing blow. No real harm done."

"But . . ." She moved to feel his head, but he fended her off.

"Georgia, behave yourself. You shouldn't even be here."

She considered him. "Perhaps not, but I'm a widow, not an innocent miss, and you're a guest in this house and injured."

It sounded very well, but she wasn't surprised that he looked skeptical.

"And," she added, "I'm insatiably curious. Tell me all about it."

He shook his head at her, but he was smiling too. "On your head be it. If we're caught . . ."

"It will be by my parents, who will scold us both but invoke secrecy. What happened? Start from the beginning. I was told you'd been summoned to the Admiralty."

"I was, and there I met some old, landlocked friends who carried me off to dinner. After dinner we went to a tavern to talk of old times, and eventually we rolled on to another establishment."

"What establishment?" she asked.

"You wouldn't know it."

"I *thought* you meant one of those establishments. Which one?"

"You're incorrigible. Mirabelle's."

"My husband said it was an excellent place."

He glared at her. "It's a brothel."

"Among other things. Maybury liked to game there whilst watching the living statues."

"Do you know how little those living statues wear?"

His outrage made her want to laugh. What a strange model of her he carried in his mind. "Nothing but a veil, but often a very pretty veil."

"You've *been* there?"

"Of course not, but we had something similar for an entertainment at Sansouci. Male as well as female."

"That's not decent!"

She had to laugh then, just a little. "The men wore a kind of codpiece. But if it's decent to have naked statues around a house, why not the same thing in the flesh, with veils?"

"It's different and you know it."

"Don't be provincial."

"You're too young for such things."

She smiled out of pure fondness and leaned forward to kiss his cheek. "Dear, sweet Dracy."

He grabbed her hair and forced her lips to his.

Georgia pushed back in shock, but she'd been wanting another kiss like the one at Thretford.

This wasn't like the one at Thretford. He was kissing her with passion and possessive skill, as if her mouth was his to explore without restraint. A forbidden kiss, but she cradled his head and kissed him back, shifting to an ever-more comfortable position, silk slithering and rucking up all around her. *Mind his arm. But get closer, tighter . . . ah, yes, delightful, delicious.*

The taste of him was so familiar, as if they'd kissed a thousand times through the ages and sustained each other for eons. The smell of his body, the feel of his hair, of the bones beneath, the entire shape of him was simply him and always had been.

He stilled and then gently moved her away. "Enough, enough. You must leave now, Georgia."

He was right, but she didn't.

"That was a splendid kiss." And not enough.

"I don't deny it," he said, squeezing a hand on her hip.

Georgia realized that she was straddling him! And a hard ridge lay between her thighs. It moved, sending a hot ache through her innards, stealing her breath.

So easy. So easy. Simply shift some clothing and move a little that way. . . .

She stared at him and he stared back, eyes dark, reflecting her hungers. Magnifying them.

She wanted him. Wanted to join with him here as she'd never wanted such a joining before. If only she'd felt like this with Dickon, how glorious it . . .

At that thought, she scrambled off him, off the bed, pushing down her clothing, backing away, feeling on the brink of adultery.

"Wise enchantress," he said, smiling his crooked smile.

His cock was visible under his nightshirt, still summoning her to the feast.

The words escaped. "I wish I could."

He closed his eyes, laughing softly. "Devastating honesty. It must be difficult to be a widow, having enjoyed bed."

She shouldn't speak the words, but there was something about this moment that demanded honesty. "I didn't," she said. "Enjoy it."

He opened his eyes. "Are you saying you're a virgin?"

"No! No. I just didn't enjoy it. I shouldn't be saying these things."

"No, but . . . I'm sorry that you were deprived of pleasure. That's something to try to ensure with your next husband."

"How do I do that, sir, without ruining myself?"

"You're here and unruined."

"I'm not likely to sleep so close to a suitable man," she pointed out.

"The unsuitable man craves your pardon."

She put hands to her hot cheeks. "Oh, don't! I'm sorry. I didn't mean . . . But you *know* it would never work!"

"I know one way it would work."

She did too, and still ached with the need to prove it.

"You're not unique," she reminded him.

"We're all unique, but you're correct. Many men have the ability to pleasure you, but many don't, and some won't."

"I know. But . . ."

"You're not thinking of it, are you?"

"What?"

"Trying out men."

"Of course not!"

"'Struth, you're a poor liar. You mustn't do that, Georgia."

"Don't 'must' me!" she snapped and turned to pace away from the bed. "No one understands. . . ."

"No one? You discuss this all around London?"

She whirled on him. "Of course not. Only Lizzie—Lady Torrismonde. And it's not what you think." She spread her hands. "I would hate to disappoint, you see."

"Disappoint? I promise you, Georgia, that's not possible."

"You can't be sure. No one can until it's too late. Oh!" She ran to the window. "My parents are back. I'll go down to tell them about the attack on you."

She ran out, fleeing discovery, but also temptation accompanied by an aching sense of might-have-been. All the time they'd been talking she'd been fighting a pull back to the bed, a pull so strong that he might as well have been drawing on a rope.

If her parents hadn't returned, she might have succumbed, might have tried out a man in completely the wrong way.

Dracy lay back against the pillow, fighting to calm his body. He wasn't sure if he'd been most tormented by the vision in white linen and green silk, by the caring conversation, or by her enthusiastically inexperienced kiss.

A sin against all that was holy that such a woman had been shackled to an uncaring dolt. Or perhaps he should pity Dickon Maybury a little. Married young, and raised by an overprotective mother, the earl had certainly not had the benefit of the education he'd enjoyed around the world.

He heard footsteps and got himself under the covers.

Lady Hernescroft came in, also swathed in green—a dark green cloak over a fine dress of deep gold, emeralds glittering on an overexposed bosom. The contrast was almost amusing.

"A shocking thing, Dracy. You have all the care you need?"

"Yes, thank you, ma'am."

"A lesson to you not to wander the night streets alone."

He was growing weary of that advice, but it was inarguable.

"I will station a footman outside your door," she said. "If you require anything in the night, you need only call."

"That's not necessary—"

"You are my guest, Dracy."

She swept out and her husband entered. "Scandalous," Hernescroft said, perhaps a little unsteady with drink himself. "Any chance of catching the caitiffs?"

"None, I'd think. Common thieves."

Hernescroft nodded. "Wish we could round up the lot of 'em and sweep 'em into the sea. My wife's right, Dracy. Don't wander the night streets alone."

Dracy was finally left in peace, and he savored it, in an empty-headed sort of way. He was drifting off to sleep when he remembered something.

He climbed out of the bed, still having to favor his arm. He checked his side but saw no sign of blood. He opened the door.

A footman sat in the corridor. At least they'd provided him with a chair.

The young man shot to his feet. "You require something, your lordship?"

Probably the task had gone to the most junior, and he looked as if he'd been hauled out of bed for it.

"Yes. Come inside."

The footman did.

"Is there a truckle bed beneath this one?"

The footman bent down to look. "Yes, sir."

"Pull it out and use it."

"Sir?"

He was probably about seventeen and terrified of making a mistake.

"You're instructed to be alert for my needs, yes?"

"Yes, your lordship."

"I prefer you to be closer than the corridor. I might turn weak and unable to bellow. Close the door, pull out the truckle, and at the least spend your vigil lying down. I won't take offense if you nod off, as I'm sure you'll awake if I fall into a fit, start choking, or run around naked and witless."

The lad's lips twitched, but he managed to control it. "As you say, your lordship."

Dracy nodded, extinguished the candle, and arranged himself carefully in bed with the least discomfort.

*Don't walk the night streets of London alone.*

He wouldn't forget that, but he intended to spend as little time as possible in the foul place. Only Georgia and her cause kept him here.

But could he bear to leave if she didn't accompany him?

# Chapter 21

Georgia was wakened out of a deep sleep by Jane with her morning chocolate and a letter. "Said to be urgent, milady."

Georgia grabbed it. Was it from Dracy, saying he was shaking the dust of London from his shoes after the attack last night? She broke the seal and unfolded it.

Alas, no. It was from Portia Malloren. Georgia had completely forgotten her excuse for moving into Town. She scanned it quickly.

"Oh, my. There's some problem with the water supply at Danae House, and Portia is about to leave Town. I must go. A simple dress, Jane. A water problem sounds messy."

"As if you'd have to muck around in it, milady. And you need to have a final fitting for your costume. The masquerade is tonight."

Georgia put a hand to her head. "There's time for both. Hurry, Jane, one of my Herne dresses. We brought at least one, didn't we?"

"Those dull things?"

Georgia hesitated, for she might be seen. "One of those dull things," she asserted.

She sat to write a reply to Portia and dispatched it so the Mallorens could be on their way, then put on the country stays that fastened at the front.

"I can dress myself in this," she said. "Go and ask how Lord Dracy is. If he needs a doctor. Ask specifically about his temperature. And order a chair for me."

A part of her wanted to go to see for herself. Another part wasn't sure she could ever face him again. She heated at the memory of that kiss. It had been memorably magnificent, but she shouldn't have allowed it for a dozen reasons. Shouldn't, in all truth, have gone back to his room, or if she had, should have dressed beforehand. She could have put on this gown.

She sat to brush out her hair, and Jane returned to take over the arranging. "Just put it in a knot," Georgia said. "How is he?"

"Well, milady. No ill effects other than a sore arm, or so Jem the footman said."

No excuse to visit.

Not even for conversation. They'd talked so easily in the intimacy of dim candlelight, but such easy talk was dangerous. He'd shown how little he understood her or her world, and she feared the more he learned of her, the less he'd like her. She shouldn't have admitted knowledge of Mirabelle's, or that she'd hired living statues for an entertainment, but without honesty, all was dust.

She pulled on her light gloves and was checking her appearance when there was a rap on her door.

Dracy?

No, he wouldn't come here.

Jane opened the door a few inches and a footman said, "Lord Sellerby has called to see her ladyship."

Georgia pulled a face at her own reflection. She could deny herself and then linger until he left and was well away, but she couldn't always avoid him. He was behaving in a foolish way, but the only correction was her continual, firm denials.

"Come down with me, Jane, but then you must go to Mary's to assist her, and to tell her I'll go later for the final fitting."

"You'll go off with just the chairmen, milady?"

"And what could you do if they attacked me? They're my father's servants and completely reliable. Come."

She went down, pleased to be in hat and pelisse, ready to leave, and that her chair was waiting.

"Sellerby," she said as she went into the reception room, smiling. "How kind of you to call, but this is the day of the masquerade, you know, and I'm very busy."

He kissed her hand, looking sane, thank heavens. "I understand perfectly and won't delay you, my dear. Can I tease a hint as to your costume?"

"Now, you know better than that!"

"I do, but I had to try. Does Lord Dracy attend?"

"I believe so, but we can't expect him to match our standards of costume."

That pleased him, but she remembered she wasn't supposed to please him. How difficult it was to be cold to an old friend.

"I have heard strange rumors, Georgia, my dear."

She tensed. What new disaster?

"You aren't in truth considering Dracy as husband, are you?"

Ah, only that. "Is there some reason I should not?"

He chuckled. "My dear, my dear. Is there any reason you should?"

"He's a naval hero, wounded in the service of us all."

"There are a thousand such, some more grievously harmed. Marriage is not a reward for service. You have nothing in common with such a man, and it is not well-done of you to use him in one of your games."

"I'm not using him," she protested. "How could you think that of me?"

He stared at her. "You are in fact considering him?"

She hated to lie. "My father favors him, so there are discussions. . . ."

"They share an interest in horse racing, but you can't

be traded like a horse yourself. You would never suit. His fortune, his appearance . . ."

"I think it vastly unbecoming to sneer at his scar, Sellerby!"

"What? No, of course I never meant such a thing. I refer to his style of dress."

"He can dress well enough when called for. This is becoming tedious. I admire Lord Dracy and enjoy his company, and that is not nothing. If there is any consideration of a match, it's in the early stages, and as you say, there are considerable counts against it. So be at ease that I will not decide rashly. Now I must be away."

She went into the hall, and he came with her to hand her into her chair. He retained it. "Consider me, Georgia. You know we would suit."

"I will consider all my suitors, Sellerby, but only when the masquerade is over."

Would he try to escort her, and how would she deal with that?

He took his leave in decent form, however.

"Don't leave yet," she said to the chairmen in case Sellerby was lingering outside. It felt silly, but he was being silly, and she'd not handled that well. Why hadn't she simply said no? It was so hard to be cruel.

"You're going out, Georgia?"

She poked her head out of the window to look behind. "Dracy? Should you be out of your bed?"

He smiled as he came alongside. "I'm tougher stuff than that. I was hoping for your guided tour of Town."

He did look hale and hearty.

"I can give you a tour if you truly are fit," she said, "but it won't be the usual sort of attraction."

"You intrigue me. Where are you off to?"

"Come along and see."

"Very well." He sent a footman for his hat, gloves, and sword.

"Jane, you see I'm adequately defended," Georgia said. "Off now to Mary's, but send word if there's a disaster."

As soon as Dracy was ready, she gave the chairmen the order to go, suppressing a wide smile. What had felt like a burdensome duty now promised pleasure.

The men picked up their poles and carried her out into the street. She left the window half down to let in some air, and so as to be able to talk to Dracy.

"Not even a hint as to our destination?" he said.

"Not even a hint."

She realized that they'd met and last night hadn't spoiled everything. A perfect day.

"We're going toward Bloomsbury Square, I believe," he said.

"You know your geography."

"Maps and charts are the sailor's blood."

"Do you truly not miss the sea?"

"I suspect we all miss aspects of our pasts, but it would be folly to dwell on them."

The men carried her chair into a quiet, tree-lined street not far from Bloomsbury Square and came to a halt outside Danae House. She climbed out, suddenly nervous about her responsibility. She was a patroness, apparently the only one in Town, but she knew nothing of water supply.

"Danae House," he said, reading the words etched in stone above the door. "Who is Danae?"

"Was," she said as one of the chairmen rapped the knocker. "The mother of Perseus. A prophet warned her father that her son would kill him, so he had her imprisoned in a high tower. But Zeus took on the form of a shower of gold and thus gained entrance."

The door opened cautiously and a round-faced, round-bellied young woman peered out. "Yes, ma'am? Sir?"

Of course she wouldn't be recognized. By the very nature of Danae House, no one stayed here for a year.

"I'm Lady Maybury, one of the patronesses, and this is Lord Dracy."

The girl opened the door wide, dipping a curtsy. "Beggin' yer pardon, your ladyship. Your lordship."

A West Country accent. What was her story?

Mistress Ossington, the manager of the house, came rushing from the back, gray hair and manner flustered. "Oh, Lady Maybury! So kind . . . I did hope . . ."

Hoped for Diana Rothgar, or one of the other older patronesses, not the young, flighty, scandalous one.

"The water's failed," the woman hurried on. "I've contacted the company, milady, but nothing's been done."

"When did the water stop?" Georgia asked, trying to seem efficient and knowledgeable.

"Two days ago, milady! At least, that's when I realized the tank was running dry. It's filled three times a week, and we must have been missed the last time, but the company won't send someone to turn on the tap to us."

"Are your neighbors affected?" Dracy asked.

"No one's said anything, milord."

"May I see the tank?"

Dracy was taking over, but if he knew anything about such things he was welcome to.

"This is Lord Dracy, Mistress Ossington. My"—she struggled for a word—"adviser."

The woman made another curtsy. "So kind of you, milord. Come with me."

Georgia followed, studying these back parts of the house with interest. She'd never previously progressed beyond the guest parlor and dining room.

The place seemed to be as clean and orderly here as in the more public rooms, which was a good sign. Most doors were shut, but in one room she saw four girls working at writing, and in the kitchen three women and two girls were preparing food. They all dipped curtsies and seemed cheerful, despite their shame. From some of the stories she'd heard, a few were shameless.

Dracy was waiting for her at the top of a short, narrow staircase. "Have you not been through the house before?"

"I've had no need to," she said, feeling defensive. "What's down here?"

"The water tank."

She went down, wrinkling her nose at the damp, moldy smell, and grateful for the simple gown, which wouldn't be ruined by dust. The lead tank sat in the dank space, a pipe feeding into it, through which, she gathered, water was pumped by the water-supply company. At her house on Belling Row, she'd never concerned herself with the working of the system. She'd paid five guineas a year to the New River Company and expected water to be available when required, and that had been the end of it.

"So the tank should be filled three times a week?" she asked.

"Yes, Lady Maybury," Mistress Ossington said.

"And that pipe rising up?"

"To a pump in the kitchen, ma'am."

"Ah."

There'd been no pump in Belling Row. The servants had gone to the tank with buckets to get water. Georgia wished she'd known better. She would in her next home.

Dracy had mounted some wooden steps and was looking into the tank. "Nearly empty, and in sore need of cleaning out."

"Let me see," Georgia said.

He came down and handed her up. The bottom was thick with slime. "No wonder no one drinks the water from a tank. Do you have drinking water, Mistress Ossington?"

"No, ma'am. We all drink small beer."

In her house Georgia had paid for barrels of both small beer and good drinking water, which had been brought from the chalk downs. She was about to say she'd pay for a supply to Danae House when she remembered how little money she had access to.

Dracy was tapping the incoming pipe. "It's possible the turncock neglected to turn on your water when he should, but I suspect something's flowed in to block your pipe, Mistress Ossington. I was told fish and eels sometimes make their way through."

"Lord save us all!" Mistress Ossington exclaimed, seeming more bothered by that than by the sludge.

Georgia remembered she was supposed to be in charge of this crisis. She descended the stairs. "I'll make sure the company comes to check the pipe, Mistress Ossington. How are you managing for now?"

"The girls are going to the open pump in Black Bull Lane and bringing water in buckets, ma'am."

"I'll arrange for pump water to be delivered in barrels for now. I can authorize that expense."

She led the way upstairs, feeling she'd executed her duty, and relieved to return to clear light and fresh air. As she passed through the kitchen, she paused, then went to where a plump girl of about seventeen was slicing quince for preserving. "It must be thinner," she said gently, "or it won't preserve well. Watch," she said, and took the knife. She cut a very thin slice.

She gave the girl the knife back and observed. "That's it exactly."

She left the kitchen suspecting that the girl would return to cutting thick slices as soon as she could. It was a sad fact that some didn't want to be diligent and hardworking, no matter how kindly they were treated. One girl had run away from Danae House, taking a pile of shifts from the laundry room with her. Diana Rothgar had refused to pursue and prosecute, but she'd had locks installed on most storage rooms.

Georgia promised to send a report to Lady Rothgar and to order the water, and then left the house, Dracy at her side. "Fish in the water pipes?" she asked.

"So I'm told."

She paused by the chair. "How do you know about such things?"

"I've become interested in the way this great city works. London is riddled beneath with sewers, streams, and conduits for water."

She looked down. "You make me feel that this pavement is only a thin crust."

"Over the foulness that washes down from the streets."

"And a country farmyard is sweet?" she challenged. "Or the air, when the muck's being spread in the fields? At least there's amusement here and a variety of company, which you admit to have enjoyed."

"I confess it. Now tell me the purpose of Danae House."

"It's a charity specifically for younger servants who become pregnant. In many cases it's through seduction or even rape by the men of the house. That tank should be cleaned out regularly. I believe I can authorize that too."

"How very brisk you are. And surprisingly knowledgeable about domestic management."

Georgia took her seat in the chair, tucking in her skirts. "A lady should understand her servants' work, even as a captain, I assume, should understand the meanest tasks on board his ship. That doesn't mean that the captain has any desire to scrub the decks."

He smiled. "You won't be making quince preserves?"

"I sincerely hope not."

"Thank you for a tour of an unexpected part of London. May I reciprocate and take you to a place you do not know?"

She looked up at him. "I doubt there are many of those that are decent."

"My naval friends introduced me to an excellent place where we can dine on pie and ale."

"Dine on pie and ale?"

"My poor Lady May, you have not lived." He gave the chairmen the direction.

Three hours later, Georgia left Dolly Pott's Pie House arm in arm with Dracy, in high spirits, which might have had something to do with the strong porter served there. One way or another, she felt spun around. She hadn't always stayed within the confines of aristocratic London, but she'd never before dined on steak pie and strong ale at a long plain table in the company of a dozen or so naval officers.

The men had been startled by her arrival, and indeed, there'd been few ladies eating at Dolly Pott's. They'd been even more startled when Dracy had introduced her. Her being a countess would explain the surprise, but she could see some also knew she was Lady May, and perhaps the layers of her scandalous reputation.

No one had been discourteous, however, or even cool, perhaps from good manners, or perhaps from consideration for Dracy. It had rapidly become clear that he was liked and admired.

She'd delighted in that, as if she could take credit for it, which she certainly could not. She'd also delighted to see him at ease in his own milieu, even though it was far, far from hers.

She'd soon come to feel at ease, which could well have been the ale. It had been dark and strong, an odd taste at first, but she'd quickly become accustomed. The men had flirted with her a little, but none had crossed the line. She felt they'd have behaved the same with any young woman out of good manners, for no woman likes to be ignored, but that overall they'd treated her as if she were a male friend Dracy had brought along. An outsider, a landlubber, but welcome.

She'd been fascinated by stories of naval life and foreign lands, though aware that they were selecting those suitable for a schoolroom. The pie was delicious, as was the ale, and the atmosphere cheerfully uncomplicated. Heaven.

She'd sent her chair home from the pie house, so now they strolled down Pall Mall toward Hernescroft House.

"I enjoyed that as much as anything I can remember," she said.

"Then reward me with a hint about your costume."

"Certainly not!"

"As we'll travel together, there can be no secrecy."

"Which is why I intend to make my own way."

"Cunning, but I'd lay a thousand I'll know you."

"Do you have a thousand?" she challenged, smiling at him.

"Not that I can afford. What fair terms should we put on our wager, then?"

"Wager?"

"That I recognize you before the unmasking."

"To be fair, it would need to be a wager over who recognizes whom first."

"True, but hard to pin the prize."

"We're so unequal," she agreed. "Male, female. Poor, rich . . ."

"We each have an equal amount of time," he said.

"Time?" Georgia became aware that this conversation might be drifting into danger, but she was too ale addled to be sure how.

"The winner gains fifteen minutes alone with the loser, to do with as they wish."

That sobered her. "Definitely not."

Instead of argument or persuasion, he said, "Wise lady. We should put a limit on it. The loser must not be distressed."

"Then what's the point?"

"You *want* to be distressed?"

"I might hope to be excited."

He smiled. "Indeed, what other point in a wager? You

could hope to be excited as winner too. What might you demand of me for fifteen minutes?"

It was a challenge, a dare, so she spoke the most outrageous thing imaginable. "Would you strip naked for me?"

"Here, if you wish."

She looked around the Mall with its scattering of people of all ages. "You wouldn't!"

"You mean *you* wouldn't."

"Of course not. I'd be ruined."

"I wouldn't. And nor, I think, would you for seeing it if you screeched loudly enough."

"I'm very tempted to call your bluff, sir."

"It's not a bluff. Men strip all the time among themselves—after battle if all bloody, or to swim, or in some sorts of bagnios. It means nothing to me."

Georgia knew she should be screeching at this conversation, and running away too, but it was irresistible, as was the wager. Only a quarter hour, after all, and she was not to be distressed.

Good sense fought with her ale-loosened mind and lost.

"Let's have the stakes clear. If I detect you before you detect me, I will have fifteen minutes alone with you during which you'll do all I command."

"As long as I'm not distressed," he reminded her, but with a wicked glint in his eyes.

Stripping for her would not distress him, which had her heating from her own thoughts, perhaps even sweating. She'd never seen a naked man in the flesh....

"And if I win," he said, "I will gain the same from you."

*Strip?* No, he couldn't mean that. After all, it would distress her a great deal. All the same ...

She'd held a bird once whose heart had raced like this.

Fear of the unknown.

Fear of a new, unforgivable scandal.

But above all, fear of the very excitement burning through her.

Good sense won. She walked on. "I can't afford more scandal."

"We live in the same house," he said, "and your parents sleep some distance away. No one will know, and even if I win I won't distress you. I would never do that, Georgia."

She glanced at him and saw truth. In fact, she'd always known it. She could trust Dracy in every respect, which made the adventure possible.

"Very well," she said. "After all, I'm sure of victory. You are quite distinctive, and I defy my mother to detect me."

"You do realize you've just narrowed the field."

"Perdition, but I'm still sure I'll win. And thus, if I wish, I can dictate the fifteen minutes be spent reading sermons."

"You could," he agreed, "but you won't."

She tossed her head at that, though the damnable man was right, and the outrageous wager lent the night ahead a lot more spice.

But then she remembered. The masquerade. Her costume.

"What time is it?" she asked.

He took out his watch. "Half past four."

"Gemini! Only four hours before I must leave for the masquerade. Hurry," she said, switching directions. "I must go to my mantua maker for a final fitting. You'll leave me at the door, Dracy," she said severely. "I won't risk you learning the smallest detail."

As they hurried in their new direction, Dracy asked, "What's the cleverest masquerade costume you've ever seen?"

"Apart from my own?" she said. "A river maiden, complete with the illusion of sitting on a rock."

"An achievement, but difficult to manage, I suspect. Like the one I saw in Naples where a man attended as a galley."

"However did he manage to dance?"

"He didn't. Nor did the two who dressed themselves as a camel."

"Poorly thought out."

"Will your costume allow you to dance?"

She shot him a frown. "You won't catch me that way, sir."

He laughed. "Nevertheless, I'll know you, Georgia, even in a suit of armor."

"Joan of Arc? Most inappropriate for the theme, but here we are, and you are dismissed."

They were outside the mantua maker's house.

He kissed her hand. "Thank you for an enchanting day."

"Thank you for a novel and delightful dinner. I will see you at the masquerade. Before," she added, "you see me."

He smiled as she went in and then walked away, adrift, simply because she wasn't by his side.

Today had given him hope, however. As she'd once said, people had many facets, and she was a diamond. The peacock Lady May was also a patroness of a charity, and willing to attempt to fix a lowly water problem dressed appropriately for the task. She was a woman knowledgeable of housewifery, even if she denied any application of it, and she'd been kind in correcting a clumsy girl's work.

She'd been only momentarily dismayed by the low-beamed, straw-floored pie house set with long tables, where all types mingled. She certainly hadn't been deterred by the company of men, and in no time she'd charmed his friends, but perhaps had been a little charmed herself. She'd been interested in their stories and asked intelligent questions, enjoying learning about different ways and foreign lands. Would a country manor house not interest her too, and the society around it?

He reined in his optimism. A country estate was not a ship of the line or a spice island. It wouldn't even be new to her. She'd lived in the country to the age of eighteen, and if she'd been trained in all levels of household management, she'd have experienced dairies, brew houses, laundries, and kitchen gardens. And learned to dislike them, it would seem.

Dracy was a great deal smaller than Herne. Cozier, he could say, if he were optimistic, but he needed a wife who knew not only how to slice quince, get rid of moths and beetles, and repair curtains and hangings, but who was also willing to actually do it.

He'd never been a dreamer, so perhaps he had been ensorcelled by sirens after all. That didn't prevent him from anticipating the masquerade, and the result of their wicked wager, win or lose.

# Chapter 22

It was nearly nine when Georgia checked her appearance one last time, assessing its ability to conceal her identity. Surely Dracy wouldn't know her with almost every inch concealed.

It hadn't been easy to design a costume portraying the dove of peace that was comfortable, flattering, and could be made rapidly, but they'd achieved it, and at very little cost.

The headdress had been the most work, but it perfectly resembled a dove's head, with the beak projecting above her nose. The feathers fed down the back of her head to blend with her hair, which fell loose to her waist and was powdered white.

It had been Jane's genius to point out that real doves' feathers would be too small to be in scale, as well as being too hard to find in quantity. The solution had been white goose feathers, which continued down the flowing back of the gown to end as the fan of a dove's tail.

At the front Georgia had wanted to wear a classical robe, but Jane had argued in favor of decent convention, so she wore stays under a high-necked gown of white silk. She wore no hoops and only a roll at her hips to spread the skirt a little. The skirt had an overlay of gauze cut into feather shapes and a trimming of down.

Intent on challenging Dracy, she'd applied a bold red rouge to her lips and purchased a different perfume. It was delicate because she disliked heavy scent, but distinctly of rose.

She smiled at the book that had arrived an hour ago, a gift from him. According to Jane it was a book about the language of flowers, but it was also perfumed, so Georgia hadn't touched it. She'd rebuke him later for trying to trap her with a distinctive, spicy smell. She'd had Jane wash her hands thoroughly before adjusting the costume.

That trick made her all the more determined to win the wager, so she'd practiced speaking in a high, whispery voice. It would work, and thus tonight would be a wicked revelation—if she were brave enough to demand that prize, that he strip naked for her.

Before that, she had to face the beau monde en masse.

Lady May had never lacked courage, and she would ignore the slight churning in her belly, but she was grateful that for the first hour she would be disguised.

She nodded at her reflection in the mirror. "Ready for the fray."

"It's not a battle, milady."

"Oh, yes it is," Georgia said.

Her strategy was simple. She was presenting herself as the very image of purity and would behave to match. When she removed the dove's head to reveal herself, the impression should linger. It wouldn't wipe all away—that was the work of time—but it should help.

The flurry of scandal about the letter had died down simply because no letter had been produced or published. That had been the promise at the ball, so now, according to Babs and others, most people dismissed the rumor as spite. Some were even ashamed to have believed it so quickly, and thus more well disposed through guilt. Eloisa had done her a kindness, which would doubtless choke her if she knew. Dracy had done her a greater one by taking that letter. She might not have thought of that on her own.

Georgia put on a voluminous black hooded cloak that hid all of her except her face. If Dracy was cheating by spying on her, he'd not learn much. Jane was carrying the head in a red cloth bag. Red to further mislead. Her parents had agreed to let her go separately. They'd already left and would send the coach back for her, and it already awaited.

She was soon on her way with only Jane for company, if one didn't count a coachman and two armed footmen. Soon the coach joined a stream, all approaching Carlisle House.

Georgia looked ahead at the brilliantly lit house. "Splendid decorations."

"That they are, milady," Jane said. "Illuminated pictures of peace and prosperity in a whole rank of windows."

"And garlands of lamps in the form of crowns. Madame Cornelys has outdone herself. We must do the same. The head, Jane."

"You'd be better to wait until we arrive, milady. There'll be a dressing room."

"No, I want to arrive in full disguise."

"I don't know why you're so anxious not to be recognized, milady. Within the hour everyone will shed the more cumbersome parts of their costumes for the dancing."

"I need to remain anonymous that long. I have a wager with a friend. Hurry."

She shed the cloak. Jane took out the dove's head and settled it carefully in place, then smoothed the feathers at the back into Georgia's hair.

"Does it look well?" Georgia asked. "I wish I had a mirror."

"There'll be mirrors in the dressing room," Jane pointed out.

"Dear Jane, humor my foibles as you always have."

"And sometimes when you've gone too far, milady."

"I plan no improper behavior at this masquerade, I promise you." That was honest as far as it went.

She perched on her seat so as not to disturb anything, telling herself again that Dracy could never detect her.

"Here's your mask for later, milady," Jane said, sliding it into a pocket, "and your fan. And here we are. I hope all goes well."

"It will, Jane. Enjoy yourself in the servants' room."

She stepped carefully out of the coach, leaving the cloak to Jane, and delighting in the reaction of the crowd of onlookers. So often she'd arrived at a grand event in a spectacular gown, sparkling with jewels, and the crowd had applauded and called out, "Lady May!"

"The dove of peace," someone said, and she was applauded.

Georgia smiled and swept into the heart of the beau monde.

Lady May was back, and tonight would go perfectly.

The interior of Madame Cornelys's house was often decorated to represent Venice, for the lady came from there, and the Venetian masquerade was her specialty. For this event, however, it remained a handsome English house, decorated only with banners hanging from the ceiling.

*Clever,* Georgia thought. They resembled banners of war but instead were banners of peace and prosperity. She saw joined hands, abundant countryside, a lion and a lamb, and a merchant ship.

"A dove of peace," said a gentleman in a toga. "Clever."

Georgia inclined her head to Lord Sandwich but moved on. She didn't care to dally with members of the ministry. She behaved the same way with two other gentlemen, and the second said, "I suppose doves can only coo."

"Coo," Georgia said to him and went upstairs, delighted that Waveney hadn't recognized her. No one was recognizing her, and that meant that for the moment she was free.

Free of the past.

Free of expectations.

Free of scandal and suspicion.

"O happy dove!" declared a crusader, seizing her hand to kiss it.

"Coo" was rather limiting, so as she pulled her hand free, Georgia adopted her high-pitched voice. "You are inappropriately dressed, sir. How can a knight partner peace?"

"I'm Richard the Lionheart, pretty dove, great warrior of England. I guard the peace."

"Only with bloodshed, sir." She spotted another armed warrior and challenged him.

"I'm Saint George," he declared, thumping his spear. "Slayer of the dragon of France. Accompanied, of course, by beauteous Britannia."

Lord Trelyn, she realized, and the voluptuous Britannia was his wife, whose narrow mask was no disguise at all. As portrayed on the coins, she wore a helmet and carried a spear and shield. Rather overencumbered in Georgia's opinion, but then Nerissa Trelyn was overendowed as well.

"So many weapons," Georgia sighed. "The dove of peace could weep."

"Weapons keep the peace, silly dove," Lady Trelyn said. "Flutter away."

The Trelyns moved on, saving Georgia the effort of responding, but she wondered if she'd been recognized.

She and Nerissa Trelyn had been rivals in beauty at one point, but not in other ways. Lady Trelyn was a model of dignity and virtue, which Lady May had never claimed, but she lacked the noble virtue of kindness. When people had been stirring the scandal broth about

her, Nerissa Trelyn would have wielded a very large
spoon. If she'd been at Winnie's ball, Georgia would
have consided her as chief culprit of the letter.

That reminded her that the creator of the letter was
still at large and could be here. Most likely was here. She
put aside any fears in case they showed, and tried to
spot Dracy. He'd had little time to get a costume and
lacked her expertise. Surely he'd be wearing something
simple. While dealing with light flirtations, she eliminated many men because they hadn't his height and
trim build. But then she wondered if he might attempt
a deep disguise.

She assessed a tall, turbaned Arabian with a great
belly. . . .

"Pretty dove, do you carry an olive leaf?"

She had to turn to the togaed man. In answer to his
question, she opened her fan, revealing that each spoke
was painted to resemble an olive leaf. "And you, sir, do
you argue for peace in the senate?"

He chuckled. "Only if the terms are right."

She rapped him with the closed fan. "Then the dove
will have nothing to do with you, sir."

She moved on from Lord Holland, who would have
been better costumed as a moneybag. He was said to
have accumulated half a million when paymaster to the
forces during the recent war.

The turbaned man had disappeared, but she didn't
think he'd been Dracy. She felt she'd know Lord Dracy,
no matter what the disguise.

Dracy scanned the room for Georgia.

There were a dozen redheaded Queen Elizabeths. A
Tudor gown made a concealing costume, but not concealing enough. In any case, none of them moved with
the light grace of Lady May.

There were even more Britannias, some better suited
to the costume than others, but most were showing too

much flesh. Georgia wouldn't come here scantily dressed. She was too aware of her situation for that.

That eliminated the many other women in classical robes, presumably portraying one goddess or another. Some wore wreaths of flowers or Grecian tiaras, while others carried cornucopias or sheaves of wheat. He gave careful study to one in a gown and headdress encrusted with fruit and flowers. Would Georgia be cunning enough to wear such an ungainly outfit? Not even to win a wager. Nor would she attempt to portray a cornfield, like another lady, who was leaving a trail of ears of wheat.

So where was she?

And would she recognize him?

He didn't care if he won or lost, but pride demanded that he present a challenge, so he now regretted having chosen to portray Neptune, god of the sea. The hint was too broad. He hoped he was disguised by the overlarge robe, belted so that it bunched about him in a way that made him look fat, and by the simple fact that his headdress concealed much of his face.

He'd made sure it covered the damaged part, at least.

The seamstress who worked for the theater had cut green cloth into seaweed shapes and attached them to a hood as hair, with some hanging around his face. In addition, she'd made a green mask that came down on both cheeks, concealing his scar. With Nugent's glue, he'd stuck on a gray beard and mustache, which itched. The trident was also a nuisance, but he'd be able to abandon it when the dancing began.

"I challenge you, sir," said a husky foreign voice. "You come to a masquerade of peace, weapon in hand."

He looked at the masked woman, who was magnificently dressed in a green silk gown.

"You, ma'am, don't seem to be in costume at all."

Her painted lips smiled. "Green is the color of hope, sir, and fertility, and as hostess I have the right of challenge. Your weapon, if you please."

He bowed. "Madame Cornelys, you and your talents are famous. And clearly well deserved."

"Flattery is all very well, Lord Neptune, but in the spirit of this event, I am confiscating all arms."

She held out an imperious arm, and he surrendered his trident.

"Delighted to oblige, ma'am. It's a damnable nuisance. But how will you confiscate the ladies' beauty?"

She passed his wooden trident to an attendant servant, who already had a sheaf of such. "There, you gentlemen will have to survive as best you can."

She swept off on her mission, and Dracy realized how cleverly this was being managed. Even more than the ball at Hammersmith, this masquerade brought together the many fractious sides, but to talk, not fight, so anything close to a weapon was being confiscated.

A wooden battlefield and toy weapons. How long it seemed since he'd said that to Georgia, when she'd come to London to equip him for the ball. The weapons were real, she'd warned him, and she'd been correct. Real, and often concealed.

Which was she? He needed to be by her side.

Nearby, a woman said, "Shaldon! In virginal white. How droll."

Dracy turned to see a man in Elizabethan dress, and as the Queen Bess confronting him had said, in pure white. The costume showed off magnificent legs, which the woman was frankly ogling.

But here was someone he'd been seeking—one of the men at the Maybury duel, and perhaps a crony of Vance. For some reason Shaldon didn't encourage the queen, who flounced off.

Dracy moved in before some other lady tried her luck.

"Sir Harry Shaldon, I believe?"

"Hardly in the spirit of the masquerade, Poseidon."

"Neptune, which amounts to the same thing. Can I breech protocol for a moment to speak with you?"

Shaldon wore only a narrow mask, so it was easy to see annoyance war with curiosity. "A moment and no more," he said at last. "Shall we go apart?"

They went together to a quieter part of the house. Later it would be used for trysts, but at the moment the guests were all enjoying the charade.

"I beg your pardon for accosting you, Shaldon. I'm Lord Dracy, and if you're to be in Town tomorrow we can simply make an appointment."

"Dracy? Your horse beat Fancy Free."

"It did, sir."

"Alas, I plan to ride to Lambourne tomorrow as soon as I rise. Or without sleep if the night provides lengthy amusement. Is it a matter I can help you with now?"

There was no choice but to be blunt. "I'm attempting to help Lady Maybury by discovering more about the duel."

"Got you in her web too, has she? If you're poking into the reason for the duel, I don't believe Georgia Maybury had a liaison with Vance, but you'll never prove it."

"Were you at the duel as a second?" Dracy asked.

"No." After a moment, Shaldon said, "It bothered me, so I went along to see fair play. We were all rolling drunk the night before, but I sober up quickly. I thought to talk them both out of it, but Vance said he'd been challenged, and Maybury was sticking to it. You know the way some weak men get when pushed to it?"

"Yes."

"Vance was making light of it, anyway. Implying—though later I couldn't pin down the words—that it would all be for the form of it. Kellew, Maybury's second, was little use, as I expected. Green from the drink and trembling with nerves. I went along to keep an eye on things, but everything was done correctly. It was a fair fight."

"If it's fair when a skilled swordsman fights an unskilled one."

Shaldon shrugged.

"It wasn't for the form of it in the end, was it?" Dracy asked. "I read the inquest. Your testimony didn't reveal much, but from Kellew's words, Vance struck to kill. Was that nerves speaking?"

He thought Shaldon wouldn't answer, but in the end he said, "No, I think Kellew was right. Poor man's been a wreck over it ever since."

"Why did Vance kill Maybury?"

"Devil if I know," Shaldon said. "He had to flee the country over it."

"You know that to be true?" Dracy asked.

Shaldon frowned at him. "You think he might still be in England? No one's seen him since, and he'd not be able to stay away from his haunts this long. Anyway, he sent a letter from Cologne, didn't he? Even turned up at Lady Thretford's ball."

"In fact, it did not. That was all rumor. Do you know his handwriting?"

Shaldon snorted. "What? You think we exchanged letters? A scrawled IOU and that's about it. Now, if you'll excuse me . . ."

"You have no desire to rescue Lady Maybury from unjust scandal?"

"I don't tilt at windmills, Dracy, and I recommend you cut free before she traps you too into fatal folly. Adieu."

Dracy had to let him go. He'd learned nothing new but had one detail confirmed. Charnley Vance had deliberately killed Lord Maybury.


"A dove, Georgie?"

Georgia turned to the broad-shouldered man in white Tudor dress. "How did you know me, Shaldon?"

"Your hands."

Georgia frowned over that. She'd left off her wedding ring but not thought that her hands were themselves recognizable.

"I should have worn gloves. What does your costume have to do with peace?"

"It's white like a flag of truce, and shows off my legs remarkably well."

"Do you think Queen Bess dictated trunk hose for her own enjoyment?"

He chuckled. "If I were monarch I'd dictate trunk hose for ladies," he said. "You're remarkably well covered. I remember that goddess costume. . . ."

She rapped him with her fan. "Don't play games like that. I need to ask you something. Did Charnley Vance ever write to you?"

"What?"

"Do you know if he had family? Family he might write to."

"Dammit, Georgie, there wasn't anything between you two, was there?"

"No!" She was hard put not to shriek it. "No, Shaldon, no. It's to do with trying to find him, to make him tell the truth about me."

"Like that Neptune over there. Leave it be. It'll blow over."

"That Neptune?" Georgia smiled at the baggy-robed god with seaweed hair. Not a bad attempt. "Thank you, Shaldon!"

"Thank me with a kiss?"

She chuckled. "It can only be a peck," she said and tapped his chin with her beak. Then she headed toward Dracy, victorious. Fifteen minutes of power . . .

"The dove of purity. A perfect choice."

*Sellerby.*

She considered ignoring him, but he was odd enough these days that he might call after her. She turned to exchange a few polite words.

But heaven help her, he was dressed as an angel, complete with robes, halo, and rather awkward wings. At the

thought of the Annunciation, she had to fight a giggle.
She didn't quite succeed.

"I amuse you?" he asked coldly.

"I do apologize, Sellerby! Only a remembered joke."
She glanced behind. Dracy had gone.

"At my expense?"

She turned back quickly to him. She was being appall-
ingly impolite.

"Of course not," she said kindly. She knew Dracy now
and would easily find him once she was rid of Sellerby. "I
can't explain. You know such jokes don't survive a second outing. It's a splendid costume. I compliment you."

He inclined his head. "Yours too is well-done, but
your perfect lips need no enhancement."

"All part of the game of disguise. Now I must go—"

"And yet I knew you."

She paused to ask, "How?"

"I have my ways." He smirked, and she had a sudden
suspicion.

"Bribing servants? Sellerby, I'm shocked."

"The rules of fair play do not apply in love or war."

"But as this is neither, adieu, Angelicus."

He grabbed her arm. "You've neglected to provide
the dove with wings, Georgie. Won't it be hard to fly
away?"

"A bird can also walk," she said, trying to pull her arm
free. "Stop this. People are noticing."

"Noticing one of our lovers' games."

"I was never more serious, my lord. Let me go."

He released her and she turned to walk away. She'd
taken only one step when a tug on her gown halted her.
He'd put a foot on her dovetail train.

Without turning, she said, "Release me, sir, or I will
scream." She was obliged to speak loudly and could have
wept with fury at being made the center of a scene.

At least he obeyed. She whirled to give him a very
sharp piece of her mind, but found him red faced and

choking, because a Neptune was dragging him back by the wings, which were supported around his neck.

Dracy! But, by the stars, he looked fit to do murder.

"Let him go!" she cried.

Dracy did, adding a shove. "Fly away, angel, or you might find yourself with your fellow, Lucifer."

Sellerby turned on him, fists clenched, but Madame Cornelys swept in. "Gentlemen, gentlemen! This is a festival of harmony. Will you fight over a dove?"

Someone drew—compelled—Sellerby away. Another man attempted the same with Dracy, but Georgia went to him. "Thank you, my lord Neptune."

"I couldn't see the dove of peace assaulted, especially tonight," he said clearly for all to hear.

"And I shall reward you with the first dance," she said, offering her hand.

He took it, kissed it, and then led her away from the stares and whispers.

"I would like to kill Sellerby," she hissed.

"You might have good reason to."

But she'd remembered the wager. She paused to grin at him. "I know you, Dracy."

"I already knew you."

"You can't prove that."

"Would I rescue just any dove? You're too fond of birds, my sweet."

"Damnation," she muttered, and he laughed. "I renounce birds forever. As for recognition, I'm sure I'd have riddled out the Neptune as soon as I saw you, though your lack of a trident is cheating."

"I came with one, but Madame Cornelys and her people are confiscating all weapons. Wisely, as it turned out."

"I doubt Sellerby came armed. An angel, after all."

"Haven't you heard of flaming swords? What was he up to?"

"I don't know. We were talking about costumes. I admit I laughed, but it wasn't exactly at his costume, but at angels. A joke with Lizzie, that's all. He took it amiss, but then we conversed. Squabbled over something. Ah, yes, would you believe he bribed someone to reveal my costume? Positively dastardly. Then when I walked away, he tried to stop me."

"I'll deal with him."

"No violence," she said, gripping his arm. "I'll have no more violence over me."

He put a hand over hers. "Then there won't be."

She looked directly at him for the first time and smiled. "A gray beard and mustache? I don't think it suits you."

"It's beginning to slip and a prickly nuisance." He grabbed one side and ripped it off. "There. That's better. The things I do to win a wager."

"But who's won?" she challenged.

"Perhaps we both have. Fifteen minutes each?"

She went hot and cold at the same time, an extraordinary sensation.

She should say no, she should say no. . . .

"Very well," she said. "When?"

"After this event is over."

She'd expected that, wanted that, but now pattering panic tangled her tongue.

"Delaying will change nothing," he said.

"Everything can change in a moment. We both know that."

"So we do. Then *carpe diem*, Georgia. Let's pay our debts tonight."

"Seize the night, you mean. Very well. As soon as the house is settled I'll come to you."

# Chapter 23

A change in the music heralded the dancing, and all around revelers shed the more cumbersome pieces of their costumes into the arms of waiting servants. There was much laughter and some genuine surprise and even applause as identities were revealed.

Georgia let Dracy help remove her dove's head and then put on the slim feather mask instead. Dracy passed the dove's head to Jane, who had joined them to help with the unveiling and was grinning at the show around her. Then he put his seaweed wig headdress on top.

His green mask cleverly hid almost all his scar, all except the slight twist to his lips. As a result, she saw only clean-cut beauty, framed by thick, curly hair that hung loose to his shoulders, sending her heart pattering for new reasons.

"I do believe that in times of yore you could have grown a periwig of your own."

"I can't imagine living with that much hair to take care of. I've been tempted at times to shave mine off and wear a wig."

"No," she said, before she could control it.

He smiled. "You like my hair."

She could hardly deny it.

"I like yours too, though it's a shame it's powdered."

"For disguise. For the whiteness of the dove."

"I can't admire your scarlet lips."

She rapped him with her fan. "Don't echo Sellerby."

"'Struth, did I? You can punish me with forty lashes."

"You're echoing him again."

"I'll cut my throat. Let's dance."

They went hand in hand into the ballroom for the first dance. Everyone placed importance on the first dance, and Georgia was delighted to be with Dracy. After all, it fit with their pretend betrothal, and if people were thinking that Lady May was having to settle for a lowly husband, let them. They'd see the truth in time.

And yet, her high ambitions felt strangely hollow.

"Don't let the oafish angel clip your wings," he said softly.

She smiled at him, encouraged by him, anchored by him, and ready for all her challenges, both here and later. She would have liked to stay with Dracy all night, but after the first dance, she had to accept another partner for the next.

Waveney, Porterhouse, and Shaldon competed for the honor, which salved her pride. She chose Shaldon. A dance with Waveney would upset his wife, and Porterhouse, in a plain toga, felt too safe. Shaldon wasn't a safe man, but she understood him. Dracy was captured by a Queen Bess who was actually showing her nipples beneath the most gossamer silk gauze. She was sure he'd enjoy that.

"Causing fights, Georgie?" Shaldon asked as they took their places.

"Is everyone speaking of it?"

"Alas, yes."

"A curse on Sellerby," she muttered. "Why would he behave so ruinously?"

When the dance brought them together again, he said, "Desperation. I never had any hope, but he did."

"I never gave him reason," she protested, but then remembered to smile.

"You are reason, unless a man has a very strong head."

And she'd delighted in it, she admitted as she wove the patterns. Perhaps her beauty was a cursed gift, but she couldn't wish it gone.

She danced next with Harringay, another safe partner. She enjoyed it, but she'd feel she was making progress only if she was asked for a dance by someone who was not a close friend.

She saw Beaufort in a nondescript toga, and Bridgwater in a robe with various engineering implements dangling from a belt. She suspected he was representing the Grand Engineer.

Neither approached her.

At least Richmond came to speak to her. His toga was silk, and he wore a golden wreath in his hair that might truly be gold. They were discussing the costumes when a man said, "A plain white gown with a ragged overdress. You are meant to be . . . ?"

Georgia whirled. "Perry!" She managed not to fling her arms around her brother, but she felt as if all clouds had blown away. Perry was back and he'd make sense of an insane world. "How *dared* you stay away so long?"

"It's only been three weeks," he complained, "and over a week of that was travel there and back." He greeted Richmond, who was as delighted to see Perry. Her brother was an arbiter of fashion and style.

"That's why no one ever goes so far from Town," Georgia said. "And the roads are appalling in the north."

"They're appalling in many places," he said, looking her over. "I still wonder at your clothing."

"With the headdress it was a wonderful dove of peace, wasn't it, Richmond?"

"Oh yes," he said. "Brilliant as always."

"As for you," Georgia said to her brother, "that's your Dionysus costume from the Olympian Revels. I expect more novelty from you."

"Have pity. I only arrived back in Town this afternoon."

"A paltry excuse."

"A sound one."

A buxom young lady in extremely filmy robes "accidentally" brushed up against Richmond, and in moments he was off with her.

"She should be dressed as a fox," Georgia said.

"And he as a chicken? His guardians will keep him safe from predators such as that. I'm surprised you were dallying with him. A new taste for the infantry?"

Georgia glanced around to be sure no one was close enough to hear. "I'm rather short of admirers."

His brows rose. "Delusions?"

"No. The scandal. Now you're back, I'm sure we can do something. You are staying in Town?"

"Of course."

"Did you hear about Sellerby?"

"No."

"He . . . Oh, it's too complicated, but he spread word that we were to wed and is generally behaving like a lunatic."

"You shouldn't have—"

"Encouraged him. I know, I know. Then there was the letter incident at Winnie's ball."

"In a pickle again?" he said with a smile. Then, "Now what has you in a giggle?"

"Pickle!" she gasped, trying to control herself. "That was Dracy's last ship. Can you believe it?"

"Ceddie Dracy? No—"

"The new Lord Dracy. Have you been so very out of touch? His horse beat Fancy Free."

"Ah, I remember that. I have been busy, love, but I remember now. Naval officer. Captain of the *Pickle*?"

"Lieutenant only. Oh, and there's something else. We are pretending that he's first in the running for my hand. Don't look at me like that. It is all Mother's doing."

"The world's run mad and is best left for the morrow. What do you want me to do about Dracy?"

"Nothing. He's not a problem. In fact, I like him. I . . . I do worry that this device might break his heart."

"Not if he has any sense."

"He's very sensible. Apart from a fixed dislike of Town."

"A madman, then," he said with a smile.

"He makes no secret of it, can you imagine? He's anxious to return to his muddy estate."

"Then doubtless he and the mud deserve one another. Ah, what's this?"

Footmen were passing through the rooms ringing small bells and announcing that the dove of peace would be displayed in the central hall.

"Me?" Georgia gasped in a panic.

"An automaton," Perry soothed. "The king has sent that automaton that the Chevalier d'Eon presented to him a while back. The one representing peace and harmony. You must have been there."

"No, I had a horrid sore throat. But I heard about it. Silver, mother-of-pearl, gold, and diamonds."

"And like all women, your eyes glitter at the thought."

"You're not so indifferent to jewels, brother. Hurry, let's get a good position."

The hall was crowded, as were the staircase and the gallery around. People were seizing any spot with a good view of the huge silver dove on a plinth in the center. Georgia wanted to be close and wriggled through, hand in hand with her brother, pleased that she wasn't wearing hoops.

"It's very glittery," she said when they were almost at the front. "Feathers made of mother-of-pearl and silver. Are those diamond eyes?"

"Probably not. Ah, Rothgar's in charge of the display. I heard that he took the dove into his own workshop for improvement. As delivered, it was rather simple and awkward."

"Then it's probably improved," Georgia said. "I attended a lecture he gave on such toys when he put some up for auction in support of the Smallpox Hospital. Dickon bought me one," she remembered. "A pretty dancer. I've not seen it since. . . . It must have remained with the house."

"That could be contested."

She was tempted, for it was a pretty toy that held happy memories, but she shook her head. "Hush."

The marquess made a short speech on behalf of the king, thanking them all for celebrating peace, prosperity, and the patriotic heart. But then he said, "As we have a charming dove among us tonight, I think she should switch on the machine."

He was looking at her.

Georgia was swept by a prickly heat of nervousness and was shocked. Lady May, afraid of being so much the center of attention?

Perry took her hand and forced her forward, so she summoned Lady May with gracious posture and a bright smile. Perry handed her up the steps and Lord Rothgar showed her the switch.

"You need only push it down, Lady Maybury."

It moved easily, and with a whirr of machinery the bird flexed its neck this way and that.

"It should have real feathers," she murmured, but then pressed her lips together to silence any other unwise comment.

Then the bird lowered its head, seized an olive branch off the ground in its beak, and straightened as it spread its wings to reveal words picked out in gold underneath.

Peace. *Paix*.

Everyone applauded, including Georgia, for it was prettily done.

Then Madame Cornelys announced that Signora Terletti would sing a new song in praise of peace composed by Mr. Clemson. As the lady swept toward the dais, Georgia happily went down, Lord Rothgar at her side.

They listened to a blessedly short song and applauded the performance. People then dispersed—to refreshments, cards, or dancing, or to simply sitting in various small rooms, many talking politics.

Lord Rothgar smiled at her. "You're correct about the feathers, Lady Maybury, though real ones do tend to fall apart in time, whereas silver and mother-of-pearl should last longer than any peace ever has."

"An interesting dilemma, my lord. Perfection in the moment, or compromise and long delight."

"Repeated in much of life. Welcome back to Town, Perriam. I thank you for your efforts on behalf of my wife."

Georgia looked between them. Perry and Diana Rothgar?

"I also saw benefit to my friend Malzard, my lord."

"How blessed we are to gain numerous benefits from one act. Speaking of which, I'd be obliged if you'd wait on me tomorrow."

Perry bowed. "Your servant, sir."

Rothgar bowed in return and moved away.

"What was that about?" Georgia demanded.

"Diana Rothgar was visiting her northern estates, her baby with her, when the infant started a tooth. I rescued her from an inn in York and took her, her entourage, and her howling, drooling monster to Keynings, the Earl of Malzard's place. My dear sister, that journey was a noble sacrifice."

"And the benefit to Malzard?"

"His wife needed a cloak of approval. I'll tell the whole story later."

"I may get it from her—Diana Rothgar, I mean. She and I are acquainted."

"Oh, yes, Danae House. Ask her about the pageantry in Darlington."

"Do they have pageantry in Darlington, wherever that is?"

"Ignorance is never a matter for pride, Sister."

"A convert to the wonders of the north, are you?"

"It was a pleasant diversion."

"But now you're back where you belong. Why are you summoned to Malloren House?"

"For my sins, I'm sure. After my exertions in the north I deserve delightful idleness, but it seems Rothgar seeks to employ me, and I'm sure Father has demands. And here you are, not as happily situated as I'd like."

"I thought you lived a life of leisure."

"I may not toil at the routine work of my sinecures, but I've been given them so I can toil in other areas. I'll always be at your service, however."

She put a hand on his arm. "I know you will. It's such a comfort to have you back. I do need to talk to you, Perry, privately. There are so many things...."

"So it would seem. Send to tell me a good time tomorrow."

*Which would be after tonight.*

"What's amiss?" he asked, and she quickly smiled.

"Nothing but my scandal."

"Come and dance your worries away."

As they went that way she said, "If anything could, it would be a dance with you. Though Lord Dracy is almost as fine a dancer."

"Is he?" Perry asked.

"I was surprised too, but apparently a life in the navy includes time ashore, sometimes in elegant surroundings. Sometimes with fine ladies."

She did not want to think of his fine ladies.

"He tells you of his adventures?"

"We converse easily, on many subjects," she said as they took their places. "Ah, there he is in the ugly robe. He looked better as Neptune, but he's freed himself of most of the costume."

"I heard he was disfigured."

"The mask hides it. It's not so terrible when one gets used to it."

"Is it not?" Perry said, looking at her. "I rejoice for him."

The dance began, and Georgia stepped out lightly, feeling almost carefree at last. Perry was back. He was master of Town and court intrigue and had always been her best adviser and friend. He'd soon smooth out everything.

A good thing he didn't know about the wager and tryst, however, or he'd sort that out too.

Dracy watched Georgia, though he made sure not to insult his partner by it. He'd worried when she'd been summoned to a leading role in the demonstration of the dove, but he should have known that was Lady May's milieu.

He'd been jealous of the Dionysus she'd greeted with such joy. Merely a brother, he'd learned—the fribblous Peregrine Perriam, come as the god of drink and mayhem, but able to make her happy, damn him.

He saw a family resemblance, even though Perriam had brown hair and clean-cut features. It was in the eyes, perhaps, and in expressions and gestures.

Dracy made himself look away and relax. Georgia would be safe with her brother, perhaps safer than she was under his protection. Perriam must understand the choppy waters of the beau monde far better than he. But, he suddenly wondered, would the brother's arrival interfere with their nighttime tryst?

That would not be allowed.

# Chapter 24

The clocks were striking two when Georgia left Carlisle House accompanied by Dracy, Perry, and Jane. Her parents had returned home earlier and were probably already in bed.

All the better, as long as Perry didn't take the notion of coming with her to Hernescroft House to talk about her problems instead of returning to his own rooms. If he suggested that, she'd protest that she was too tired. In truth, she was wound up like that silver dove of peace, as if she could spring into action at a touch.

It was all so ridiculously dangerous, and she was trying to be sensible and good. . . .

She could claim that as they'd both won, neither had, and therefore neither owed a debt.

The carriage stopped by the building where Perry had rooms, and he climbed out, saying his good nights. One problem averted, but they'd soon be home, where she'd have to make her decision. She was sure Dracy was looking at her, but she concentrated on the darkness outside.

"We're here."

The carriage had stopped. He climbed out first, then assisted her and Jane to alight.

A footman knocked at the door, which opened, and they were home. Her august ancestors looked down in the candlelit gloom, and it was as if they all frowned at her.

"Good night, Dracy," she said, calling the wager off.

"Good night, Lady Maybury," he said, accepting her unspoken decree.

There, and it was better so, she told herself as she went up to her room.

Jane assisted her out of the gown and stays.

"What shall I do with the gown, milady? There's not too much to it without the head."

"Put it away somewhere. It might form the base of another. But remind me never to assume the guise of a bird again."

"Very well, milady, but why?"

"I don't like to be predictable. Bring my washing water and then get to your bed. I'm sure you're as tired as I am."

"You've powder in your hair, milady."

"And there it will stay until morning. But I will need a bath then."

"Very well, milady." Jane curtsied and left, and Georgia turned to the mirror.

How oddly pale she was, in her white shift and powdered hair, loose and tangled. Her scarlet lips did look grotesque. She tried to rub away the rouge with her shift, but a stain remained.

Soiled dove.

Scarlet woman.

Where was Dracy now?

Jane returned with a jug of steaming water and poured some into the basin. "Are you sure there's nothing else you need, milady?"

"Nothing. Good night, Jane."

Jane curtsied and left and Georgia knew she'd have no more interruptions unless she sought them.

Her white linen nightgown was spread on the bed with the green silk robe beside it.

She draped the nightgown over the screen around her washstand and went behind to take off her shift and wash. Even when alone, that was her habit, a habit she'd been trained in from infancy. She even bathed in a shift, in a tub with curtains modestly gathered around.

How could she ever have imagined standing naked in front of Dracy?

But she had imagined it, and him undressed as well....

She washed, whirled in confusion. She could keep to her room and keep safe, but Perry was back and soon Dracy would be free to return to Devon. She might never have such an opportunity again.

She dried herself and put on the nightgown, but she didn't go to bed. She paced. Why was it so *hard* to be sensible and virtuous? All she had to do was get into bed and stay there. She knew Dracy wouldn't invade.

She picked up the robe from the bed to put it on a chair.

But why? She already knew she was going to do it.

Her nightgown. It dated from before Dickon's death. Had she worn it for him?

No. It was a plain one, and she'd always worn finer ones when he'd told her he'd visit her bed. As on that last night ...

She buried that memory.

Tonight would be sinful, but it wouldn't be adulterous. Neither she nor Dracy were committed to another. All the same, she wished she'd purchased new nightgowns. The plain ones she had were in excellent condition, so it would have been an extravagance, but she'd never considered such things in the past.

Would Dracy really ask her to strip naked for him?

Could she do it?

How strange that she could mingle with hundreds in a costume that gave the illusion of bare breasts but faltered at the prospect of exposing them to one person.

\*   \*   \*

The footman brought Dracy hot water. He would have assisted him, but Dracy sent him away, only asking him to first bring port. He stripped off the classical robe and raised his hands to untie the mask. Then he paused to consider his appearance.

He'd been a handsome boy, youth, and man and given no thought to it apart from appreciating that it provided a choice of lovers. He hadn't grieved the loss of his good looks for long, especially when he'd found it didn't limit his choices. But when he'd put on this mask, he'd been reminded of what had been.

He'd minded then.

Because of Georgia Maybury.

He took off the mask, then turned from the mirror to wash, scrubbing the remains of the glue off his face. With so many obstacles in his way, it was madness to think his disfigurement important, but he wished it gone.

He was still naked when the footman brought the port, but it was Jem, who thought nothing of it.

"Are your wounds healing well, milord?"

"Yes, thank you. I've always healed well. Good night."

Jem left and Dracy poured himself some wine.

Beauty and the beast. If he succeeded in winning her, that would be how many would see them.

The ticking clock seemed to mark time slowly. Had it been as long as he thought? Would she come?

He shouldn't be waiting for her naked. He reached for his robe but then went to drawer to take out another. A gift from a high-born merchant's wife in Batavia, and of Chinese make. Red silk embroidered with a black dragon. As beautiful and impractical as Georgia's finest gown.

He put it on, fastening the long line of tasseled buttons at the front. If she came, if she asked him to undress, he could make something of the process. Laughing at himself, he sat in the armchair facing the door, the one she'd sat in a few nights ago, in fine white linen and pale green silk.

Beauty and the beast.

If he won her, the beau monde would speculate about why she'd entered such a mismatch. They'd say that Lady May needed to flee her shame and bury herself in the country. That Lady May had found her grand suitors gone and had to take the only man who'd have her. That Lady May had a taste for monsters. As with Charnley Vance.

She wasn't coming, and he should be glad of it.

He wasn't, selfish bastard that he was.

She'd revealed a chink in her armor—her sadly wanting marriage bed and her curiosity about the possibilities. Even a kiss had revealed the untapped passion that seethed in her.

He could release it. He silently toasted the ladies of his past who'd found it exciting to teach an angelic youth how to pleasure them. Some had liked it sweet, some had liked it naughty, and some had needed to be pushed to the edge of fear to achieve their full release. Those were the ones who'd favored him most after the wound.

He would discover Georgia's tastes and pleasure her until she was bound to him forever.

He rose to set the stage. He extinguished all the candles but one, and set that far from the bed. It was possible Georgia had never seen a naked man and never been naked herself in front of one. He wanted to pleasure her, not shock her.

If she came.

He touched the decanter of port. Rich, strong, and sweet. He'd no idea why ladies rarely drank it, for they always liked it when they did. There was only one glass, but sharing would be part of their pleasure.

He picked up the vial of oil he'd purchased from an Oriental shop far from the fashionable parts of London. The glass was a swirl of jewel-like reds and oranges ornamented with gold. Held to catch the candlelight, it glowed like fire. Like the fire he intended to ignite.

If she came.

He'd had them blend the perfume of the oil to his design—spicy and musky. It was completely unlike her perfume, for there was nothing of pretty blossoms about it. He'd no wish for the oil to tell tales, so he'd used it on himself here. He'd sent Georgia a book scented with it to explain any trace she carried back to her room.

If she came.

He set the vial by the bed and turned down the covers to expose the sheets. Then he sat in the armchair again, sipping port and appreciating the cool breeze that came in through the window. The clock ticked away the minutes, and then he heard another noise. He watched the door handle move down.

She had come, and his heart began to thump.

She slipped into the room, wide-eyed, hesitant, but blushing sweetly in that sea-foam robe. Quickly, quietly she shut the door, but stayed against it, looking at him.

She was dressed as before in robe over white nightgown trimmed with a frill at neck and wrists. This time, her loose, disordered hair was powdered white. He regretted that, but it created a magically fey effect.

In all his preparations for this moment, he hadn't anticipated the erotic power of Georgia Maybury, fairy princess.

# Chapter 25

She whispered, "Dracy?"

He rose and went to her. "You're like a creature from myth and magic."

"So are you. Dragons?"

"Never fear. They only eat virgins."

Her brows rose. "How many virgins have they eaten, then?"

He laughed at her way of picking up on an idea, but softly. Her parents slept on the far end of the corridor, but noise could carry.

"None, but they've nibbled their way through many more experienced women."

He wanted her to know that, to remember what he'd said before and believe it. He brought her hand to his lips, and instead of kissing it, nibbled gently on a finger.

"I should be shocked," she said unsteadily. "You're a thorough rake."

"To be condemned to rake coals in hell? Surely to deserve that fate a man must be cruel. I assure you, I'm never cruel to ladies in the night."

He dipped one of her fingers in the wine and then sucked the wine off.

Her breasts rose and fell from just that.

He dipped his own finger and offered it to her.

After a moment, she licked the wine off.

His heart pounded, but he said, "Do you like it?"

"It seems a good enough port."

Again he laughed. Why had he thought she'd not have tasted port wine? This was a woman who'd smoked a pipe for the experience and held an entertainment of living statues, male as well as female.

But with the males emasculated.

He offered her the glass. "More?"

She took it and sipped.

"Who goes first?" he asked.

"What?"

"Our quarter hour of power."

Her hands tightened on the glass. "I'm not sure either of us should. It would be wicked."

"This is wicked. Who goes first?"

She licked wine from her lips, which did nothing for his control, then said, "You."

"Why?"

When she didn't answer, he said, "You go first."

"Why?"

"Because you're not sure what to demand and are hoping to learn from me. If you go first you'll follow your instincts and desires." He stepped closer and put his fingers over hers on the glass. "What do you truly want, my fey Circe? What do you want to see, to do, to have done to you?"

She took a step away from him, and her back came up against a bedpost so that the port sloshed in the glass. She took another drink, a gulp, and swallowed. "I want what we spoke of. To see you naked."

"Too easy," he said and moved away from her to give her a better view.

Slowly he unfastened the buttons; then he peeled the robe back to let it slither to the floor.

She watched the whole time, wide-eyed and then slack jawed.

But then she started out of her daze, collecting herself, and sipped the wine.

Now she studied him, up and down, meeting the challenge, but concentrating as if expecting an examination later. Concentrating particularly on his rising erection.

"Turn, please."

Amused by the squeak in her voice, he did so, slowly, but continuing until he faced her again, which he was sure was not what she'd intended.

She surprised him by looking seriously at his face. "You have a lot of scars, in many places."

"None serious."

"I forget your navy past. That you've fought in a war. You seem . . . I'm not sure 'gentle' is the word, but . . ."

"I hope I'm a gentleman, and I have no natural taste for violence of any sort."

"But you did your duty, and you're always ready for it, aren't you? As when you were attacked by thieves. I see the wound."

"Old habits take time to shed. I hope to become a thoroughly easygoing country gentleman in time."

She smiled. "You'll need some fat on your belly and a lazy way of moving."

"Moving?"

"You move like a warrior, ready to command."

"I was only a lieutenant. I obeyed far more orders than I gave."

"If you'd stayed in the navy, you'd have become an admiral. I'm sure of that. You don't regret leaving?"

"Georgia, we can discuss my navy career at any time. Will you waste your diminishing minutes? I'm still yours to command."

She glanced at the mantel clock and her breasts rose and fell. "Will you come to me so I can touch you?"

"I'm yours to command," he reminded her.

She put aside the glass of wine. "Then come to me."

He did so, cock high, trying to tame it and the beating

drum of desire. He was almost pressed against her when she finally put her right hand on his chest to stop him. He covered it before he could even try to control the movement, loving to have her soft hand there where it belonged.

Every part of him said, "Mine."

She looked at their hands, and hers moved a little. "Do you think married couples do this sort of thing?"

"Shame if they don't."

"We didn't. Dickon and I. He came to me when I was in bed."

He raised her hand and kissed it, drawing her eyes up to his. Her big, beautiful, perplexed eyes. "I pity him. I fear he had no notion of the possibilities. If you were my wife, I'd see you naked every night."

"Every night? Oh, do you want me to . . . ?"

"This is your time," he reminded her, but he put her hand back on his body, but lower, on his belly not far above his cock. "If you hadn't done this, I would have asked you to when I have command."

"Touch you?" she asked, flexing her fingers again as if longing to explore.

"I'm yours to command, Georgia. What do you want now?"

He expected her hand to move lower, but she surprised him by saying, "Turn around. I mean, turn your back to me."

He did so smiling. No, a man would never be bored by Georgia Maybury. Georgia Dracy one day soon if there was any way to make it so. She touched him on his nape; then a fingernail traced down his spine, sending a shudder through him.

She stilled. "Does that hurt?"

"No."

"Then why did you shiver?"

"For the wonder and wickedness of it."

"Is it wicked, then?" she asked, continuing her gently abrasive exploration. "It doesn't seem so."

"Liar. But it's pure pleasure, which can never be wrong."

"I doubt most would agree with you on that."

He turned. "Do we care about the opinions of lesser mortals?"

She stared at him. "No."

"Now you've seen a naked man. What do you think?"

"That you're probably a finer specimen than most."

"Flattery. I like it."

"Truth. I've seen statues, cold and living, and pictures. None rivaled you."

"Pictures?"

"In books. Are you shocked?"

"No. Touch me again."

"I'm in command," she reminded him, teasing now, the minx. "I was shocked. I was trying to find out if we were doing things wrong."

"Because you didn't conceive."

She nodded, looking away. Brave Georgia Maybury had this one pit of sorrow, perhaps even of shame.

He turned her face back to him. "I'd never blame you for not conceiving, Georgia, remember that. But again, we can talk of such things fully clothed and by daylight. What do you want?"

She chuckled. No, it was a giggle, reminding him that though she'd been a wife for years, and even ruled her little world, she was still young and to be cared for.

"Command me," he said.

"Lie on the bed, then. I want to explore you from that angle."

'Struth. Young and bold.

"I obey," he said, but he passed her the perfumed oil. "If you wish, you may use this."

She took out the stopper and inhaled. "It's the perfume you put on that book, trying to cheat."

"Cheat?"

"So you'd detect me at the masquerade by smell."

He laughed. "I wish I'd been so clever. I sent the book so that any hint of that perfume on you would be explained. I used it here for the same reason."

"I smelled it when I came in. It's unusual, but I think I like it."

"It's for wicked nights, not elegant days."

She inhaled again, smiling like an ancient goddess. Heaven save him.

He lay on the bed, mischievously lying on his front, though it took a bit of adjustment.

He heard a sort of humph, but then oiled fingers slid across his back. He muttered into the pillow, praying for strength.

How typical of Georgia Maybury that in all innocence she found a novel sensation. He'd been massaged by professionals, and some of them had also been lovers, but he'd never before been tenderly, hesitantly, stroked in this way.

Both sets of fingers slid across his shoulders, then came together again to slip down his back. They went away, but then oil dribbled into the small of his back and her hands settled there, circling and then pushing up and down.

Down, down, and her oiled hands settled on his buttocks. He sucked in a breath, and she asked, "Should I stop?"

"No. But I wish there were a mirror so I could watch you, all green and white, stroking me, looking at me, I hope with pleasure."

"A mirror? You're a shocking man, Lord Dracy."

"You could spank me for it."

She giggled and slapped him.

"I see I'll have to provide you with a switch."

"Don't be silly," she said, soothing the spot where he'd hardly felt her blow.

He smiled, but then put the erotic images aside. Control was hard enough as it was.

She flexed her hands on his muscles, then slid them down onto his thighs, squeezing, then stroking. Then she lightened her touch so she barely stirred the hair there.

"Witch."

She chuckled in a way that celebrated her growing awareness of her power. "Such hard muscles," she said, running fingers down his calves.

"And other bits. I'm turning over."

He did so and she shifted back. "I'm not going to ... even when it's your turn. I can't. . . ."

He sat up and took her hands. "I know. It's all right. I need to deal with it, though."

"Deal with it?"

He glanced at the clock. "Your fifteen minutes are over. My first command is that you wait here for me."

She wrinkled her brow, but said, "I obey." Then with a wicked twinkle, she added, "In ripe anticipation of your commands, my lord and master."

Dracy swept up his robe, putting it on as he left the room. She learned quickly, far too quickly, and he adored her more by every moment. He went no farther than the corridor, where he indulged in memories of her touch and visions of complex pleasures as he shot his seed into a handful of the robe, doubtless ruining it.

It was a part of his past he no longer wanted, and perhaps he was now safe for fifteen more minutes with Georgia Maybury. He returned to his room.

Heaven help him, but she'd perched on the side of the bed, hands in her lap, ankles crossed. Embroidered green silk slippers peeped shyly from under her pure white hem.

"Are you deliberately looking like a schoolroom miss?"

"Do I? I'm sorry."

"How little you understand men. No, I'm sorry. I didn't mean it that way. It was a tease."

"But I don't understand," she said, "and I've been

thinking what a handicap it is to me. Not understanding. It makes selection of a husband like buying a horse without the slightest idea of breeds, points, or conformation."

He leaned back against the door, fighting noisy, outright laughter. "You are completely delightful, Georgia Maybury."

"Because I'm an ignorant wigeon?"

"Because you're frank and ready to learn."

"Only with you," she said. But that clearly struck her, for she quickly added, "What are your commands, my lord?"

He walked forward, put his hands at her waist, and swung her off the bed, showing his strength before putting her slowly down a yard or so away.

A small cloud of hair powder went with her and they both laughed.

He took her place on the bed and said, "Strip."

She'd been expecting it and showed only the briefest hesitation before unfastening her robe and letting it slither off to pool on the floor.

"Wait," he said. "I want to enjoy each layer."

She obeyed, but said, "It's a very plain nightgown."

"It's perfect."

Her white linen nightgown was completely concealing, but it pleased him more than any of the veils of Madame Mirabelle's living statues.

"Go on."

She looked down as she undid the first of the six buttons leading down from her neck, but as she undid the second she looked at him, attempting to be bold. Her gaze slipped by to some spot behind him.

A better man would give her a reprieve.

He was about to do that, when she shifted her gaze back to his and held it as she worked down the buttons to the sixth and last, the one between her high, firm breasts. As she unfastened that one she suddenly smiled in knowing pleasure of the effect on him.

Goddess that she was, she then took her time over untying the laces that kept her ruffles snug at her wrists.

Then instead of taking off the nightgown, she removed her pretty slippers and placed them neatly, side by side.

Then, only then, did she raise the voluminous garment by the hem and take it off over her head, gradually revealing all her secrets. He was breathless and speechless — but then she coughed at a new small cloud of powder. Laughing, she shook her head, generating more as she tossed the garment aside, and he had to laugh too.

She stood there proudly and looked him in the eye. "What now, my lord and master?"

Heaven save him. He wanted to fall to his knees and kiss her pretty toes.

"Turn," he said. As she obeyed, he said, "You're perfectly formed. Do you know that?"

She peeped backward at him. "Everything seems in the right place, I admit."

"And everything is just as it should be. That's the prettiest arse I've ever seen."

She continued slowly in her turn. "That doesn't mean much when they're normally covered by hoops and skirts."

"Depends where you are," he said with a grin. "Now come to me."

She stayed where she was. "I told you, I can't risk getting with child."

He loved that her brain and sense of caution were still working. It meant he could push her harder.

"I'll not put you in danger. Trust me."

He thought perhaps she wouldn't, but then she obeyed, as supple and elegant on bare feet as in heeled shoes, hips swaying, high breasts moving just a delicious bit.

He put his hands on her waist, feeling her tremor. "Your husband truly never enjoyed this?"

She shrugged, and it was not a sensible question. He commanded himself to sense.

He oiled his hands, rubbing them together, then put them on her sides and slid them down, enjoying her caught breath, a sway of reaction.

He slid his hands around her buttocks. "So round where a woman should be round"—he settled at her waist a moment—"so trim where a woman should be trim." He cupped her perfect breasts. "So plump where a woman should be plump. And so proud where a woman should be proud."

He leaned forward and gently sucked on one jutting pink nipple.

She jerked, but he ignored it, holding her firmly as he completed his homage to one breast and then attended to the other. Her hands clutched his shoulders, breath catching, and he wanted to go down to hell to thrash her husband. No, the poor lad had probably been as ignorant as she, thinking his brief pumping pleasure the best to be had.

She was quivering now, and he smiled into her wide, anxious eyes. "I will command, but you can refuse if I distress you. You remember that?"

She nodded, but then whispered, "This is . . . this is . . . normal?"

"Too tricky a question for now, sweet Circe."

He kissed her gently, wanting above all to give her that, the gentle loving that was in his heart. He tasted her soft lips, her warm mouth, holding her soft, silken body to his.

He could enjoy this for hours, but he had so few minutes.

He slid his mouth to her ear. "This is very normal. We could do this in our drawing room, in our garden, or beneath an apple tree in our orchard."

He was painting a picture. Was she listening?

She shifted to look him in the eye. "Rather more clothed, I hope? For now, if you please, something we could not do in all those places?"

He took her mouth more forcefully, glorying in the way she melted into him, sharing the passion in her soul, the passion that matched his. He could have kissed her like this too for hours, if they had hours, but too many minutes were gone.

She wanted something more, something she hadn't yet even imagined.

He would give her that.

# Chapter 26

He broke the kiss and said, "Step up onto the bed."

"Up?" she asked.

"Yes."

He handed her up the three steps, admiring her feet, her toes, her neat ankles and shapely legs. A lady's legs were the great mystery, and sometimes a disappointment, but nothing about Georgia disappointed. Nothing could. If she'd revealed herself to be thin hipped, her breasts an illusion of padding, and her legs as straight as tree trunks, it would have made no difference to his besotted mind, but as it was, she threatened his sanity.

She stood on the mattress, her head brushing the fringed valance, looking down at him. "This excites you?"

He smiled up at her. "It will. Hold the rail on either side of your head."

She did so, but said, "This is peculiar."

"You'll need something to hold on to. I hope the bars are sturdy. Spread your legs."

"What?" He saw hesitation and the beginning of rebellion, but then she shifted her feet sideways on the down mattress.

"More."

She spread them more, but frowning now. "What are you going to do?"

"Mystery can be part of the pleasure. Are you uncomfortable?"

"I'm not sure I like this. Tell me what you're going to do. You said I could object."

He ran an oiled finger up the inside of her right leg to brush her inner thigh. "Pleasure you. You can always escape. Where you are now, you could knee me in the nose."

"An unusual opportunity, I'll grant. Why are you doing that?"

He was using both hands now on her thighs. "Don't you like it?"

She wriggled slightly. "Perhaps, but this is your time, not mine."

"My only desire is to pleasure you. Permit me, but remember that you can stop me with a word."

"What word?"

"Stop," he said and moved one hand slowly, gently, into the dusky pink folds between her legs.

Georgia gripped the rail tighter, sure she should object, for decency's sake if no other. She'd agreed to this wager knowing it would be wicked. But she'd had no idea what wickedness might mean.

Heaven help her, he was touching her *there*. No wonder it was sinful. Sins so often seemed to be wickedly pleasurable.

She made a noise, and her legs quivered. He murmured something she could make no sense of, but it sounded pleased, or encouraging. Encouraging of what?

She was aching down there now, low in her belly, between her legs. It had happened before, at odd times, and she'd been aware of a hunger, a need. She'd never connected it to Dickon's messy invasions, but now she did.

Now—yes—now she wanted, needed, to be invaded. To have that hard thrusting. There. Now. "Please . . ." She'd said it. "No. I mean . . . we can't."

"Hush, hush . . . Hold on tight and remember to be quiet."

"Quiet?"

She looked down to where he looked up, from between her legs.

"You don't want your parents to hear," he said.

"Heavens, no . . . Oh . . ."

His mouth!

She held on as tightly as she could as the rest of her body seemed to shake and melt into jelly.

His tongue. It must be his tongue. Firm and hard, thrusting.

Not like Dickon.

Nothing like Dickon.

"Oh stars, oh stars, oh stars . . . Oh!" She managed, barely, to choke it back. She was swaying as if storm tossed, bucking against the hands that gripped her hips, holding her for his ravishing.

She strangled sounds as best she could as waves of pain and pleasure shook her to her core, and then something sent her rigid in the most wonderful way, again and again and again, sapping all her strength.

He caught her.

She'd let go of the rail and collapsed, but somehow he'd caught her and laid her on the bed. Now he covered her, naked to her nakedness, kissing her.

Kissing her as she'd never been kissed, with a taste on him that she recognized as perfume and herself, her heart still pounding against his, his hands running over her, soothing her, pleasuring her.

His mouth on her breasts again. Her aching breasts, her needful breasts. Creating instant, greedy need. His hand between her thighs now, his fingers inside her.

"No, oh no . . ."

He went still. "No?"

Her body throbbed in rebellion. "I'll break."

He laughed and kissed her, gently now, as if sipping

from a cup, his touch so gentle, one finger stroking over slick flesh, so she floated as if on a boat on a river of pleasure, drifting, drifting. His mouth on her earlobe, her neck, her shoulder, her breast. Only slowly licking to her nipple, then so gently there as an ache built and her hips raised up off the bed, seeking, demanding.

His hand moved faster, his mouth demanded, and the pleasure surged through her again and again, arching her and releasing her, and everything went black.

"Did I faint?" she asked, limply prone, his body hot over hers.

Stroking her, but oh so softly, so undemandingly, he said, "Perhaps. A little absence to recover. It's commoner for women than for men, for women can take so much more pleasure at a time."

"I'm . . ."

"Don't try to explain it, Georgia."

She fell silent, deliciously amazed by a satisfaction so deep it felt like a new existence. She couldn't remember ever being so relaxed before, and she'd certainly never enjoyed the astonishing comfort of a big, hot body over hers.

But normality crept back, and along with it, thoughts.

She pushed up and shifted, rolling over to look up at him. He moved to one side, head resting on a hand, smiling at her in a way that seemed a wonder of its own.

Oh, sweet heaven, she'd vowed not to break his heart.

"Now I'm more confused," she said, trying to be matter-of-fact, which was hard when he put a hand on one of her breasts. "I see why Babs enjoys her marriage bed so much and misses Harringay when he's away, but Lizzie seems only mildly pleased by hers yet quite content."

He leaned to kiss the tip of the nipple. "Perhaps she is. Or perhaps she thinks it a private storm, not to be spoken of. There are many variations on this theme, and we can explore all of them."

That book. Those pictures . . .

She put a hand to his face. Because of how they lay, it was to the scarred side of his face, but she didn't mind. She wanted to touch it now, as if her touch could magic the hurt and damage away.

"It would be too dangerous to do this again," she said.

"I kept my promise. You're in no risk of conceiving."

"Not that."

"Then what?"

"Being caught."

"That's not what concerns you."

"Very well. That I raise your hopes."

"If I'm willing to bear the disappointment, it needn't distress you."

"Then that I come to like this too much."

"What danger in that?"

"You understand. I can't marry you."

"A license and a church and it'd be done." Before she could respond, he went on, "I've made no secret of enjoying many women, but I tell you truly, I've never enjoyed pleasuring one as I have you."

"A decent woman should not be pleased by that."

"But you are pleased." He stroked her cheek with his knuckles, looking into her eyes. "You're made for this, Georgia, and for so much more, and you've always known it. That's why you knew your marriage was lacking, even though you didn't know how. Think about this. Remember this. What does rank and fortune matter when we can weave such rare magic for the rest of our lives?"

It was the temptation of Satan, but she pushed his hand away. "I command you not to say such things."

"You're past your fifteen minutes."

Fear collided with wicked desire. She rolled off the bed and grabbed her clothing.

He watched her, smiling wryly.

"You're not unique," she threw at him.

"No, I'm not, though you are. What other woman would have this conversation here and now? In case you're unwise enough to settle for less, my lovely Georgia, there are ways you can pleasure yourself. I could teach you those too."

She ran for the door, but he said, "Slippers."

With a hiss of annoyance, she dashed back to pick them up and then escaped, running naked across the corridor to her own room.

She stood there, heart galloping, half fearing pursuit.

He wouldn't, however, and in some way that seemed tragic.

# Chapter 27

Jane woke Georgia the next day with her chocolate. "It's gone noon, milady, and Lord Dracy has asked to see you."

Georgia felt the blush rise. "He'll have to wait. I need to bathe and get the powder out of my hair."

Jane was sniffing. "That book's making a real stink, milady. You should get rid of it."

Her cheeks were getting hotter. "No, not yet. Order my bath, please."

Jane left and Georgia tried to reassemble herself into some normal form, but she felt taken to pieces and put together differently. She looked up at the rail around this bed, drowning in memories, understanding at last why some women threw away honor, reputation, fortune, even family out of lust for a man.

That would not be her.

Dracy had opened a door for her, but . . .

But she couldn't imagine going through with any man but him.

"Yet," she said aloud.

She simply needed time to work through it all. And other things. Perry was back. He'd untangle her scandals, and by the time that was done, Dracy would be back in Devon. She'd be sane, and she'd have sane suitors again.

Jane returned and drew the bed-curtains to provide privacy from the servants who were bringing the bath and jugs of water.

In a shadowy nest, Georgia sipped her chocolate, allowing her mind to return where it willed. She'd experienced a new world and must understand it.

Her chocolate seemed more delicious, her pillow softer. Every part of her seemed alive to new sensation, and she fizzed with questions. Definitely not ones she could ask of Jane.

Not of Babs either, for all that Babs could answer them. Babs, so unabashedly in lust for her husband, and he for her, but deep in love too.

She wanted that in her marriage.

She remembered her idea of trying out men until she was with child. Dear heaven! Difficult enough to contemplate lying under potential husbands as they did the necessary. Doing the sorts of things she'd done last night!

With Beaufort or with Bridgwater?

A suppressed giggle made her choke.

Jane poked her head through the curtains. "Are you all right, milady?"

"Yes, yes!" Georgia gasped, trying to conquer the coughing.

"Your bath's ready, milady."

Georgia had heard the tub thump down on the floor and busy footsteps, but she'd been in another world.

"In a moment, Jane."

She'd been in the world of Dracy's skilled hands and mouth, and his hard, warrior's body. She'd never seen Dickon's body, but Dickon had never had to exert himself more than he cared for, and never, as best she knew, had to fight for his life.

Except, of course, at the end.

She cradled the cooling cup. How disloyal to think less of Dickon for that. Hard-muscled sporting men were two a penny—like Shaldon, Crackford, and Vance. Good, kind ones were precious.

Dracy was good and kind, and admired by his friends. And a skilled lover.

Unfair to compare Dracy's expertise with Dickon's lack of it. All the same, she knew which she preferred.

And she knew what she wanted.

She wanted to see what else Dracy had to teach her.

"Milady, the water's growing cold!"

Georgia pulled herself together and climbed out of bed. She went behind the screen to exchange her nightgown for her plain bathing shift. After last night modesty seemed silly, but to alter a lifetime's habits now would be to wave a flag. Strangely, it would still feel wrong to be naked in front of her maid.

She climbed into the tub and set to scrubbing her body with soap and cloth. It was ridiculously awkward with the sodden shift in the way. In time, she *would* change this, modesty be damned.

"Put your head back now, milady."

Georgia did so, and Jane began to wash her hair in a bowl. "Perhaps I'll give up powder entirely."

"Not as long as fashion requires it, you won't. And it was a very pretty addition to your dove costume."

"Yes, it was, wasn't it? There were some clever costumes. Lord Dracy's was quite good for someone inexperienced, don't you think?"

"A tolerable effort, milady."

Irresistible to talk about him. "He rescued me from Lord Sellerby."

"I heard something odd went on, milady. What did Lord Sellerby do?"

"He was distinctly discourteous, and when I tried to walk away, he stepped on the dove's tail of my gown."

"The monster!"

"Angel, actually, and quite a fine one until Dracy dragged him off by the wings."

"Oh, dear, milady, that must have been a scene."

"Yes and some people will hold it against me. It's so unfair. I am not at home to Lord Sellerby, Jane. Ever again."

"Very well, milady, but what a shame. He was such a fine gentleman, and you enjoyed his company."

"Perhaps too much. But Perry's back, so I'm sure I can be restored, plus the matter of the dove of peace was to my advantage, I think."

"Your costume, you mean, milady?"

"No. Perhaps you didn't hear. The king sent that automaton that the odd Chevalier d'Eon presented to him when acting as French ambassador—a silver dove of peace. I missed the occasion because I was ill, but everyone spoke of how pretty it was, but how Rothgar's had been the better. Are you done?"

"Just the rinse now, milady."

"The king sent the dove to the masquerade under the marquess's care, and Lord Rothgar summoned me to set it in motion. I was somewhat alarmed after the Sellerby debacle, but I think Lord Rothgar meant it well, and perhaps it served. I was presented to all in my costume of peace and purity, and with Rothgar's approval, which counts for something."

"The marquess likely knows your connection to his wife, milady."

"Certainly, and has always been kind, though I find him somewhat awe inspiring."

"It's to be glad something inspires you to awe, milady. There, done." She wrapped a towel around Georgia's head. "As well we didn't use much grease, or the powder would have been much harder to remove."

"Though the powder didn't stick as well. I dusted my partners in the dance, and it's all around this room. . . ."

And Dracy's room!

And he hadn't been powdered.

It was as if the water had turned icy cold.

Georgia surged out of the bath, grabbing the towel

from Jane. How could she have been so foolish? Even now, were servants whispering about the hair powder and coming to scandalous conclusions?

She sat at the desk.

"Milady! You need to get into dry clothes."

"I remembered a note I must send."

"Surely it'd wait—"

"It won't." Georgia dipped a pen and wrote quickly, struggling for innocent words.

> *My dear Lord Dracy,*
> *I believe we were to meet today to discuss carpets for your Devon house. There was also the matter of cleaning them, and how to remove a variety of scattered matter. I will shortly be at your service, sir.*

She regretted those last words, conventional though they were, but every moment might count.

She scrawled her signature and folded the sheet. No candle lit for sealing wax, so she gave it to Jane. She trusted Jane.

"Take it directly to Lord Dracy, please. Yes, now."

As the maid left, Georgia went behind the screen, peeling off her clammy shift, fighting a need to run across the corridor and check Dracy's room.

Jane returned. "Lord Dracy's gone out, milady, but I left the note with one of the footmen."

Thank heaven she'd chosen her words so carefully. She realized that it was all pointless anyway. It was gone noon and a maid would have cleaned the room as soon as Dracy left. She hugged herself, feeling newly vulnerable, and this time she *was* guilty of a sin. She'd taken solace from the fact that she was innocent of any sin connected to Dickon's death. In truth, it may have saved her sanity....

"Milady?"

Georgia had to put on a dry shift and emerge, just as she had to face her life. There was no true escape short of flight into exile, and even then a person had to go to a remote spot indeed not to be found. She wasn't made for such misadventures.

Jane helped Georgia into her wrap. "Sit you down, milady, so I can comb out your hair. It'll be such a job after you sleeping with it unplaited."

Georgia obeyed, but she had to probe for any hint of scandal.

"Is there talk among the servants this morning, Jane?"

Jane began to gently tease out the knots. "Talk, milady? About what?"

Stupid to even raise the thought. "About Lord Sellerby's behavior last night."

"Nought's been said that I've heard, milady. And that fracas was not to your discredit."

"I'm sure some will make it so."

Georgia couldn't press for more, but surely if the servants were whispering about Lady Maybury's hair powder on Lord Dracy's carpet, Jane would have heard.

Perhaps there hadn't been as much as she'd thought, or it had been trodden in. It seemed she'd escaped that disaster, but she couldn't face the world yet.

"I'm going to enjoy a quiet day, Jane."

"A good idea, milady. You're looking a bit peaked."

Georgia couldn't even bear to be fussed over. "I set you at liberty. You have the day to do as you wish, though I recommend that you leave the house so you won't be pulled into some other work."

"Thank you, milady. I'd like to visit my friend Martha Hopgood. She was a maid with me at . . ."

Georgia listened with surprise to a story out of Jane's earlier life, for her maid rarely chattered of such things. Her friend Martha had married the keeper of the Three Cups in Clerkenwell.

"Didn't she find that a change from being maid in a nobleman's house?"

"A change for the better, milady, for she became mistress of her own house and now has five fine children."

"Ah yes." Georgia understood that. "Do you ever wish you'd married, Jane?"

"Never had an offer I liked, milady. No husband's better than most, I reckon."

"Perhaps that's why God invented love. To overcome our good sense. You've never been in love?"

"Not that I've noticed, milady, and from what I've seen, there's no mistaking it. Fit for Bedlam some are, when it hits them. Why, I remember one maid who could hardly walk straight she was in such a daze, and of course there's many a one—man or woman—who's tipped into a ruinous mismatch by it."

Georgia kept a slight smile, as if her conscience was as clear as a nun's.

"Can a mismatch never be happy? The lady who runs off with the footman? The gentleman who marries the dairy maid?"

"I doubt it, milady. I know of a young lady of high birth who ran off and wed a coach maker—can you believe it? A fine figure of a man, to be sure, and a sound business, but back she came to her father's house, a babe in arms, weeping at the hard life she had, with no fine clothes or parties, and too few servants."

"What happened?"

"Her husband came to claim her and the child, and the father released her to him, for he had the right of it. She'd chosen her path. A lady must live at her man's level, and I doubt many like to live lower than they're used to, no matter how lusty he is. It's little better for the foolish gentlemen, even though they don't sink in society. Caught by a pretty dairy wench and end up with a wife who doesn't know how to make a fine home and who's a figure of fun to his friends."

Was Jane deliberately sending warnings? She'd seemed

to favor Dracy at one point, but perhaps she'd come to her senses.

Marry Dracy. That was the thought that bounced in her head like a ball in a *jeu de paume* court. Her sinking wouldn't be as far, but she wouldn't enjoy the lack of fine clothes and adequate servants.

Dracy would be as ill served. She knew how to make a fine home, but only with money. His friends wouldn't laugh at her, but would they be comfortable around her?

She'd felt at ease with the naval officers, but Dracy's Devon friends would be the gentry around Dracy Manor, which meant the sort of ladies who made a fuss about their one or two new gowns a year and were interested only in children and household nostrums, generally for revolting conditions like the bloody flux.

"There, milady, I've worked the knots out, but it'll take a while to dry, thick as it is."

Georgia stood, fingering her damp hair, thinking of Dracy's thick hair beneath and around her fingers. . . .

"Do you want your letters, milady?"

"Letters?"

"I mentioned them before the bath, milady, but you didn't seem interested."

Lost in foolish thoughts. Georgia looked through the three. One was from Althea Maynard, one from Lizzie, and another from an H. True. She knew no one by that name.

She was about to the snap the seal when Jane said, "Which gown, milady?"

She'd promised Jane the day off, and she'd no need of anything fine for a day at home. But she'd be speaking with Dracy and would like to look her best. . . .

Enough of folly. "The same as yesterday," she said.

"What if someone comes to call, milady? I sponged off the dirt as best I could, but there are stains near the hem."

"I won't be at home unless it's Perry. Or Lord Dracy,

of course." Georgia hesitated, for she truly wanted to look her best for him. *Enough of folly.* "Do find it, Jane, and then you can be off to see your friend."

Jane produced the gown and jumps, and then Georgia shooed her away and dressed by herself.

It was oddly pleasant to fend for herself, to be alone. Except in the night, it so rarely happened.

What a strange mood she was in.

It didn't take long to dress, and then she surveyed herself in dull blue, thinking she looked a little like a countrywoman—except that no decent countrywoman would go about with her hair hanging down her back.

Decent woman.

Hair powder.

She went to the door, opened it a little, and looked out. All seemed quiet. She could cross the corridor to Dracy's room and see if the powder was still there. If it was, perhaps she could get rid of it, but she had no brush other than her hairbrush. . . .

She went back into her room and closed the door. This house was properly run, so the room would have been cleaned. The other reason for giving up the plan was that it seemed scandalously sinful. Yesterday she would have invaded his room without a qualm, secure in her innocence. Now it was as if it would brand her a whore.

A whore.

As bad as she'd been painted.

There'd be no more such frolics, and the sooner she told Dracy that, the better.

When he returned they must meet on safe, neutral ground. She took her correspondence to the small drawing room. The sun was shining in, and she raised a window and moved a chair so she could let it dry her hair as she read.

So delightfully warm on her back. She fingered her hair to let the warmth reach the lower layers and slid back into sensuous memories. Of Dracy's fingers in her hair, against her scalp. She circled her own fingers there, and it was almost as sweet. But only almost.

She remembered the wild storm he'd created for her, and the gentle sweetness that had rocked her as power-fully in the end. There'd been smiles and laughter, and warmth, such warmth, for body and for soul.

With such a man she need never be cold, or alone, or afraid. . . .

Knowing she shouldn't, she allowed herself to relive the pleasures of the night.

Dracy had slept until gone ten, but once awake he'd quickly dressed and left Hernescroft House. He didn't trust himself there when the need to return to Georgia burned so fiercely in him. Perhaps the greenery of the parks would sooth the heat and calm his need to possess her. By force if necessary.

What if she persisted and chose another?

He'd go mad for fear that she'd be miserable.

Many men were selfish. They didn't understand the pleasure of pleasuring a woman. Their whores would pretend pleasure at even their crudest attentions, requir-ing no thought or effort from them. He'd heard some men claim that decent women had no interest in passion, and one that he'd whipped his wife for suggesting a lack and never trusted her since.

What if Georgia fell into marriage with a man like that? If he'd left her in ignorance she might have been content.

But she'd never been content, and her natural passion would explode one day, wreaking havoc. She could end up as a truly scandalous countess, the sort of highborn lady notorious for lying with any lusty man who could slake her hungers. Like the fine ladies who'd visited Vance's "lair."

Conscience warred with desire, and logic tormented him over both.

When he'd seen the hair powder on the carpet, he'd been tempted to leave it there, for he knew the scandal of it would force her to wed him.

He'd cleaned it away, however, and made sure no other evidence lingered. He wanted no wife against her will, and he saw all the ways his world would not suit Georgia Maybury. But he wanted her anyway, to the point of madness.

He could remove one obstacle by abandoning Dracy and living the frivolous Town life she adored. Perhaps applying himself to politics and doing his best for the navy would salve his conscience. Politics didn't pay the bills, however, and he'd not take bribes. They'd have to live on Georgia's money.

Could they?

What would be the interest income on twelve thousand? No more than a thousand without taking foolish risks, and probably no more than six hundred. They'd need at least a third of that to rent a decent house.

Madness. She'd need servants and a carriage, and then there was her love of fine clothes. He'd read that one grand gown for the queen's birthday celebrations had cost three thousand pounds. They'd end up spending the principal, and that was a sure road to ruin.

In any case, he didn't want to live in London year-round. The parks, pleasant though they were, couldn't compare to true countryside, and no labor here could be as rewarding as bringing Dracy back to prosperity. In time that income could at least match the investments, but it would be a long time unless he used much of her dowry on the estate and stud.

Georgia Maybury wasn't for him, and if not for the business of Fancy Free and Cartagena, he'd never have dreamt of reaching so high.

He'd reached. He'd touched. But she might as well be the moon.

He turned wearily toward the nearest coffeehouse,

but halfway there, he changed direction to return to
Hernescroft House. Dolt that he was for letting his lust
and miseries blind him to important matters.

He still hadn't shared his thoughts about Sellerby.
They'd seemed outrageous, but after the man's behavior
last night, perhaps less so, and the incident last night
could have pushed him to new menace. He'd been publi-
cally rejected by Georgia and then manhandled in front
of his precious beau monde. He'd left the masquerade
immediately after the incident, but he would be today's
breakfast snigger. It served him right, especially if he was
the one behind that letter, but he was the sort of weasel
to need to bite back.

When he entered the house and inquired, he was told
that Lady Maybury was in the drawing room. The world
seemed brighter as he went quickly up the stairs. He
went in and paused to smile at the vision she presented.

She was sitting by an open window in yesterday's
plain gown, her hair, a mass of copper and bronze in the
sunlight, forming a halo around her glowing loveliness.

But then he realized she was staring into nowhere like
a dead person.

# Chapter 28

"Georgia?"

She blinked and looked at him wildly, her hand moving to cover some paper in her lap.

Some proof of her guilt?

Sick, he went forward. "What is it?"

"Nothing!" She'd have crumpled the paper, but he snatched it from her.

"Don't!" she cried, but then thrust a knuckle between her teeth.

He smoothed it out.

Not an incriminating letter, but a cartoon, the sort of satirical drawing seen everywhere. But this one . . .

He shoved it in his pocket and pulled her into his arms. "Forget it."

"How?" she wailed, and burst into tears.

He held her, rocking her. Then he carried her to the settee, where he could hold her in his lap as she wept her misery.

The clearly etched picture had shown a filly, labeled "Lady M**b**y," tail high in invitation, with Maybury and Vance, swords in hands, arguing over the finer points of her legs, breast, and rump. In a bubble from her horse's mouth came, "Cease your squabbling, gentlemen. I need one of you to mount me for a rollicking ride."

In one corner another picture showed a man lying dead, a sword still in his chest, while nearby, a couple embraced.

The paper wasn't new, so it probably dated from the time of the duel. Hundreds must have been printed, perhaps thousands, and she would have realized that.

Her family must have kept such things from her. It had been intended as a kindness, but ignorance makes a person vulnerable, and in this case it had led her to underestimate her scandalous reputation. He too had had no idea it went so far. A wonder she'd been accepted as much as she had. Testimony, he supposed, to her family's power and influence, and to her own true nature. But perhaps this explained her parents' puzzling drive toward her marrying him.

They'd not believed she could fully recover from the disaster and sought a husband who would take her away from London and the cruel beau monde. They probably had investigated his character and found him adequate, but above all they'd wanted no more scandal in the family.

They'd thought to trap her at Thretford House and settle matters there, but Georgia had plotted her escape. So, then, the spurious betrothal, intended to pave the way to a real one. Had the placement of their bedchambers so close been part of the plan?

He damned the Hernescrofts even though their plotting might take him where he longed to be.

Not like this, however. Not like this, with Georgia brokenhearted in his arms.

Who had sent this poison? No attempt here to increase the scandal—only to hurt.

Sellerby, taking revenge for last night?

Miss Cardross, venting her spite?

Some other viper, simply outraged that the scandalous Lady May had dared to appear so carefree, had been chosen to stand high above all in switching on that damned dove?

When would it stop?

Her sobs eased and she dragged out a handkerchief to blow her nose.

"I'm sorry. So silly . . ."

"Not silly at all. That disgusting drawing must have been a shock."

She could only nod.

He pushed back hair that had fallen near her eyes. "I'm sorry you had to see it, but it's always best to know your enemy."

"But I don't want to *have* any enemies!"

He cradled her face and put a soft, soothing kiss on her unsteady lips. "Be brave, Georgia. . . ."

Someone cleared a throat.

Georgia pushed off Dracy's lap. Dracy swiveled to face danger. But saw only a slender man in a plain but elegant blue suit.

Dionysus.

"Perry!" Georgia said, running to him. "Do shut the door." She did it herself. "That wasn't . . . Well, it was. But I just received a horrible shock!"

"What shock?" the Honorable Peregrine Perriam asked, but his manner raised Dracy's hackles. He realized he might be facing an enemy to all he wanted.

"Oh, I don't want to talk about it," Georgia said quickly. "Come and sit. Do you know Lord Dracy?"

Perriam bowed with the expertise of a dancing master, and Dracy felt obliged to return it as best he could. He passed the crumpled cartoon to Perriam.

Georgia turned and went to the window.

"He'll have seen it already," Dracy said to her back.

Perriam put it in his pocket. "Yes. I'm sorry, Georgie. How did it reach you?"

She turned, superficially composed. "Enclosed in a letter. I mean, there was no letter, but it formed a packet for it."

Perriam went to pick up the paper from the floor and

inspected it. "Blank seal, and from H. True. Clearly a false name."

Dracy ached to take Georgia back into his arms. She looked so vulnerable standing there alone, and Perriam had already seen them embracing, but he suspected that she didn't want any more coals on that fire.

"Eloisa Cardross?" he said to her. "Or even someone who envied your costume at the masquerade."

"Nerissa Trelyn was spiteful."

"There you are."

"But it could have been anyone!" she exclaimed. "And that's the problem. It seems I have a host of enemies, and I can never know what she, he, or anyone will do next. I didn't know it was as foul as that. Why did no one tell me?"

He put his arm around her. "You've been protected too well, but perhaps it served. If you'd known, could you have returned to the beau monde so bravely, chin high?"

She looked up at him, tears still on her lashes. "No, but now I know. . . ." She leaned her head against him. "I don't know how I can go on."

"Courage, Georgie. You're a Perriam," her brother said.

Dracy could have throttled him, but it did seem to brace her.

"This is new to you," Perriam went on, "but old news to Town. It changes nothing unless you permit it."

He was making no objection to the embrace, but Dracy still felt the chill. He was Georgia's favorite brother and she put great store in his advice.

"Now we've dealt with that," Perriam said, as if all anguish was past, "order tea, Sis, and we'll discuss your situation in depth."

Georgia moved out of Dracy's arms to ring the bell. Had that been the intent? She had some of her courage back, however, so perhaps her brother knew how to handle her.

"In depth?" she asked.

"In depth," Perriam said. "It seems a great deal has been happening in my absence."

"I didn't ask you to go north at such a time!"

"No, but a friend did, a duty that supercedes care for a sister. Or so it seemed at the time."

A footman came in and was sent to bring the tea.

"I anticipated no great problems in my absence," Perriam said. "My apologies."

"Nor did I," she said, sitting wearily on the settee. "Or, nothing like the ones I've faced."

Dracy wanted to sit beside her but took a chair.

It seemed unfair when Perriam sat beside her and even took her hand. "Tell me what's been happening."

"Father wouldn't permit me to come directly to Town, so I visited Winnie in Hammersmith. She held a ball for me, though it turned into a political affair. I intended to dress demurely in order to obliterate any scandalous notions, but in the end I couldn't. It wouldn't have been me," she said. "You understand that, don't you?"

He smiled. "Perfectly. What did you wear?"

"The peacock."

"Perfect."

"Truly? I've thought since, that if I'd . . ."

"No. When the beasts are circling, never show fear."

Dracy agreed but said, "That's a trifle harsh, Perriam."

Perriam looked at him, but whatever he might have said was silenced by the entrance of servants with a tea tray and plates of thin biscuits.

When they'd left, Georgia busied herself with the making of the tea, and perhaps a purpose helped her.

"Were you at my sister's ball, Dracy?" Perriam asked.

"I was."

"And your assessment?"

"People were intensely curious. Some wanted to believe the scandal and some didn't. Some, of course, being jaded, hoped for trouble to provide amusement."

"Such behavior is as common in a village as in Town," Perriam said, "and as common in the navy as in the coffeehouses, I'll be bound."

Unwillingly, Dracy said, "A point, sir, I grant you." Peregrine Perriam seemed a Town idler, but he might have as many complex depths as his sister.

He accepted tea from Georgia, and Perriam did the same, choosing a biscuit with irritating precision. The man looked up. "My sister's ball?" he reminded.

"Ah yes. Matters turned awry. People murmured about a letter, but I lack the charts for these waters and I couldn't track the problem. You'd tell it better, Georgia."

She sipped her tea. "It was the dowager's letter, Perry. The one she claimed to have but never showed anyone, and which didn't turn up after her death. We assumed she'd invented it to add fuel to her spiteful fire, but . . . At Winnie's ball, the rumor started that someone actually had it, and would show it to trusted people before publishing it for all to see."

"Who?" Perriam asked.

"We tracked it down to Eloisa Cardross, and she admitted it."

"Eloisa Cardross? Why would that ninny do such a thing?"

"Because she's a ninny," Georgia said. "But also out of jealousy. You know she and Millicent were considered great beauties in Gloucestershire. When her family compelled her to move to Herne to play companion to Millicent during her time, she was confronted with me. It was all pettiness until the dinner after the horse race. Beaufort was there, and Richmond. They, Sellerby, and a number of other gentlemen made much of me. Only because it was my first appearance, of course, but she took it amiss."

"But how could she have the letter? I would have sworn it didn't exist. The dowager would have nailed it to a church door if she'd had it."

Dracy took the letter from his pocket and passed it over. "I think it's a forgery."

Perriam read it through. "Almost certainly. I doubt Vance could write such sound sentences, and he had no reason to spew those lies." He considered the front. "Addressed to Major Jellicoe, his second. A plausible recipient." He produced a small magnifying glass and studied the address and other marks. "Yes, I think you're right, Dracy, though I'll have an expert opinion. I'd lay fifty that stamp from Cologne is painted on."

A very interesting gentleman, the Honorable Peregrine Perriam. Not as shallow as he seemed, and not a man he'd choose as an enemy.

"Who could have forged it?" Georgia asked. "Who hates me so much?"

Dracy shared his suspicion. "Sellerby."

"Sellerby!" Georgia exclaimed.

"Sellerby?" Perriam asked. "The man doesn't hate Georgia. He's mad with love. And he was her staunchest supporter when the dowager first spoke of such a letter."

"I found it as hard to believe as you," Dracy said, "and for the same reasons, but he sought me out a few days ago when word of our supposed betrothal first leaked out. He was anxious to advise me of how absurd a notion that was, even that it might be a revenge by the Perriam family for my victory in the horse race."

The two Perriams were staring at him as if doubting his sanity.

"When talk turned to Georgia's choice of husband, he commented that with the reviving scandal she might have little choice. There was something in his manner. The smugness of having a secret and of being sure of winning in the end."

"You have to be mistaken," Georgia said.

Her brother added, "He wants to marry Georgie, so why cover her with scandal?

"I know, I know, but at least consider how it might

have been. Sellerby was one of your constant admirers, Georgia, during your marriage. Perhaps even a friend?"

"Yes. I enjoyed his company, and he was often my chosen escort to some sorts of affairs."

"To you he was only a friend, but he fell in love with you. That was no matter until you become a widow. Then he has unexpected hope of happiness. He waits patiently for a year."

"Not so patiently," she said. "He wrote a correct letter of condolence, but then a few weeks later another to, he said, raise my spirits. It was all Town froth! When he wrote again, I had both returned with a note to say I was not corresponding with gentlemen."

"Perfectly correct, and a blow, but if you were not corresponding with any gentlemen, he was willing to wait. But then things changed."

"No," Georgia said. "I won't hear any more of this. He's become odd, but what you're suggesting would be vicious!"

Perriam took her hand. "I want to hear him out." His expression was unreadable.

"Consider the dinner after the race at Herne. Sellerby was there, but am I correct that he's not a racing man?"

"Not at all," Georgia said. "He's not much fond of riding, but then, neither am I."

"Nor I," Dracy said. "Not a skill that gets much practice in the navy. I thought his country wear a trifle underused. He turned up to woo you."

"Before your mourning year was over," Perriam said. "Did he?"

"I'm not sure," Georgia said. "I've never thought of him in that way."

Dracy felt a trace of pity. "Your sister didn't give him the attention he expected, Perriam. She was warm and, yes, friendly, but nothing more. At the same time, she had dukes pressing for her attention and was dancing dutiful attendance on me."

Perriam raised a brow.

"All to do with Fancy Free," Georgia told him. "An irrelevance here, except that Dracy's right. Sellerby probably did expect more from me."

"Did he write after that?"

"Yes, twice, and becoming a little silly."

"He waits impatiently for your mourning to end, for you to return south, into his orbit. You don't return to Town—a disappointment, I'm sure—but there's to be a ball. His milieu par excellence."

"He came out to Thretford to inquire about his invitation," Georgia said. "I'd thrown his away." She grimaced at them. "I shouldn't have been so unkind, but I knew he'd press his suit."

"I wonder if he suspected anything," Dracy said. "I doubt it. He's the sort of man to be able to overlook evidence that doesn't fit his case. He arrives at Thretford intent upon courtship, but there's the Duke of Beaufort again, getting in his way, and other gentlemen of some eligibility. What's needed is to revive the scandal."

"Doesn't make sense," Perriam said. "If he made sure Eloisa received the letter, he brought it with him. In fact, prepared it well ahead of time. That forgery is professional work."

"I bow to your knowledge, sir."

"See!" Georgia exclaimed. "It's nonsense."

"Not necessarily. I've considered that aspect. He saw the danger at Herne—that you still had eminent suitors—and commissions the letter in case of need. At any time, he can fan the fire to flame again and scare your other suitors away, leaving him as your sole support."

"Except that I then had you," Georgia said.

"So you had," Dracy said. "Even as future husband, if rumor was to be believed. I became his bête noir. He said as much to me in our conversation, but he wouldn't be aware of any special connection early in the ball."

"But where does Eloisa come into this?" Georgia asked.

"They went into dinner together at Herne, I believe."

Georgia groaned. "I did my little best to throw them together, intending a kindness to both. I believe I mentioned her favorably in a letter to him."

"Salt in his wounds," her brother said. "I wonder if he has come to hate you as much as he adores you. He'd have Eloisa's measure quickly, for she's shallow as a plate. She couldn't resist hissing jealous spite to me, even. By the way, you dye your hair and use belladonna in your eyes." He turned to Dracy. "You lay out a plausible thread, but you've no evidence."

"I know it. But someone forged that letter, carried it to the ball, and then used it to turn most of the guests, and especially the suitors, away from your sister. Who else?"

"Was it very bad?" Perriam asked Georgia.

"Horrible. If Dracy hadn't been there . . ." She sent him a look that sparked hope but looked away in a manner to dowse it. "Thank heavens he took the letter from Eloisa. When our parents refused to invite her to Town, she might have been furious enough to send it to someone who would publish it."

"Then she may have sent you that picture," Perriam said.

"Oh, no," Georgia said, looking close to tears again. "It's not all her fault, Perry. She too was immured at Herne, and whilst I could escape Millicent, she couldn't. Millicent is convinced I haven't suffered a fraction of what I should for bringing such shame on the family."

Perriam whistled. "What are the odds that *Millicent* sent that picture to her sister with encouragement to use it? I wouldn't put it past our dear sister-in-law to have hoarded that drawing for a year."

"Lud! Eloisa writes bitter complaints to Millicent, not mentioning her malice, but dwelling on my shamelessness and cruelty. Millicent sends back a weapon. Not to increase my scandal, for she truly does feel it stains the family, but to wound me."

"A delightful family, the Perriams," her brother said to Dracy. "Sure you want to join it?"

"Yes," Dracy said before he had time to think. He looked at Georgia. "But I promise not to be a Sellerby about it. Speaking of whom, if I'm right, he's struck once and could try again. How do we stop him?"

"Wait!" Georgia said. "Could Millicent have sent that letter to Eloisa?"

Dracy considered, but Perriam said, "Won't work. She wouldn't know how to find a forger, especially around Herne. And if she was going to send it to Eloisa, it would be through the post, not during the ball. You'd rather it be her than Sellerby?"

"Yes," she said sadly. "I'm accustomed to Millicent's dislike, but Sellerby? I truly thought we were friends, in the past, at least."

Perriam patted her hand and rose. "I'll go in search of the forger. We aren't looking to prosecute, so I might get the right person to talk. Confronted with a witness, Sellerby will be defanged. He'll do anything to avoid becoming a scandal himself." He kissed his sister's cheek. "Courage, my dear."

# Chapter 29

Georgia smiled after Perry, comforted by his being back to help her, but troubled by that brief exchange. The words echoed in her mind.

*A delightful family, the Perriams. Sure you want to join it?*

*Yes.*

She knew Dracy would never harass her as Sellerby had, but she couldn't bear to break his heart. She should never have allowed last night.

"More tea?" she asked.

"No, thank you. We have another day to explore Town, if you're free of appointments?"

She looked at him, torn between exasperation and tenderness. Of a certainty, he was no Sellerby. "I'm entirely free, except from guilt. I've created a madman."

"Nonsense. The rest of the men in England have managed not to tip into insanity over you."

She chuckled at that but had to ask, "Including you?"

"Perhaps the jury's out on that," he said, but so lightly she couldn't persist. "Where shall we go? What about the menagerie at the Tower?"

His lightness was not froth but steel, a mesh of it, protecting her. He couldn't protect her from everything, however, and for his sake, he must not try. After seeing that cartoon, she wanted to hide away, but as Perry had said, it was new only to her. The streets would be no more hostile today than yesterday, and she must walk them for the rest of her life.

"Very well," she said, "but I must change."

"You wore that yesterday."

"It's a rag," she said, deliberately adding, "and Lady May must dress in finery." But then she halted by the door. "I've given Jane the day off."

"I'm sure there are other maids," he said. "Or if necessary, I know how to fasten a lady's stay laces."

She stared at him, remembering too many things, and even thinking, shockingly, that if they went to her room they might be able to adventure in the day.

"I'll make do as I am with hat and gloves. I doubt we'll meet anyone we know on a visit to the Tower."

They didn't, which, as far as Georgia was concerned, was perfect. They toured the ancient fortress and the menagerie of exotic animals sent to the kings of England as gifts.

"They seem sadly confined," she said as they left that part of the Tower and walked across the lawn.

"Some of them were born there, it appears, so perhaps they would dislike change. As, you claim, Fancy Free would dislike removal to Dracy."

"Dracy is inferior to Herne," she pointed out. "That race seems so long ago. How goes the substitution? I haven't noticed you or Father discussing it."

"We're awaiting developments," he said, but she could tell there was something amiss.

"Is he not being fair? I'll speak to him about it."

"No, his offer is more than fair."

"Then why do you not take it?"

His lips twitched. "Perhaps because it would end your application in the cause."

"What?" She laughed. "I've given no thought to that in days."

"Good." He looked at the large piece of wood, darker in the middle. "The headsman's block, where so many paid with their lives."

"I've recently felt for Anne Boleyn," she said.

"Why?"

"She was unjustly treated, perhaps because she fascinated men, frightening them and upsetting the women. Then her son was stillborn. I know how a twist in life can have drastic consequences. At least I can't lose my head over any of my troubles."

"But you could lose your life."

She understood him. Her life in the beau monde. If Perry couldn't clear her name and spiteful people stirred new trouble, she might lose the battle.

She shrugged. "We all have many lives. You've made a drastic change twice. Once when you went into the navy, and once when you left."

"A third, when my parents died. Not as drastic as it might seem, as they were often away and Dracy Manor was my second home."

"Tell me more about your boyhood, then," she said, and enjoyed listening as they left the Tower and returned to Mayfair in the Perriam carriage.

They arrived back only just in time for dinner, and Perry was already there.

"You went out in that thing?" he asked, looking at her dress.

"Why not?" She enjoyed his surprise and then his exaggerated shudder when she confessed to visiting the Tower. Such a plebian amusement, but she didn't care.

Their parents didn't dine at home that afternoon, so there were just the three of them. They took chairs at one end of the long table.

"The letter?" Georgia asked as she started her soup. Perry would know how to discuss the matter with the servants in mind.

"As we thought, but I don't know the source. I've set that in hand. Our friend wrote, or rather scrawled, some specifications for a new pair of pistols."

So it wasn't Vance's writing. She smiled at him. "That's delightful to hear."

"Isn't it?" he replied.

"You do know these waters," Dracy said, looking at Perry rather coldly. Lud, not more acrimony over her.

"Navigated them all my life," Perry said, "and showed a natural talent from a young age. I would have been all at sea in the navy."

"I'm not sure Arthur isn't all at sea there," Georgia said, referring to her youngest brother.

"Could be time for a different line of work, yes."

They served themselves from the other dishes and talk turned to the heat, the limited amusements in the rapidly thinning Town, and some quirks of fashion. It was unbalanced, for Dracy knew little of such things and cared less, so she shared the story of the water problem at Danae House and the possibility of a fish blocking the pipe.

"A fish," Perry said, feigning horror, but he had the same curiosity as she, and soon they were all discussing London's erratic water supply.

When the dishes were removed and the second course laid out, she dismissed the servants. As the door closed behind the last of them, she took some veal sweetbreads and fried artichokes. "Now we can talk."

"We were talking," Perry said, selecting from the dishes, "and most enjoyably. But yes, if you need confirmation, the letter is a forgery and not in Vance's hand. I assume Sellerby, if it was he, didn't have a sample and didn't think it would matter, Vance being far, far away."

"Do you have any idea where Vance is now?" Dracy asked. "He would be the best witness to a number of things."

"None at all," Perry said.

Georgia saw Dracy's irritation. Perry's light matter could have that effect. "What effort has been made to find him?" he demanded.

"Every effort, from the first," Perry said crisply, "and even now there are people at all consulates and embassies with both his name and a reasonably accurate illustration of his face. We have also made known a substantial reward."

Dracy still looked irritated, but he said, "I apologize, Perriam. Of course you and your family would have made every effort." He looked at Georgia. "Will it distress you if we talk about the duel?"

It would, but she wanted these tangles loosened. "I can endure it, but the facts are clear. There's no mystery to it."

"I'm not so sure."

"Why?" Perry asked.

"It seems peculiar to me," Dracy said, "and has from the first. Perhaps it's only that I don't understand your world, but everyone agrees that Lord Maybury wasn't a quarrelsome man."

"Nearly any man can be goaded into issuing a challenge," Perry said, "especially in his cups and before his friends."

"But why did Vance goad him?" Dracy asked.

"Because he was mad enough to think that if Maybury was out of the way he'd have a chance with Georgia."

Dracy looked at her. "But he didn't, did he? Sellerby had a reason to believe that, but Vance?"

"None at all," she said, "as I've been trying to make clear all along. Truly, we hardly met." Dracy nodded, but then he went still, staring past her. "Dracy? Is something amiss?"

"By God," he said, still staring.

"Are you struck by an apoplexy," Perry asked sharply, "or about to strike us dumb by solving the mystery entirely?"

Dracy looked at him. "Either I'm struck by insanity or about to do just that. Not here, however. A servant might return."

Georgia's heart rate rose. Was it possible? Could she be cleared?

She stood up. "The small drawing room. Do either of you want tea or coffee?"

Dracy rose, still lost in thought. "Coffee, I think, and perhaps brandy too."

"Oh dear," Perry said. "I believe we are about to be shocked half to death."

Dracy almost sleepwalked to the small drawing room, with its rich green wallpaper and gilded plasterwork, where they soon had coffee and brandy to hand, and the door firmly shut. By silent accord they'd said nothing since leaving the dining room.

"Now," Georgia said. "Explain."

He'd put the pieces together in his head, but could it really be true, and would it make sense to the others?

"If you remember, I said that while Vance had no reason to think you would marry him if you were a widow, Sellerby might." He looked at each in turn. "What if he thought precisely that?"

Georgia frowned. "That if I were a widow I would marry him? I suppose it's possible."

Perriam was looking as struck as Dracy had been. "By God . . ."

"*What?*" Georgia asked, looking at them. "One of you explain!"

Dracy wondered too late how she'd react to the new picture, but there was no retreat. "My insane thought is that Sellerby might have brought about your widowhood by hiring Vance to kill your husband in a duel."

She went deathly pale.

All he could think to do was to push on. "Why else did Vance do it? On the surface, he gained nothing except exile. We agree that any notion of him trying to win you is unbelievable. A few days ago, I was told about a man called Curry who might have been paid to try to kill the Marquess of Rothgar in a duel. . . ."

"No," Georgia said. "No, no, *no*!"

"Definitely no," Perriam said, going to her side and taking her hands, chafing them. "I'm willing to entertain the possibility that Sellerby had a letter forged in an attempt to clear the field, but murder? He's the least bloodthirsty of men. He turns pale at the sight of blood. I've seen him faint because of it."

"He didn't have to see any blood," Dracy pointed out. "Georgia . . ."

She seemed lost in horror, thrown back to her husband's dreadful death.

What a fool he was to speak of this in front of her. He went to her, pulled her into his arms. "I'm sorry, I'm sorry. Don't think of it."

She burst into tears, deep, racking tears.

Dracy stroked her back, looking helplessly at her shocked brother. "Georgia, don't. Your husband died by the sword, and that hasn't changed, but you've grieved that and mourned that."

She wailed and sobbed on.

Heaven help him, what should he do? "He died quickly. He may not have known what happened to him. . . ."

She looked up at him, breathing hard, tears streaming. "You don't *understand*! If you're right, everyone's right. I'm to blame!"

She thrust away from him and stumbled back. When he reached to balance her, she swatted his hand away.

"Don't you *see*? Don't either of you *see*? All this time I've taken comfort from one thing—it was nothing to do with me. Whatever caused Dickon to challenge Vance, it couldn't have been about me. Whatever drove Vance to kill, it couldn't have been me. But it *was* me. It was *all* me. *Dickon was killed because of me!*"

"No." He went to her, but she beat him away with her fists.

"Don't. Don't come near me! You were right to call me Helen. I get men killed. I won't . . . I can't . . ." She looked wildly between them and then ran out of the room.

Dracy took a step to follow, but Perriam gripped his arm. "I'll go. I'll make sure she's cared for. Wait here, if you will. We have much to discuss."

Dracy was left alone, wishing he'd kept his damned mouth shut.

Georgia ran toward her room, but she'd be found there. She ran up to the unused schoolroom with its neglected toys and over-read books and stood there, beyond tears now, unable to see any way forward.

She turned at a footstep, but it was Perry.

"Don't argue with me," she said. "It's true."

"Even if it's true, the fault doesn't lie with you."

"Does it not? It's not only my appearance. You know that I like to flirt, to charm, to bewitch, even. You warned me more than once about my court. It was a sin of carelessness, not deliberation. But I killed Dickon."

"It's a wild guess. There may be nothing in it."

"What if there is? And I can see it, Perry. Sellerby has become more and more peculiar in his behavior. Maddened by me."

"Georgia, you have a leveler head than this."

"Have I? I can't see it any other way."

"The way, as always, is forward. What's between you and Dracy?"

She put a hand to her face, shaking her head, unable even to find words.

"He loves you."

"To his peril."

"He seems a man able to take care of himself. And take care of you."

She laughed at that, a bitter sound. "Until some other man who desires me plots murder!"

"Madmen are rare."

"Except that I create them, like the enchantress who turned men into swine?"

"Yes, the Greeks knew a thing or two, but come down from the heights, love. If Dracy's right, it's a terrible thing and Sellerby will pay, one way or another, but it was his sin, not yours. You have your life to live, and I don't think you're suited to a convent."

"What am I suited to, then?"

"Perhaps Dracy."

Georgia couldn't believe Perry was suggesting such a thing. He, more than anyone, knew her nature. "I'd bankrupt him in a year."

"I'm sure you're capable of being frugal if you try."

"But I don't want to try! And if I suffered frugality for him, he'd know it and be miserable. I can't face him. He'll have to leave. Oh, I don't know what to do!"

"You need to get away from here," he said steadily, "for your safety as much as anything else. If Sellerby is a mad murderer, he might try to do you harm. Where do you want to go? To Winnie's?"

"With Eloisa Cardross there?"

"No," he agreed with a smile. "Where, then?"

Georgia saw one path clearly. "To Brookhaven. To Lizzie Torrismonde. Now. I want to go now."

So she could avoid Dracy. So she wouldn't weaken. Before spending another night under the same roof.

"I'll make the arrangements," Perry said.

His calmness spread to her, but didn't they talk about a dead calm? She couldn't think, and couldn't see her future beyond one point, the point she clung to, Lizzie and Havenhurst. Calm, sensible Lizzie and her tranquil home. Lizzie's steady, amiable husband. Her children. There was hope of sanity at Havenhurst, and perhaps even a path beyond.

"Go and have Jane pack what you need," Perry said. "You won't need much."

Georgia burst out laughing, on the edge of tears again. "I've given her the day off!"

"I'm sure you're capable of packing your own clothes if you try."

"What challenges you're setting me. I know where she is. I can send for her. Thank you, Perry."

"I've failed you all around, but I'll clear everything up now."

"You can't do that," she said wearily. "If Sellerby hired Vance, there's no proof of it, and Sellerby will never confess. Vance is far, far away. If by some miracle you found him and dragged him back, if he confessed all, I'd be little better off. The world would know the duel was all because of me, because of Lady May's foolish, flirtatious ways, and many will choose to believe I was Sellerby's whore."

"Sometimes it would be easier if you were a wigeon. Yes, you will always have some of that story hanging over you. But you can dilute it every day by being yourself, especially if no one else stirs the pot. We can easily deal with Millicent and Eloisa, even though Pranks is scared to stand up to his wife. Soon Sellerby will trouble you no more."

She clutched his arm. "No duel. Promise me, Perry. No duel!"

"It would be simplest, but I doubt I'd get him out, so I promise."

"And make sure Dracy doesn't take that route."

"I will. You don't intend to speak to him before you leave?"

"It's better that way. I . . . I don't know if I love him, Perry, but it will break my heart a little to cut him free. I have to do it, however." She sadly turned the globe, thinking of all the places Dracy had been, all the women he'd pleasured, and would in the future. "We're like creatures from different worlds, like night and day."

"Perhaps," he said, "but a time to recover and think about it will do you no harm. He's a good man."

"Which is why I have to cut him free. Tell him that I thank him, for everything in the past and for any effort he makes in the future, but that I can't see him again."

"Are you sure?"

She nodded and went to her room. She sent a note to Jane at the Three Cups at Clerkenwell, but she also sent for her smaller trunk and began to pack for herself.

# Chapter 30

Dracy paced the drawing room until Perriam returned. It seemed a hour or more, though the ticking clock showed only ten minutes.

"She doesn't want to see you," Perriam said.

"The fate of the bearer of bad news."

"Perhaps, but her main concern seems to be to protect you from her deadly effect."

"That's nonsense."

Dracy stepped forward, but Perriam raised a hand. "All the same, you'll do as she wishes."

He could overpower the smaller man. "I'm tempted," he said, "if only to see how good you are."

"I'm sure it would amuse," Perriam said, "but so distressing to get blood on the carpet."

"Devil take it, but I don't suppose I'll further my cause with Georgia by breaking your bones. I have to watch over her."

"Against her wishes? She wants to leave Town, to go to Brookhaven, the Torrismondes' place. Lady Torrismonde is her dearest friend, and Torrismonde's a good, dependable man."

Dracy didn't want Georgia more than a few yards from him, but she'd be better off away from the beau monde and Sellerby. "Well escorted," he said. "If I'm right, Sellerby's literally mad for her."

"Very well escorted, but we can spike his guns by letting him know we suspect his part in the letter. He's sane enough to go carefully when under suspicion."

Dracy turned to pace the room. "I wish he weren't. I want to see him hang."

"So do I—Dickon Maybury was a good fellow—but the evidence would have to be very solid to convict a peer, and thus far all we have is suppositions. I see no hope of more unless we first find Vance and then force him to incriminate himself."

Dracy grimaced at that prospect. "He'll get away with it? Apart from the injustice, will Georgia ever be safe?"

"He won't get away with it," Perriam said, in a tone that chilled the air. "And Georgia will be safe."

"A duel?" Dracy said, studying him. "She—"

"She's forbidden it. If necessary, I'll kill him in cold blood, but only when I'm sure without doubt that he's the monster we think he is."

Dracy was shocked. He no longer thought the Honorable Peregrine Perriam a silly fop, but he'd met few men who could make such a statement and be believed. He believed in this case.

A twitch of Perriam's lips showed he read these thoughts. "Are you willing to stay in Town and help pursue proof?"

"Of course," Dracy said, though half of himself was with Georgia above stairs, longing to be closer, and stay closer.

"Then you'd best remove to my rooms. I'll explain the two departures to my parents."

"You'll tell them all?"

Perriam laughed. "By no means! My father's temper is chancy at best, and Mother can be a Gorgon when the family's threatened. I will simply say that Georgia felt the need for some country calm, and you don't wish to impose any longer. Time to leave," he prompted. "I'll arrange for your belongings to be packed and—"

"No, dammit!" Dracy exploded. "It's madness. She can't travel without one of us. We're the only ones who know the real threat."

"We can warn the outriders. . . ."

"And if the Earl of Sellerby stops them and spins some story, they'll deny him?"

Perriam glared at the obvious answer. "Devil take it. I'll go."

"Where's the sense in that? You're the one who knows Town waters, so you'll get to the bottom of the forgery far quicker than I. Georgia's wishes should be respected, but not beyond reason. Tell her that I will accompany her. I won't bother her—I won't even speak to her if that is her wish—but I will guard her with my life. I insist on it. And if Sellerby gives me an excuse to kill him, I'll do that too. On my honor, I will. "

After a moment, Perriam nodded and went out.

"No, Perry, no!"

Georgia turned away, refusing to allow any persuasion. She wouldn't endanger Dracy further, his life or his heart.

"Shall I leave, milady?"

At Jane's voice, Georgia turned, seeing her maid in the doorway, still in cloak and hat.

"No, Jane. I'm sorry to drag you away from your friend, but I've decided to visit Brookhaven. I've begun to pack." She waved vaguely at the open trunk, half full of clothing and other items.

Jane opened her mouth, then shut it again. Hardly surprising. Packing was not as easy as it seemed.

"Very well, milady. You leave it to me. How long will we stay?"

"I don't know, but I leave soon, so don't pack much. I can send for more." Georgia looked at her brother. "Adieu, Perry."

He didn't move. "Someone who knows the situation must be with you, but I'm needed here. This can't entirely be your decision, Georgia. Dracy won't distress you."

At those words, she put her hand to her mouth and turned away, fighting tears. And losing.

"Milady?" Jane said, rising from her knees by the trunk.

"This doesn't concern you," Perry snapped, and he'd never normally speak so sharply to Jane. "Georgia, you will do as I say."

He'd never normally give her such an order.

She turned on him. "Damn you! You don't know what you ask."

"I'm concerned for your safety. Dracy goes with you."

"Very well, then. He may ride escort."

"He's not a practiced rider and you'll be traveling at speed."

"Then he can sit on the box!"

"You're afraid to be alone with him?" Perry asked, and she read a host of new problems in his tone.

"No," she said quickly. "I don't fear him at all." *Only my own weak folly.* "Oh, very well, let him come. Let him travel in the carriage with me. Let it all be as you say. I'm sure you know best."

He stepped toward her as if to comfort her, and then halted.

Very wise. She was ready to scratch him, or worse.

He turned and left without another word.

"What's going on, milady?" Jane asked quietly.

Georgia turned from her too. "I'm going to Brookhaven, and Lord Dracy will accompany me. Finish the packing, for the coach could be ready at any moment."

Indeed, a footman came only ten minutes later to say

that her father's traveling chariot awaited. He carried down the small trunk, and Georgia followed with Jane. She'd realized only at the last minute that she still wore the dull gown, but she wouldn't delay to change.

Dracy awaited in the hall, and she felt his concern press on her. A part of her longed to rush into his arms, but she passed him without a word. She didn't deserve him, she wanted to protect him, but she was also angry at being forced to have his escort.

At sight of the equipage, she gave a short laugh. Six horses in the traces, and four armed riders alongside. People would think royalty went by.

She settled herself on the thickly stuffed carriage seat, and Jane sat opposite, eyes wide with curiosity. Dracy entered and sat beside Jane, and then the coach rolled down Piccadilly, on its way out of Town.

They traveled in silence, and Georgia looked outside to avoid looking at Dracy. When she flickered a glance, he was doing the same thing. Jane was pretending to doze. Georgia knew it was pretence because her maid's mouth always fell open if she truly slept.

They didn't stop for a change, for the six prime horses could do the thirty miles if handled well, and there'd not been time to send others ahead, as the family normally did when traveling.

She'd been blessed with a life of luxury, in which everything was arranged for her comfort and pleasure, and only see what she'd done with it. One man dead and another mad, and another too devoted for his own good.

She saw a finger-post and realized they were approaching the place where the road to Hammersmith went off. Perhaps she should go to Thretford, confess her sins to Winnie and Eloisa, and endure their smug condemnation as penance.

No, she wasn't saintly enough for that. She wanted sanctuary, not confessional, and she wanted Lizzie. She'd sent a message to Brookhaven as soon as she'd made the decision, so the Torrismondes would have some warning. She'd given no details, but she was sure her tone had betrayed distress and urgency.

The first touch of evening was softening the ivy-clad house with gold when the coach slowed and Georgia saw Lizzie and her husband come out to greet them. She scrambled out of the coach and into her friend's arms.

"Georgia! You know you're welcome, but what's amiss?"

"Everything. But I can't speak here."

"Then, come inside. Come, love. I'm sure nothing can be as bad as it seems."

# Chapter 31

Dracy watched the two women go into the house, pre-paring to explain the situation to Lord Torrismonde, who was remarkably unreadable. On slight acquaintance, Dracy would have said the very ordinary viscount was easygoing and amiable, but he knew the signs. Torrismonde was assessing what danger had come to his home and his family and was ready to eviscerate the culprit.

"As you'll have guessed," Dracy said, "Lady Maybury is in some trouble, and possibly in some danger. Should I have some of the Perriam men stay?"

"Danger? You're serious?"

"Very serious. Most likely of abduction."

"Then perhaps you should. I have only the normal complement of servants." Clearly he wished normality could be maintained.

Dracy spoke to the armed outriders. Two were chosen to stay and sent round to the stables. Once the horses had been cared for, the rest would return to Town with the coach.

When Dracy went back to Torrismonde, the viscount said, "Are you, too, staying? Welcome, of course," he added without sincerity.

"I don't know," Dracy said honestly. "I'd better tell you what's going on and we can decide together."

Torrismonde pulled a face, but he took Dracy into the house and offered him wine, tea, coffee, whatever he would like.

"Coffee, if you please," Dracy said, taking a seat in the small library. "Strong and black."

Despite the tension of the moment, he couldn't help liking the cozy, well-worn room lined with books that looked as if they'd been lovingly read. Because Ceddie's only interests had been in Town, he'd left Dracy Manor untouched except for pillaging it of anything of value, but once it had had a similar well-worn comfort. Perhaps that could be restored without great cost. . . .

But such thoughts led toward paths closed to him as yet.

Once the order had been given and the servant had left, Dracy said, "I'll be blunt. Perriam and I have reason to believe that Lord Sellerby is a deep-dyed villain, willing to go to any lengths to possess Lady Maybury."

"Sellerby?" Torrismonde said, staring. "He's certainly extreme in his feelings for her, but so many are. Not for Georgia particularly," he said with a wave of his hand, "though she's plagued by admirers, but in matters of the heart. Florid declarations, threats of suicide, ridiculous extravagances as if they lived on a damned theater stage."

Dracy was amused by the assessment, for he had no doubt the phlegmatic viscount adored his wife just as passionately.

"Lady Maybury took Sellerby's devotion as dramatic rather than deeply felt," he said, "for after all, she was happily married. He felt matters more deeply, but probably didn't see any path to his desires—"

"Of course not," Torrismonde interrupted, glaring.

"Of course not," Dracy echoed, wishing he was more skillful at handing delicate situations. "You've no need to assure me of Georgia Maybury's virtue. By desires, I meant marriage, which was completely out of reach."

He broke off as a footman entered with the coffee tray and poured for them both.

When the man left, Dracy had seen another way to come at the situation. "Do you remember a fatal duel involving the Marquess of Rothgar a while ago?"

Torrismonde sipped his coffee. "Of course. It was an occasion of note. Two years ago, as I remember, and the marquess fortunate to escape without criminal proceedings."

"As I heard it, talk was that Curry had been paid to kill the marquess by his political enemies."

"Gossip, only," Torrismonde said, but then allowed, "yet possibly true. Enemies in England and in France."

"That event might have sown the seeds in Sellerby's mind. It would have taken him time to find the right man and to put the proposition to him, but I judge Sellerby to be patient, despite his madness, and in Maybury he had a man who'd be much easier to kill."

Torrismonde had listened impassively, but now he put down his cup and saucer. "Are you suggesting that the Earl of Sellerby hired Sir Charnley Vance to kill Lord Maybury in order to make his wife a widow, and eventually wed her?"

Dracy truly admired such a pithy analysis.

"Succinctly put. Yes."

"You have proof?"

"No. But," Dracy said before Torrismonde could protest, "we are on the way to proof that Sellerby had that letter forged—the one that troubled the Thretford ball—and gave it to the person most likely to use it."

"That's hardly the same matter as murder, sir!"

"I know it, but consider Vance's lack of motive. Any talk of him seeking to win Georgia is unbelievable, as is any thought of a liaison between them."

"It certainly is."

"So why kill Maybury unless for profit? I've read the inquest, and it seems clear to me that he struck to kill. It was no accident."

Torrismonde's lips were tight, but he didn't argue.

"If he was paid," Dracy went on, "by whom? No one suspects Maybury's heir, and Maybury had no enemies, political or personal. Who, then, would gain?"

Torrismonde didn't like the idea at all, but in the end he said, "Perhaps you have something there, but no proof, Dracy, no proof."

"I know that, but we seek it. Perhaps Vance confided in someone, though the most likely person is his second, a military man now in India. Letters have been sent, but it could be a sixmonth before we hear back. Perhaps Vance can be found."

"After a year? I understand that Georgia's family has made great efforts."

"Yes. He seems to have managed to disappear...." But then Dracy put down his coffee and rose. "Your pardon, Torrismonde, but may I have writing materials? I must send a message back with the coach."

Torrismonde's brows rose, but he took Dracy to the desk and made sure he had what he needed. "Am I to share your enlightenment?" he asked drily.

Dracy smiled at him. "I'm taxing your patience, I know. My apologies. I must write to Perriam because I suspect the danger may be even greater than we thought. Vance has not been found, despite, as you say, the Perriam family posting rewards and sending notifications to all British embassies and consulates, along with descriptions and even pictures. What if he's dead?"

"That's certainly possible if he's gone wandering in the lesser-known foreign parts."

"I mean, what if he never left England? What if Sellerby eliminated the one person who could incriminate him, also eliminating the need to pay the large sum Vance would have demanded?"

"Gads, man, you talk of the darkest villainy! And still without a shred of evidence."

"If we could confirm Vance's death, that would be

evidence, wouldn't it? His death within days, perhaps within hours of that duel."

Torrismonde looked almost theatrically exasperated.

"And how are you to do that, a year after the event? If he was killed, there would have been a corpse. If there was a corpse, it would have been identified. I ask you, Dracy—where is Vance's corpse?"

"In a pauper's grave," Dracy said, dipping the pen. "By your pardon, Torrismonde, I'll explain my thoughts in a moment."

He chose words that wouldn't give away too much if read by the wrong person.

> *My friend,*
>
> *We arrived safely after a smooth journey, and all is well. Lord Torrismonde has kindly offered me hospitality, and I will stay for a little while. I have a small commission for you if you would be so kind. I find myself concerned about Sir C, wondering whether he may have had a mishap before going abroad. A great deal of time has passed, but I was told that he had a feature that would probably be remembered by anyone handling his remains, even if they were beyond identification. A somewhat equine endowment. Perhaps you could make inquiries and put my mind at rest.*
>
> *I pray you take care of your own health, sir, in this chancy season, and most especially of what you consume. We spoke of the dangers of London's waters.*
>
> *I remain obliged to you, sir,*
> *Dracy*

He folded and sealed the letter, hoping the last part was a strong enough warning against poison. "If you would be so kind as to alert the coachman that he's to take a message? And then I'll test my new suspicions on you."

Torrismonde opened the door and gave the order and then returned. "I do not like this, Dracy, any of it."

"I don't like it either. I'm very fond of a tranquil life."

"More than can be said for Georgia's brother. I'd call him a gadfly if I didn't suspect some of his dealings were more serious."

That confirmed Dracy's suspicions, and that Torrismonde was a very shrewd man.

"You asked, where is Vance's corpse? Why wasn't it identified at the time? But if the body wasn't found for some days or even weeks, his remains might not have been identified, especially if his body had been in the river."

Torrismonde grimaced. "True enough, and no one would have been inquiring about him, as might be the case when a person goes missing. But a year's gone by, and any unidentified corpse will be bones by now. You'll never prove your case."

"I'm not looking toward the current remains, but toward the corpse. It would have been examined for foul play and anything that would identify it, then put in the hands of an undertaker, I assume, for a pauper's burial. I believe that anyone handling Vance's remains would remember him. He was, if you'll pardon the expression, hung like a horse. Unless the fishes nibbled it off, people would notice that, gossip about it, even show off the corpse to cronies. It might even have been mentioned at the inquest."

"This matter becomes more distasteful by the moment. I'll have no mention of it before my wife, Dracy."

"Of course not," Dracy said, though he'd tell Georgia. She had a right to know, and she might well tell her friend. "This new idea is speculation, but it feels right to me. There's another aspect. If still alive, why hasn't Vance returned? The inquest raised a few questions, but there was nothing in it that could lead to an accusation of murder."

"But how would Sellerby kill Vance? The one, effete. The other close to a brute, but quick with his fists and a sword."

Dracy had worked this out. "Poison. According to Perriam, Sellerby can't take the sight of blood and even faints if faced with any amount of it, so he couldn't have used a blade or pistol ball. He's the type for poison—coldhearted and cunning. Therefore, it would be best to be careful about food and drink coming into Brookhaven."

"By God, sir! Is there no end to it? My family is in danger?"

"I don't believe there's much risk," Dracy assured him. "Sellerby is in London and won't want to use someone who would then become a witness. But any unexpected gifts of food and drink should be treated with caution."

Torrismonde paced the room, hands clasped behind his back. "A damnable affair. And I doubt this part of your tale. Sellerby could administer poison, but how then could he get a very large corpse into the river without being seen?"

"A skeptical mind is useful. Thank you. Very well, let's imagine that he appointed a meeting to pay Vance, and took a room at a tavern that overlooked the river. There are any number of those. Vance arrives, Sellerby proposes a toast, but only pretends to drink, then watches Vance die. He'd remove anything that might identify him, including his boots, which would have the maker's mark, and his jacket, which would be of gentlemanly quality. He'd get him to the windowsill in some way, put stones or lead weights in his pockets, and tip him out. Quite likely he'd wait out the day until dark."

"In the room with his victim?" Torrismonde protested.

"I doubt he has any of the finer sensibilities, despite his exquisite airs. He'd certainly have to wait until high tide, whenever that was. I must add this to my letter."

He sat, broke the seal, and did so.

"It's a remarkable story," Torrismonde said, "but I say again, you have no shred of proof."

"But chance of some, now. We might find evidence that Vance died, and even the place of murder, with people remembering Sellerby and Vance there."

"It still might not hang an earl."

"That's for later. Now, we must remember that Sellerby is a very dangerous man. If I'm right, he killed by his own hand, despite his aversion to blood. I'm even wondering about his valet. Perhaps Sellerby's capable of bashing in a man's skull when desperate." He impressed his seal with force. "He must not be allowed close to Georgia on any pretext, for I fear by now his passions might teeter between adoration and hatred."

"Damned theatricality! And beneath my own roof. I don't hold you to blame, but by God, I do not like it."

Dracy could only say, "Nor do I. I assure you, I'll work as hard to protect your family as I will to protect Georgia Maybury. And that is with all I have."

"What lies between you?" Torrismonde asked.

"I wish I knew. We're close, but we're also a mismatch, and now this. I neglected to tell you that this new idea has hit her hard. She holds herself responsible, and I can only hope your wife can restore some balance. Georgia didn't want me to come here with her, in part because she sees herself as a danger to men who love her."

"Do you love her?" Torrismonde asked. He was not a man to ask such an intimate question without cause.

"Yes, but I won't be like Sellerby about it."

Torrismonde nodded. "I thought there was something between you at Thretford, and so did my wife. I wish you well there."

"Thank you," Dracy said, surprised. "But I'm committed to a country life."

"As am I, but some time in London never comes amiss, especially when we have our duty to Parliament."

"It's expensive, especially if Georgia were to be with me. Alone, I could take a simple room, but she would want more."

"Stay at Hernescroft House. It's large enough, and thus most of your costs are blown away."

Dracy wasn't sure how Georgia would regard that, but it was a thought; indeed it was. "And her adoration of expensive fashion?"

Torrismonde acknowledged that with a grimace. "A problem, I grant, but she delights in the ingenuity of design. She might embrace the challenge of creating wonders on little money."

"She might," Dracy agreed, but dubiously.

"She's young, Dracy, and will surely change in one way or another. This might be a natural time for her to progress out of extravagance."

"Some never manage that, not even in their dotage," Dracy said, "but I thank you for some hope. First, we must keep her safe."

Georgia was sitting on the settee in Lizzie's boudoir, in her friend's arms. She'd wept again. She was very tired of weeping. She felt a little better, but not free of guilt and hopelessness.

Lizzie had said, "You can't blame yourself, Georgie. As well blame the sky for lightning. If Sellerby devised that plan, he's an evil man and always has been. You didn't make him so."

Those had been pleasant words, but she couldn't believe them. "Without me, Sellerby would never have taken such steps."

"You need rest," Lizzie said, "and time to regain your balance. I prescribe good country air and food, long walks, and time with the children."

"I pray you're right, but Dracy's come with me. I fear he'll want to stay."

"He's welcome here."

"But I'm trying to push him away. I can't allow any man close to me again! Not one I care for."

Lizzie straightened them both and looked Georgia in the eye. "No theatricals. You know how much Torrismonde dislikes them. I mentioned lightning. Would you avoid walking through a field because someone was once struck by lightning there?"

"No, but I'd avoid walking there during a thunderstorm!"

Lizzie chuckled. "Always practical. You won't live in a constant thunderstorm. Only think. Who else among your admirers turned demented? Shaldon—he's untouched. Beaufort, still with his sense. Porterhouse, as well-balanced as always. I know you don't believe this now, but you will—you are not to blame for Sellerby's vileness. Let me take you to your room. I recommend a quiet supper and an early night. You look worn-out."

Georgia remembered the adventures of the night before—an eon ago—and didn't wonder at looking exhausted.

Dracy would be under the same roof again . . . but she wasn't the slightest bit tempted to engage in wickedness again tonight. She could be tempted by other things, however, by his tenderness and his strength. . . .

"I think you're falling asleep as you are," Lizzie said, helping her to her feet. "Come, Jane will take care of you, and truly, love, everything will seem a little brighter tomorrow."

# Chapter 32

Lizzie was wrong. Georgia's mind had trundled around and around horrors all night, and she wasn't sure she'd caught much sleep at all. Morning found her sluggish and hopeless. All very well for everyone to tell her Dickon's death wasn't her fault, but she knew the truth. If she'd been a sober, quiet wife, her husband would still be alive. She washed and dressed without a care for the details and could hardly face her breakfast.

Jane had brought a letter with her breakfast, a letter from her mother expressing shocked disapproval of the possibilities and a stern instruction to Georgia to behave with dignity and avoid all hazards.

"Yes, Mother," Georgia murmured as she refolded it, but she wondered if there'd been a touch of caring in those last words. What was she coming to if she longed for solace from her mother?

There was also a letter from Perry, but it didn't tell her much.

*My dearest sister,*

*I hear a good report of your journey and arrival, my dear, and urge you to enjoy your time at Brookhaven to the full. As for myself, I have been busy on many fronts and have yet more commis-*

*sions. You must ask Dracy about one of them, and
also about the creator of letters, about whom I've
written to him.*

*Be kind to Dracy, sister. He will do you no harm,
nor you him.*

*Your exhausted but devoted brother,*
*Perry*

That must mean he'd found the forger. She supposed
that was good news, but that laid the way to a dreadful
path. She wanted Dickon's murderer hanged at Tyburn
for his crime, but that would pillory her—the cause of it
all—far beyond her sufferings so far. Five years ago, Earl
Ferrers had been tried and hanged for the murder of his
steward. A peer of the realm, publicly executed. That
would never be forgotten, nor would the execution of
the Earl of Sellerby for arranging the murder of the Earl
of Maybury for love of his wife.

Doubtless his wicked wife. Many would assume she'd
been Sellerby's lover!

The sun was shining and it was a glorious late June
day, but when could she ever be carefree again?

Jane came in and tutted at the scarce-touched breakfast. "You must eat something, milady. Starving yourself
won't do a bit of good."

"I'm not starving myself," Georgia protested, but she
saw that she'd taken only one bite from a piece of but-
tered bread and one sip from her chocolate.

She drank the chocolate and refilled the cup, then
took another bite from the bread. Too theatrical by far
to faint for lack of nourishment, and dear Torrismonde
did dislike theatricality.

"There's another letter, milady," Jane said, offering it.
"From Lord Dracy."

Jane looked as if she expected Georgia to refuse to
read it, but she was determined not to go to extremes.
She considered the seal, however, for she'd never seen it

before. She'd never received a letter from him before. A coat of arms, presumably the Dracy ones. Two animals supporting a shield with perhaps a helmet on top.

Similar to so many others.

Not a matter for fascination.

And yet she broke it gently because it was his.

She unfolded the paper.

*My dear Lady Maybury,*

So formal, she thought.

> *I am kindly invited to stay at Brookhaven and intend to avail myself of a respite from Town for a few days at least. I will be often away from the house, for Lord Torrismonde has graciously agreed to let me attend him around the estate so I may learn more of my business.*

He was telling her that he'd keep his word and not bother her with his close presence.

> *I ask for an opportunity to speak privately with you about a recent matter, and as soon as may be convenient. Of course you may have your maid in attendance if you trust her with sensitive matters.*
> > *Your obedient and humble servant,*
> > *Dracy*

Obedient, perhaps, but humble? Never.

He had things to tell her, and she realized what she needed. She needed him to tell her a great deal more.

"I must dress, Jane. What gowns do I have?"

"I didn't have time to pack many, milady. The blue lustring, the yellow sprig, the floral damask. That thing you wore yesterday."

Georgia was tempted by "that thing," for it seemed

suitably penitent, but she said, "The yellow, Jane. And pick out that lace from the bodice. I won't pretend to be a silly sixteen again."

In due course, Georgia was dressed in the yellow gown she'd worn to Lady Gannet's musical evening. It had been restored to its low-bodiced simplicity, but she wore a linen fichu to make it suitable for day wear. Her hair was simply dressed beneath a small, plain cap.

She thought of wearing the mourning bracelet, but that would be theatrical, so she placed it in front of the miniature of Dickon. He'd have been better off married elsewhere, but there was nothing she could do about that now except make sure that his murderer was punished, no matter what the cost to herself. She did want the Earl of Sellerby tried before the House of Lords and hanged at Tyburn before a jeering mob, and she'd do anything in her power to achieve that.

She met with Dracy in the small breakfast parlor, but it felt too confined, as if she couldn't breathe.

"I need us to talk outside," she said. "We can walk in the garden."

"As you will," he said, and they left the house.

Fresh air did help, but Georgia shivered slightly despite the warm air. "I need you to tell me about the duel," she said.

"Why?"

They were walking a gravel path between beds overflowing with summer flowers. It was beautiful, but the blossoms might as well be shades of gray.

"I need to make sense of it," she said. "I need it to be clear in my mind."

"You'd be better off without it in your mind."

She looked at him. "And how can that be? Tell me, Dracy."

"I wasn't there."

"But you understand it, don't you? You've thought about it and you understand it."

He sighed. "Perhaps. You're certain you want to do this?"

"Yes," she said, looking ahead. "Start with the quarrel."

"Remember, this is only my interpretation. The men spent the day racing their carriages and drinking. In the evening, they ate and also drank more. Vance said something cutting about your husband's driving ability. That would cause a little spat, but it grew, presumably because at some point Vance insulted you. It might have been a play on horse and filly, and the ability to manage and enjoy them."

"Like the cartoon."

"Like that cartoon. It seems no one was sober enough to remember any details, but I think Vance had been preparing the way. A man called Cavenham remembered Vance hinting about having you in his bed. He probably did the same in various places, and your husband might have caught wind of it."

"He'd never have believed it."

"No, but it would rankle, and he'd know some men would make a duel of it. I can only think it boiled up and he threw his wine in Vance's face. Vance couldn't issue the challenge, you see, not with them being so unequal in swordsmanship, so he had to provoke your husband to do it."

"Dickon turned up at Lady Walgrave's ball," she said, "still somewhat drunk. He insisted I return home with him. . . ." She didn't say the rest, but she wished he'd told her what was afoot. She'd have stopped it. "Tell me about the duel."

"I spoke to Shaldon at the masquerade, and he said he expected it to blow over in the sober morning, but of course Vance didn't want that. He insisted on the duel going ahead but gave everyone the impression it would be only for form's sake. A little light sword work, at most a minor wound, and a merry breakfast afterward." He stopped her with a slight touch and turned her to face him. "That means, I think, that your husband wasn't afraid. From the account at the inquest it went exactly that way until Vance made the killing blow. If you're disposed to be kind, you might think that Vance wished to cause as little pain and distress as possible."

"Am I supposed to *thank* him?"

"Perhaps. It could have been more brutally done."

"It should not have been done, especially for money. Wherever he is, I hope Charnley Vance is suffering the horrors of the damned."

"Now, that is very likely."

She stared at him. "What?"

"I had a new thought yesterday. I wrote to your brother about it but haven't yet received his response, but I think Sellerby killed Vance."

"*What?* No, no. Vance was a big brute of a man. It's impossible."

"Not with poison."

Georgia listened to a story bizarre enough for Mr. Walpole, author of *The Castle of Otranto*. She put a hand to her head. "I think I must have fallen into a fevered dream."

"Into a web of evil," Dracy said steadily, "but we will keep you safe. I will stay close, and you must be suspicious of any unusual food or drink."

"Suspicious . . . You think Sellerby would try to poison me? But why? He wants to marry me!"

"He may have tipped beyond reason. I don't think it's likely, but it's best to be aware. If a box of sweetmeats or some sweet cordial arrives as a gift, don't sample it."

"Lud! I've heard of whole families killed by rat poison in a stew instead of salt."

"Calm, calm. Torrismonde is aware, and any items that arrive will go first to him or me."

"This seems . . . it truly does seem fit for the theater."

"Evil is unfortunately real. Sellerby has paid for one

man to be killed and poisoned another. He might have killed his valet himself."

"Killed Gaspard?"

"His murder seems too convenient."

"But Sellerby was distraught. He truly was."

"Possibly over having to commit violence. Or just from losing a highly skilled valet. He said that to me."

Georgia sat on a wooden bench, feeling slightly faint. "How do we stop him before he hurts anyone else? Dracy—the supposed betrothal. You might be a target."

"Then I'll stay here, safely with you."

He was teasing her, but Georgia stared at him, cold with dread. She rose and gripped his arm. "That attack. That was Sellerby too!"

"What?"

"After Mirabelle's! You said the linkboy had led you. . . . Sellerby paid them to kill you!"

"By heaven . . . He heard about the false betrothal, then I confirmed it. I always thought that attack odd, that the ruffians struck to kill rather than steal."

She thrust away from him. "*See?* You could have died that night, and all because of me! Keep away from me, Dracy. Return to Devon and to safety. Forget all about me!"

She turned and fled back to the house.

# Chapter 33

Dracy watched her run away, sick with despair. If only he'd thought of that for himself, he might have prepared some defense, some rationalization.

He followed her back to the house, seeking some way to overcome this new barrier, but also urgent to send a new message to Perriam. Perriam wouldn't be caught in such a foolish trap, but he needed to be constantly on guard.

At least Georgia would be on guard against poison. He hadn't mentioned abduction, however, which might be Sellerby's next move.

He halted and then walked around to the stables, where the Perriam men were housed, and spoke to them.

"You're to take turns in patrolling around the house and keep an eye open for any strangers, day and night."

The men masked any surprise. "Very well, sir."

Dracy wished he could bring in an army to encircle the house, but he was being extreme. Sellerby was in London and now knew he was suspected of the forgery. He wouldn't act hastily, for he was a cold sort of madman, full of cunning.

In time, Dracy was going to have to talk to Georgia again, to discuss many aspects of this and try to bring her to reason, but for now, he'd leave her be.

He wrote the letter to Perriam and sent it off with a groom, then faced the day. He couldn't bear to stay under the same roof as Georgia, knowing her to be in such pain. He might as well take up Torrismonde's offer to tour the estate and learn more about land management. With or without Georgia, he'd soon have to return to Dracy and do his duty by the place.

Georgia huddled in the coverlet on the bed, wanting only to be alone, but Lizzie found her there and insisted on being told all.

"Upsetting," she agreed, "but only more proof of Sellerby's vileness. Once he's dealt with, all will be well."

"But Dracy could have died!"

"Yet is alive and well. He must have come close to death many times and avoided it, so perhaps he's particularly fortunate."

"Not to have met me."

Lizzie gave her a look, and Georgia sighed.

"Oh, very well. I couldn't bear that, but it seems I can't fly in alt forever."

"Thus, you might as well enjoy this lovely day. Come with me to visit the children, and then I'll drag you around my daily tasks. There's nothing like work to settle us."

She wouldn't be refused, and by dinnertime Georgia accepted that she was feeling more herself, entirely because of her surroundings.

She'd visited Brookhaven only once before, at Christmas, with Dickon. It had been delightful, but the house had been full of family and friends and awhirl with entertainments. The gardens and the estate had been mostly gray, without even snow to enchant them.

This visit was different. Outside, everything was deliciously fresh and alive, and inside the house was tranquil. Harmony breathed from the mellow wood and worn furnishings, and from the gentle blend of fresh air and indoor herbs.

In her own homes Georgia had delighted in the new and elegant, and Herne had been done over in that Italian style thirty years ago. Brookhaven had simply been cared for over the generations and had developed a patina of comfort.

A new pattern for country life took shape for her, a pattern that might even be possible at a place like Dracy Manor. Could she be content with it, however, year in, year out? Her misadventures in the fashionable world had left a sour taste. She'd miss a great deal about it, but she might welcome something close to Lizzie's life.

As they strolled down from the nurseries toward the dining room, Lizzie asked, "Better now?"

"Better, but guilty about that. I felt so vile and knew I deserved to. I'm not sure I should allow ease."

"And who is served by your misery?"

"I'm sure there's some biblical requirement for sinners to suffer."

"You've committed no sin."

"I'm sure I have, but I don't seem to be able to suffer as I should. I fear I'm a shallow creature."

"Simply practical. Despite Lady May, you are a very practical person. It's why we're friends."

"And I give thanks for it." Georgia paused on the landing. "Lizzie, I must tell you something, even if I disgust you."

"You never could."

"I'm not so sure. I want Sellerby dead. I truly do. No Christian forgiveness or turning the other cheek. I want to dance on his grave."

Lizzie did look shocked but said, "If he'd arranged for Henry to be killed, I think I might feel the same."

Georgia hugged her. "Thank you! For understanding. I forbade Perry from calling him out, but now I dither even about that. Dracy suggested that he might kill himself."

"That would be a very good thing."

"Lizzie, I'm shocked!"

"I'm a little shocked myself, but I've never encountered such evil. He needs to be stopped, and why should his blood be on anyone else's hands? What's more, he'd be buried in an unhallowed grave and burn in hell." She nodded. "We'll pray for that."

Georgia gasped, but it became a giggle. "Oh, Lizzie, thank heaven for you."

The men hadn't come home, so they dined in Lizzie's boudoir.

"They'll be eating at a farmhouse somewhere and enjoying it mightily."

Georgia told Lizzie about the pie house, and somehow she spent the whole dinner relating the various adventures she'd enjoyed with Dracy.

But not all of them. She couldn't share the nighttime ones.

Perhaps one.

She recounted Dracy coming home drunk and wounded, making light of the wounds, for in truth there'd been nothing to them. She confessed to returning to his bedchamber and finding him in his nightshirt.

"Really, Georgia, that wasn't good of you," Lizzie said, but she was amused. In fact, she was smiling at the evidence of Georgia's feelings for Dracy, and Georgia couldn't fight it at the moment.

"He has very fine feet," Georgia said and, to her amazement, blushed.

"Perhaps you should write a poem to them," Lizzie said, lips twitching.

"His name is Humphrey. Don't use it, though."

"I'm sure it was a very noble name in the middle ages."

Georgia almost spilled his amorous career, but thank goodness she didn't, for he came in with Torrismonde, both looking hearty from fresh air and simple food.

"I returned to find a letter arrived from your brother."
He made sure the door was shut and said, "He had little
trouble in finding someone who remembered a corpse
that was probably Vance."

"Dracy! I didn't tell Lizzie about that."

"Then my apologies, Lady Torrismonde."

"No, no," Lizzie said, bemused. "Sir Charnley Vance
is dead?"

Torrismonde said, "I think I should explain this new
matter to you, my love."

"Indeed," said Dracy and tilted his head, sending
Georgia the clear message that she should leave with
him.

"What?" she asked quietly when they were in the corridor. "Why is it a secret?"

He grinned. "There's a detail. Back to the breakfast
room, I suppose."

"Oh, don't be foolish. This is my room. Come on." She
led the way into the room and then shut the door when
he was in. "Now, tell me, and don't frown at me. I trust
you not to leap on me."

"I was worried about my virtue, as it happens," he
said, but with a twinkle in his eye. "Very well, the delicate matter is how Perry could find out about an unidentified corpse a year old. Charnley Vance was rather
monstrous in his manhood."

She frowned. "Rather . . . Oh, you mean his enormous
cock! Dickon told me about that, and there were some
cartoons. In one it was a flagpole."

He leaned back against the door, shaking his head.
"You're the most well-informed innocent in the world."

"I'm not an innocent."

He smiled. "You're not as innocent as you were. No."
He pushed straight. "None of that. From what your
brother says, the corpse was fished out of the river four
days after the duel, dressed in shirt and breeches. A bag
of stones had been tied around the waist, but the corpse

had eventually been stranded by a low tide. It was assumed to be a suicide. People do that sometimes. Add weights so they will drown quickly."

"How horrible to be so despairing."

"Of course no one looked for murder, and I doubt there would be any sign of poison after that time. In view of the suicide, he was buried in an unmarked spot in unhallowed ground."

"So we have our proof," Georgia said, "but not enough for a murder trial."

"No. It would be easy for a lawyer to argue that Vance was so overcome by having killed your husband that he took his own life. It gives us greater certainty, however."

"What happens now?"

"Given the lack of hard evidence, your brother proposes another forgery. Another letter written by Vance, but this time entrusted to someone before the duel. If anything were to happen to him, it was to be delivered to the Chief Justice, and of course it contains a description of the plot."

Georgia was staring at him. "That's . . . that's . . . *wicked*. But wonderful. Hoist with his own petard! If word spreads that Vance is dead . . . Wait, wait! The letter isn't real."

"It is now. Vance gives someone—let's call him Hermes—the letter. Vance disappears after the duel, but Hermes assumes he's fled abroad. Today, with all the world gossiping about the possibility that Vance died, Hermes decides he must act on the letter. He—in this case your brother—sends the letter anonymously to Lord Mansfield, the Chief Justice."

Georgia stared at him, slightly breathless. "Oh, the justice of it when Sellerby used forgery as a weapon. What will happen?"

"Such an accusation against an earl is a weighty matter. Most likely Mansfield will summon Sellerby to privately answer the questions raised."

"He'll deny the whole thing, and that will be that." But then Georgia inhaled. "If he were warned, however . . ."

"Being devious must run in the Perriam blood. Sellerby will be warned somehow, with an added detail about the place of Vance's murder. Your brother hasn't found it yet, but he agrees it must exist, so Sellerby will hear that a witness can place him at the spot with Vance on the day of the duel."

"I wish I could see his face."

"As do I. But the end will satisfy, assuming he either flees the country or puts an end to his miserable existence. If he flees, remember your brother expects to truly find the place and witnesses, so he can be hauled back to face justice."

She sat down, shivering slightly. "It suddenly seems real. More real. More horrible. He planned it. He planned Dickon's death, and planned Vance's murder. He poisoned Vance, watched him die, then threw him in the river like rubbish. Then he waited patiently, so patiently, to claim the prize—me. So cold, so cold. I could imagine that his blood runs icy rather than hot."

He came to take her hands, to hold them between his big, warm ones. "He is vile, and you are his victim as much as your husband was." He drew her up, saying, "I'm breaking my word," and wrapped her in his arms.

She shivered there for a moment, but then his warmth comforted her and she snuggled close, suddenly sure. "Home," she said.

He stroked her back. "You want to go home? Where is that?"

She looked up. "You. You are home."

He lowered his head and kissed her, softly, warmly. She played her lips against his, drawing in some essence that she needed, that fed her and made her whole.

She drew back. "I'm breaking my word too, and being selfish as well, but I want you forever. I need you by my side, as my husband and my dearest friend. Please."

She saw the joy in his eyes, a promise, a blessing. "It's I who should beg, but I need to tell you something first."

"Tell me something? I don't like the sound of that."

"It's a confession of sorts, yes." He led her to the small settee, so small they had to sit closely side by side. "You've probably wondered why your mother constructed the false betrothal."

She shrugged. "Still playing Father's game to keep Fancy Free."

"True, but not the game you thought. Your father's plan to keep his horse is based on an exchange, but the exchange has always been you."

"What? What are you talking about?"

"At Herne, after the race, he offered me you as wife, along with your large dowry, in exchange for Fancy Free."

"I can't believe that."

"Would I lie? He ordered you down to dinner so I could see the goods."

She gaped at him, but then anger raised her from her seat. "He had no right to do that. I'm free to marry whom I choose!"

"He seemed to think he could command you to it."

"He was wrong," she said. In fact, she almost growled it. "How could he?"

"Don't be too angry, Georgia. I think he was a very worried man. You didn't realize the full extent of the scandal, but your parents did, and I think they were concerned about your treatment by the beau monde. They were probably also concerned about your future behavior, for your father mentioned my well-honed ability to impose discipline."

"Discipline!"

"I know, I know. I was hard-pressed not to discipline him by a fist to his fat nose. . . ."

Georgia covered a giggle at that image.

Dracy smiled. "He was led astray, of course, by my face. It makes me seem much more ferocious than I am."

She had been furious, but humor had broken it, and she shook her head. "I can imagine it all. Father believes he's God as far as the family is concerned, no matter our age or legal status. So I was to be saved from shame by being shackled to a tyrant who'd bury me in the wilds of Devon and beat me if I misbehaved."

"And who was poor enough to be tempted by such a bitter prize."

She narrowed her eyes at him. "You were tempted, weren't you? And willing to do everything in your power to grab the prize!"

"Don't start along that path. I was tempted by you—I admit it. By your beauty, yes, but almost as instantly by your kindness. You looked me in the face from the first."

"I'd take shame not to."

"I know, but most would not. I came to Herne, I saw you, and I was conquered, but I never expected to win such a prize, and I would never have taken you against your will, even if your father found a way to force you. That was true then, and it's true now." He drew her into his arms. "But I'll willingly marry you, my love—once you've seen Dracy Manor."

"What? Why?"

"It's not Brookhaven, Georgia. It's a ramshackle mess. I need you to know what you take when you take me."

It did daunt her—she couldn't deny it—but she said, "Then I'll travel there with you, as soon as possible. And if there's work to be done, we'll decide how to do it."

He rested his head on hers. "I hope you feel the same way when you actually get there." He stepped back so that they only held hands, then slowly slipped free even of that. "I hope for calmer days too, and the end of this madness, so you can choose without fear or anguish."

"You're being noble," she complained. "It won't matter. The simple fact is I can't live without you, you dratted man, so even if it's life in a pigsty, so be it!"

He laughed and swept her up to whirl her around—but her foot caught a vase and sent it flying to smash into a pane of the window.

He put her down, and they stared at each other, aghast but laughing. He quickly flung open the door as a serving maid and the Torrismondes came running.

"My deepest apologies," Dracy managed, but sent her a wild appeal for help.

"He annoyed me," Georgia said, "so I threw a vase at him. And missed. I'm so sorry, Lizzie. I'll pay for the damage."

"Of course not. It doesn't matter, but . . ." Lizzie's lips were twitching, and probably some of the joy still danced in the room. "Come away and let Betsy clean up the bits from the floor. I'm not sure what can be done about the window."

"It's a summer evening," Georgia said. "The breeze will be welcome."

The breeze was indeed welcome that night, Georgia thought as she sat by the window, too full of thoughts and dreams to sleep. She suspected that Dracy was awake too, but she wouldn't go to him. This was a quieter time, a thoughtful time. But even though she tried to think practical thoughts about country living and expenditures, the truth kept dancing through. The truth she'd spoken. *She couldn't live without him.*

She'd brought Dickon's picture to the window ledge. At first it had upset her that moonlight leached the color, making him ghostly, but then she found a peace from that. He was gone, and she could only pray that he was in a good place, a true heaven.

He wouldn't want revenge. "But you'd want Sellerby stopped, wouldn't you?" she murmured to him. "I fear he's like a bad dog. He's learned to bite, and so he'll bite again—if not me, someone else."

*If you have any power,* she thought to him, *wherever*

*you are, help us put an end to his menace, and keep every-
one safe. I worry about Perry, even though I know he's
alert for danger. I'd worry about Dracy if he wasn't here
with me. Please don't let danger come to Lizzie and her
family.*

Moonlight shone on something. For a startled moment she thought it was a sign, a message, but then she
saw a splinter of glass remained in the leading around
the empty rectangle. Someone had removed the jagged
pieces, but they'd missed one bit.

She pulled on it, but it was firmly fixed, and in trying
again, she cut her finger. "Idiot," she muttered and
sucked the nick, playing her tongue over it.

That stirred dangerous longings, so she went reso-
lutely to bed.

# Chapter 34

Georgia woke early the next morning, before Jane had come with hot water and her morning chocolate. How rarely she'd seen the hour after dawn except through sleepy eyes, and what a waste that was. She flung open both casements of the window to breath the exhilaratingly fresh air, to smile at the birdsong and at the jewel-like effect of dew on spiders' webs.

It was completely glorious.

Then she became aware of a young man looking up at her, grinning. As soon as she saw him he ducked his head and hurried on. She backed away from the window, but she couldn't help a chuckle at the gardener's reaction.

Attracting men.

She reached out for the guilt and sorrow she should feel, but it eluded her. She would try to do better. She would be careful how she behaved with men and flirt only in the most innocent way, and only with elderly gentlemen. As Dracy's wife.

Lady Dracy.

No more Lady May, and she felt no regret over that.

Lady Dracy, hardworking country wife, wearing sensible clothes . . .

Most of the time. There would be parties and assemblies, and perhaps even masquerades.

There might be children.

She put her hand low on her body, as if she might be able to sense the truth there. Dracy wouldn't blame her—she believed him about that—but now she wanted children so desperately. First Winnie's and now Lizzie's darlings had stirred a deep longing that could break her if she allowed it.

God's will, Lizzie would say, but would God punish her for her sins with barrenness?

She shook that away. She'd go out to enjoy the morning beauty.

She pulled open drawers, seeking her jumps and her plain dress, feeling like a girl again, slipping out of the house on some mischief. Soon she was decent and she slipped downstairs, her shoes in hand....

But of course there were servants up in the house as well, preparing for the day. They dipped curtsies before continuing with their tasks, but she put on her shoes, feeling foolish.

She knew this world from her childhood, but in recent years she'd lived in that other one, the one that went to bed at dawn and woke at noon or later. She'd forgotten the servants' world that lived life in reverse, like the gardener at Thretford who never smelled the night-perfumed flowers.

*Balance,* she thought. There had to be a balance between the two.

She went out through the door in the morning room and down a shallow flight of stairs to the path through the rose garden, where many blooms held a diamond of dew.

The grass was damp, but she walked across it, remembering Winnie's ball, and the terrace, and ruined shoes. These ones were leather and sturdy. She walked all around the house, feeling simple and free in this newborn world, washed clean, even, as if christened all over again.

Smiling, she returned the way she'd come and entered her room just in time to prevent Jane from crying the alarm.

"Milady, I couldn't imagine what had happened to you. And there's blood!"

Georgia looked at the white-painted windowsill. "A very little bit of blood, Jane. There's a sliver of glass left in the pane, that's all."

"Oh, I was so afraid! All these carryings-on, I don't know. I've brought your water, but you're already dressed!"

Georgia hugged her. "Dear Jane, my apologies for upsetting you, but all is well. I'll take off these clothes and wash and then you can dress me more becomingly. But after I have my breakfast. I do believe I'm developing a country appetite."

Jane gave her a look but hurried away.

Georgia ate a hearty breakfast, but she had another appetite. She hungered to be with Dracy. She sent Jane to ask if he was free but received an unsatisfactory reply.

"How dare he be out looking at trees?"

Jane just rolled her eyes.

"Are there no messages from anyone?" Georgia demanded. She needed news from Town.

"I'd have given you them if there were, milady."

It occurred to her that she'd never sent Dracy a letter—a scribbled note didn't count—and sat to do so. *Saying what?* she wondered, stroking her chin with her quill.

Biting her lip, she wrote,

*My dearest Dracy,*
*I am quite bereft that you prefer trees to me, and you'd be justly served if I were to address you as Humphrey at all times. That would steal your dark demeanor, would it not? I shall expect more careful attendance in future.*

> *For now, I will insist that Lizzie teach me frugal
> household management. I believe people can sub-
> sist entirely on offal and potatoes if necessary.*
> > *Your helpmeet in training,*
> > *Georgia*

She folded it, but following the maiden's game, she
drew a little heart by the join before dripping wax there
and pressing on her seal. She glanced at Dickon's picture,
for she'd done that during their courting time, but she no
longer felt any conflict there. Dickon and Dracy were
very different, but she felt they'd have liked each other
if they'd met, because they were both honest and kind at
heart.

She gave the letter to Jane, to have it placed in Dracy's room, then sought out her friend. She found her in
the stillroom, looking through a book.

"Frugal housewifery?" Lizzie asked. "You know how
to run houses, extravagantly or economically."

"But I've not practiced the latter. Beyond some girl-
hood lessons, I've never managed a stillroom. I had none
at the London houses, and at Maybury, the dowager
ruled there. What are you doing?"

"Looking for a cure for the evil sleep."

"Whatever is that? A poison?"

Lizzie looked up. "What? No, of course not. The evil
sleep is an affliction of pigs, and there's a case at the
home farm. The pig sleeps too much, especially in the
middle of the day."

"That could describe Father when he's rusticating."

"Georgie! I don't suppose your father neglects his
food so he's in danger of starving to death."

"Quite the opposite. What's the cure?"

"I know I have something here. Ah, stonecrop. Come,
we'll collect some."

Georgia went off with her friend but noticed the man
who followed. One of the outriders, keeping an eye on

her in case Sellerby attacked. In her new, brighter world, the very idea seemed ridiculous, but she was glad he stayed in sight.

They found the yellow flowers on a wall near the orchard and gathered a basketful, then carried their haul to the farm.

"Why isn't the farmer's wife doing this?" Georgia asked.

"It was that way at the Maybury home farm. The still room at the castle was used for household concoctions."

"Mistress Pennykirk is an invalid—a tragic fall, which has left her crippled and melancholic—and her daughters are young. So I help in such matters."

Farmer Pennykirk was a short-legged, robust man who seemed weighed down with care. He was truly grateful for their help, as was his poor wife, who sat in a chair by the fireplace, bolstered with cushions and with a rug over useless legs. She was eager to do her part by bruising the flowers in a big bowl, encouraging her two young daughters to help.

A young maidservant was cutting up some bony meat for a stew.

Lizzie went off with the farmer for some other ingredient.

Some flowers spilled on the floor, and Georgia returned them to the bowl. "I'm sorry for your injury, Mistress Pennykirk."

Tears started in the woman's eyes. "I'm such a trial to everyone, your ladyship. I sometimes wish I were dead, and that's the truth."

Georgia almost said something bracing, but her heart knew better. "Perhaps you would feel better if you were a little more mobile. I've seen some chairs with wheels. With one of those, you could at least push yourself around the kitchen. And perhaps with a low table you could do some of the things you used to do, like cut up meat. . . . Oh, I'm sorry, I'm afraid I have a managing disposition. I shouldn't try to rearrange your life."

"Oh, no, your ladyship," the woman said. "If such things were possible, it'd be a godsend!"

"Well then, a lower table should be easy enough to arrange, perhaps even to sit in front of your chair. As for the wheeled chair, when I return to London I'll see what I can learn."

Lizzie returned with a pungent mash and added it to the bowl. "When that's thoroughly mixed, it will be ready. By God's blessing, the pig will recover."

"Thank you, your ladyship," Mistress Pennykirk said. "And to you, your ladyship."

The woman had tears in her eyes. Georgia only hoped she could make good her promises. As they left, she asked, "Are you sure that potion will work?"

"It works some of the time, which is the best anyone can hope for."

"I wish there were a cure for paralysis. Sometimes life seems so unfair."

"Which is why we should count our blessings—and not seek out suffering," Lizzie added pointedly. "Are you going to marry Dracy?"

Georgia felt herself blush. "I rather think I am."

Lizzie hugged her. "I thought as much. Torrismonde's very impressed with him, you know. Sadly lacking in knowledge, but keen to learn."

"He says I must visit Dracy before committing myself. He assures me it's a dreary mess. What if I can't face that? Truly, I don't think I could marry into dire poverty, no matter how I loved."

"The Dracy estate can't constitute dire poverty, and if it's run-down, you'll have a home to improve. You've always delighted in that."

"Not one about to fall on my head!"

"It can't be as bad as that. It probably needs a thorough cleaning and some coats of paint, and then it will be ready for you to make beautiful."

"With virtually no money."

"A challenge," Lizzie said. "I do not doubt you."

Georgia held on to that thought as they returned to the house, and then went to her room to write some letters. She would write to Lord Rothgar about wheeled chairs, for he was interested in many devices besides automatons. If he didn't know about such things, he'd know who did. However, that reminded her that she'd not sent a report to Diana Rothgar about the water situation at Danae House.

She was in the middle of that letter when someone knocked at the door. She opened it herself and found Dracy there. She couldn't help but smile, and he smiled back.

But he sobered. "A letter from your brother. The plan is in hand."

She pulled him into the room and shut the door. "What does he say?"

"Read it."

> Strange events at the Cocoa Tree last night, where there was a considerable company, including Waveney, Brookdale, Sellerby, and others, all gathered to hear more of the rumor that Sir Charnley Vance has been discovered to be dead and buried in an unmarked grave. No one speaks of anything else.

"Sellerby," she muttered. "Of course he couldn't stay away."

"Especially not when rattled by the news. It improves."

> It seems to be true, for the undertaker remembers the well-built corpse with the significant attribute, and he also noted a long scar on the corpse's thigh, which many know to have resulted from a riding accident some years ago.

Georgia looked up. "Is the scar real?"

"I assume so. Convenient."

"It really was Vance. Sometimes I think we've invented it all."

*There's a lively search to find his remains, but how anyone hopes to identify one skeleton from another, I've no idea, nor the point of it. The inquest said suicide, so he can't be reinterred.*

*No sooner had this tale built up steam, but Henry Dagenham comes in with news of a letter he'd seen that very afternoon at the offices of the Chief Justice where he works . . .*

"Dagenham's a friend of Perry's," Georgia said. "Convenient again."

"Or reason to choose the device." She read on.

*. . . a letter written by Vance a year ago. He claimed that he couldn't reveal more or lose his position, but that the letter cast doubt on the judgment of suicide, and that Vance feared an enemy. An enemy he named. Dagenham even hinted that Lord Mansfield has set in hand questions about Vance's movements after the duel, and placed where he might have met his end.*

"Spoken in Sellerby's presence! Oh, I wish I could have seen his face."

"Sick as a dog," Dracy said. "Read on."

*Speculation ran wildly, but with no conclusion, for Vance was a man disliked by many and feared by some. Of course the Maybury duel was mentioned, but as the letter had been written before the event, his death could not be revenge. As well for me, who could be seen as a suspect there!*

*All will be revealed, I'm sure, and in the meantime people are fleeing Town. There's sickness in the air, which afflicts rich or poor. Lord Sellerby left the club early last night looking unwell. It's to be hoped he is not attacked by it.*

*Your servant, sir,*
*P. Perriam*

Georgia refolded the paper. "That all happened last night. Sellerby could have killed himself by now. I wish I knew. I wish I knew."

"Your brother will write as soon as there's news."

"The fastest courier takes nearly three hours." She eyed him. "We could return to Town."

"No, Georgia. If Sellerby is still resisting his fate, he's particularly dangerous."

"Oh, damn you, but you're correct. Now, I suppose, we must go down to dinner and pretend none of this is happening."

"I think it's best not to share these stratagems with your friends. They're honest people."

"And we are not?"

"You can certainly be cruel. Would you really call me Humphrey?"

"If sufficiently provoked."

He grinned and kissed her. "You're a remarkable woman, Georgia—soon, I hope, Dracy."

She kissed him back, but as they left the room she said, "Only think, if you were a duke's younger son you'd be Lord Humphrey. No hiding it at all."

"But in that case," he said, "you'd soon be Lady Humphrey. How would you like that?"

"I'd have to achieve a title for you in order to be saved!"

After dinner Dracy went off with Torrismonde to go over accounts, so Georgia suggested she and Lizzie do the same thing.

Looking on from the side, she pointed out some errors. "You need to keep your columns more neatly. Your figures tend to drift."

"Yes, ma'am," Lizzie said with a look.

"I like numbers," Georgia said. "They're precise."

"Mine aren't." Lizzie pushed the ledger over to her. "You look at that while I go over the inventory."

Georgia began but said, "I wonder what state the Dracy accounts are in."

"A magnificent mess, I'm sure."

Georgia smiled at the thought. Lizzie rolled her eyes but chuckled.

Georgia enjoyed putting Lizzie's ledger in order, and when she was with Dracy again, she asked, "Is the book-keeping at Dracy in a shameful state?"

"Completely neglected for years. Now, what has you looking so cheerful?"

"I enjoy numbers."

"Can I hope that extends to cards? I think whist is proposed."

"How good are you?" she asked.

"Tolerable."

"Then we'd best play for tiny stakes. So impolite to beggar one's hosts."

He was better than tolerable, and they began to collude not to win, for Lizzie in particular was a careless player, preferring to gossip rather than watch the cards.

At ten o'clock they all ate a light supper, and then the Torrismondes went to bed. Georgia and Dracy remained in the drawing room, for the safety of it, she knew.

"Another activity in which we're well suited," he said.

"I enjoy cards, but not true gambling."

"I feel the same."

She began to build a tower with the cards, but the deck was old and the cardboard often bent. He helped, and they reached a seventh story. A foolish pastime, but Georgia knew they were both waiting, hoping for news.

When the clock struck eleven, however, she couldn't hold back a yawn. She had been up very early.

They jointly demolished their ramshackle creation and went up together, hand in hand, as they had been that night on the terrace at Thretford. Possibilities danced like hot temptation. There was nothing to restrain them except themselves.

They were to marry.

It wouldn't be so terrible a sin.

Yet they parted with a kiss at her door. A simple kiss, a gentle kiss. It was enough for now, for this waiting time, when there was the certainty of more.

# Chapter 35

Georgia readied for sleep in a fog of weariness, but when Jane had left and she approached the bed, she was too restless to get between the sheets. That bright moon shone in again, and she saw that the pane hadn't been replaced, nor the splinter of glass removed.

It didn't matter. The night air was only pleasantly cool. She opened both casements wide to enjoy it.

With a smile she accepted that she was acting the plaintive lover. She should be declaring, *Dracy, Dracy, wherefore art thou, Dracy?* She knew where he was, however, and was denying herself.

She inhaled, seeking night perfumes, but couldn't detect anything in particular. Night-flowering plants mostly gave out the strongest perfumes in the evening and early dark, and now it was nearly midnight.

An owl hooted, and somewhere, a fox barked.

The door opened behind her.

She turned, surprised, but sinfully pleased that Dracy's will had broken.

But it was a servant.

An outdoor servant in breeches and frieze jacket.

With a pistol in his hand.

*Dear God, it was Sellerby!*

"Make no sound," he said, closing the door. "Or I will shoot you."

"But you can't stand blood!"

"By the time you bleed, you'll be dead."

He was calmly rational, even smiling, but terrifying.

Georgia frantically weighed it. A scream and Dracy would be here in moments followed by others. But if Sellerby fired at this distance, she would be dead.

She didn't want to die.

"What do you want?" she asked, her voice strangled.

"You. My lovely, darling Georgia, all I ever wanted was you."

"I was married," she whispered, knowing it was nonsense even as she spoke. Her heart seemed to pound in her throat, and she couldn't think.

She had to think.

"And now you're a widow." He held out his left hand. "Come, my love. I'm here to set you free and give you everything your heart desires."

Georgia shook her head, dumbstruck, but trying to find an escape. He stood in front of the door. The window was to her right, but it was far too high. She'd die from the fall.

"We'd never get away," she managed.

*Play along with his fantasies. Play his warped lover's game.*

"The house sleeps, poorly guarded. So easy to avoid those watching and to break the glass in one ornamental door. Come, I have a horse nearby. We can ride for the coast and take ship to heaven."

"Leave England?" she asked, simply to delay. She glanced toward Dickon's picture beside the bed. *Help me, love.*

Sellerby strode over and snatched up the picture. "We have no need of that, do we?" Smiling at her, he threw it out through the open window.

Georgia choked back a scream, but if she'd held the pistol she would have fired it.

Her head was clear now, however. Sellerby, or rather Dickon, had given her a plan.

She ran to the window and looked down. "Why did you do that?"

"He wasn't worthy of you. Where would you like to live? Not France or Germany. Too close, too easily found. Russia perhaps, or the East. Would you like India?"

She turned back, pulling shut half the window, as if from annoyance at his action. The side with the broken pane. "India would be too hot. I'd sicken there."

"Then America, north or south."

"I don't want to leave England," she said petulantly, turning half away from him. "All my friends are here."

She pressed the heel of her hand against the sliver, trying not to flinch or wince as she dragged her flesh over it.

He noticed something. "What are you doing?" he asked, raising the pistol, coming toward her.

Georgia thrust out her hand, her bleeding hand, and he fell back a step.

"Blood, Sellerby. *Blood!*" She smeared it over the front of her white nightgown. "Dickon would have looked like this, bleeding from the heart."

He stared, shocked, even horrified, but he hadn't fainted!

He waved the pistol at her. "Get away. Get away from the glass."

She scurried sideways, squeezing the gash she'd made in her hand to get more blood, but it was stopping. Why hadn't she pressed deeper? Why wasn't the blood having the right effect?

He was unsteady, at least, and leaned against the windowsill for balance. The pistol shook but still pointed toward her, and now he was furious. "They've turned you against me."

*Moonlight,* she realized. Everything in shades of gray, even her blood. The full effect on him must be in color.

"Alas, it must be the other way, then," he said. "I will shoot you and then take the poison I've brought. You'll see the truth in the next life."

He was serious.

*Smell!* Blood had a particular smell.

As he steadied the pistol, Georgia forced open the wound so a bit more blood oozed and then ran toward him to thrust her hand at his face. He raised the pistol to shield himself and she fisted it out of her way and drove her bloody hand onto his nostrils.

"No!" he choked. "No . . ."

"Yes. *Dracy! Someone! To me! Sellerby's here!*"

She pressed her hand harder and harder. "You killed Dickon," she snarled. "You killed Dickon. You killed Dickon. . . ."

She couldn't stop saying it, couldn't stop pushing, even as he whined and struggled to get away.

And then he went over backward, out through the open casement. She almost went with him but grabbed the casement at the last moment, clung to it in horror as he landed with a horrible crunch on the ground beneath.

Arms came around her, pulled her away from the window. "What's happening? What are you doing? Blood!"

"Sellerby!" she gasped. "I . . . I think I killed him."

Everything went black.

Dracy caught her up in his arms as the Torrismondes ran in.

"What's happening?"

"Georgia!"

Dracy put Georgia on the bed. "Take care of her. See what wound she has." He ran to the window and looked out. "Dear God."

Torrismonde was by his side. "Sellerby?" He turned

to some servant behind. "Someone's fallen out of the window. Go and see if he's dead."

Dracy returned to the bed. "How bad is it?"

"She's not hurt at all," Lady Torrismonde said, "except on her hand. See, she's coming to. It's all right, Georgia, love. It's all right."

Dracy climbed onto the bed and took her in his arms. "It is all right, love. You're safe now."

She stared at him. "I *killed* him. I didn't mean to kill him!"

"Hush, hush."

He pulled her against his chest, but she whispered, "Could I hang for killing him? That would be an even greater scandal, wouldn't it? A countess hanged for killing an earl."

"Hush," he said again, feeling helpless. "Of course that could never happen." He looked at Lady Torrismonde, but she didn't need to be told.

"Sweet tea and brandy. As soon as may be."

The servant returned. "Dead, milord. I don't know who he is!"

"I'll deal with this," Torrismonde said and left.

Georgia wriggled free, still shocked, but showing her strength. "My robe . . ."

He found it for her and helped her into it.

"He's truly dead," she said.

"Yes." He was about to reassure her, to comfort her, but she said, "I am very, very glad."

He smiled at her. "You should have gone to the masquerade as Joan of Arc."

"Not a happy fate. To talk of costumes! He outdid himself in rough clothing. I might not have recognized him on the street. But down there, he looked like a broken doll."

"Never mind, love. . . ."

"He said if I called for help he'd shoot me," she said, "and I think he would. The blood didn't work."

Dracy took her back into his arms. "You tried to scare him off with blood?"

She nodded. "But the sight of it didn't make him faint. Then I thought of smell. . . ."

"Don't try to explain now, my love."

"But I need to explain how he came to fall. I realized that blood smells. I pushed my hand to his nose, and he was desperate to get away. So he went backward through the open window. He threw Vance out like that, so it serves him right, doesn't it?"

"I'm sure it does. . . ."

But she tore from his arms and ran over to the window. "Please, can someone bring up Dickon's picture? He shouldn't be down there with him."

Dracy swept her up into his arms and carried her away to his room just as Lady Torrismonde came with sweet, brandied tea.

He sat with her in his lap, feeding her the tea. "My brave darling. Is it possible to adore you more?"

"You don't mind that I killed him?"

"I crown you with golden laurels. I only regret that you were terrified."

"I'm sorry for being silly."

"Hardly silly," Lizzie said. "You're a heroine. I don't know what I would have done."

"But he came here," Georgia said, sitting up straight. "I brought evil here. I create danger wherever I go!"

"One man brought danger into your life," Dracy said, "and you vanquished him. Now he will harm no one anymore. Drink more tea."

She obeyed and relaxed again, but said, "There'll be a new scandal attached to me. He fell from my window."

"We'll arrange things as best we can. Don't worry about it now. You're sleeping here tonight," he said, looking a challenge at Lady Torrismonde. "With me."

Georgia smiled a little. "Thank you. I don't want to be alone."

\*        \*        \*

Georgia awoke aware of someone in her bed, and of
comfort.

A moment later, she opened her eyes and rose to look
at the man beside her, his scarred face relaxed in sleep.
She'd recognized him before she'd seen him, by instinct.

Memory returned with shocking clarity, but it didn't
shake her, because he was with her. Her steadfast guard-
ian, her anchor.

And then she smiled. She shouldn't smile at a death,
not even the death of evil, but she did. Lord Sellerby was
dead and she needn't fear he would hurt anyone else she
loved.

She reached out to touch, but then hesitated, inches
away. It seemed wrong to intrude on a sleeping person,
but then she placed her hand on his warm shoulder, covered only by his linen nightshirt.

His lids fluttered and then he woke up, smiling, but
also searching her face.

"I'm all right. I'm not," she added, "distressed."

Smile turned to grin, and he captured her hand to kiss
it, playing his lips there and then sliding them up her
sleeve, across her shoulder until he found the exposed
skin of her neck.

She stretched slightly with pleasure, and he explored
behind her ear and all around it, sending shivers through
her.

"We are not," he whispered softly, "going to do more
here, my sweet lady."

She slid her eyes to him. "We're not?"

"I hope we'll have thousands of mornings and thousands of nights. . . ."

"The time for wickedness."

"All times are ripe for wickedness, and pleasure. But
this is not ideal, not for our first full discovery. Let's arise
and explore the morning of our new days."

She smiled and kissed him, yearning, but knowing he

was right. There should be a special time for that, and this was not it, with stories still to spin and questions to be answered, and with Dracy Manor still to be visited.

"Come with me back to my room so I can find some clothes."

"Of course. I can show my skills with stay laces."

She swatted him on the arm and led the way, and he did know how to tie stay laces as well as Jane. But Jane couldn't spice the process as he did, with scattered kisses, some soft, some firm, and some very sweet nips.

She pushed him away when he was done, hot and tingling all over, and aching deep inside. "Get dressed. I can manage from here."

"Are you sure?"

"I'm sure, but I warn you, Lord Dracy, I will not let Jane go when I move to your pigsty!"

# Chapter 36

They returned to London first, to explanations to her parents, who heard the truth, and eventually to an inquest, which heard most of it.

Georgia hated having to give her evidence in the crowded room, with people from all stations packed in to hear more about the Maybury Scandal, as it was now known.

That evening, she wrote to Lizzie about it in her room.

*Dear Lizzie,*

*It was quite horrid. So many people, all staring at me, and the heat and smell. I feared I would faint. Perhaps it would have conveyed a good impression, but pride forbade it. I completely understand that you could not come, because your husband didn't want you involved, so don't distress yourself on that. I had so many other friends to support me, including Diana Rothgar and her husband, which made a considerable impression.*

*All was helped by Lord Mansfield having made known the contents of the Vance letter in the days before. The beau monde now feasts on Sellerby's reputation, not mine, and many even see me as an innocent victim of a madman rather than an adulterous ac-*

*complice. It's odd, isn't it, that the world found it easier to believe I was Vance's whore than Sellerby's?*

*All the same, recounting that night was difficult, especially as Dracy says I'm a poor liar. Everyone told me it would be best not to confess to my attack, so I did my best. It wasn't hard to convey the terror of being confronted by death, but I claimed the cut to my hand was an accident. Sellerby's reaction to blood was well-known, and no one seemed to think of the effect of moonlight on the color of blood, so there was no need to mention smell. The coroner accepted that in his distress, Sellerby thrust away from me and fell to his death.*

*The jury decided it was accidental death, complicated by the victim being insane. So thus, it is over.*

*Dracy is insisting that Vance's death be revisited so that the judgment can be murder and his bones can be reinterred. I still can't feel any kindness to that man, but I make no protest. Perry is beside himself at letting Sellerby slip by him in London, for he had him watched and never imagined he'd put on lowly garb. It will do him well to be brought low, just a little, in my opinion, for he is generally intolerably right about everything.*

*Tomorrow I fulfill Dracy's final condition and travel to Dracy Manor, which is like to take four days. Four days from Town! Once I couldn't have endured it, and even now I quail a little. I know the state of Dracy cannot turn me against him, but my next letter will be from there with a full and complete description of the horrors, and pleas for solutions for myriad disgusting problems.*

*Your challenged friend,*
*Georgia*

Georgia would much have preferred not to have her mother as chaperone on the journey to Devon, but apparently everything must be done with perfect propriety now.

Her mother's presence meant they had to travel in full state, in the traveling berlin, with two coaches of servants, bedding, and other comforts, and six outriders. There was pleasure to be in the same carriage as Dracy, but no scope for true conversation. At night, after they'd supped, she was taken off to the bedchamber she shared with her mother and their two maids.

"I might as well be in a convent," she muttered to Dracy one day as he handed her into the coach.

He kept her hand long enough to kiss it. "Many men find nuns arousing, you know."

"Do you?"

"If the nun is you."

Such little things fed her love and desire, and she grew eager to arrive at Dracy only to have this test over. But when they arrived, she had to hide her feelings.

He'd told the truth when he'd said this was no Brookhaven, and nothing was helped by them having traveled the last half day in pouring rain. There was no porte cochere, so they all had to slog through mud to get inside.

Her mother immediately insisted on a room, a fire, and dry clothes, but Georgia looked around, wondering if such things were available. The walls were grimy and soot stained, and some patches looked suspiciously like mold. She shivered in the damp air and wrinkled her nose at the smell.

Two servants hovered, but one was a terrified young girl, and the other a hunched old man.

She turned to Dracy and saw endearing apprehension.

She smiled, and it was genuine. "I've always enjoyed improving houses, and delighted in a challenge."

He laughed. "I take pride in providing one, then."

"Where is my room?" her mother asked, ominously.

"I would remove to an inn except that I saw no such thing this past hour and I will not venture out again into that weather."

"Begging yer pardon, your ladyships," the serving girl said in a squeak, "but there be fires in the best bedchambers. Mistress Knowlton arranged them."

Georgia looked at Dracy. "Housekeeper?"

"Friend," he said. "I wrote ahead."

She didn't like the idea of a woman friend, but her mother was being led upstairs and so she followed. Pale spaces on the wall marked where paintings had hung, and out of the corner of her eye she saw a mouse scurry.

A cat.

Maybe a few cats.

The room allocated to her mother was more promising than Georgia had hoped for. A musty smell was almost masked by potpourri, and the fire burned cheerfully without spilling smoke into the room. Though as grimy as elsewhere, it didn't seem damp, perhaps because of that lively fire. A fire in summer—that told the tale.

She quickly checked the sheets for damp and found them dry. "I think you'll be comfortable here."

Her mother snorted. "I am having doubts about this, daughter. Dracy, go away and see that I have hot punch to warm my bones, and sustaining food. Georgia, stay with me."

Georgia wanted to defy her mother, but old lessons were hard to ignore. Once they were alone, she said, "You planned to marry me to Dracy, Mother."

"I did not realize the extent of the sacrifice."

"I can endure it. I love him."

"You were always difficult, Georgia. Your reputation is mostly restored. There's no need for this." She indicated the room and the whole house.

Perhaps old lessons could be overcome.

"Mother, you plotted and connived to marry me to Dracy for the sake of a horse! Oh, I know you thought it best for me, but I was a pawn to you. I'm not a pawn anymore. My money is my own, I am mistress of my own fate, and I intend to marry Lord Dracy and, yes, live here at Dracy Manor."

Her mother stared and Georgia braced for an explosion, but Agatha, her mother's maid, came in, and the fire turned against her. "There you are at last. Get me out of these wet clothes before I catch an ague. Go away, Georgia. You exasperate me; I declare you do."

Georgia escaped and found Dracy awaiting her in the corridor. She wondered how much he'd heard. He only smiled. "Let me show you to your room. I would have done better by it with more time."

He took her down the corridor to a room also warmed by a fire, and where some flowers stood in a pottery vase. Lady Knowlton again?

"Tolerable," she said, ignoring the moth holes in the hangings and the stained plaster in the ceiling. When she reached the window she ran a finger along the windowsill and held it up wet.

"Not quite fixed everything yet," he said.

"Is the roof sound?"

"Mostly."

"I can see we'll need my twelve thousand." This was his home, however, and thus hers. "You spent much time here as a boy. What was it like then?"

"I liked it. Never elegant, but cozy."

"Then we'll make it cozy again. Truly," she said when he appeared to doubt. "I see no fallen plaster, so when the roof is repaired, paint will restore most, and the paneling in the entrance hall will be lovely when restored. Which is your room?"

"Have wicked intention, do you?" he asked, and she went hot at the look in his eyes. She supposed she had passed the last test, given that she was already planning restorations.

"How could anything be wicked between us?" she said.

He grinned. "I like a challenge."

He took her to the end of the corridor to another room, flinging open the door. "The chamber of the Barons Dracy!"

It was large and had once perhaps had grandeur—a century or two ago. The walls were paneled here too, and the fireplace a cavern of stone. The carved oak bed, however, was the most baronial aspect. It was enormous, more than six feet wide.

"All the better to roll around in," he said.

They looked at each other, but then her mother called, "Georgia? Where are you? Come here."

Georgia pulled a face but went.

"Sit," her mother said. "Eat. The rain has stopped and we have hours of daylight. We can do a first inspection of the garden. There must be something promising about this place."

Georgia sent Dracy a silent apology. He smiled and went away.

Soon her mother was demanding pattens, and they were equipped to keep their shoes and skirts out of the mud. Dracy appeared to escort them, and Georgia muttered, "Boots. If I'm to attempt this sort of country living, I shall wear boots."

"You'll probably set the fashion."

"Not here, I won't. I can only hope no one ever sees me in this milieu." But she sent him a smile. Truth was, she saw a challenge and she couldn't wait.

Looked at clearly, the stone house was solidly pleasant. Much of the ivy could come off the walls, especially that hanging over windows, and perhaps some flowering plants could be trained there instead. The drive needed gravel, and there would have to be some sort of shelter for arriving coaches, but all in good time.

"I see sheep cropping the grass," she said. "Why not more of them?"

"I've had a lot of demands on my time."

"But frittered some away at horse races."

"I can't regret that," he said.

She couldn't resist. She kissed him.

"Besides that," he said, "Carta won me a fair sum, cash in hand."

Georgia's mother was ahead of them, looking around. She began to call suggestions, most of them far too expensive to implement. Georgia didn't argue, but she saw other needs.

"We must have a pond."

"It would be in danger of overflowing at the moment," Dracy said.

"Not if properly constructed. You promised me a naval battle, sir."

"I don't have twenty servants."

Georgia considered the problem. "Don't you think we could find twenty willing children from the village? Where is the village?"

"Crux Dracy? About a mile beyond the long coppice. Over that way. And, yes, I'm sure we could find willing children. When we have a pond."

"We" was a most delightful word, and the sun was struggling out from behind the clouds.

They progressed around to the walled kitchen garden, where beans climbed poles and cabbages thickened amid a number of other plants.

"This could easily be brought back into full production," her mother said, and Georgia agreed. Only a third was in use, but it was decently tended.

"The few servants my cousin left here saw no reason not to grow food," Dracy said. "Quite likely they passed any surplus to their families, or even sold it. I've not inquired."

Her mother sniffed at that and went off to inspect a neglected herb area.

Dracy said, "Come and see the stables."

"I'm more interested in the orchards. We'll need to

provide for ourselves as much as possible. What's the state of the home farm?"

"Later. Come to the stables."

She went, but as they approached she said, "The stable roof looks sound. And new."

"It was in the worst state, and with Carta showing such promise . . ."

"Are you desperately attached to the Dracy racing stables?" she asked. "I don't think we can afford it, and I won't like my husband to be often away at race meetings."

"Demanding, are you?"

Georgia felt a twinge of fear, fear that she would ruin all this, all her dreams for this, but she said, "Yes. I'm willing to put my all into Dracy Manor, but for us. It must be about us."

"All I want is us. There's Carta over there in the field."

She smiled at the black mare. "Our Cupid. Without her we might have missed each other in the night."

"Perhaps I'll rename her, or name her first foal that. But no. You're right about the stud. Perhaps I only dedicated myself to that because it seemed possible, and the house and estate defeated me. With you at my side, no longer."

She snuggled up against him. "It's a powerful challenge, but I can see it now, a mellow house in blooming gardens, well-drained land, and plentiful produce."

"You really can bear to live here most of the time?" he asked.

"As long as it's us."

"I have an idea. Carta's too good a racer to keep here. How much do you think your father would pay for her?"

She grinned. "With persuasion, a good deal."

They came together for a kiss but eventually found the resolution to break it. No lovemaking in the muddy gardens, but Georgia longed to be closer to him, together in each other's arms.

"Torrismonde had an interesting idea," he said, taking her hand as they strolled on. "About Town living."

"Yes?"

"I will need to spend some time there in winter for Parliament. What would you say to living at your father's house?"

"What?" she exclaimed in instant rejection.

"Think about it, love. Hardly any expense, and otherwise, we can't afford any kind of elegant accommodation. You wouldn't like a tiny room on a third floor. Perhaps your parents would provide a suite of rooms where we could be private in a way."

"Damnation, Dracy, you heap hardships upon me!" But she made herself consider the idea. "I will pine a little for a neat Mayfair house of my own, and that's the truth, but it would be ridiculous to have one for only a few weeks a year. I will insist on that suite, but if that's the worst hardship I ever face, I will be blessed. I am blessed," she added, and they kissed again.

She decided she loved these little kisses, like tasting kisses, or sips of nectar. Nectar they could drink deeply of one day. Soon.

She linked arms with him and they strolled back toward the house. "So we toil here from spring to autumn and enjoy a little of the beau monde in the winter. And perhaps an occasional visit elsewhere? Bath is not so very far."

"Bath is not so very far," he agreed. "Come, you missed something in the garden."

He took her hand and led her back to the house, to an unkempt flower bed against the wall. Part had been dug over, and in it . . .

"Nicotiana!" she exclaimed. "How did you manage that?"

"After the ball I asked Lady Thretford to donate her plants. I didn't know if they'd survive the journey, but here they are, and with a blossom or two." She smiled at him, but before she could comment, he added, "They're carefully placed beneath my bedroom window. If you were to visit tonight after dark, you might catch the perfume."

That night she slipped into his bedroom. He was waiting for her, this time in a plain woolen robe. She was wearing a pretty, new nightgown and her green robe.

"It seems so long," she said.

"It's been an eternity," he said, taking her into his arms and kissing her, and kissing her. She could have kissed like that for eons except that she had more in mind for this night.

She pushed him away and shed her silk robe. Slowly, she undid her buttons.

With a smile, he unfastened the ones on his own robe, watching her.

She chuckled and slowly raised the skirt of her nightdress, teasing him.

He peeled off his robe and tossed it aside, naked.

"Are you going to stand there like that all night?" he said. "I don't mind. We do have all night. If we're caught at this, they can only make us wed."

She laughed and pulled off the nightgown, tossing it aside as he had. "No hair powder tonight."

"For which I thank the heavens." He plunged his hands into her hair, raising it up and then letting it fall. "It catches fire in the candlelight."

"I worried about that powder," she said. "That a servant would know."

"I cleaned it up, though I was tempted."

"Tempted?"

"To leave it, to compromise you. To force you."

"But you didn't," she said, melting with love. "You are the most perfect man in the world." She went on tiptoe to kiss his scarred cheek. "I want you to take me to your bed and make me completely yours."

He was caressing a breast, but his hand stilled. "Why?"

"At one time I considered taking my chosen husband to bed before the wedding, because if I didn't conceive, I could jilt him. I didn't want to disappoint again."

He shook his head. "I doubt you could have done it, love, and I've told you, if we have no children, I'll not complain."

She put her hand on his chest. "Then what difference will it make? You'll not escape marrying me, Lord Dracy, so take me now. Make me completely yours."

He did, with all his skill, but simply, which for Georgia was skillful perfection. He caressed her to passion as she explored his wonderful body, and then sank deep into her, slowly, gently, sliding sweetly, making her arch with breathless delight.

He kissed her as he moved, commanding her, guiding her in the pounding rhythm to a passion beyond even that they'd shared before. She filled her mouth with his hot, salty flesh to stifle cries of pleasure as her body jolted with fulfillment and then collapsed into another drowning kiss and limp completion.

Eventually the power of speech returned, but what to say?

"I love you," she said into his sweaty skin. "And I love lying here like this, tucked against you, safe from all harm. Did I tell you you're my anchor?"

"I'd rather you fly, Georgia, than be tethered by me. I adore you," he said, kissing her hair, "and I adore being in bed with you so much that I fear Dracy will crumble around our besotted heads."

Georgia chuckled and turned to nuzzle into him, inhaling a sweeter and more magical smell even than flowering tobacco. "Let it."

# Author's Note

A *Scandalous Countess* was great fun to write because I found some new elements with which to play.

First, there was a widowed heroine. I haven't featured a widow in one of my novels for a long time, but my story idea called for one. However, I also wanted a heroine who was vulnerable to her family's pressure to marry, and I decided that meant she must be a young widow. In the eighteenth century, widows generally had a rare degree of power and independence, but I assumed that at twenty years of age Georgia would be powerless.

When I plunged into the research, I discovered I was wrong. No problem. I love to learn something new.

I discovered that a widow or widower was free to marry whomever they wished, even if less than twenty-one. I assume the rationale was that their father surrendered authority at the first marriage and couldn't get it back. A widow also had possession of her jointure no matter how young she was.

Thus Georgia could have lived independently, but it makes perfect sense to me that she doesn't. She is shocked by bereavement and unjust scandal, and gladly accepts her family's support, even though it comes with control. Even as she recovers and begins to resent restrictions, she's still not ready to set up house for herself. She doesn't want to be independent and alone. She wants to win back all she has lost in position and possessions.

Scandal was another new story element for me, and it was interesting to see how a powerful family and a strong heroine would deal with it.

The third new element was the seriously scarred hero. I didn't know how that would work out, but, as I wrote, I liked the fact that Dracy takes his disfigurement without bitterness. I only discovered slowly that he'd been extremely good-looking, but it adds to the novel in many ways. It gives him an interesting sexual history and plays against Georgia's dependence on her beauty.

Writing a young widow was an adventure in another way. I experience the developments with my characters as they happen, so I was with Georgia as she discovers that overnight she's gone from being a wife—with wealth, a high position in society, and complex homes to run—to having nothing but the dowry she started with, returned almost to the schoolroom.

Such a situation would have been rare. Even back then, not many young ladies married at sixteen, and hardly any were then widowed at twenty. To be widowed and childless was probably close to unique. If Georgia had had a son, she would have remained in her homes as he grew up, but, as it is, she is in effect evicted.

Have you wondered about marriage settlements, dowries, and jointures? It can seem quite complicated, but I'll try to explain.

When a bride brought a dowry to the match it was usual for her parents or guardians to negotiate legal settlements, mainly to protect her interests.

The first point to be hammered out was the income the bride would have during the marriage—what was called "pin money." Also, if the groom was a minor, the settlements would specify what income his family would provide so he could support his wife until he came into possession of his property at twenty-one.

The second point was the amount to be set aside for any daughters and younger sons to be born of the marriage. The oldest son would in time inherit the estate, so he wasn't covered by the settlements. However, a lump sum was usually put in trust to provide for any other children. As they came into their teens and found professions or husbands, they received their share, which is why each person's part was called a "portion." As you can see, a large family could result in small portions and an only child could have a large one.

The third negotiation point was the income for the bride if she became a widow, which was called her "jointure." This was an amount per annum, and usually about ten to twenty percent of the amount she brought to the match. So a dowry of two thousand pounds would lead to an annual income as a widow of two hundred to four hundred pounds to be paid from her deceased husband's estate by his heir. Sometimes this was to cease if she remarried, but that was negotiable.

Georgia's large dowry provided for a large jointure, which certainly would have been a burden on the Maybury estate if she never remarried and lived a long life. The scandal that surrounded Georgia could easily have made it hard for her to remarry, so it's not surprising that the new Earl of Maybury thought it a better gamble to return the dowry and be done with it.

That leaves my heroine, Georgia, a rich woman, but, looked at another way, it emphasizes the fact that she's been returned to her life of age sixteen, almost as if her marriage had never happened. I found her situation, and the way she deals with it, rewarding to write.

I'd like to share a bit more about research.

When I'm writing a book there are always new things to learn, large and small. Nicotiana and London's water supply are each almost incidental to the plot, but digging around the subjects was fun.

Many thanks to Margaret Evans Porter, who has a particular interest in the history of gardening, for sharing knowledge about flowering tobacco in the eighteenth century.

As I said in the book, the perfumed tobacco was rare

in the 1760s, but I liked the word play about tobacco, and many people were importing exotic plants at the time.

I've enjoyed nicotiana for years. The plants are rather plain and ungainly, but the perfume is heavenly as evening settles into darkness. If you want to try it in your own garden, you'll probably have to grow it from seeds, because the bedding plants in garden centers are usually the small, colored varieties, which don't have much perfume. Look online for seeds for the large, white variety. Some sorts can grow to four feet or more, and the big plants seem to have the strongest scent. It's quite easy to grow.

When Danae House needed help, I considered a range of problems and chose the water supply. My general reading had taught me about London's problems with water. A little more research gave me the details, and also the nice touch of a fish blocking the pipes. Yes, it really did happen, because the water was pumped up from the river. No wonder people didn't drink water—it wasn't safe unless you were rich enough to have it brought from pure wells or springs.

The usual drink in Georgian England was small beer, a quickly brewed, low-alcohol beverage. They didn't understand why it was safer than water, but the secret lay in the liquid being boiled as part of the process. As tea became cheaper, it would replace beer as the common drink, and again the process involved boiling water.

The Malloren family played only a small part in this novel, but you can see that it's still set in the Malloren world, with aspects from other books coming into play. If you're new to the Mallorens, please visit my Web site to check out all the books in the series. You can also find out about all my other books, most of which are available new in print and e-book. You'll also find a sign-up box on most pages for my occasional e-newsletter, and you can contact me by e-mail at jo@jobev.com.

Happy reading always,
*Jo*

Please read on for an excerpt from
another historical romance by Jo Beverley
set in her exciting Malloren world,

# An Unlikely Countess

Available now from Signet

*Northallerton, Yorkshire*
*March 1765*

He was drunk, but could still see well enough in the dimly lit street. Well enough to detect ruffians at work. And that the victim was a woman.

Catesby Burgoyne grinned, drew his sword, and charged. At his battle cry the ruffians whirled toward him, eyes white rimmed, mouths agape. And then they fled.

Cate staggered to a halt, flailing his sword. "Come back!" he roared. "Come back, you scum, and meet my blade!"

Only their fleeing footsteps answered.

"Damn your blasted eyes," he muttered. "A bit of slaughter's just what I need."

A breathy sound made him turn, sword rising again, but it was only the woman, leaning against a house wall, staring at him.

The narrow street was lit only by two feeble house-holder lamps, so all he could see was pallor and shadows. Pale face surrounded by loose, pale hair. A dark gown that covered her neck to toe. Gown was respectable. Hair wasn't. Couldn't be respectable, could she, out alone at night?

He shoved his sword back into its scabbard. "You must be new to the trade, sweetheart, to dress so dully." Damnation, where were his manners? No need to be crass because she was a whore and he was at odds with the world.

He bowed. "Catesby Burgoyne, ma'am, at your service. May I escort you to your destination?"

She shook her head, mute.

He walked closer to see her better. She tried to shrink back, but the wall was relentless.

"Please . . ." she whispered. A thin hand clutched a shawl at her chest as if it could be a breastplate.

Cate was trying to come up with reassurance when a door opened nearby and a flat Yorkshire voice asked, "Wot's going on 'ere, then?"

The stocky man carried a candle that illuminated his face and straggling hair more than them. Even so, the woman turned away as if to hide her face.

She had a reputation to lose?

"The lady was attacked, sir," Cate said, striving to hide all trace of gin from his voice. "The villains have fled and I'll see her safely home."

The man peered, but like all sane people, he didn't go looking for trouble. Probably Cate's aristocratic tone helped him along that path. "Good night to ye, then," he said, and shut his door.

Cate turned back to the woman. She still stared at him, but the intervention of someone from the ordinary world seemed to have restored her voice.

"I must thank you, Mr. Burgoyne," she said on uneven breaths. "But, please, there's no need to delay you longer."

A well-bred voice. Her left hand bore no ring. Where was her father or brother to permit this?

"I may not be the most perfect of gentlemen, ma'am, but I cannot leave a lady to walk the night streets alone."

"I live very close by. . . ."

"Then this will delay me little."

He gestured her onward. He'd commanded men in battle. Surely he could command one ordinary woman. She did move forward, stiff with wariness.

Or anger?

Now, that was interesting. He assessed her as best he could in the gloom. Hard to judge her looks, but her features seemed set in . . . resentment. Yes, that was it. Resentment. She might have reason to be wary of him, but why in Hades should she resent him? She was also dawdling, but he would not be put off.

"Your direction, ma'am?"

She quickened her steps as if she might outpace him—a thin, sour thing, all sharp angles and antipathy.

He kept up without effort. "Unwise to venture out alone so late, ma'am."

"I merely wished to walk."

"I have no pressing engagements. If you desire a stroll, I could escort you for miles."

Her angles became harder, which vaguely amused him. A blessing that, on such a dismal day.

They'd arrived at the main street of the town. He saw no one else on foot, but this was also the Great North Road, lined with inns, all still open, hoping for late trade. A coach rattled by and turned through the arch to the Golden Lion, the best inn in town.

To the left lay the Queen's Head, a mangy, ill-run place where he'd failed to drown his sorrows. He'd escaped into fresh air, but fresh March air was cold up here in Yorkshire, and the next London coach didn't pass by until early morning. He'd need a bed for the night somewhere, but could only afford to share a room with others.

The woman was simply standing there.

"Forgotten where you live, ma'am?" he drawled.

She turned sharply to face him. "Why are *you* walking the streets at night?"

"A man is allowed to, ma'am. Especially one with a sword, who knows how to use it."

"Men are allowed anything, whilst we poor women have no rights at all."

*Ah.* "What man in particular has offended you? I have a sword and know how to use it."

She gave a short laugh. "You'll not call out my brother."

"He wouldn't fight?"

"Only in court. He's a lawyer."

"The lowest form of scum."

He meant it as the general, common gibe, but she said, "He is indeed."

What had the fraternal scum done to her? Something he could avenge? He was done with war, but at this moment bloody violence would be immensely satisfying.

"His name and location?" he demanded.

"You're ridiculous."

"Perhaps he has an excuse for scumminess if you flail him with such a razor tongue."

"You'd be sharp if . . . *Oh!*" It was pure exasperation. "I suppose, being a man, you'll insist on having your way. Very well."

She marched across the street and into a lane lined by rows of small cottages, where she stopped by the fourth door. "Good night, sir."

The breathy hiss was angry, but cautious. So, she didn't want to alert the neighbors to her improper behavior. The only light here escaped from a couple of shuttered windows, but Cate could tell her small house probably had only two rooms on each floor. From her bearing and speech, she'd come down in the world.

"Is your brother inside?" he asked quietly.

"No, thank God."

"Will he be back soon?"

"Live *here*? Aaron?" She laughed, but quickly covered her mouth with her hand.

Something was wrong here, and he found lame ducks so hard to ignore. It was the bane of his life.

"If you were to invite me in, ma'am, perhaps I could advise you."

*"Invite you in?"* She looked around frantically, seeking listeners. "Go away."

"I'm not planning a rape. You need help, but we can't discuss your situation here."

"We can't discuss it anywhere. Go away or I'll scream."

"Truly?"

She hissed in a breath. "You wretched, drunken—"

A door opened nearby. "Whosur? Woyeruptuh?"

The old man's accent was so thick Cate could hardly understand the words, and he was Yorkshire born and bred. The meaning was clear enough, however.

He pressed down the latch and pushed her inside. He followed, having to duck to save his head, and shut the door. They both froze in place, listening, and Cate was aware of her bony angles conflicting with a sweet smell. She took the trouble to store her clothes with herbs.

A dog whined.

Cate turned to face new danger, but the small dog looked to be a spaniel, a gentle breed. Hard to tell its mood when it stood in front of the candlelit back room, but dogs didn't whine a threat.

The woman pushed past Cate and hurried to the dog. "It's all right, Toby." She fondled its floppy ears and the tail wagged.

Woman and dog went into the kitchen and so Cate followed, instinctively hunching, even though the beams cleared his head—just. The floor was beaten earth, the air damp, and the front room held only one dip-seated chair.

Had all the rest been sold off so she could survive?

What was the story here?

He ducked into the kitchen—to face a knife, held firmly in a bony hand. It was only a short kitchen knife, but probably sharp enough to do some damage.

The dog only whined again, the cowardly cur, but she, with her weapon and her fierce, determined eyes, pale hair glowing in the candlelight—she was magnificent.

Cate raised both hands. "I intend no harm, ma'am. My word on it."

"And why should I trust your word? Leave. Now."

"Why?" he asked, taking evidence from the room.

The tallow candle gave too little light and too much odor, but it illuminated poverty well enough. The tiny kitchen, like the whole house, was cold. If there'd been a cooking fire in the hearth it had long since burned to ashes. He saw no sign of food.

The only furniture here was a deal table with two chairs at it, and a rough sort of sideboard holding cheap pottery. Alongside pots, however, sat a few pieces of pretty china and glass. Remnants of the better life that showed in her well-bred accent and proud demeanor?

Why was this goddess alone and in such desperate straits? Why was she bedraggled and dressed so poorly? Her encompassing gown was a particularly dismal shade of black, her knitted shawl an ugly brown.

Had she truly been out on the streets attempting to earn some pennies in the only way available?

Her thinness told of hunger, but it etched strength into a face worthy of a Roman empress—high brow, long straight nose, perfectly curved lips, and a square chin. Not a face to conquer the fashionable world, but, by God, it was in danger of conquering him.

"Go!" she commanded again, but without confidence. The cowardly cur whined again, somewhere amid her skirts.

He realized his height was frightening her and sat, placing his hands on the table. Holding her eyes, he said, "I admire your courage, ma'am, but you won't scare me away, and if it comes to a fight, you'll give me no more than a scratch. Simpler by far to sit down and tell me your story."

She tried to hold on to her strength, but her lips quivered.

*Oh, 'struth.*

Cate quickly took the leather flask from his pocket and put it on the table. "Have some of this."

"What is it?"

"Dutch courage."

"What?"

"Geneva. Gin."

*"Gin!"*

"Have you never indulged? It can sweeten bile."

She changed her grip on the knife. Startled, he half rose to defend himself, but then she drove it, two-handed, deep into the rickety table.

"My, my," he said after an appreciative moment. "Do please sit, drink, and tell."

"You've already had too much to drink, sirrah."

"It's never too much unless I'm unconscious. You have glasses, I see. We could even be elegant."

Suddenly she laughed. It was ugly, but a release of sorts. She pushed straggling hair off her face, then took two glass tumblers and slammed them on the table. She went back to open a low cupboard and returned with a bottle.

"Brandy," she said, putting it beside the glasses. "My mother's medicinal supply. I'll get some water."

"Seems a shame to dilute it." Cate picked up the bottle and unstoppered it. "Your mother is abed upstairs?"

"My mother is dead."

"My condolences."

"Four months ago."

Cate cursed his drink-blurred mind. He was being tossed pieces of a picture but couldn't quite put them together.

She sat down opposite him, straight and proud. "Pour me some, then."

The knife stood upright between them. Some vague reference to the sword of Damocles struggled to form, and failed.

He sniffed at the brandy. Not good stuff, but perhaps not atrocious. He poured half an inch into one glass and pushed it over to her. He poured the same into the other.

He'd normally take more, but even half an inch might be enough to send her under the table. He didn't want her sozzled, only loose tongued.

And in his arms?

No, he had no place in his life for folly like that, but he'd help her if he could.

# Jo Beverley

## *The Demon's Mistress*

The first in a trilogy of passionate Regency-set stories
AVAILABLE ONLY AS AN eSPECIAL

Lord Vendeiman has returned from war to find his estate
bankrupt and his father dead. When wealthy widow
Maria Celestin offers to hire him to pose as her fiancé, he
agrees, but forbidden passion ignites between them. Dare
he reach for happiness? But what will happen when
Vandeiman learns the truth about the woman he has
come to love?

**Available wherever books are sold or at
penguin.com/especials**

From

# JO BEVERLEY

The long out of print novella

## *The Demon's Bride*

### NOW AVAILABLE AS AN eSPECIAL

Rachel Proudfoot has enough trouble resisting
the temptation of rakish Lord Morden without
supernatural intervention. When she plays the
traditional role of the demon's bride, however, a
mighty earth spirit wants to use them both to
return to the world.

From
*New York Times* bestselling author
# JO BEVERLEY

# An Unlikely Countess
*A Novel of the Malloren World*

Prudence Youlgrave is out to marry above her station
and secure a happy life. Catesby Burgoyne is out to
continue his noble family's good name. When fate
pushes them together, they are married—but this
inconvenient marriage of convenience quickly turns
into something much more...

**Available wherever books are sold or at
penguin.com**

"A delicious...sensual delight." —Teresa Medeiros

**New York Times** Bestselling Author
# Jo Beverley

AN UNLIKELEY COUNTESS
THE SECRET DUKE
THE SECRET WEDDING
A LADY'S SECRET
LOVERS AND LADIES
LADY BEWARE
TO RESCUE A ROGUE
THE ROGUE'S RETURN
A MOST UNSUITABLE MAN
THREE HEROES
SKYLARK
WINTER FIRE
SECRETS OF THE NIGHT
DARK CHAMPION
ST. RAVEN
LORD OF MY HEART
MY LADY NOTORIOUS
HAZARD
THE DEVIL'S HEIRESS
THE DRAGON'S BRIDE
DEVILISH
SOMETHING WICKED
LORD OF MIDNIGHT
FORBIDDEN MAGIC

**Available wherever books are sold or at
penguin.com**

S0027